AUTHOR'S NOTE

Dear Reader,

Thank you for joining me on this adventure. You are about to dive into a series where each book is a crucial piece of a larger puzzle. For the fullest experience and to grasp the evolving story, it's important to read them in order. This sequence ensures you won't miss the unfolding mysteries and the journey of our characters. I've crafted this series with great care, aiming to take you on an unforgettable journey. Start at the beginning of book 1 and enjoy the ride—each book brings you closer together to the big ultimate reveal.

With all my love,
    Sara

TIMEBOUND

BLADE OF SHADOWS
BOOK THREE

SARA SAMUELS

BLADE OF SHADOWS

BOOK 3

TimeBound

SARA SAMUELS

Timebound

Book 3 in the Blade of Shadows series

Published by Sara Samuels

Denver, CO 80237

First Edition

Cover image copyright Krafigs Design

Editing by Rainy Kaye

Formatting Storytelling Press

"Heroes rise, villains plot, destinies change, and secrets hold the power to rewrite all. Come closer, dear reader, fear not. The twists within these pages, will change you forever."

"To my past self, for dreaming. To my future self, for believing. To you, dear reader, for journeying through time with me."

CHAPTER ONE

What kind of man guts you with a blade so sharp you don't feel it slide inside until blood oozes from the wound? A man who's a demon, that's who. And not just any monster—he was the darkest of the dark, the kind of demonic presence feared by all, whether human foe or supernatural fiend.

And, currently, said demon was retrieving something to tend to the wounds he'd inflicted on me.

As I waited for this sinister beast, while lying on a filthy bedframe, I stared at my ragged, bloody flesh. A long, wicked gash had been sliced from my belly button to my pelvis. My torso was bare, and the fly of my deerskin breeches had been unbuttoned and pulled apart, revealing my lower abdomen. My feet were free of the moccasins I'd worn a short time ago when I trekked across the plains.

A sudden chill overtook me, and beads of sweat covered my head, neck, and torso. A queasy feeling rocked my stomach like a churning sea.

Holy fuck, am I going to die? I slumped back onto the bed and closed my eyes.

"Wake up!"

Whack! A slap landed on my cheek, whipping my head to the side.

My eyes flew open, and my gaze collided with Balthazar.

The light of a thousand candles illuminated the room in Balthazar's lair. I'd been heading for the Catskills a short time ago with my wife, Emily, and the bitch Olivia. Now I was in Balthazar's hideaway in some undisclosed location. How he'd transported me here was anyone's guess. The only thing I remembered was arriving at John James' house to find him decapitated. Then, Balthazar appeared. And then I thought I was dead, felled by the demon's blade. But how did we arrive here?

It was too much to comprehend and made my head throb.

Balthazar held an elegant glass vial with a delicate handle in a silver holder. "Ready? This will make you feel *so* much better. It's a healing tonic."

I nodded, feeling my life essence wane. The agony of my wounds was too much to bear. I needed help, or I wouldn't make it.

Balthazar poured some of his so-called "healing tonic" into my belly.

I shrieked like a stuck pig. The liquid sizzled and burned as it landed inside the wound, scorching my intestines.

"Stop acting like a little bitch." Balthazar snarled, his long teeth yellowed by his centuries of existence. "I procured this substance from a necromancer in Italy in the late fifteenth century."

Pain ripped through my insides like bolts of lightning. The only response I managed to make was a scream.

"The necromancer said he got the recipe from a corpse. Or maybe he sourced it from the corpse's lingering spirit. It's been so long. How can I remember such details?" he said with a swish of his hand.

I'd been injured a lot in my lifetime. In the eighteenth century, I'd been assaulted by arrows and tomahawks. As a gladiator in ancient Rome, I'd been mauled by lions and tigers, harpooned by the three-pronged trident known as the Fascina, and skewered by razor-like scimitars called siccae. But nothing had prepared me for the kind of injury imposed by a master of depravity. When it came to inflicting harm, no one compared to Balthazar. And no one took as much delight in hurting others as he.

The grin on his face when he poured another stream of the tonic into my wound was evidence enough.

I nearly blacked out from the pain this time.

But Balthazar, now sneering, whacked my face with his hand. He seized my shoulders and shook me. "Don't lose consciousness. The healing properties won't work if you're inert."

"Who told you that?" I wheezed. "The necromancer? Or the dead man?"

Sweat pooled beneath my body as I lay on the feather and straw mattress. My skin was drenched, and a sick odor emanated from me.

"It was one of them. I don't recall. Like I said, it was a long time ago." Balthazar separated the edge of my wound with his clawed fingertips and peered inside. "The elixir seems to be working. Show some gratitude."

I said, "It's hard to be… grateful… when I can barely… think. You weren't supposed to… gut me… like that." My words sounded strangled. "You were only…"

I paused to catch my breath. "Supposed... to scare them… away."

Good God, it felt like I was being burned alive from the inside out.

Balthazar circled his hand, causing the candle flames closest to us to flicker. "Oh, I think Olivia and Emily were suitably horrified. I sure love to mess with them, especially Olivia. It gives me great satisfaction to see her scared and suffering."

He chuckled. "Anyway, I had to make it look believable. I couldn't tell them you have been working for me this whole time, now, could I?"

An angelic smile spread across his devilish face.

"I suppose… not…" I was about ten seconds away from passing out. "Still… I didn't think I'd be in…this…much… *pain*."

Balthazar removed his fingers and picked up the vial again. "I missed a spot."

"No!" I cried out, my arms flailing.

"Oh, yes. Be the warrior you are and my strongest soldier yet."

Another stream of silvery liquid landed on my intestines. Steam issued from my belly, along with a hissing sound.

I screamed in agony. A man was not supposed to look down and see his pinkish-white entrails. But that was what I saw when I lifted my head.

Balthazar flattened me against the mattress with his palm. "Stay still and let the medicine do its magic. I've witnessed its results before, you know. I'm not just using you for torture."

The pain lessened to an aching throb that pulsed through my tissues. I wiped the sweat away from my brow with my forearm, then exhaled a long breath.

"You weren't supposed to hurt me like that," I said again.

"I pledged to work with you based on my love of being dark, not my desire for anguish."

Utterly wiped out, I struggled to prop myself on my elbows.

"When I summoned you, I told you to follow my orders and not make your own choices. Did I ask you to marry Emily?" Balthazar's lip curled. "She's nothing but a whiny human. Do you want lovers? I can provide you with lovers. A man like you craves dark sexual desires. You should have never settled with Emily. No, you need someone much darker."

He moved the vial to a small, polished table shoved against the wall.

I eyed the glass container as Balthazar stepped away, hoping he was through with the tonic torture. When I looked back at him, he had moved across the room to lean back against his fireplace mantel.

The burning logs behind him crackled, sending sparks against the iron grate shielding the opening. Shadows highlighted his features, and an orangish glow backlit his body.

"I'm waiting," he said coolly.

"For?" It took too much effort to hold myself up, so I slumped to a prone position again.

"Your justification for marrying a *human*. Especially *that* human. And for making your own choices without consulting *me*." His face contorted as he spoke.

"I had my reasons." I groaned and tried to pull my knees to my chest as a new wave of pain shot through me. But the act of lifting my legs proved too tricky.

"And what are they?" Balthazar took slow, measured steps across his stone floor in my direction. As each footfall struck the solid surface of this cavernous room, the sound blasted through my ears like bullets.

"She's Olivia's sister. So, I married her. I had to make it appear…" I closed my eyes and panted. When I managed to catch my breath, I continued. "It had to look… realistic. I had to pretend…"

The agonizing pain wrapped around my belly and squeezed. "I had to pretend I was a changed man."

Balthazar's eyebrows drew together, and his chest rose and fell rapidly. "What did you say? The first part?"

He loomed over me.

I weakly tried to shove him away. "Emily…she's Olivia's sister." Burning pain tore through my abdomen. "Alina gave birth to two children." I moaned and writhed. "Different fathers."

"That means Emily is a Timebound!" Balthazar's head fell back, and his loud roar shook the rafters.

I drew my hands over my head for protection. When he didn't strike my head, I tried to distract him, hoping to change his sour mood. "What is a Timebound?"

"Fuck Alina!" he said, ignoring my question. "She gave birth to two bastards and never gave *me* a child! Instead, I have a son who is an idiot and a complete failure."

A son? Balthazar has a son? This was news to me. But the information whirled out of comprehension as I fought to stay conscious. I felt like dogs gnawed at my entrails while I suffered through each bite and tear of flesh.

Balthazar stormed around the room, each footfall shaking the bed, the candles, the ancient books lining the book-shelves. Even the logs in the fireplace sparked and blazed, caught up in this madman's outburst.

He stopped at the side of my bed, closed his eyes, and took several long, deep breaths.

I tensed in anticipation of what might come next.

When he opened his eyes, they were the color of rubies.

He ran his tongue back and forth across the tips of his sharp incisors, staring at my belly. His fingers drummed his thighs. If he had a tail, I was sure it would twitch back and forth like a wildcat.

"You should have brought this information to me sooner. Why didn't you?"

"I didn't think it was important."

"You didn't think it was important? Telling me that Emily is Olivia's sister is fucking important, you dumb fuck!"

"Forgive me, master. I promise next time it won't happen again." I loathed bowing and scraping before Balthazar. I was no man's bitch. But there I was behaving like a serf.

Balthazar looked at me, his expression contorted with rage. But then, a softness spread across his face. "Are you feeling better?"

I blinked, realizing the pain had subsided again. "Yes."

"Good." A chilling smile spread across his face. "I need to close this wound, so you don't get infected. Ready?"

I gulped. "I guess so."

He lowered his hand to my stomach and pressed.

The stink of burning flesh filled the air, along with my howls.

Balthazar's teeth were bared as he burned me with his hand. His arm trembled and shook as my skin blistered, turning a waxy color.

I couldn't endure the pain, and I blacked out.

When I became conscious, Balthazar sat upon a velvet upholstered chair angled to access the fireplace heat and watch me. He held a golden goblet.

"How do you feel?"

I took stock of my body. I didn't feel as bad as I thought I would feel. My skin was damp and cold, but no shooting pain pulsed through my system. But then, maybe I was numb from the chest down.

I propped myself on my elbows and stared at my belly, expecting to see charred, blackened skin. Instead, the skin looked pinkish-brown and healthy.

"Better." I remembered what we were talking about before I'd passed out. "Why didn't you tell me you had a son?"

"I didn't think it was any of your business." He sipped his drink. "Besides, you didn't tell me about Emily. Why should I mention my son?"

I ran my tongue around the inside of my parched mouth. "Master, I asked you for forgiveness and assured you it wouldn't happen again. I'm loyal to you and want to be your soldier. Please, tell me about your son. Who is he? Where does he live?"

"I still don't think it's any of your business. Let's just say my son is an idiot whom I can't stand. I wanted to get back at Alina—cause her significant emotional pain—so I had an affair. I didn't expect her to get pregnant with another man's bastard." He bared his teeth, much like a growling wolf. "So, this line of questioning is *closed.*"

In a fluid movement, he got to his feet and crossed to where I lay. "Open your mouth."

I did so, and he poured a drizzle of wine into my mouth.

I coughed and shook as I attempted to swallow it. When I managed to get myself under control, I croaked, "More, please."

"That's enough. The backwash of my saliva contained in that swallow should prove restorative." He stalked back to the chair and sat.

My stomach recoiled at the thought of drinking Balthazar's spit. I worried I might vomit up whatever I'd managed to get down my throat. "No one ever knew about the child. How is that possible?"

Balthazar glared at me, his eyes glowing red. Clenching his teeth, he said, "I don't want to talk about it." He squeezed the goblet so hard that a dent formed in the gold. He threw the now-deformed chalice across the room, where it clanged against the wall, spilling the remnants in a crimson stain against the pale stone.

He assessed me with his reptilian-like eyes. "Now that you are feeling better, you will answer my questions. Where's Roman?"

"I don't know." I closed my eyes. My body grew pleasantly warm from the wine.

Or maybe it's from Balthazar's slimy spit. Bile shot into the back of my throat at that unsavory thought.

"He's missing," I said, curling on my side. "Ever since the battlefield, he's been gone. I returned to get him since he was severely wounded, but he was no longer there. Maybe he's been devoured by wolves. Perhaps he's with Eyan Malik. That's what Olivia suggested."

Balthazar appeared by my side, his hand around my throat in the blink of an eye.

"What did you say?" he snarled.

I had enough strength to shove him off me. "Get your fucking hand off me! You've already done enough damage to my body."

"Tell me what you said!" he yelled, spittle spraying from his mouth.

I jerked my head out of the way—I didn't need to partake of any more demon spit.

"According to Olivia, Roman could be with Eyan Malik. What's the problem?" I rubbed my throat.

"There's no fucking way Eyan Malik is alive. He's dead." Balthazar began to pace, his hands gripped behind his back. "This is impossible."

"Do you know Eyan Malik?"

Balthazar didn't answer. "How did you hear about Eyan Malik?"

"John James told Olivia and me about him." I continued to palpate my neck, sure there would be a bruise tomorrow. The tissue felt sore and manhandled. "When Olivia was informed about Malik, she seemed to have met him or something. I wasn't really paying attention when she mentioned it to me." I was lying through my teeth, when in truth, I'd paid attention to every detail. But Balthazar didn't need to know that.

Balthazar's agitation rolled from him in palpable waves, sending a chill around the room. Yet, the fire continued to crackle beneath the hearth.

"We went to find out more about Eyan Malik from a man named John James, but all I heard was his name. From what Olivia said, it all sounded like he had some kind of terrifying power—like he was another version of you, capable of doing the same evil things. I couldn't believe that two people like you could ever exist, and yet here we were. It scared me to think of how much destruction he could cause if you two were together." I rubbed my stubble-covered jaw. I pushed up to sit and swung my legs off the bed, surprised by the apparent healing proficiency of Balthazar's Necromancer tonic. Then, I pinned my gaze on Balthazar as he wore grooves in the stone floor with incessant pacing.

Balthazar was in such a foul mood I needed to keep my wits about me.

"What else did James say about Malik?" Balthazar asked. "He must have said more!"

I desperately ran my fingers through my hair, racking my brain for anything I could remember of the conversation between James and Olivia. My palms were slick with sweat, and I felt like my heart was beating out of my chest.

Balthazar's intimidating presence filled the room, causing me to tremble in fear as he pressed me for more details. Then it suddenly clicked, and I hastily snapped my fingers. "Oh! Right! James said you raised Malik and looked after him like your own—is he your son?"

"No! Malik was *like* a son to me once. I took him under my wing and watched over him. I cared for him. And what did he do in the end? He betrayed me…going against the man who showed him his dark side and guided him through everything. The son who carries my blood is alive. Malik is long dead, rotting in his grave," Balthazar added as an afterthought, continuing to prowl around the room.

I reeled back. Is he lying? Lying comes as effortlessly to Balthazar as breathing. Does he really have a son who is alive and walking among us?

I squeezed the back of my neck, trying to ease my tension. "So, who killed Malik?"

"Who do you think? I did. I killed him long ago when Malik became a threat to me, and I could no longer control him. His anger fueled him to be reckless and untrustworthy. He had to go, just like John James."

A tick pulsed in my temple. So he's the one who killed James and separated his head from his body.

A brittle silence filled the space between us.

I eyed Balthazar, how one might watch a predator hungry for its next meal.

"What else did James tell you?" Balthazar stopped before me, towering over me.

I got to my feet so I could feel equal to him.

"He was a strange man. He said a lot of things," I said, waving my hand in the air.

"Don't try my patience, Marcellious. Tell me everything that crazy old man told you and Olivia," Balthazar said. His ruby-red eyes glowed. He wrapped his hand around my throat, and he bore down, digging into my flesh with his pointy fingernails. "I know you have more information. Don't try to lie to me. I can smell a lie, Marcellious, even when it's miles away."

I couldn't pry his fingers from my neck.

"Okay, okay, I'll tell you what else he told me," I wheezed. "Release me so I can tell you."

Balthazar removed his hand, and I gulped in greedy gasps of air, coughing violently.

"I'm listening," he said.

When the coughing subsided, I croaked, "He mentioned something about Malik living in the Catskill Mountains and being alive, planning and biding his time to kill you."

I fingered my mangled neck. There would definitely be more than one bruise there tomorrow.

A deep fissure formed between his bunched eyebrows. "How is this possible?" he said as if to himself. "It can't be. I killed him. I watched his body be consumed by fire. He has been dead for hundreds of years."

"James also mentioned that Alina found one of the missing blades...either the sun or the moon dagger. I can't remember which blade exactly, but she found one for sure."

"There's no way! They've been missing for thousands of years!" A sheen of sweat glistened on his forehead and cheekbones.

I narrowed my eyes. *Balthazar's scared.*

"I knew my Alina was up to something when I was hunting her. That's why I need that damn journal. I knew she would find one of the blades and write down where she hid it. I felt it. Is there anything else? Tell me everything you can remember about what John James said." Balthazar resumed his restless prowl.

I stroked my jaw. "Let me think. James said that Alina hid the blade somewhere safe and gave her journal to Malik for safekeeping."

Balthazar stopped before me and drew himself up to his full height. He leaned forward slightly.

I buttoned my trousers and did the same.

"You're going to help me find Malik," he said, his eyes glittering. He licked his lips like he could taste the blood.

I grew excited by the power rippling from his muscles. This was why I worked for Balthazar—for the powerful feeling that came from plotting acts of evil and executing them.

A sense of exultation washed through me. "Of course, I will help you—I will always be of service to you. Olivia went to look for Malik, and she had the map John James gave her to find Malik. I glanced at the map when Olivia was studying it. I know where to look. I will locate the journal and the daggers. You have my word, Lord Balthazar."

I bowed before Balthazar solemnly and silently, swearing my allegiance to him.

When I rose, Balthazar stroked his goatee and eyed me. The trim facial hair, the color of midnight, gave him the chilling appearance of Satan's evil brother. "You've always been a good servant, Marcellious. But I'm not one hundred percent convinced of your loyalty."

A slight quaver shook my knees. "With all due respect, I have proved my loyalty to you since you first summoned me. I have done everything you asked for. I have told you everything I know. I have betrayed my brother and my people and will continue to serve until my last dying breath."

Balthazar appeared to think, saying nothing.

Beads of perspiration bloomed on my face and neck, dripping down my torso.

A smile spread across his face. "We shall see. Finding Malik and bringing me the journal will prove your loyalty."

The thought gave me a heady rush, replacing the terror. Now that I was back with Balthazar, I could let my darkness out and relish the thrill of evil.

I pulled my head back. "I'm ready to leave right now. I can head for the Catskills at once to find Malik. And I can prove my loyalty to you anytime by killing anyone that comes our way."

"You've forgotten one thing." The smile turned into a leer.

"What's that?" I said, frowning.

"You're healing." He pointed at my abdomen.

I patted my now-hard belly. "I don't know what you're talking about. I feel great. That healing tonic really worked."

"That was only the first treatment. It's a process." A wicked-sounding laugh erupted from his throat. He whirled and stepped toward the door at the back of the room.

Searing pain seized my limbs, and I crumpled to the ground.

"I'll be back soon to administer more elixir," he called before the door snicked shut.

As I lay there, writhing in agony on the unforgiving stone floor, I couldn't help but wonder if I had made a grave mistake in allying with Balthazar. But then again, perhaps this excruciating pain was the cost of my ascent into darkness, the inevitable toll I had to pay to become the ruthless killer I had always dreamed of being.

I gritted my teeth and clenched my fists, determined to emerge stronger and more powerful from this ordeal than ever before. For now, all I could do was endure the suffering and wait for the moment when I could finally rise from the ashes of my old self, reborn as the ultimate predator. If, of course, I survived…

CHAPTER TWO
ROMAN

Images of blood and death filled my mind as I rocketed to consciousness, with the shouts of fighting ringing in my ears.

I opened my eyes. I'd either died and gone to the afterlife or time-traveled again to some strange new world. I hoped for the latter as I stared at all the peculiar objects surrounding me. I had no idea what any of them were—they were shiny, noisy, and loud.

People spoke to me from a wall box. I yelled at them, trying to get their attention, but they ignored me.

Music floated through the room from somewhere else. It sounded metallic and harsh—unlike the orchestras I'd attended with my mother in the 18th century. Nor did it match the trumpeting fanfare of the tubicines, the blasts from a cornu, or the water organ which played before a gladiator fight in Rome.

I jammed my hands over my ears to quash the sound.

As I looked around, blinking at unfamiliar objects. Time-pieces glowed brightly displaying numbers and dates. Floor lamps held delicate white orbs that emitted soft golden light while a cone-shaped thing protruded from the ceiling radiating light from a large round globe. The music blasted from somewhere behind the closed door, like an entire band was nearby.

The room began to spin, and orbs of light flashed in front of my eyes. Unable to comprehend my surroundings, I slipped away, dragged back into an abyss of dreams.

The dream started promising—a small deer I'd shot hung around my shoulders. Its antlers bounced against my arm as I tromped through the forest, eager to see my wife and children. I would present my prize to my beloved, and she would thank me with kisses before skinning and gutting the beast and preparing its meat. Then, I would bounce my children on my knees and tell them tales of the wild.

I could hardly wait. My pace quickened like when my horse Tempestas knew we were heading home with the promise of warmth and a good meal.

Tempestas…I no longer have that horse. That was at a different time. Where am I now?

The air smelled fresh and clean as I pushed through the woods, my boots crunching across the dead leaves. The bright promise of snowfall appeared overhead in the somber sky. This deer would keep us fed through the winter, with the root vegetables stored in the cellar and the preserves my wife had put up in the late summer. We would survive another cold season.

When I emerged from the trees, the acrid scent of smoke filled my nose with dread. My steady stride transformed into a jog until the deer became too heavy. I flung the deer to the ground and took off at a sprint.

Flames shot from my house just ahead. Four figures emerged, engulfed in fire. Their screams and cries would haunt me for the rest of my existence. All three of my children stumbled and fell. My wife, whose beautiful hair was now consumed by an orange blaze, tried to pick them up.

I kept running and running, faster and faster, but I couldn't reach them. With arms outstretched, I tripped and fell into a dark chasm, chased by the memory of my family being burned to death. Heaving sobs left my mouth, making a terrible caterwaul as I fell. When I landed, sure that I would meet my loved ones in the afterlife, I opened my eyes to see a face hovering above me.

I was back in the strange bed, in this unfamiliar room, awake.

I let out a strangled yell and shoved the stranger back.

The man's arms pinwheeled and he caught his balance. "Whoa, whoa, whoa, there, son. I'm a friend, remember?"

I pushed up on the soft bed that smelled of lavender and soap, studying the man.

His thinning gray hair and the spectacles perched on his nose caused him to appear innocuous. The shirt and pants he wore weren't like any clothes I'd ever seen. The shirt, covered with flowers and musical instruments, was as loud as the blaring music. The pants hung loosely from his hips.

I glanced behind him and noticed the people in the box were gone.

"Is my music too loud? I usually listen to the classics. You know, Bach, Beethoven, and the like. Sometimes I like jazz. Miles Davis and John Coltrane…those guys can stir the soul. But today, I needed a mood boost, so I flipped on some 70s tunes. Those old rockers could really belt out a tune." He propped his hands on his hips.

70s tunes? Old rockers…like rocking chairs? Jazz?

"Am I talking too fast for you? Or, is the Hawaiian shirt too colorful? I usually don't dress like this, but I decided to try something new for a change." He cocked his head to the side like a small bird. "Cat got your tongue? You were badly injured when you arrived. I've been tending to your injuries for weeks. I thought you were a goner there for a while. Glad to see you're still here."

I lifted the clean white bedding covering me and examined my body. Pink scars and fresh scabs adorned my torso, along with small squares of white. I reached down to pick at one of the squares.

The man stilled my hand through the bedding. "Easy now. Some of your wounds are stubborn, and we don't want them to get infected. I've applied an antibiotic and sterile gauze to those ones."

I frowned as a memory surfaced of hundreds of Kiowa warriors astride thunderous galloping horses.

And then I was stabbed through the belly. Who was that man who sliced my palm with my dagger and repeated the sacred scripture, sending me here?

The man before me frowned, scratching the side of his head. "Do you understand me at all? We had a conversation a couple of weeks ago. Don't you remember? You were hiding in the closet over there. You gave me a fright when you emerged, wandering around the room muttering like the devil. And then you saw this…" He picked up a silver frame and pressed it to his chest. "You are married to my Olivia."

His eyes moistened.

Fragments of memory flitted through my rattled brain. Yes! This man is Jack, Olivia's father! I'd woken up in this room, yelled at the box on the wall, studied the strange surroundings, and spoke to Jack. But I thought that was a dream. Am I still dreaming?

I patted my naked chest to check.

I feel solid. I guess this isn't a dream. I'm in the time when Olivia was born.

Thoughts of Olivia and our unborn child sliced through my heart.

Olivia, where are you? Burning hot rage slammed through me. Who sent me here, away from my love, and why?

I pushed aside the bedding and swung my legs, now covered in soft leggings, over the side of the bed. I stared at the flimsy covering.

"Sorry, I had to dress you in some old sweatpants. They were Tristan's. You're a big guy. Olivia had some of his clothes in her Jeep, and we needed to dress you in something, so…" His expression clouded over. "At least I was able to find a use for his belongings. I hope he burns in hell, that son of a bitch. Please forgive my coarse language."

Tristan. He was the man whom Olivia had loved. He'd betrayed her and killed her father. Now I must kill him and make him pay for his mistakes and for hurting my beloved. He put her through pain and hell.

I bolted to my feet and towered over Jack. "How is it that you're alive? Olivia told me you were killed by Tristan—she watched you die."

A lone tear tracked down his wrinkled face. He eased away the photo he'd been clutching to his chest and reverentially set it back on the side stand.

"And that's Olivia's last memory of me? Oh, dear, my darling Olivia doesn't know. I thought I was a dead man. Yes, I did. I survived because of Lee—he saved me." He glanced at Olivia's image and stroked her face with his fingertip. "That was eight months ago. My daughter has been gone since then."

None of this made any sense. I staggered around the room, still struggling to find meaning. "That's impossible! Olivia's been gone for two years, not eight months! We met two years ago!"

Jack's face became pale, and he patted his leg. "My good-ness, son, how is that possible? Oh, I have so many questions. Where is she now? How did you meet her?"

I headed toward the door. "I need to get back to my wife. I need to be with her."

I winced as a stab of pain shot through my chest.

"No, son. What you need is to rest, heal, and gather strength." He gently grabbed my arm. "Please, go back to bed. I will call my neighbor, and he will know how to advise us."

I wrenched my arm away. "No! You don't get it! I've got to be with Olivia. She'll think I'm dead!"

A pain in my chest flared to life, and blood seeped through one of the white patches Jack had placed on me.

Slight as he was, he seemed to grow in stature. "Please, son. Get back to bed. This wound is the worst." He indicated the bleeding area. "Lee and I have worked hard to keep you alive, and we won't lose you now."

I staggered back to the bed and fell upon it with a groan. Moon Lee was Dancing Fire in my time. "Moon Lee is here at this time? He is the man who raised Olivia?"

Jack bristled. "Well, I'm her father. But he helped raise her, yes. He taught her to defend herself. She was a highly trained martial artist."

"A what?" I furrowed my brow, both with pain and confusion.

"A, um, what you would call a warrior."

A surge of pride rocked through me. Olivia and I had fought side by side. But the agony of my wound took prece-dence in my mind, forcing me to focus on its intensity.

Jack seemed to sense this. He retrieved a small, dark gray rectangular device and pressed it.

The device glowed with light.

I jerked in alarm. "What is that?"

"It's a phone. A mobile phone. I'm calling for help. This is how we communicate to one another in this century." He tapped the front of the phone and held it to his ear. "Damn. Voice mail. Hey, Lee, this is Jack. You've got to call me back. He's awake. And that darn wound opened up again."

He pressed the side of the phone, and the illumination disappeared. "He'll call us back."

"What do you mean, call us back? Like, shout through the window?"

Jack chuckled. "No, son. There is much to teach you. But right now, you need to focus on healing. I'm going to get some supplies and redress that wound. I'll be back in a jiffy."

"In a what? What is this jiffy?" All this new information made my head hurt.

Jack smiled. "I'll be right back."

After Jack changed my bandages and gave me a small white pill to dull the pain, he invited me into the kitchen for food. My stomach growled in response, and I followed him through his house.

The house was larger than the one I grew up in with my mother and filled with many peculiar things.

Jack directed me to sit at a table in the kitchen corner, and he bustled around, preparing a meal.

Olivia's time had so many marvels. There was a giant silver box that kept food cold. Turning a dial on the stove yielded instant flame. Jack poured ground coffee beans into some sort of device. Several minutes later, the room was filled with a heady and familiar aroma. Yet it was nothing like the fragrance of coffee that I remembered.

"Here," he said, resting a mug of coffee before me. "Do you like cream and sugar?"

"I don't know," I said, taking a long sniff of the beverage.

"Let me prepare it the way I like, and then you can decide for yourself."

He crossed to the silver box and returned with a container formed of sturdy waxy paper. He opened the top of the container and poured white cream into my mug. Then, he reached for a small glass jar of sugar and poured in a small amount, stirring it with a silver spoon.

"There," he said, smiling. "Try it."

I took a tentative sip. The warm, sweet liquid was like nothing I'd ever tasted.

"Do you like it?"

"Yes, very much so."

"Excellent. I'll prepare bacon and eggs next." As Jack bustled about his kitchen, he peppered me with questions. "You've brought me much joy, son. My Olivia is alive! And you seem like a stalwart young man. I never liked Tristan. I knew there was something evil about him. I felt it in my gut."

He poured a stream of yellow eggs into a pan.

"Stalwart?" I said, taking another sip. *Heaven.*

"It means hardworking...loyal... You seem to possess those attributes."

I nodded. I was indeed hardworking and loyal. No question there.

"And where is Tristan now?" I planned on killing him and swiftly returning to Olivia with the news that I had vanquished her betrayer.

A deep frown creased Jack's forehead. "We don't know. He's been missing since the night he shot me. No one can find him. Not Lee or me, or the local authorities. He is like a ghost."

I drummed my fingers on the table. This wasn't what I wanted to hear.

Jack retrieved several slabs of meat wrapped in something transparent and flimsy. He placed them on a large flat pan and slid them into the oven.

Soon the welcome smells of sizzling pork fat teased my senses. "How long was I unconscious?"

"Oh, maybe two weeks." Jack scratched his jaw. "You woke up, took water and nourishment, fell back into your slumber. Lee insisted we keep you out of the hospital. He kept me out of the room while he did his mumbo-jumbo Native rituals on you. But I was afraid you would perish without proper care." He paused for a moment. "I'm sure it was a shock to wake up in my bedroom. I think you're on the healing path now, though."

Healing path? I frowned and took another gulp of coffee.

Jack retrieved two plates from a cupboard and scraped the pale yellow cooked eggs onto each plate. Then, he put some sort of cloth glove on his hand and retrieved the bacon. He slid several slices onto each plate and placed one in front of me and the other across from me. Next, he retrieved two forks and set one in front of each of us.

I took several bites of eggs, then bit down on the bacon. The food here tasted so different from what I was used to, but it was flavorful. "What should I call you, Jack? Father?"

"Jack will do," he said with a sweep of his hand.

"Thank you for the food, then, Jack."

"You're welcome. I'm so glad you're here, son." He looked at me. "Do you mind if I call you son? What should I call you?"

"Roman, if you don't mind."

Hearing the word "son" stirred an inexplicable ache in my heart.

"So, tell me what period you're from, Roman. And how you came to meet Olivia." Jack beamed as he munched his breakfast.

"I'm from the 1700s, but Olivia and I met in ancient Rome. I time traveled to Rome and became a gladiator." I regaled Jack with stories of my time in the Americas, growing up in England, and life as a gladiator under Emperor Severus.

Jack sat across from me, his gaze transfixed, absorbing every word.

"When I met Olivia, she had already killed some of the emperor's men. She was an oddity in ancient Rome. No one knew how to regard her, so the emperor gave her to me."

Jack chuckled. "Oh, I'll bet she didn't like that. She's very independent."

"She is. At first, she and I butted heads. She was often rude to me and my housekeeper, Amara. We had to battle out our differences." I pushed away my empty plate and mug.

"Rude? She was raised with good manners. I'm sure she felt frightened and alone. She didn't know she was a time traveler until too late. I should have told her when she was younger, but I was afraid. I didn't want to frighten her. I told her when it was too late." His face seemed to melt into remorse.

"I'm sure. It's a bewildering experience." I took a moment to gather my thoughts. "So, she and I learned to fight side by side. I'm convinced it was fate that brought us together. She is my one and true love. We have endured so much together. I believe we will always find our way back to each other."

A wistful feeling coiled through my chest. I missed Olivia with fierce longing.

I leveled my gaze at Jack. "She's pregnant with our child. I must get back to her."

Jack clasped his hands beneath his chin. "Oh, my goodness! I am to be a grandfather. How exciting! I'm so happy for you both, my daughter finding love in another time, and for bearing a child and becoming a mother. I thought I had lost her that night. But Lee kept reassuring me that everything was going to be ok."

His eyes glistened with tears.

The wistful pang turned into a throbbing ache. I had to speak of other things.

I cleared my throat and said, "After Olivia and I left Ancient Rome, we came to the 19th century and learned about your late wife, Alina. Could you tell me more about your marriage to her?"

Jack removed his glasses and wiped his eyes with his thumb and forefinger. Then, he procured a handkerchief from his pocket and blew his nose.

"I'm sorry," he said after a beat. "My marriage to Alina was a godsend for me. But I don't think I was anything more than duty and obligation for her. Alina's heart lay elsewhere. She held many secrets from me and always kept her distance. She was a mystery in our marriage. When Olivia was born, she became even more distant from me. Only after she was killed did I truly learn who she was and why she sought me out."

He sniffled again and wiped his nose with the handkerchief.

"Look at me. I'm an old fool. I was in a really dark place in my life when I met Alina. She saved me, even though she only found me for her own reasons." He forced a smile and said, "Alina gave me Olivia. I will be forever grateful to my wife. And she proved the theories I'd been studying my whole life. She was a Timeborne, like our daughter. I didn't know this until after she was dead. She never confessed her secrets to me."

His smile turned upside down. "But our marriage became rocky when Olivia was born. Alina worked late to find some ancient artifact. She and Lee were always conspiring with each other. At first, I thought they were having an affair together—they were always so close. But then I learned after her death that Balthazar had her heart. I was just a man she felt bad for."

"You know about Balthazar? That he was Alina's lover?" I pressed my palms into the worn table and leaned forward.

Jack shuddered. "Yes. Horrible man. Despicable. I never met the man, nor did I want to. But Lee told me all about him. He told me she was in love with the darkness and couldn't help herself. That's why he killed her. What Alina saw in him was beyond me."

He rubbed his arms before continuing.

I weighed my following words carefully. How will Jack take the truth that Balthazar is hunting Olivia and me?

"He's after us, you know."

Jack stiffened like a frightened sparrow sensing a hawk overhead. "He's after who? You and Olivia?"

"Yes. Balthazar is hunting all Timebornes. He wants to kill Olivia and me—even my twin brother."

Jack's eyes widened. "You have a twin brother?"

"I do. I thought I lost him when I was cast into Rome, but it turned out he was thrown there, too. We were separated at birth." I gazed at the ceiling. "In Rome, we were gladiators. I was stronger and faster than Marcellious. I won more fights. He loathed me for that and made me kill my best friend,

Marcus. I thought Marcus was my brother. I hated Marcellious for a long time. We both hated each other."

"Marcellious…" Jack said softly. "That's your brother?"

I reeled my mind back from the memory that snagged me and said, "Yes. I have to credit Olivia for bringing us together. Marcellious and I were pitted against one another in the Colosseum. It was a fight to the death. I was about to kill my brother, my flesh and blood, when Olivia transported us all to the Americas. She felt Marcellious, and I were more than just enemies." My heart surged with love for my beautiful bride, my heart song, the flame of my life. "She's a good woman. I sometimes wonder if I deserve her."

Jack reached across the table and patted my hand. "Don't say that. I can tell you love her and that you are a good person, Roman." He stared out the window before saying, "Alina was a good woman, too. At least I try to tell myself that. I often wish she had told me the truth about who she was, her purpose here, and her lover. Then, she might still be alive."

His voice cracked at the end.

"She might not be." I shook my head. "I don't know how much you know about Balthazar, but he's pure evil."

Jack frowned. "Lee told me about him. Why would my wife love a monster?"

His eyes creased at the corners.

"The darkness…" I said. "It has compelling sway over people."

Thoughts of Balthazar soured my stomach. I needed to turn this line of thinking around.

I glanced toward the device that had made the coffee.

Jack noticed where my gaze skittered off to and said, "Oh! Would you like some more?"

"Yes, please," I said.

He bolted to his feet and rushed around, pouring coffee, and retrieving the sugar and cream.

Once we both had more of the warm beverage before us, he said, "Has he..." His expression grew cloudy. "Has he ever harmed my daughter?"

"Balthazar has tried. He tried to poison Olivia, then tried to poison her mind. He turned her against me, and she nearly killed me."

Jack's mouth formed an O.

"That must have destroyed Olivia. I can't imagine what she felt when she came out from his spell." I thought he might cry, but then he continued. "When I discovered Alina's lies and secrets and the true reason she found me, I tried to protect Olivia."

He ran a hand through his sparse hair, then wiped his face with his palm. "I tried to shield her from the truth about her mother. If she'd found out, I knew she would have been deeply hurt."

"Balthazar told her everything. It broke her." I clenched the mug.

I'd hated watching Olivia's anguish over her mother's behavior. A daughter should not despise her mother. But, then, the mother should not give the daughter reasons to hate her like Alina did. It was like mothering was an afterthought for Alina.

"I can only imagine." Jack's eyes moistened, and he blinked back the tears.

"Did you know Alina had another child? Her name is Emily. She's with Olivia now. They met in the 19th century."

Jack rocked back and forth in his seat. "Oh, that must be a comfort to Olivia, to have a sister. And it doesn't surprise me that Alina had another child. She was a wild one. She was..."

His fingertips flattened against the table like he was trying to control his emotions. He pulled his phone from his pocket and pressed it into illumination.

He tapped the front of it and held it up to his ear. "Lee, where are you? Call me when you get this message. Roman and I have been chatting, and we need your advice." With a sigh, he tapped away the light on his phone. "I don't know where he is. This isn't like him. He is always here when I need him, especially when you first came here. He was so happy to see you here, and now I can't seem to reach him."

We sat in silence, drinking our coffee.

Finally, Jack said, "Oh, I nearly forgot to mention this. When you arrived, you held a piece of paper in your hand. You clutched it so hard I had to pry your fingers to get you to release it."

"A piece of paper?" I repeated, frowning.

"Yes. You kept saying you were in danger."

"Do you still have it?"

"Yes. Let me go get it." He hurried out of the kitchen. When he returned, he slapped the paper on the table before me. "Here it is."

I lifted the brittle parchment and read it.

Roman, if you're reading this letter, you have healed and survived your wounds. You're probably wondering who I am. All you need to know is I'm your ally. Olivia is safe, and you will see her again soon. I need you to do the following things soon.

First, find Tristan. When you find him, bring him to me under the full moon. You will find me in 1597 Italy. When you arrive, meet me at the following address-Via Antonio Cecchi 63, 30122 Sant'elena Venezia, Italia. It is a villa. You have less than a month. Once you return, Olivia will be waiting for you.

Yours, Malik

I re-read the parchment several times.

Where have I heard that name before? I think I should know him, or perhaps we have met? Did I run into him in the Americas? In England? In Rome?

My mind returned nothing but an empty hole. He felt familiar, but I couldn't put the pieces together.

"What does it say?" Jack reached across the table and grasped my wrist. "It felt like an imposition to read it while you were unconscious. You know, like prying into your business.

"I'm supposed to meet someone named Malik. I think Malik is the fellow who saved me from Balthazar. Perhaps he's the same man who sent me here. He keeps saving me and assures me he's an ally. I believe we know each other and have known each other for much longer." I lifted my gaze to Jack. "He asked me to find Tristan."

Jack released my wrist and said, "That's impossible. We've been searching for him for months. He left without a trace."

I bolted to my feet. "I've got to find him!"

"And I've got to reach Lee. He's the only one who can help us." Jack picked up his phone, which he'd set down on the table, and performed the same ritual.

I sat anxiously, hoping that this Moon Lee, the man I knew as Dancing Fire, would answer.

CHAPTER THREE

OLIVIA

Emily and I were on the run from the demon Balthazar. Our lives were on the line—he'd made it clear when he found us at John James' house, he'd destroy us the next time we met. It had been two long months of endless running and looking over our shoulders. I spent my waking hours in a state of paranoia and terror. When I slept, nightmares assaulted my sanity. But I couldn't let go of my quest: finding Eyan Malik before Balthazar discovered us and ended our lives.

Late winter snow started falling several days ago, making the trip much more arduous. So far, the snowfall was only a few inches, and our horses still found forage to eat. They would paw the ground, grazing on shrubs and dried grasses, then head for the streams and rivers we followed.

We'd made a camp last night and nibbled on our waning food supplies. I'd fallen asleep hungry and frustrated.

How long until we got to the Catskills Mountains?

As dawn stirred, I awoke, snuggled next to Emily for warmth. I blinked, yawned, and stretched, propelled to move forward despite needing more sleep. We needed to create a vast distance between us and the bastard demon who so relentlessly hunted us.

A light smattering of ice crystals had seeped through the branches we'd stacked together for shelter. I brushed myself off and sat up, disturbing Emily.

"Can't we sleep some more?" she said. "What does it matter how early we start? We just seem to go in circles."

I arched an eyebrow and looked at her prone body. Her head was huddled under the furs with her back facing me. Emily seemed to be in a mood of complaint lately, and it was getting on my nerves.

"No, Em, we're not going in circles. We're heading north for the Catskills."

"Well, I haven't seen them yet. Have you?" She flopped on her back, flung the robe from her head with an impatient gesture, and glared at me.

"Good morning, Emily," I said with a smile. "Did you not sleep well?"

"I haven't slept well in weeks. Ever since we started this horrible journey." She pulled the fur up to her neck. "Brrr. It's freezing."

"Just stay there. I'll start the fire and make us some tea."

She tugged the hide over her head again without a "thank you," a "yes, please," or an "I can help."

I gritted my teeth and crawled free of our shelter.

Our horses stood beneath the nearby trees, their breath shooting from their nostrils in white clouds.

Only a few flakes of snow drifted from the gray sky.

"It's not snowing," I called to Emily.

"Who cares? It will start again as soon as we head out," she called back.

I shook my head and stacked branches from the pile we'd collected last night. Then, I started the fire by scraping my knife against the flint I carried, aiming it at the gathered leaves and tinder.

Within minutes, a blaze started. Soon, tea was ready. I poured some into our tin cups, retrieved a few pieces of jerky from the saddle bags propped against a tree, and brought everything back into the shelter.

Emily sat up and ate and drank without speaking.

After breakfast, we packed our belongings and mounted the horses. We traveled north, using the sun and the terrain as our guide and a map depicting rivers, streams, and trails. The snow lay in patches on the land, and we pushed the horses into a frantic gallop between short rests. We said little, in keeping with Emily's sour mood.

When the sun was high in the sky, we stopped beneath a copse of maple trees, somewhere in the state of New York— or so I assumed based on our progress. I dismounted, dug around in my satchel for the jerky, and handed a piece to Emily.

Emily climbed from her horse, too.

"I think we lost the route, Olivia," she said, peering at the map. "This map is useless."

"It's not useless. It's upside down," I said, smiling as I turned the map around.

"I know that," she snapped. "I was just seeing if it made more sense upside down. It doesn't seem to matter."

I huffed out a sigh. "Emily, what's wrong with you?"

She threw up her hands, startling the horses foraging a few feet away. "Everything's wrong. My husband is dead. I'm tired of traveling, running, just plain *tired!*"

I stared at her, unsure what to say.

"I don't think I can do this anymore." She batted at a few errant strands of hair that had fallen on her face. "We don't know if we're going in the right direction or anything. As far as I'm concerned, Balthazar can take me! I can't do this anymore! I'm exhausted. I'm just plain *done!*"

My jaw dropped open. "You can't mean that, Em."

"I can, and I do." She flopped on the frozen ground and folded her arms over her chest, appearing like a sullen child.

My temper flared. "Look, Em, I'm tired, too. I lost my child, my husband, *everything*. At this point, the only thing holding me together is *you!*"

Emily began to shake. Her voice rose to a high-pitched shriek. "Well, that's a mistake. I'm so angry! We keep running and running, and everything is so hard." Her arms flailed about. "We barely have enough to eat. Everything about this trip is getting harder and harder. And we don't even know if this Malik fellow exists!"

I blinked as I stared at her. I'd never seen my sister behave this way. I took a deep breath and tried to gentle my voice.

"Look, Em, I know we're both exhausted. But I also know Malik exists. He's the one who brought Roman back from Balthazar's dungeon. And when I was in the teepee with Grey Feather, we did a ritual with my dagger… The dagger showed me an image of Roman, alive, with a man next to him. I think that man was Malik and that he knows where Roman is." I reached out to touch her shoulder. "I'm sorry you lost your husband, Em. I truly am. But maybe he's still alive. Balthazar can be cruel, but I don't think he kills without cause."

Emily's eyes looked dead when her gaze met mine. "How can you still be full of hope, Olivia? I might be carrying a dead man's child. I love Marcellious with all my heart, but I can't have this baby without him."

A few tears trickled down her soiled, smudged face.

"Oh, no!" I gasped, my hand flying to my mouth. "You're pregnant? How long have you known?"

"I haven't bled since before our wedding night." Her shoulders slumped, and her hands fell in her lap, listless and unmoving, like dead fish.

"Why didn't you tell me sooner?"

A few tears clung to Emily's long lashes. "How could I? You just lost your own child. I was scared you'd be distraught." Tears cascaded down her cheeks. "I'm sorry I've been so cross. I just don't know what to do. I feel so lost and confused. Everything is so hard for us."

I reached for her, and she didn't resist. She wrapped her arms around me, crying into my shoulder. Her body felt bony, all sharp angles.

But relief poured through me at our truce.

I eased her back and wiped her face with the edge of my dirty sleeve, creating a brownish streak across her face. "We're both grieving and exhausted. But we have to keep fighting, keep on with our quest. We must pray that Marcellious finds us soon. I think he's still alive, Em. I really do. He is a strong man, and he can endure anything. But even if something did happen to him, I won't ever leave you, Emily. We will raise the child together, I promise. "

"Oh, Olivia, what would I do without you? I'm so sorry for my behavior. I truly want Marcellious to be alive. But I think believing him already dead protects me from heartbreak. If I already believe it, I won't be shocked when I find out it's true." She sniffled. "I can't seem to carry your optimism."

I let out a bitter laugh. "I'm not sure about optimism. It's more like desperate determination." I glanced up at the sky. "We should get back on the horses and make headway. The sky is clear, and we should make good progress."

I pushed to standing, groaning from the cold ache in my muscles. "Spring is coming soon. I can hardly wait."

The horses picked our way down a hill, heading for a stream. We let them fill their bellies with water and dismounted to take several gulps ourselves. When I lifted my gaze from the water, I spied something out of place upstream. I shielded my eyes from the sun and peered at it.

"Look, Em. It appears to be a carriage on its side."

Emily lifted her head and frowned. "Oh, no. Let's go check. Maybe we can help."

We trekked the creek's edge until we stood in front of the wreckage.

The wagon's wheels lay twisted and mangled, and the leather reins lay listlessly in the water, undulating like seaweed.

"I don't see the driver anywhere," Emily said, staring into the distance. "Maybe he left to go find help."

I looked further down the stream.

Two shapes lay across the water, blocking its progress.

"I don't think so, Emily. They were flung from the wagon." I pointed.

Emily let out a shriek. "Oh, that's awful!"

"We need to drag them out of the stream, so they don't spoil the water for animals and travelers," I said.

"Ew! Do we have to?" Emily shuddered.

"Oh, God! Did we just drink water infested with bacteria from a rotting corpse?" I propped my hands on my hips.

"Ugh! No, that's a horrible thought."

I picked my way into the creek with Emily behind me.

It took us forever to drag the soaked man and woman from the creek. The term "dead weight" had come into our language for a reason. But finally, they lay side by side a yard or two from the waterway with small stones over their eyes with respect for the dead.

That task accomplished, I looked toward the carriage. "Maybe there's something useful in there. They certainly don't need it anymore."

"Good idea," Emily said.

We trekked back to the wagon and sorted the sodden goods, finding some much-needed food in leather pouches and utensils, a knife, bowls, and tin cups. We placed them all on the creekbank so we could decide what to keep and what to leave.

The snap of a breaking branch sounded, sending me on high alert.

Balthazar. Has he finally come to kill us?

"Be quiet, Emily," I whispered. "Someone or something is out there."

We both crouched in the water, scanning our surroundings.

I eyed the horses who still stood in the stream. We could get to them in a few seconds if we sprinted.

But then a tiny child peeked out from behind a tree.

"Oh! It's a little girl! I didn't think to look for survivors." I rose and started heading toward the trees without consulting Emily.

"Wait, Olivia! What if it's a trap?" she hissed, scurrying behind me.

I ignored her and kept moving.

The child ducked behind the tree as we approached.

"Sweetie," I said, "we won't hurt you. We're here to help."

I stepped around the tree trunk and found her crouching near a small bush.

"Honest," I said, holding out my hand. "Emily and I are here to help."

The child stood and took a few tentative steps toward me. Her pale face appeared somber, hovering at the edge of sadness. Her enormous eyes stared back at me, and I reeled backward.

They looked exactly like Roman's eyes. In fact, this child, with her dark tousled hair and child-sized Patrician features could be Roman's child.

I sucked in a breath. How is this possible? She looks exactly like my husband.

"What's your name, sweetheart?"

She ducked and regarded me through the longest eyelashes I'd ever beheld.

"I'm Olivia. And this is Emily," I said. "Can you tell me your name?"

"I'm Rosie," she said in a high-pitched, lilting voice.

"What a beautiful name!" I crouched, inching closer. "How old are you, Rosie?"

Rosie held up five fingers.

"You're five," I exclaimed. "Where are your parents?"

Rosie's chin began to quiver. She lifted her chubby hand and pointed toward the stream, which was out of sight through the trees and brush. "They died."

I prayed she hadn't seen us haul her parents from the stream. "What happened? Did the horses pulling the carriage spook?"

The little girl shrugged, clasped her hands at her hips, and twisted back and forth.

"Do you think anyone's looking for her?" Emily whispered from behind me.

"Look around, Em. There's no one for miles. We haven't encountered anyone for days," I said. "Let's care for her."

"Are you crazy?" Emily hissed. "Balthazar is hunting us, and we're in danger. Do you really want to put this child in harm's way?"

I tugged her out of earshot. "Not so loud. She could have heard you."

"You can't honestly want to drag a child into our misery, can you?" Emily's contorted face was red with rage.

"It could be a sign," I said. "Can't you see how much Rosie looks like Roman? Maybe fate has put her in our paths so I can protect and care for her since I lost my child."

"Don't be ridiculous." Emily gestured as she spoke. "She needs proper care, not to be hauled on horseback by two women who can barely care for themselves."

"But we have more food now! You saw the goods her parents had. That will last us a good long while! She'll need to eat, too. You can't just expect us to take her family's food and leave her to fend for herself. She's only five!"

Emily grew silent, perhaps moved by my guilt trip. At last, she said, "Fine! But if she slows us down or anything happens to us because of her, I'll be the first to say I told you so. I'm scared for her. I don't want anything to happen. Especially since Balthazar is hunting us."

"Nothing's going to happen to her or us. We've made it this far, haven't we?" I grinned.

Emily huffed out an exasperated breath.

I turned to find the little girl, but she was gone. "Rosie? Rosie? Where are you?"

One of the horses whinnied.

I whipped around, expecting to find Balthazar. Instead, little Rosie was patting the horse's muzzle.

"Oh, thank God," I said, pressing my hand to my pounding heart. "Sweetheart, guess what? Emily and I are going to take you with us."

. . .

We traveled another week with Rosie perched behind me or in front of me on my horse, Daisy.

Rosie was a remarkably even-tempered child who gave us little fuss. I found her a ray of sunshine in her willingness to laugh at snowflakes, stick her tongue out to catch them, or sing songs to the horses.

Eight days after finding her deceased parents, we came upon the majestic Catskill mountains.

"We did it, Emily! We found them," I exclaimed.

"Thank goodness," she said.

We guided our horses to a trail that snaked up the mountain's side. When we neared the top, we came upon a stately old house tucked in a grove of trees. I sent a prayer of thanks to whoever might be listening. Orange, peach, and purple clouds filled the sky, and soon it would be dark.

The massive wooden house, perched atop a stone foundation, had a large, wraparound deck and two gigantic stone chimneys along one side. Greenish shingles covered the roof, and huge boulders surrounded the weathered house.

"This looks just like the house John James described. I think this is it!" I dismounted, saying, "Stay here. I'm going to see if there are any occupants. It doesn't look like it—the windows are all boarded up."

I retrieved my gun and my dagger from the straps on my thighs.

"What are you doing?" Emily asked, her voice higher than usual.

"I'm protecting myself. What do you think?" I strode toward the entrance, even though my heart hammered erratically. Pounding on the door, I yelled, "Is anyone there? Hello?"

No one answered.

I tried the doorknob, and it gave way. I gently pushed open the door.

It made a chilling creak as it opened to an empty foyer.

The only light inside came from the waning sunset. Shadows fell across the parquet floor. Spider webs draped from the dusty chandelier, the walls, and the banisters coiled alongside an enormous, bifurcated staircase, divided into two separate flights of stairs at the top, each leading in a different direction. I could picture an actress sweeping down the steps, a martini in her hand.

The vast emptiness of the place spooked me, and chills marched up my spine like an army of ants.

This can't be the place. It looks like no one has been here for decades.

The door gave a shuddering creak, and I jumped, crying out.

"It's only us, Olivia," Emily said in a hushed tone with Rosie by her side. "We didn't feel safe sitting out there alone."

She gripped Rosie's hand, and the two tiptoed into the foyer.

"My gosh, look at that staircase!" Emily said. "And that chandelier. There must be hundreds of crystals joined together."

"Right? This place was once a masterpiece." I looked up the stairs, swallowed my fear, and said, "I'm going to go upstairs. You wait down here. If you hear or see anything strange, get outside as fast as possible, understood?"

"I understand," Emily said in a quavering voice.

I slowly ascended the steps. They groaned and creaked

under my weight. I reached the first landing and turned my head right and left.

Which flight should I take first? Deciding on the right-hand stairs, I proceeded with my climb. When I reached the top, I stilled, my heart galloping in my throat.

At the end of a dark hallway, backlit by a small window at the end, stood a tall, muscular man. Cobwebs draped from the ceiling over his head.

He stared at me with dark intensity radiating from his eyes.

It could only be Eyan Malik.

CHAPTER FOUR

OLIVIA

The man lurking in the shadows at the end of the hallway sent chills up and down my body.

I was so shocked to see him, finally finding him after all this time, my body shook. Was it rage I was feeling? Exhilaration? Or was my body finally releasing all the pent-up feelings of despair and exhaustion I'd been carrying?

I didn't know, didn't care.

Standing at the top of the stairs, I stood tall and took several long, deep breaths to stop the trembling. Then, I said in a strong, clear voice, "Who are you? Stop hiding in the shadows and reveal yourself to me."

He didn't move, didn't flinch, didn't even seem to know I'd said anything. He simply stood with his hands by his side, taking slow, measured breaths, evident with the rise and fall of his broad chest.

"You must be Eyan Malik. I've been on a long journey to find you," I said, clenching and unclenching my hands.

He said nothing.

"I'm tired of finding you in the shadows, always hiding.

Please come out and face me. Reveal yourself to me." I pressed my palm to my heart to soothe its erratic beating.

A scuffling noise sounded downstairs.

I whirled around.

Emily stood clutching Rosie. Both of them stared up at me, their eyes unblinking.

The floorboards in the hallway creaked, and my head whipped back around.

Malik seemed closer like he'd taken a step.

Or am I seeing things? I wiped the perspiration from my upper lip. Come on, Olivia, get a grip on yourself.

"Well? Are you going to reveal yourself to me, or should I turn around and flee?"

The thought of leaving after our arduous journey made my body slump, pulled by the strings of fatigue.

Rosie whimpered.

My head spun around to look at her.

The floorboards groaned.

I jerked back around.

Malik seemed closer still.

What if it isn't Malik? What if it's some insane man who only knows one thing—murder?

I swallowed, willing moisture into my parched mouth. My hands resumed opening and closing like bellows. I pressed my palms to my dirty deerskin dress to stop the continuous movement, but then my fingers began to tap my thighs. The anxiety was killing me. I shook my hands out, then shook my entire body.

Malik was closer.

How did he do that?

It unnerved me.

I glanced over my shoulder at Emily and Rosie.

Emily continued staring at me, but now she was crouching, her arms around Rosie. Both seemed to tremble like autumn leaves clinging to a winter branch.

Rosie had buried her face in Emily's bosom.

When I turned around again, Malik stood directly before me. I yelped and stepped back, nearly tumbling down the stairs.

He grabbed my upper arm to steady me, and tiny stars tugged at my brain, drawing me toward a black abyss. I had to get myself together.

Malik fixed his intense gaze on me yet continued to stay silent. Once he seemed satisfied I wouldn't fall, he let me go and drew the side of his finger down my cheek.

I shuddered. There was something about him. He had a strange magnetic force that drew me closer. I was looking at a work of art made by a master's touch. He was, in a word, stunning.

His shoulder-length hair hung in waves around his sculpted face. His eyes were hypnotic, a cross between the dusky blue at twilight's edge and the green found in a mossy bed beneath massive redwoods. A light shadow of beard growth covered his chiseled jaw, highlighting his full lips. The arteries in his thick neck pulsed in a slow, steady beat, hypnotizing me. Even his scent was captivating—he smelled like petrichor heralding a rain or the sharp fragrance of a field following a lightning strike.

I wanted to reach out and trace the hollow of his neck, collarbone, and massive muscles that radiated strength like coiled electricity. All those lines and angles invited exploration. I wanted to peel away his knee-length coat, shirt, pants, and boots, all in the color of night's shadows, and behold the potency rolling from his body. I longed to touch his olive skin, tanned by the sun, smooth and unlined as if he had been born yesterday. Yet, ageless wisdom shone through his eyes, belying his age.

He could be nine hundred years old for all I knew. Yet, he looked to be around Roman's age.

Malik's eyes softened as he gazed at me, and his lips curved up in a hint of a smile. He exhaled, and it was like a breeze of comfort and tenderness wrapped itself around me.

I became aware of the quietude that surrounded me as if we existed in a place where space and time didn't live. We were nothing; we were everything; we were…

With a growl, I shook myself out of my fascination. Malik was probably tricking me, playing with my mind, causing me to feel all these impulses that betrayed my allegiance to Roman. After all, he was the darkness, just like Balthazar.

"What have you done to my husband? Where is he?" Fat tears came unbidden and rolled down my cheek. "It's been two months! Two months! Is my husband dead? Where did you take him?"

I fell to my knees, unable to bear my own weight. Sobs burst from my lips.

Malik crouched before me, still damnably silent. All he did was watch me impassively as if from miles away.

The stillness, the maw of vast nothingness, shook me to the core. I couldn't take it. I wrapped my arms around myself, sobbing violently, pouring forth the ache of everything I'd ever endured.

Finally, I said, "*Please* tell me what happened to Roman. I miss him so much. I can't bear not knowing. I don't want to suffer anymore."

I was going to wisp away like dust if I kept crying, but I couldn't seem to stop.

Malik reached across the emptiness between us and

stroked away my tears. He sucked them into his mouth like consuming exquisite, golden gemstones.

The room began to vibrate, or maybe it was just me. I could hear Rosie and Emily breathing and sense their stares on my back. Yet, we were all held captive by the power emanating from Eyan Malik.

He cupped my chin and regarded me the way you might consider a child who just fell and scraped her knee.

I felt soothed and embraced by his touch.

At last, he spoke. "I am indeed Eyan Malik. I've been waiting for you for a long time. And finally, you have found me."

The timbre of his voice was rich and melodious as if ancient trees could talk. He kept caressing my cheeks, stroking my forehead. I fell into his embrace, beckoned by need and longing.

Remember Roman. He's your husband. This Malik is nothing to me. He's tricking me, luring me into his world. I'm betraying my husband.

I shoved him away. "Stop. Where is Roman? Where are you holding him?"

"I don't have your husband. He's not here."

The words came sharply, like broken glass hurled at my ears.

I seized his lapels. "But you know where he is. I saw you take him. I witnessed through my dagger that you were holding him."

Malik rocked backward, and I was forced to release him. Then, he swayed back and forth as if stirred by wind only he could sense. Once again, he said nothing.

I felt like the silence would swallow me whole, and I snapped, *"What have you done with my husband?* Did you kill him?"

SARA SAMUELS

I cocked my arm back and let loose to strike Malik, but he caught my wrist. Then, he unfurled my fist and stroked my palm.

Once more, I fell into his charm, swaying in rhythm with his body, back and forth in a breeze no one could sense but us.

"I took him to a place to heal, Olivia. You will see him soon. I had to send him to another time to heal and gather things for me."

Roman is alive! I jerked my hand away. "What kinds of things? Where is he?"

Malik's only answer was to stand, drawing me with him. "You and Emily are exhausted and hungry. You must eat. Rest."

He started to guide me down the stairs, but I surged away from him.

"I'm not going anywhere with you."

Malik ignored my protests, placed his hand on my back, and continued down the stairs.

I moved with him, buffeted by the force of his dominance and power.

"How do you know our names? How do you seem to know so much about me when I know nothing about you?" I said as we reached the foyer.

"You're a Timeborne, and Emily is a Timebound," he said, and his voice seemed to float across a canyon. His hand disappeared from my back, and he glided past me, moving in ways that didn't seem bound by gravity.

"What do you mean, Emily is Timebound?"

As always, Malik said nothing and ignored my question. Instead, he surprised me by crouching in front of Rosie and kissing her forehead.

"Hello, little friend," he said, smiling. "Where did you come from?"

Rosie shifted side to side shyly, but she didn't shrink away. Instead, she reached out and touched his cheek.

"You're a sweetheart," he said gently. "Do you have a name? My name is Eyan Malik."

Rosie looked at me, then back to Malik.

"Her name's Rosie," Emily interjected. "Olivia and I found her at the site of a carriage crash. Her parents died."

Malik tapped Rosie's nose. "That's such a sad thing for a child to experience. I'm glad you are here. I'll help you in whatever way I can."

Rosie's bright button eyes seemed innocent and earnest as she regarded him.

Malik stood and directed his gaze at me. A seductive smile curved his lips, and his eyelids lowered.

I sucked in an inaudible gasp. Malik was the most mysterious and compelling man I'd ever met.

"You and Emily are strong women. Rosie is fortunate to have found you. You've traveled far and endured arduous conditions to arrive at my humble dwelling. Here you can rest, restore, and renew." He reached for Rosie's hand.

She willingly took it, as magnetized to his presence as I was.

"Allow me to show you to your rooms. You must be exhausted." He headed toward the stairs with Rosie by his side.

I stood there like a gaping goldfish, utterly speechless.

Malik and Rosie ascended the stairs, turning left instead of right as I had done. As they trekked, they kept up a barely audible conversation.

"Can you believe this, Olivia? He's showing us nothing but kindness," Emily said.

"I don't trust him, Emily," I hissed. "The darkness can easily manipulate others and they are ruthless killers. Malik was trained under Balthazar. I don't believe him, nor trust him for a second."

Emily placed her hand on my upper arm. "He wants to take care of us. And isn't he kind to Rosie? Children know whether it's safe to trust someone."

"I don't know, Em. Malik could have hypnotized her. He's extremely compelling." I propped my hands on my hips and watched them disappear into the upstairs hallway.

"You don't know him," Emily said. "I say we give him a chance."

I shook my head. "You're right. We know nothing about him. But, again, he's the darkness. At this point, I trust no one and definitely not him."

I raced up the stairs, anxious about where he was taking Rosie.

The left upstairs hallway looked completely different than the one on the right. Sconces along the wall glowed from lit candles inside them. No spiderwebs hung in the corners or from the ceiling. The air smelled like beeswax and lavender.

Still, I was suspicious.

Rosie and Malik chatted amicably from a room up ahead.

I stormed into the room.

Malik looked up and smiled as if greeting an old acquaintance.

I gawked at the room—it was lovely.

Rosie perched atop an impressive four-poster bed, complete with a canopy and heavy blue silk sidepieces that draped around it. Underneath the luxurious fabric covering was most likely a featherbed lying atop a husk mattress. Beside the queen-sized bed was a much smaller one; perfect for Rosie's size.

A huge dresser stood opposite the bed, and in the corner of the room there was a hassock and chair. Along the other wall was an armoire. A stunning carpet filled the floor, with blues, golds, and reds twirling together. Gold stripes lined every wall except for the one behind the bed, which had been papered with an elegant blue instead.

The memory of Balthazar's lair came to mind with its cockroaches and foul mustiness. This was the exact opposite.

Emily pushed past me and assumed the same mouth-open expression as me. "Oh, my! What a beautiful room!"

"This can be your room, Miss Emily," Malik said.

Emily crossed to the bed and flopped on top of it. "It feels like heaven."

All sorts of warning bells clanged through my head. *Don't get seduced! This is a trick!*

"Would you and Miss Rosie like to take a bath, Miss Emily?" Malik said, ever the charming host.

"Would we ever," Emily gushed.

"I'll have one of the maids draw one for you." He took a step, but I put out my hand.

"Hold on there a second. How do we know we can trust you?"

An easy smile played along his lips. "What harm can come from a warm bath, a good meal, and an excellent rest?"

The thought did sound inviting.

Malik probably sensed my indecision because he said to Emily, "I'll have the maid retrieve you when the bath is ready. There are fresh clothes for you to wear in the armoire. I'll show Olivia to her room."

"Thank you," Emily said.

Unable to think of any other protests, I followed Malik. We proceeded down the hall, and into another bedroom.

This chamber was larger than the one assigned to Emily,

with everything decorated in rich burgundy and gold tones. The bed called to me like a siren's song, and my eyelids drooped.

Maybe a bath and a rest would be nice. After that, I'll be able to think more clearly.

Malik glided from place to place with no discernible movement.

I was startled and pulled away. "Stop doing that."

"Doing what?" he said, smiling.

"That…that now you're there, and now you're here kind of thing." I waved my hands all around.

He ignored me and asked, "How are you feeling?"

His eyes were vast pools of mysteries, like staring into a nebula might be.

"What?" I took a step back. "I'm utterly fatigued. That's how I'm feeling."

"The last time I saw you, you were grieving the loss of your child. Have you sufficiently healed?" He ran a lazy finger across my collarbone.

"No!" I shoved his hand away, already starting to feel under his spell. "How does one heal from such a violent loss? My child died because Balthazar assaulted me! I'll never recover from such a heinous act!"

I took a step backward, wanting to escape his influence. "Why are you asking me these questions? What do you want?"

Malik's expression solidified into stone and steel. Slowly, he stalked around me. "Are you saying you could have healed all by yourself? That no assistance was required?" He appeared to move in a blur, appearing before me, disappearing behind me, then in front of me again.

The effect was dizzying.

"Why did you come here, hmmm?" His voice snaked through my mind like liquid silk.

I pivoted, trying to track his whereabouts. "I came for the journal. You have Alina's journal, and I need it."

He slid behind me and whispered into my ear, "You came here because you think I can defeat Balthazar."

His breath was warm, so very warm, that I nearly fell back into him. But I caught myself and stiffened.

"I can help you defeat him. You mustn't be afraid of me."

"Who says I'm scared?" I said, closing my eyes, savoring his effect on me.

"Your heart is beating like a bison chased by a bear," he said, still so close to me that his breath tickled my neck.

"I'm not afraid of you," I said, prying my eyes open. "I'm simply tired."

"You're scared of Balthazar."

Now his voice came from my other side. How did he do that? I didn't feel him move.

I whirled to face him.

He laughed. It was a mocking sound.

"You have my mother's journal. I need it. It has important information in it. I'll be on my way if you just hand it over." I kept my voice even and calm, so it didn't betray the quivering fear shaking my bones. Or my longing to stay in Malik's presence…

He seized my jaw and bore down.

I tried to wrench my face away, but his grip proved too strong.

"You're not in a position to make demands. I would be cautious with your words, Olivia. Your stubbornness could get you killed. I am just as dangerous and ruthless as Balthazar." His eyes became tornadoes and violent storms, tearing apart everything in their way.

The intensity emanating from those twilight orbs turned my muscles to jelly, my bones to liquid. I couldn't move. All I could do was tremble in Malik's grip.

"I could kill you," he said, his breath searing my skin.

"You're a demon, just like Balthazar."

"And yet you came to me for help." He released my face with a flick of his wrist.

I opened and shut my jaw to ease the ache caused by his grip.

"Why are you so nervous?" he said, resuming his circling of my body.

I pivoted as he blurred in and out of sight, appearing and reappearing. I yearned to be close to him. I loathed his nearness, and I hated how he made me feel.

"My servants will draw a bath to you. You will find clothes in your armoire," he said. "Then, you shall be shown to the dining room where a repast is prepared for you."

"What if I don't care to dine with you?" I said, well aware I was playing with fire.

"You'll be there," he said, ghosting out of sight.

I fell back against the door and slid to the ground. Somehow, in a way that made no sense, I *knew* Malik. There was something about him, but I couldn't place it from where or when. And I had to find out how I knew him before it was too late, and I wound up dead by his or Balthazar's hand.

CHAPTER FIVE

ROMAN

I feared what my dreams would reveal whenever I closed my eyes at night. I traveled through vivid landscapes fraught with violence. I would wake up soaked in perspiration, my bedding tangled around my limbs, my heart beating wildly in my chest. I would bolt upright and wipe the sweat from my face with the edge of the sheet before replaying the nightmare, turning it over and over to find meaning.

Yet, tonight was different. I found myself dreaming of Malik, this strange man I'd never met. How he'd saved me from Balthazar and brought me back to Olivia's time. How I'd lay dying on the battlefield, stabbed by a Kiowa warrior, and he'd lifted me like a lamb and transported me here to get help.

And then, in the dream, we were hunting together, our bellies on the ground, our bows and arrows poised, ready to shoot.

Ahead stood an eight-point buck, his head lifted, his ears cocked forward, listening.

"Now!" Malik whispered.

The deer's head pivoted, and he looked directly into my eyes as I let loose my arrow. It flew steady and straight, piercing the buck's chest.

With a bellow, the buck stumbled and fell to his knees. He struggled to get up as blood dripped from the wound.

Malik put out his arm, preventing me from rushing toward the dying animal.

"Wait," he whispered. "He's gathering his song to sing to the spirits."

The deer staggered several meters before collapsing onto his side.

"Now, he is ready," Malik said, rising.

We tread through the forest toward the fallen animal. When we reached the animal, it lay sightless, staring at the beyond.

Malik turned to me and embraced me.

The exchange felt warm and deep, like two brothers sharing the thrill of the hunt and its subsequent victory.

Next, we rode without saddles, our horses galloping across the plains. Our lives together were whole and rich, the kind of life I had only imagined. This was the kind of brotherhood I had longed for with Marcellious. Instead, I found it in abundance with Malik. A pleasant feeling like warm water surged through my chest. As our horses galloped, I threw up my arms and shouted. I loved my life, my family, and the man that became a brother to me.

Then, the skies grew dark as thunderclouds rolled overhead. Deep, bellowing thunderclaps shook the air, followed by lightning strikes. The grasslands ignited, and fire spread across the plains. Soon, the world was on fire, claiming everything I loved—my wife, children, and our home.

I ran to my wife and scooped up her burning body.

"My love." I sobbed as the flames charred her flesh. I

gently lay her down and kissed her scorched lips. Then, I retrieved the blackened bodies of my children and set them beside her.

I would never see any of them again.

My heart exploded like a cannonball had been fired through my chest. I awoke drenched in sweat, fighting against the sheets wrapped around my legs and gasping for air. These relentless nightmares—they had to cease. I couldn't take it anymore.

With a groan, I yanked aside the covers and swung my legs off the edge of the mattress. I propped my elbows on my thighs and hung my head in my hands. This was all too much. The dreams would come every night. And each night, they got worse and worse. And in the end, everything was on fire and burning. I lost everyone; my dream family was gone. The dreams felt surreal, and I couldn't understand why they were happening.

After dressing, I staggered out of the room, disoriented, my head in a fog.

How could I get these nightmares to stop tormenting me?

In the kitchen, I pulled up short, gripping the edge of the doorway, blinking wildly. "Dancing Fire!"

Dancing Fire's weathered face broke into a grin. He carried himself tall, emanating pride. Ageless wisdom shone from his coffee-colored eyes. Here in this century, he wore his hair in two long braids that fell down his back.

Jack sat next to him at the table, sipping coffee.

Dancing Fire rushed toward me and wrapped me in his embrace.

He felt smaller than I remembered but still carried the same strength in his limbs.

When he released me, he gripped my upper arms. "I

haven't heard that name in such a long time. Please, call me Lee. Or, Moon Lee if you prefer."

He studied me, his eyes shining.

My eyes were damp, too.

"So good to see you, son!" he said, patting my arm. "The last time I saw you, you were a young man. Look at you. You're bigger than me now. You were puny before. Look at this muscle."

He squeezed my biceps.

My throat was choked, and I couldn't speak. At last, I managed to say, "I can't believe I'm with you. It's been a long time."

"Too long! Come. Sit. Eat. We have much to catch up on." Lee turned and resumed his seat at the table.

I sat opposite him and Jack. "Good morning, Jack. What a welcome surprise you've brought this morning."

Jack patted me on the back. "Lee finally got back to me. What can I get you for breakfast? Coffee and eggs? Bacon?"

"Yes, please," I said. Since consuming this 21st-century fare, my two favorite things were coffee and bacon.

While Jack bustled about his kitchen, Lee fixed me with a somber look.

"Tell me everything. Fill me in on what you've encountered since last we met."

"Oh, boy," I said, leaning back in my chair and dragging my hand through my hair. "Where to begin?"

I told him how I'd landed in Rome and become a gladiator under Emperor Severus. I shared my alliance with Marcus, my closest friend, and my endless conflicts with Marcellious, including the setup to kill Marcus at Marcellious' request.

Lee's expression darkened as I told him of Marcellious' misdeeds.

"Who is this Marcellious man?" he asked.

"Marcellious is my twin brother. Olivia suspected it and time traveled us all to the Americas, where we found your brother Grey Feather. He helped us on our journey."

Lee's head jerked backward. "You found your twin brother?"

I nodded.

"He was Hunting Wolf when I knew him. My boy, the little boy I raised, turned into a man, a warrior. How much I wished to see him again and embrace him. I miss him dearly. The name Marcellious comes from a story I used to tell about when he was a boy. Marcellious was a great warrior that slayed all demons and was always victorious."

A mirthful smile spread across his face.

"Interesting," I said as Jack sat before me a mug of steaming hot coffee. "He tried to kill me many times. He was in a dark place in Rome."

Lee's frown deepened.

I told him about meeting Olivia, our initial conflicts, and how we fell in love and got married by Grey Feather in the Americas.

"How is he?"

My expression fell. "Much of Grey Feather's tribe has been killed. I'm sure you're familiar with the history and probably know more than I do. But his people are struggling to survive."

We didn't speak, lost in our thoughts.

The smell of bacon filled the air, stirring my stomach into growls.

I took a sip of my coffee, savoring the rich, earthy beverage.

"I'm so glad she found you. I sent her to Rome for a reason. I needed her to take you out of there. She's such a smart girl," he said, his eyes misty. "I knew she'd figure it all out."

He lifted his mug to his lips.

"It was you who sent us there," I said as the coffee in my belly tossed and turned into something acidic. "You threw me there when I was twenty-one, and then you sent Olivia to me years later. We always wondered if you were truly a time traveler. Grey Feather confirmed it for us."

A pan clanged against the burner as Jack continued with breakfast preparation.

He set a plate of scrambled eggs and bacon before me, and I began to devour it, waiting for Lee to speak.

Lee pulled himself out of his reverie. "So, Jack called me few weeks ago and said there was a strange man who appeared near his home. It was you. Who brought you here?"

"I don't know, but I have a note." I wiped my mouth with my napkin.

"Might I see it?"

"Sure." I headed for the bedroom to retrieve the parchment. When I returned, I handed it to Lee.

He studied the note, his lips moving as if repeating the words silently. "Have you met this man? Have you met Malik?"

I shook my head. "I haven't, but I feel as if I know him on deeper levels. It's as if we're bound by fate. He's saved my life on several occasions."

Lee bobbed his head. "If Malik sent you here, the mission has begun."

A sensation like feathers trailing up my spine made me shiver. "What's that mean?"

"The letter says that you must find Tristan, but Jack and I have been looking for him for months. It's like he became a ghost." Lee splayed his fingers. "Poof. Gone."

The remaining food on my plate no longer appealed to me. I shoved it away from me and leaned on my forearms. "Do you know Malik? What can you tell me about him?"

"Malik is like a son to Balthazar. Balthazar raised him as his own. But Malik is ruthless and dangerous—he's not to be trusted." Lee's gaze swung to the window as if seeking his following words among the trees. "Still, he was friends with Alina. She trusted him."

"Did you ever meet him?" I asked.

"No," Lee said, with a shake of his head. "I did not. But before she died, she returned to Malik's time and gave him her journal."

He sighed. "Her journal was her most prized possession. She was always writing in that damn thing. It contained all her secrets and adventures and the mysteries of her past."

Excitement bloomed in my chest. "Yes! The journal! Olivia and I have to find the book containing her writing."

"You'll never find it," Lee said, clouds storming his eyes.

I stiffened. "Why not?"

"Because Malik has it."

Both Lee and I grew silent as I digested this news.

Jack continued to scurry around the kitchen, rinsing dishes and placing them in what I'd recently learned was the "dishwasher."

If Malik has the journal, how will we ever find it and how will we find Tristan?

Lee interrupted my thought process. "I wonder why Malik needs Tristan. I always found Tristan strange and mysterious, but I couldn't put my finger on it. He must be important if Malik insists you find him."

"Well, we'd better locate him. I need to time travel with him in tow." I pushed away from the table, wincing at the wound in my chest.

SARA SAMUELS

"No," Lee said, placing his palm on my forearm. "You need to rest and get better."

I slammed my fist against the table. "I need to time travel! Balthazar is hunting us!"

Shock rolled from Lee's skin like a black wave. "Tell me more about Olivia. How has she dealt with Balthazar?"

"Olivia is terrified. She struggles with comprehending him and with her own darkness. She tries to fight against Balthazar, but, so far, she has been unsuccessful. None of us know the extent of depravity wielded by Balthazar or the supernatural skill with which he moves through the natural world."

Lee stroked his chin, staring out the window.

"Olivia—my wife—is pregnant. And I'm not there to help her or protect her from that hideous demon."

Lee's burnished skin seemed to pale. "There must be a way to find out how she is, even from another time and place."

Jack continued to clatter around the kitchen.

"There is a way," Lee said at last. "When you married Olivia, did Grey Feather bound your daggers?"

"Yes," I said. "During the ceremony, Grey Feather cut our hands and repeated the ancient scriptures. He said that we were now bound, meaning if we ever got separated, we could find one another through the blade."

Lee's face brightened, and he sat upright. "Where is your dagger?"

I shook my head and turned toward Jack.

Jack wiped his hands on a dishtowel. "I put it away for safekeeping. I'll get it."

He shuffled away and returned carrying a parcel of red silk. He placed it on the table before me and reverently peeled back the layers of fabric.

My dagger glistened as the light touched it.

I picked it up and held it, glad to have it back in my possession. It was as essential to me as my own skin.

"May I?" Lee said, extending his hand, palm up.

I gripped the handle, not wanting to part with my dagger.

Sensing my reluctance, Lee said softly, "We need to find her and see how she has fared."

My loose-fitting garments felt too tight, and a quivery sensation rolled through my belly.

I get to witness my love, my beloved Olivia.

My hand shook as I extended the blade to Lee.

Jack took a seat next to me. His eyes shone as he readied himself to see his daughter.

I knew he would not be able to witness what the blade revealed—Jack wasn't a Timeborne.

I squeezed his forearm. "I'll tell you everything I see."

He wiped at his eyes and gave a slight nod.

Lee gripped the knife and gestured toward my open palm. Then, once I'd extended my hand, he pressed his fingers against mine and used his other hand to slice my skin.

I winced and almost jerked my hand back.

As blood seeped from my palm, Lee recited the sacred scripture. His voice rang true and clear.

A sun ray appeared through the window, casting its beam directly over my hand. The kitchen became shrouded in quiet mystery as the dagger began to glow.

Jack's mouth formed a small O. "The blade—it's glowing."

"Shhh," Lee said as he and I peered at the gleaming surface of the knife.

Olivia, my beautiful, courageous wife, lay fighting for her life in a teepee with Emily by her side.

"I can't save them!" Olivia cried. "I can't save any of them. The Kiowa are nothing but ruthless warriors!"

My heart squeezed.

The scene shifted to one of Balthazar physically fighting with Olivia, then, shoving her violently to the ground.

Olivia let out a scream and wrapped her arms around her belly.

I let out a mangled cry.

Lee pressed my hand into the table.

"What is it?" Jack whispered, but I shook my head, unable to speak.

"I'm not sure," I whispered. *Is our baby all right?*

Then, I saw Olivia in her teepee, inconsolable.

"I lost the baby!" she wailed.

Red rage thundered through my veins. I wanted to kill Balthazar, to wrap my hands around his neck and squeeze with all my might, taking the life from him that he had stolen from me. My head fell back, and I bellowed. Pain lanced my heart with jagged slashes.

"Stay with us, son," Lee said. "You can do this. Olivia needs to feel this shared connection."

Tears streamed down my face as I continued to watch, and my breath hitched in my throat. My cheeks burned with shame at my weakness, tears, and inability to help my wife.

The blade grew dark, and I had to peer through a haze of gloom at the next scene. It felt as if I was looking through Olivia's emotions. I watched, helpless, as my poor, gaunt wife rocked side to side with unseeing eyes. She seemed to have given up on life, me, everything.

That desire to murder Balthazar roared through my bloodstream, transforming my sorrow into white-hot anger.

Then the scene changed, softening the wild pounding in my ears.

A man stood next to Olivia, offering comfort—it was the same man who had saved me. It was Malik. Curiosity twisted through my heart. It wasn't precisely jealousy, yet I didn't understand why Malik reassured my wife.

Before I could make sense of the scenario, a quaint cottage appeared. A man who looked remarkably like Jack sat around a worn wooden table, along with Marcellious and Olivia. The trio sat engaged in conversation.

The image shifted again, showing Olivia's face contorted in terror as Balthazar plunged a blade through Marcellious' abdomen.

Balthazar turned to Olivia and Emily and roared, "You'd better run. Run for your lives, ladies. And I'll be right on your tail."

My muscles became rigid as the reality of the situation shimmered before me. I could look, but I was helpless to do anything to change it. And that monster had stolen another from my life.

I bolted to my feet. "I'm going to destroy Balthazar!"

Olivia and Malik shimmered before me in what looked like a mansion, again mollifying my rage.

What's she doing there? And why is she with Malik? The memory of my dreams last night washed through me, Malik and I racing across the plains on horseback, bound by loving camaraderie.

Malik's voice echoed through my brain. "I am a monster, but you treat me like a brother."

My unspoken reply followed. "You might have been born a monster, but you will never die as one. Even the darkest monsters can transform. One day you will change and be the hero."

The images disappeared, swirling into the dust motes bouncing through the air.

The sound of a grandfather clock ticked from the other room.

The smells of bacon and coffee still lingered in the air.

Jack clutched my forearm and said in a croaking voice, "What did you see?"

Slowly, I shook my head, unable to form a meaningful sentence. My heart lay crushed in my chest. My brother had been gravely injured or killed, my breathtaking wife had been broken, and I was far away from her time or place. There wasn't a thing I could do except to bear witness.

"Tell me," Jack said, his voice cracking. "Tell me what you saw."

His bony fingers dug into my flesh.

"The baby is gone," Lee said, answering for me. "The girl I raised into a powerful woman is hurt. She is not the same Olivia that I time traveled eight months ago. She has become a shell, afraid of her own shadow."

"Oh, god," Jack said, his voice splintering. "My grand-child...My daughter...What have we done, Lee?"

He pressed his palms against his cheeks. "I should never have listened to you. We should have told her sooner and trained her the right way instead of keeping it from her. Now she is hurt, wounded, and suffering from the secrets we kept from her."

Lee's gaze met Jack. "I know, Jack. I know. We should have told her the truth and prepared her. Instead, we sheltered her, and eventually, Balthazar found her. What are we going to do?"

I slapped my unsliced palm against the polished kitchen table. "That son of bitch, Tristan. There's no more time to wait. We must start looking for him immediately. Olivia needs us more than ever."

CHAPTER SIX

OLIVIA

My evening in Malik's home was spent in a swirl of opposing extremes—at once hungry yet too tired to eat. Exhausted, yet watchful, Compelled to be in Malik's presence, then, remembering my husband, repulsed by Malik's dark nature.

Images of Roman wrapped around me as I drifted from the bath to the dining room. I felt he was with me, but no one was there when I reached for him. I ate but don't remember what was served. I conversed but I don't recall what I said.

At last, when unable to keep my eyelids open, I was led to my bedroom, where I was asleep before my head hit the pillow. Then, snuggled in Malik's soft, cozy bedding, smelling of lavender and something exotically feral, I dreamed.

"Mama! Mama!" My son's piercing wails kick-started my heart into high alert. I looked up from the garden, where I'd been pulling weeds.

My dream husband and son were ahead, struggling to carry a man down the dirt road.

I sprinted across the garden loam toward them. Each footstep produced a soft slapping noise when my sandals hit the road. "What happened? Who is this?"

"We found this man barely breathing, but he seems alive," my husband said. "With your healing skill, I'm sure he'll make it."

His arms strained from the effort of keeping this big body aloft.

My son grappled with the man's legs, positioning and re-positioning his hold.

"Set him down," I said. "Right here."

They tried to ease him to the ground, but the man fell from their grip and collapsed with a groan. His eyes popped open, and I found myself staring into a galaxy of mysterious color, from dusky blue to shadowy green.

"Easy," I said, placing my hand on the man's sweaty, warm shoulder. "My husband found you, but you're alive. You will be all right. Can you remember your name?"

"My name's… Eyan Malik. I'm in so much pain," he wheezed. "My head…hurts…" He closed his eyes.

"I've got you." I placed my palm on his head, and he seemed to fall into repose.

I awoke, groggy and disoriented, unsure where I was. It took a moment to process the safety and softness of the bedroom before sleep dragged me back into its embrace.

I dreamed of giving birth. I lay in a dark room on a bed, bearing down on my husband's hand. Sweat poured from my face and neck as I groaned into a contraction.

"One more push, my love," my husband said. "Squeeze me as hard as you must."

The act of labor felt like giant waves crashing against the walls of my body, ushering the baby down a narrow canal. I groaned and swore as I tried to force new life from my uterus. Finally, the babe was eased from my core, and I fell back, panting.

"Another push," a female urged. "You've got to extract the placenta."

I gathered strength and bore down once more.

"Beautiful," the woman said. She rested a slippery warm baby on my breast. "Here's your baby girl."

The woman began to fuss with the cord.

I started to cry as I regarded my little girl. Then, the baby began to cry. Then, my husband joined us until we were all weeping.

The midwife finished snipping the cord from the placenta and placed the placenta in a basin. With her hands on her hips, she beamed at us.

"We have another beautiful daughter," my husband blubbered. "Everything is perfect."

He placed his large hand along her tiny back, and she calmed.

A bolt of alarm shot up my spine. "Do you have news of Malik?"

"Darling, you need to rest and care for our child." My husband's eyes glistened with love and joy as he looked at me.

"But they're going to find us and kill us," I said, my gaze darting around the room, searching for the enemy. "You know how much danger we are in. They have been hunting us for a long time. We need to find Malik. Only he can help us."

"Shhh, my love," my husband soothed. "I'll take care of everything. Shhh."

His shushing noises transformed into the crackle of flames. I was propelled into lucid dreaming. My breasts hung swollen and aching with milk. I was surrounded by flames as they licked at and tore down the surrounding village.

My son lay dead at my feet.

"No!" I screamed. "No, no, no, no, *no!*"

My dream husband lunged at me, trying to calm my hysteria.

"Let me go!" I yelled and backed away from him. I seized a sword from the wall, but I was too weak to hold it.

Someone attacked me with a knife, and bright crimson spurted from my leg.

Brutish men rushed into the house and attacked my children, striking them down with sweeping blows.

My husband stormed toward me, slaying the attackers with angry slashes of his sword.

Flames engulfed my children, and the acrid smells of burning flesh wafted into my nostrils.

I clawed my way toward them, but I couldn't reach them. Each time I grabbed for one of my kids, they surged out of my grasp.

"I've got to get to my children," I whispered. "I've got to save them."

Ahead, a man raised a knife overhead in a two-handed grip and brought it down on my husband's chest.

My beloved crumpled to the ground. Then, my husband's attacker raced toward the back bedroom.

"The baby!" I screamed. "He's going to kill the baby!"

I sprinted toward the scorched remnants of the front porch stairs.

Another man shoved his sword into my stomach. I collapsed to the ground. I was dying, and my entire family was killed.

Malik appeared before me.

"Don't die," he said. "I'm sorry for leaving you. I never

should have left. I let my emotions get in the way, and now you're dying."

He had tears in his eyes.

"Protect my baby!" I wailed. "Protect her as your own.

A flaming piece of lumber struck my head. Flames licked my entire body. My life essence began to slip away.

"No, my beloved, don't die on me. Please don't die. I love you. I love you so much. I can't bear to be without you. Don't leave me. I love you," Malik wailed, his words sounding faint and far away.

I let out one last piercing scream and sat up in bed. My face was damp from crying, and the sheets and blankets strangled me, twisted around my arms and legs like lengths of rope.

"Roman!" I cried, struggling to free my limbs. "Malik! Where's my baby? Where are my children? The fire… They killed my children. My baby is gone. They burned my family. They killed everyone. Malik!"

My heart raced as panic overtook me.

The hooded clock on the mantel emitted two soft clangs, indicating the time. *2 a.m.*

Two large hands gently shook my shoulders.

I let out a cry and shoved the unseen intruder away. "Get away from me!"

Malik's voice cut through my terror. "Easy, my love. You were having a nightmare and were screaming and yelling. I heard you and came running."

He settled at the edge of the bed.

I blinked through my tears, barely able to make out his features with the moonlight filtering through the window.

He was shirtless, radiating similar warmth as the bedroom fireplace had done earlier. His broad chest glistened with a light sheen of sweat. His musky male odor taunted my olfactory senses.

I glanced at him and looked away, falling back against the feather pillow. Closing my eyes, I recalled the potency of the dream. I was in a family with Malik and Roman. My children had all burned to death. Roman had been killed or badly injured. I was dying, too, but Malik had begged me to live. Yet the fire had consumed my body, and I'd passed away.

I opened my eyes and looked at Malik.

He pushed my damp hair away from my face.

"Don't," I said, but I didn't push away his hand. "What's going on? I feel like we've met before. Have we?"

Malik shook his head. "No. I found you for the first time when you lost your baby."

"That can't be possible," I said. "The dream…it was so real."

I stared straight ahead blankly, seeing nothing.

"Everything felt so real. The fire. I was giving birth… My husband saved you. We were in danger, and people were hunting us. You were in love with me. You cried when I was dying, saying you loved me. The dream felt real, raw. I felt everything. How is it possible?"

Malik kept caressing my hair, keenly studying me but saying nothing.

I started to cry again. "I'm so tired. I miss my husband. My emotions are all over the place."

I covered my face with my hands, overcome with fatigue, frightened and perplexed by my lucid dreams.

Malik continued to soothe me, stroking and caressing. His big body pressed against me.

Why do I feel so compelled by him? Why do I feel like I know Eyan Malik?

TIMEBOUND

I put up my palm and pushed him away. "Please don't touch me. You overwhelm me, Malik."

He withdrew his hand, leaving a cold void.

I shuddered and squeezed my eyes shut, not wanting to see Malik's face or intense eyes. "Tell me where my husband is. I need to see him."

I opened my eyes and looked out the window at the half moon.

Where are you, Roman? I miss you so much. I need you here with me. I can't do this alone. I need you by my side.

"You're married to Roman. You can use your blade to find him, remember?" Malik's words sliced through my sorrow.

"The dagger! Grey Feather said Roman and I could use our knives to find one another!" I scrambled out of bed and padded across the room toward the dresser. I opened the drawer and retrieved my gleaming blade. Without preamble, I cut through my palm and began reciting the words needed to bring the dagger to life.

The polished metal started to glow, competing with the moon's brilliance.

A scene burst into the room, like a hologram. There lay Roman, my beloved husband, bandaged, in a room I knew so well. He frowned as he fiddled with my dad's television remote.

I let out a sobbing laugh. "My husband's learning how to view a television!"

Then, the sweetest vision of all met my eyes.

Papa stepped into Roman's room—my father, whom I had watched Tristan kill.

Stunned, I slumped beside Malik on the bed.

My breath caught in my throat as the truth slammed into me with the force of a freight train. My father, who I believed to be dead, was alive this whole time. It felt like a brick wall had suddenly dissolved in front of me, exposing a reality that I never knew existed. The shock left me shaking and my mind screamed with unanswered questions and raging emotions, until in a whisper I croaked out the words "My father... all this time... he's been alive?" How many other lies had I accepted as truths?

CHAPTER SEVEN

OLIVIA

The shock of seeing my father alive made me bolt to my shaking legs. I was so focused on the vision in the dagger that this bedroom in Malik's home, where I'd been sleeping a short time ago, seemed to disappear. The four-poster bed, covered with luxurious fabric, fell away, and the sturdy, polished wood armoire and dresser ceased to exist. The thick, beautiful rugs, woven in elaborate patterns, faded from beneath my feet. Even the walls, covered with sumptuous gilded wallpaper, slipped from my sight.

The only thing I could see was Papa.

All this time, I'd thought Papa dead. I'd watched that son of a bitch, Tristan, shoot him, and I'd witnessed my father as he slumped to the ground. I'd mourned his loss as I mourned my own hardships and sorrows. I'd thought I would never see Papa again.

"He's alive," I whispered, still clutching the glowing blade. "Papa's alive!"

I shifted my focus to the sight of Roman talking amicably with my father. I watched Roman's memory enacted before me, and a laughing sob escaped my throat. I pressed my free hand to my mouth and my eyes stung with tears. I could stare at this all day.

My hand shook as I gripped the hilt of my dagger. This vision before me was absolution for the loss of my unborn child, for the many tragic deaths I'd witnessed. Seeing my two loves alive and well in the future washed away the rage and terror Balthazar evoked in me.

"Olivia…"

A slight frown formed on my face. Someone was disturbing this moment of reassurance that all was not lost.

"Olivia…"

I focused on Papa and Roman, desperate to keep them with me.

"Olivia!"

Someone's large warm hand wrapped around my wrist. Still, I continued staring at Papa and Roman, who shimmered before me in the vision.

"Look at me!"

I pivoted, coming face to face with Malik.

"What do you want?" I snarled, frantic not to lose sight of Papa and Roman.

"Your hand…" He pointed at my hand still clutching the knife hilt and then the rug.

Blood, sticky and viscous, dripped from my palm. A dark stain of crimson bloomed on the luxurious wool rug. It didn't make sense—this was someone else's blood, not mine.

I yanked my arm to try and free it from Malik's grip, but it was like pulling my hand from set concrete. "Let me go!"

"No, Olivia," he said in a voice as smooth as silk and strong as steel.

I glanced back at the image produced by the dagger.

It was gone.

"What did you do?" I beat Malik with my free hand.

He caught the other wrist and held both my arms aloft.

The electricity between us was thick and rich, hot as liquid steel.

My lips parted. I wore only a flimsy nightgown, and Malik was bare-chested.

His muscles rippled and flexed in the moonlight.

"I need to heal your palm. You cut it too deep."

My gaze lifted to our clasped hands.

The blood dripped down my wrist and Malik's hand and arm, seeming to bind us together.

I shuddered and yanked away from Malik, backing against the bed.

Remember Roman, your husband. This is a trick—Malik's trying to seduce me with his power.

Malik surged forward like a wave. One minute he was several steps away. The next, he was directly in front of me with his palms on my shoulders.

I started to melt like butter in a hot pan.

"You don't need to fear me. I won't hurt you," Malik said. His eyes shone like emeralds, luring me into their depths.

I drew my head back, trying to resist his allure. "I know nothing about you except that you're a demon. John James told me you're just like Balthazar—a demon who can torture and maim me."

"Then why did you come to me if I'm so dangerous?" he said, his hypnotic gaze continuing to pull me in. "I didn't come to you."

I tried to pull away from his grip, but he was too strong. I couldn't think of an answer as to why I came.

He ran the edge of his finger down my cheek.

I shuddered.

"I'll tell you why you came. You need my help."

I blinked, recalling the reason I came here. "You have to help me kill Balthazar!"

"Do I?" He gently lifted my bleeding hand and held it close to his lips. He gently blew his warm breath upon my skin.

A curious sensation, like electric heat, spread across my palm.

"There. I've healed you." He pressed his lips to my skin and held them there.

I started to droop, to melt into the bed in a swoon. But then I caught myself, jerking my hand away.

"A simple thank-you would be nice." A soft smile played against his full lips.

"Thank you," I said, rubbing my thumb across the now-healed skin. "I'll clean the blood from your rug."

I sat down on the mattress in a feeble attempt to get some space from Malik. *Stupid move, Olivia. Now you're face to face with Malik's crotch.*

"Thank you, but don't bother with the rug. I have maids."

I waved my hands at him. "Back up, please. You're too close. I can't think straight when you're this close to me."

He smirked but obliged me. "Better?"

"A little, yes."

Oh, this is nowhere near better. Now all I see is his broad chest. Focus, Olivia, focus.

"I came to you so you could help me kill Balthazar," I repeated.

"Why should I?" The corners of his lips barely lifted, like this conversation was amusing.

"John James said you could help." I pulled my legs onto the mattress, tucking them beneath me. Then, I stared at the bloodstain, the wall behind Malik, the window—anywhere but at him.

"What does John James know?"

Malik took a step toward me, but I withdrew away from him, scooting back on the bed.

"Maybe Balthazar and I told him to make up things to tell you. Maybe we cast a glamor over him and whispered everything we wanted him to say to you." He took another step.

My breathing quickened as I stared at his thick neck…his sculpted jaw…his full lips…his—

Stop it, Olivia! Look away from him.

"What if Balthazar and I are working together? What if this is all a trap? Maybe we lured you here to kill you?" Malik's thighs were now pressed into the mattress, and I hadn't seen him move.

I closed my eyes.

Oh, God, Olivia! How could you come here, following the words of a stranger? He's right—I may have waltzed right into a trap. This could all be a big fat lie. Then I frowned. Why would he risk ushering Roman to safety?

The mattress gave from the weight of Malik.

When I opened my eyes, he sat next to me, close enough to touch.

"You're fucking with me," I said.

"Such language, Olivia." He traced the outline of my lips.

I seized his hand. "Stop this. Stop messing with me. You're not working with Balthazar. That's impossible. Balthazar destroyed my life—he's a psychopath. He assaulted me, causing me to lose my unborn child, destroyed my sanity, and crushed me emotionally. The only thing that's kept me going was the possibility of finding you. Only now that I've found you, I feel like you're playing with me, messing with my mind and emotions. Balthazar will kill me if I find the journal and bring it to him. If I don't bring it, he'll still kill me." My voice rose to an anguished yell. "I'm doomed no matter what

I do! But I'm determined to keep going, to find a way to destroy him!"

"Shhh," Malik whispered, rubbing his palm up and down my fabric-covered arm. "I won't allow Balthazar to hurt you. As long as you're with me, you're all safe—you, Rosie, and Emily."

He drew me close and held me, rocking me side to side.

I sobbed into his shoulder, letting him comfort me. "My mother fell in love with a monster! I'm chained to Balthazar because of my mom! I despise her."

Malik's arms stiffened around me like iron restraints. "Do not speak of Alina that way. Your mind is filled with lies."

I stopped breathing, sure he would strangle me.

"You know nothing but lies about your mother, Olivia."

He continued to bind me with his arms, to grip me so hard, it hurt.

"The only way to know her is to read her journals."

The sound came from across the room.

I blinked at him as he stood near the dresser. *How did he do that?*

I shivered at the loss of his warmth.

I scrambled from the bed and stormed toward him. "Don't defend my mother! She loved a monster who is now hunting me like I'm prey!"

Malik stepped toward me, and I backed up until I was against the wall.

"No, darling, I won't stop defending her." He placed one arm on either side of me, trapping me.

The word "darling" snaked into my mind and slithered down to my core. I let my head fall backward, and it thunked against the wall.

"Your mother lived a tragic life." He drew the side of his finger up and down my cheek. "Life was messy for Alina. It was dangerous and bloody. You must read the journals to find the truth."

He trailed his finger along my jawline.

I closed my eyes.

He traced a line down my neck and across my collarbone. At the hollow of my throat, he made small circles.

I exhaled a deep, long breath.

He spread his fingers, and his hand wrapped around my neck, threatening and seducing me at the same moment. He pushed his fingers beneath my messy hair and withdrew them over and over.

My lips parted, and a sigh left my mouth. I felt scared and protected… Terrified and captivated. Caged in by his arms, not wanting to go, yet desperate to escape.

He's messing with you. Make it stop.

I shook my head. "You probably loved my mother. I'll bet you fucked her, didn't you?"

"Oh, Olivia." He placed his fingertip on my lips. "You have a very filthy mouth but beautiful kissable lips."

My heart raced.

He wrapped his hand around my neck, bearing down slightly.

Oh, God. Is he going to kill me?

"I can turn your life into a living hell, just like Balthazar." His fingers tightened ever so slightly.

My pulse hammered beneath his fingers. Malik was terrifying, but not in the way Balthazar was. Balthazar was just cruel. Malik seemed to wield emotions like swords, using them to manipulate me.

Now he placed both hands around my neck. He used his thumbs to stroke from the hollow to the side.

"I'll tell you the answer to your question." He stroked my neck. "I never fucked Alina." *Stroke.* "There were only two important women in my life." *Stroke.* "Do you want to know who they are?"

I nodded, my breath still trapped beneath his touch.

"The first one was Layla. I loved her until I watched Balthazar drain the life out of her and kill her without mercy." *Stroke.* He paused, staring intensely into my eyes.

As I studied his beautiful eyes, I felt myself fall into galaxies full of vivid color and unfathomable depths of feeling.

"Who was the second one?" I whispered.

He blinked, and his long dark lashes swept up and down. "What?"

"You said you only had two important women in your life. Who was the other one?"

He cocked his head and studied me, softly smiling.

Maybe he was lost in memory, remembering whoever she was. Perhaps he found me amusing. There was no way of knowing.

Then, in that mysterious way of his, he was away from me, pacing around the room.

I touched the place where his fingers had been on my neck.

"The second woman was Isabelle," he said in a choked, strangled voice. A single tear tracked down his face.

I gasped, pressing my hand to my mouth.

"She was the love of my life. She was my everything. In the end, I killed her."

I sucked in another breath.

Malik killed Isabelle? Who's Isabelle?

He was in front of me again, one hand pressed against the wall over my head, the other stroking my hair and my face.

"Life works in mysterious ways," he said.

I hated the way he soothed me. One second he was

telling me how he'd killed Isabelle, whoever that was. Then, he distracted me with his soothing touch. His effect on me was maddening. I loathed it and craved it, all in the same breath.

His demeanor shifted into something butler-like, accommodating and polite. "I'm so sorry to have disrupted your sleep."

With a nod, he was gone.

I rubbed my eyes. I didn't see him leave, didn't see the door open and close, nothing. I staggered to the bed and fell upon it, grabbing the edge of the bedspread and wrapping it around me.

I couldn't make sense of anything he'd said. How strangely our lives were intertwined. I struggled to fit the puzzle pieces together and finally drifted to sleep.

Rapid knocking yanked me out of a deep and dreamless slumber.

"Who is it?" I said, rubbing my fists in my eyes to get the sludge from my brain.

"It's me! It's Emily!"

"And Rosie!" came the child's little voice.

"Come in, come in!" I folded the bedspread back and swung my feet to the floor. Then, I yawned.

Emily and Rosie sailed into the room like two chirping birds. Both were dressed in clean, new clothes that looked custom-made for them.

"We were so exhausted at dinner, weren't we?" Emily said, flouncing toward me. "I slept like a princess in a palace."

Rosie ran and jumped on the bed. "I love this place! Isn't it wonderful?"

She scrambled to her feet and hopped on the mattress.

I reached out for her when she landed, grabbing her

around the waist. "I'm not as awake as you are, Rosie. Why don't you just sit next to me?"

Rosie snuggled against me.

Emily sat on my other side. "How did you sleep, sister?"

Another yawn escaped my lips as I recalled Malik in my room last night. "I had nightmares. Horrible dreams of fire claiming my entire family."

I swept my fingers across my neck where Malik had wrapped his hands around my throat. Emily didn't need to know that part.

"I woke up missing Roman so much. I used the dagger to show me where Roman was—I'd forgotten we're bound that way."

"Oh, Olivia!" Emily exclaimed. "All this time, you could have known! What did you discover?"

She pushed the hair out of my face.

I turned and clasped her hands. "Roman's alive. So is Papa."

My eyes filled with tears.

"Oh, sister! What wonderful news! Your father is alive!" Emily squeezed my hands.

"Yes, they're both together in my future. Roman is learning how to use the devices of my time. I'm sure he's bewildered." I chuckled, recalling the look of consternation on his face as he pressed the remote buttons for the television.

"That's incredible, Olivia! I'm so happy for you!" Emily caught me in an embrace and held me.

Rosie jumped on the bed and hugged us both.

I was caught in the shared love between us. Then, thoughts of Malik and Balthazar stormed through my brain.

I extracted myself from Rosie's and Emily's loving arms and stood. "Let's eat. I'm famished. Give me a moment to dress, and we can head down together."

I crossed to the armoire and opened it.

Inside, an array of delicate dresses, blouses, and skirts hung from wooden hangers. I selected a beautiful blue dress of fine linen and spread it across the bed. In the dresser, I found pale white underthings.

As I donned them, Emily said, "I'd like to learn more about what Malik said when he called me a Timebound. What do you think that means? And how does a Timebound differ from a Timeborne?"

"I wonder, too," I said, struggling to get all the tiny buttons of my bodice through the equally little holes. "I guess we'll have to ask Malik and see if he's willing to tell us the answer."

I smoothed the front of my dress and twirled around. "How do I look?"

"Once your hair is combed, you'll look beautiful!" Emily retrieved a silver brush from the dresser. "Come here."

She pivoted me when I stood before her and brushed my hair to a glossy sheen.

"How does she look, Rosie?" Emily stood back and studied me.

"So pretty!" Rosie clapped her hands together. "We all look like princesses!"

We headed down the stairs and entered the dining room. An array of food, enough for an army, sat on the blue and gold table runner. Four place settings rested on placemats, and gleaming silverware sat atop blue and gold napkins next to each plate. Crystal goblets rimmed with gold sat near the dishes.

"Oh, my goodness!" Emily said.

"So much pretty food!" Rosie added, running toward the table.

Malik appeared through a door across the room. He

looked elegant, dressed in a black jacket draped to his thighs, black trousers, a black shirt, and an emerald-green paisley ascot at his throat.

When I realized I was gawking at him, I shut my mouth.

"Good morning," he said, like a well-mannered host. "Please sit down and enjoy yourselves. I don't yet know your dining preferences, so I had Cook prepare a food selection."

He swept his hand toward the table. "Besides breakfast fare, there's veal olives, raised pies, ragouts, fricassees, fruit pies, and plum puddings. There's also hard cider for the adults and fresh apple juice for Miss Rosie."

He beamed at Rosie, who smiled back at him. "Eat! Build your strength. Once you've eaten, I'll answer all your questions."

Emily and I exchanged a look, and then we each took a seat as Malik exited the door he'd entered.

"Rosie, sit with me." I waved her over, and she sat on my lap. I plucked a few green grapes from a fruit plate and held them before her.

She wrinkled up her nose and pushed them away.

I dragged a plate of food toward me. I broke off a chunk of cheese, dipped it in the honey, and held it to Rosie's lips.

She pressed her lips tight and pushed the cheese away. "No! Don't want it!"

"Want some meat, sweetie?" I carved a slice from succulent roast beef and placed it on my porcelain dish.

Rosie picked it up and flung it across the room.

"Rosie!" I scolded, setting her on the floor and crossing to where the meat fell. "Where are your manners?"

I retrieved the bloody flesh from the floor and set it at the edge of my bread plate.

"Maybe I could take a turn with her?" Emily said.

"No! I can do this on my own. I want to feed her." I'd

never raised a child, but for some reason, I needed to master the art of feeding fussy little children.

Malik reappeared with an easy smile on his face. "I'd love to feed Miss Rosie. I overheard you from the kitchen."

Rosie extended her arms to him as if this was a natural choice.

"I'm perfectly capable of feeding Rosie," I said to Malik, sniffing my displeasure at him.

"I'm sure you are. But I'd love to feed her."

I wrapped my arms protectively around Rosie, but she pushed me away.

"I want Malik!" she said.

I glanced at Emily.

She made a subtle shrug, so I lifted Rosie from my lap. "Go to Malik. Let's see if he has better success."

I doubt it…

Rosie tottered toward Malik.

He scooped her into the air and threw her high.

I rose from the table, ready to catch her when she fell—as if I could get to her in time.

But Malik caught her effortlessly. He kissed her forehead with uncharacteristic love and care.

"Let's sit down, shall we?" Malik sat across from me, at the opposite end of the table. He patted the chair next to him and handed her a spoon once she'd climbed into the seat, her head barely visible over the table.

The child scooped a bite of stew into her spoon and chomped down on it. She ate with relish, licking her fingers between bites.

"That's good, isn't it?" Malik said. He slid his napkin out from under his silverware and handed it to her. "Where are your manners?"

Rosie took the napkin and wiped her face, grinning at him.

He proceeded to place things onto her plate, selecting from several silver platters and ceramic bowls.

I sat speechless on the other side of the table.

"Shall I load your plates next?" Malik said, cocking an eyebrow.

"No!" As flames crawled up my neck, I reached for a muffin laden with blueberries.

I proceeded to eat to my heart's content while glancing at Malik and Rosie.

It must be his dark, seductive power. He's tricking her the same way he tricks me.

My mouth full of plum pudding, I chewed thoughtfully and studied him.

Malik scooped up some plum pudding and plopped it into her bowl, then added a slice of pie. "And now for dessert."

When Rosie began noisily scooping plum pudding into her mouth, much like a small dog, he wagged his finger at her. "Ah, ah, ah, Rosie. Where are your manners? You must eat with decorum."

Rosie looked at him, looked at her bowl and made a show of eating dainty bites, much like a princess in a castle.

"Much better. But use a fork for the pie." He handed her a fork.

Her little fingers closed around the utensil, and she scooped some berry pie onto the fork.

"Perfect!" Malik said.

Rosie patted her tummy. "I'm full."

"I see that," Malik said. "Why don't you go help Cook in the kitchen? I'm sure she'll appreciate the assistance." He looked so proud, like a loving father who'd just had enormous success with his child.

"Can I stay with you?" Rosie asked, her eyes the picture of innocence.

"Of course." He smiled indulgently at her. "But only if you sit in my lap." He patted his thigh.

She crawled into his embrace, smiling.

I glanced at Emily, and we shook our heads in bewilderment.

He was so, so...*patient* with her. And loving. I couldn't get my head around it. He was, after all, a demon. But, sitting with Rosie, he appeared *human*—not like the darkness.

Malik pressed his palms on either side of his plate and met my eyes. His expression was somber, stony, carved from ancient granite. "I assume you are ready with questions. Am I correct in thinking this?"

My tongue decided to tie itself in knots at his stern demeanor.

"Y-y-yes," I stammered. I cleared my throat. "Yes, we're ready."

"What are your questions?" He scooped something from his plate onto his fork, put it in his mouth, and began slowly chewing.

I side-eyed Emily and then turned back to Malik. "We only have two questions. Where is the journal, and what is a Timebound?"

I nodded, pleased to have delivered our questions without a quavering voice.

Malik continued to chew. He took another bite.

His slow, deliberate mastication continued.

My impatience grew like an ant mound.

"Are you going to answer me?" I said, eyebrows lifted.

Malik took a long sip of hard cider. Then, he forked a bite of beef.

"Are you?" I said again, leaning forward.

Emily flashed me a warning glance.

I gave a shake of my head. I was so done with this demon fucking with my mind. "Answer me!"

Malik raised one elegant eyebrow and swallowed his mouthful. "I'm not finished yet."

I picked up a silver spoon and flung it across the table. It missed Malik and landed with a tinny clatter on the floor as I bolted to my feet. "If you're not going to fucking give me answers, I'm going to leave."

Malik appeared in front of me in that strange way of his and grabbed my neck.

Emily whimpered.

I yelped and seized his wrists to keep him from strangling me.

"You will not say such dirty words in front of a child. Do you hear me?" His words came out low, but the intensity behind them felt like a blow to the head.

The message ricocheted through my body like a pinball, knocking a landslide of shame loose. Malik was right—I should act like a good role model to little Rosie. I should know better.

Tears stung my eyes. I was tired of crying and feeling like there was no safe place for my foot to land. My chin quivered.

Great. I'm behaving like an infant.

I tried to swallow back the tears, to force away the insecurity. "I apologize."

"I don't need apologies. Rosie does," Malik said with a snarl.

I blinked a few times. "It would help if you released my neck."

He stroked my neck with his thumbs in that same maddeningly seductive way he did last night.

"Apologize," he hissed.

"Rosie," I said, unable to see her through Malik's body, "I'm sorry I used a crass word."

"That's okay," she said. "My daddy used to say bad words when the cows got out."

A chunk of my heart fell to the ground. This poor child had only recently lost her parents, and I behaved like a screaming, tantrum-throwing infant.

"I'll bet he apologized to you when he did that, didn't he?" I stared at Malik.

A raging storm of intensity poured from his eyes, but he kept on caressing my neck.

"Sometimes," Rosie said. She clambered to the floor, and soft little footsteps padded toward us. She hugged the back of my legs. That was it—just a hug. But it was all I needed to start crying.

Malik released my throat.

"I'm just so frustrated," I said. "I miss my husband. I'm still tired from our journey—I'll probably need to sleep for days to recover. And all I want are answers. I need something to hold onto, some shred of hope or encouragement. Something…"

Fat wet tears slid down my cheeks.

Malik's eyes softened into pools of liquid jade.

"Meet me in my study in thirty minutes." He patted Rosie on top of her head and said, "Thank you for dining with me. Now, will you go see Cook?"

"Uh-huh," she said, gazing up at him with adoration. She tottered away, heading toward the kitchen.

Malik turned on his heel and departed.

I staggered to my seat and fell onto it.

"Oh, God, Olivia, are you all right?" Emily rushed to my side.

"I honestly don't know." I propped my elbows on the table and hung my head in my hands. "I should be grateful for his hospitality, but I feel like he crawls inside my head and makes me question everything. I don't like that feeling. I feel unstable, like I never know where to put my foot."

I blew out a breath, picked up my napkin, and wiped my wet eyes and cheeks.

Emily kissed the top of my head. "Tell you what. My question can wait. Let's go meet with Malik—if he has time, we'll get to my question. If not…"

She shrugged.

I let out a long sigh. "Thanks, Emily. You're the best."

Twenty-eight minutes later, I wandered down the lower floor hallway, searching for the study. Everything about this house was massive and sturdy, from the high ceilings to the carved wooden furniture to the ornate doors etched with unique symbols.

A doorway was open ahead on my right. I stood at the door, watching Malik as he stared out the window.

Emily crept up behind me.

Outside, a stiff wind bent the trees, and clouds raced across the sky, galloping like wild stallions.

"We're here," I said in a small voice.

He pivoted and looked at me impassively.

"Come in, come in." He maneuvered past his enormous espresso-colored desk and crossed to a sofa covered with jade-green silk. "Please join me."

He swept his arm to the side as he settled on the cushions.

I stood stiffly in the doorway.

A side table rested next to his side of the sofa. He retrieved a leather-bound book from inside.

My heart jumped.

It's my mother's journal. I longed to touch it, to hold it, to have something of hers in my hands.

He rested the book in his lap and placed his hands on it. Shifting to face me, he said, "Your mother gave me her journal before Balthazar killed her." A soft expression washed over his face, inviting me to relax. "She wanted me to tell you if you found the journal and read it, she hoped you would forgive her."

His words slid inside my chest like probing fingers, gently working their way past all the barriers and walls I'd erected toward my mother. My heart felt strange, mushy, and vulnerable.

How could we ever be reunited? In death? And, how am I to forgive her when she loved a monster who wants to destroy me and everything I hold dear?

"This book..." Malik rapped his knuckles on the worn leather. "It contains Alina's deepest, darkest secrets."

He stood and crouched before me, holding out the journal. "Here, Olivia."

I reached for the journal, and my fingers brushed Malik's. Bursts of electricity crackled between us, and our eyes met. I felt as if I looked beyond the universe as I stared into Malik's captivating eyes. Lifetimes of experience and unfathomable mysteries stared back at me.

Then, my gaze was drawn to the journal.

Malik withdrew his hands and rocked back on his heels.

The journal felt heavier than it looked. Words like "sacred" and "fragile" fluttered through my mind. I lifted my eyes to Malik's.

"Thank you," I whispered.

"Promise me you'll keep an open mind," he said softly. "I know Emily can handle what you'll soon discover. I worry about you the most."

My eyebrows lifted. "Why?"

"You're so tough."

"But isn't that a good thing?" I said.

"Not always." The tenderness emanating from him was almost too much to bear. "Read this journal here. Take your time with it. Let yourself absorb your mother's words, and please don't judge. Once you have read it, I will then explain to you both what a Timebound is. The journal is long and will take you all day to read. I will take care of Rosie while you learn about your mother."

Malik rose. I stood, too, as if guided by invisible strings. Emily's forehead furrowed, and she studied me.

I didn't understand the effect Malik had on me. There was some inexplicable longing, like silvery strands of energy binding us.

I would mull on that later. For now, I had the journal compelling me to explore its contents.

CHAPTER EIGHT

ROMAN

My head was about to explode as I paced back and forth across Jack's kitchen. I was at a dead end as to where to find Tristan. My nerves were wound tight to the point of fury and helpless frustration.

"Tristan must be located. There must be an avenue you two have missed." With a beseeching gaze, I looked at Lee who sat at the kitchen table calmly drinking coffee.

Beyond him, out the open window, the trees and bushes stood reaching their leaves toward the sun. Birds rustled about and chirped, heedless of my agitated mood.

Lee set his mug down and stroked his chin. "I used to be able to keep track of him. He's a fairly predictable guy. I could find him anywhere. Now, he's gone—no phone, nothing."

He took another sip of coffee. "He was so odd. Jack and I found him well-mannered when Olivia started dating him. But he was a mystery, too, you know? His mom had died, his dad was missing… He seemed lost, like in search of something none of us could provide."

He rapped his knuckles on his placemat.

My hands shot into the air. "How could you allow your daughter to love this man you knew nothing about?"

Lee shrugged. "We knew some things. Tristan had a good job at the hospital. And he seemed to dote on Olivia like she was the sun to his moon. What parent or caregiver could argue with that?"

He tipped back his head to drain his cup. He let out a satisfied "Ah," when he set the mug down.

"Tristan was polite. Mild-mannered." A frown creased his forehead. "But there was something odd about him, you know?"

I didn't know, so I said nothing.

"He was almost too perfect. As we got to know him, it almost seemed like he rehearsed things before he said them, like he was on stage in a play. Then, as the relationship between him and Olivia continued, Jack and I became increasingly suspicious. His perfect demeanor seemed to cover up dangerous machinations."

"Why didn't you try to stop Olivia from seeing him?"

One salt and pepper eyebrow rose on Lee's face. "You must have seen how stubborn Olivia can get."

I raked my hand through my hair. "God, have I. Olivia digs her heels in, and there's no moving her."

"That's Olivia." Lee crossed to the sink holding his mug. He rinsed it out with water and placed it in the sink. Then, he rested his backside against the counter. "The day she traveled, Jack told her the truth about who she was and that he believed that Tristan was dangerous. Jack and I felt it in our gut that something was wrong. She accused her father of jealousy, and things went downhill from there."

I sighed and settled on a kitchen chair, trying to calm my warring temper. "Where have you looked? Maybe we can retrace your steps. Perhaps I will be able to see something you have missed."

"Yeah, I don't know. We've looked *everywhere.*" He pushed away from the counter and brushed his hands together. "But maybe I've been looking at this all wrong. Maybe you're right. We can head over to Olivia's apartment."

I stood, eager to do something besides pace around the kitchen. But before I headed for the front door, I paused. "There's something I could use your advice on."

"Shoot," Lee said.

"Excuse me?" I said.

Lee chuckled. "That's a common phrase. When you say 'shoot,' it means go ahead and say what you want."

I blinked, then continued. "I've been having these dreams… These nightmares. They're horrifying. They started when Olivia and I got married."

I squeezed the back of my neck.

Lee resumed his lean against the counter, and I backed against the wall. "The dreams are so vivid, so real… They're always the same or variations of the same."

"Tell me. Describe them to me," Lee said softly.

I was already sinking into the quicksand of the night-mares, so his voice sounded like it came from a long distance away. I pressed my hands against the wall behind my hips and spoke. "I have this family in the dream. I'm content with my wife and children. I'm happy. Sometimes I race through the woods on horseback with Malik by my side. We're behaving like brothers, but I know we're not—not in the biological sense. But there's this deep bond between us. Sometimes we're hunting, sharing the exultation of felling a buck. At other times, we're striding through the woods."

I narrowed my eyes as the next part of the dream appeared in front of me. My voice emerged in a rasp when I said, "And then I see smoke. It fills the air and clogs my throat, nose, and lungs. And when it comes into view, it's my house, my children, my beautiful wife—they're all on fire, running toward me. Whenever I have a nightmare, I wake up in a cold sweat, tangled in the bedding. Sometimes I awaken with a scream on my lips."

"Roman…" Lee's quiet voice pulled me back from my tortured vision.

"There are all these bad people," I said, still mired in the dreams. "I can never get them to stop. I can't figure it out. Something happened when your brother bound us. I always felt like Olivia was my soulmate, but the bonds became more intense after our marriage ceremony."

I met Lee's gaze, willing myself to return to this house's present and safety. "They scare me. Is this something that will come to pass, or has it already happened?"

Our gazes remained locked.

Then, Lee broke the spell between us. "These dreams cannot be figured out in a moment. Let's set them aside and focus on finding Tristan. But don't worry—we'll decipher the meaning of your visions. Dreams are mysteries to unfold. They're seldom literal. Don't worry," he repeated, pushing away from the counter.

I clung to his words as I stepped away from the wall.

Outside, I followed Lee as he strode toward a green metal contraption. It looked like a strange cart with no harness.

"Will we be taking that to look for Tristan?" I pointed to the metal thing as my feet crunched against the ground.

"That's correct," Lee said.

I looked right and left. "Where are your horses?"

Lee chuckled. "There are no horses, Roman."

"Oxen, then?" I spun in a circle, looking for livestock.

"Nope. There's what's called an engine inside that will

power the SUV." Lee fished a key from his pocket and pressed a button.

The contraption chirped in response, startling me. "Is that what it's called? An SUV?"

"Correct. SUV stands for Sports Utility Vehicle. Get in. Your side is open." Lee slid behind the wheel.

I mulled over those three words as I headed for my "side." I certainly knew the word "sports" from the Roman games. And from my smattering of French studies, I knew "utility" meant useful and "véhicule" meant to carry. So this was a helpful carrying device that had something to do with sports. I opened the door and slid onto the seat. All sorts of knobs and dials covered the front of the vehicle inside.

"I remember what it was like to time travel to the 21st century." He pressed a button on the front of the vehicle. "It can be bewildering."

The vehicle lit up, and a loud noise erupted. I gripped the door handle.

"Easy, Roman. That's the engine of the Jeep."

"Jeep," I repeated. "What is this *Jeep*?"

Lee waved his hand in a circle. "We're sitting in an SUV. It's just like a wagon. But instead of a horse, there's an engine powering it. The company that made the SUV is called Chrysler. And Chrysler called this vehicle a Jeep. It's just a name, nothing more." He gave me a side-eyed glance. "Like I said, I remember coming to the 21st century. There are so many gizmos and devices it will make your head swim. But I'll help you figure it all out. Now, put your seatbelt on, and let's get going."

He helped me secure this seatbelt thing across my chest, then pulled a lever.

An image, like a television image, flashed before us.

"That's what's behind us. There's a backup camera on the Jeep. It lets me see what I'm doing as I back up."

He did something with his feet, and the Jeep lurched backward.

I clutched the door handle again as my heart tried to claw its way out of my throat.

Lee chuckled. "I was the same way. So much to learn… This old Jeep will go faster than a horse but just hang on for the ride."

He pulled the lever again, and we surged forward.

He was right—this horseless device went much faster than even a stallion.

We drove along a wooded street for a while before buildings, and more streets appeared. I gawked at everything, in awe of Olivia's strange world.

Soon we were surrounded by vehicles zipping past us. This was like a chariot race, only without the horses. Still, I probably looked foolish with my jaw-dropped assessment of our surroundings.

We pulled up in front of a tall building the color of sand.

Lee pressed the button again. The engine noise ceased, and the vehicle shuddered to a stop.

"There, there," he said, patting the steering wheel. "I should have told you—this SUV was Olivia's."

"She navigated it without supervision?" I said, surprised. "Is that what women do in this century? Travel about on their own?"

"I'm sure Olivia had to travel on her own in your century." Lee eyed me with amusement.

"Not if I could help it," I said, my chest puffing with pride. "It was my role to care for her."

Lee nodded. "And I'm sure you did your best. But Olivia is not used to being cared for by a man. Well, I take that back. She's an independent woman used to making her own decisions. I'm certain you struggled at times with who did what."

I frowned, remembering many arguments with Olivia over our roles and responsibilities. "At times, yes."

"Here's why." Lee swept his hand out before him. "Welcome to the 21st century. Anyway, let's head upstairs."

We exited the Jeep, and I followed Lee into the building. There, he guided me into something called an "elevator" that closed around us and hummed.

The pace of everything in this era was so rapid that it left me feeling dizzy. I longed for my past, where things moved at a rate I could comprehend. But mostly, I longed to be with Olivia, wherever she was.

When the elevator doors opened, I cautiously stepped into the hallway. "How is it our surroundings look completely different?"

"This is the 5th floor of the building. The elevator replaces the stairs, allowing us to swiftly travel to the respective floors."

My head ached from all this new information.

When we traipsed down the beige rug to apartment number five-fifteen, where Olivia and Tristan once lived, Lee retrieved a key and fit it in the lock.

This, at least, was familiar.

Then, he opened the door and wandered inside.

I followed him.

A musty smell met my nose as I entered the apartment, much smaller than Jack's home. A few simple furnishings sat here and there, like a couch and a couple of chairs.

The din of all those "engines" drifted into the building. I walked toward the building and gazed outside.

Many vehicles drove along the paved streets. Some of

them abruptly halted, and loud horn-like sounds came from them.

I didn't like this cacophony of noise that permeated the room, even though the windows were closed.

"Those noises are horns. Cars, trucks, SUVs—all are equipped with horns so you can yell at the car in front of you without opening your mouth." Lee laughed.

"I see." I pivoted and said, "Where should we look? This place seems bare and empty."

"It is. Jack and I have searched and searched this apartment. But go through closets, open doors, open drawers, whatever… I'll start in the kitchen."

I headed down the short hallway. Nothing in this place smelled remotely like Olivia. Instead, it smelled faintly like mold.

I raced through the house, flinging open doors and cupboards, desperate to uncover any sign of Tristan's whereabouts. My heart sank at the emptiness I found in every room until I opened a drawer and was met with an onslaught of delicate lace lingerie. It reminded me poignantly of my beloved wife, who had been taken from me across time—a longing that swallowed me whole as I touched the last remnants of her presence. Poking out from beneath the bed lay a book. Entitled *Dirty Little Secrets,* I seized it and flipped through the pages, my face heating as I glanced at the images of naked couples in various sexual positions. I scanned descriptions of things like "Reverse Cowgirl," the "Couch Grind," and the "G-Whiz," becoming increasingly agitated, embarrassed, and aroused. Finally, shame got the best of me, so I slammed the book shut and pitched it back under the bed.

I shook my head when I met with Lee in the front room. "My search yielded no results. You?"

"Same here. There's no trace of Tristan anywhere. He

took everything he could and vanished." Lee propped his hands on his hips.

My shoulders slumped in defeat. "What should we do next?"

Lee snapped his fingers. "I've got it! The last time I saw Olivia, she was at a festival in Fremont. She was worried, and I admittedly didn't pay much attention to her concerns. I was caught up in the affairs of my life."

He cast his gaze at the floor. "I wish I'd given her my full attention. Then, she might not be where she is. But then she might not have met you, either." He let out a long sigh. "Anyway, let's head there. Let's follow the trail."

We headed to the Jeep and zipped along the roads again.

We crossed over a bridge and entered a small township bustling with energy.

"This is Fremont. It's a cute little hipster city."

"Hipster?"

"Just a phrase." Lee scratched the side of his head. "It's sort of like the terms fribble, popinjay, or dandy. Or, fop."

"Oh. Someone who fancies their appearance and puts on airs?"

"Sort of. Close enough." Lee grinned at me. "You're learning."

I didn't know why his compliment pleased me, but it did.

Lee parked, and we exited the Jeep.

As we strolled along the sidewalks, I continued to gawk at everything.

"Let's buy you some new threads," Lee said.

"Threads?"

"It's another phrase. It means clothing. Attire."

"Ah," I said, staring at a storefront with pictures of people's arms, chests, legs, backs, and faces covered with branded symbols. One of the pictures depicted a nearly naked woman with a snake symbol crawling up her leg, around her hips, and up her backbone. I blushed, averting my eyes from this wanton display. "What is this place?"

"It's a tattoo shop. It's where someone puts symbols on the body, like your markings." Lee pointed at the place where my markings were on my chest and arm.

"And women get these markings? Are they slaves to the emperor?" My face continued to burn with heat.

"No slave. And no emperor. It's their choice. There are a lot of differences in women in this time than what you're used to, Roman." He reached for the door handle of the tattoo shop.

"Where are we going?"

"This is a combo barber and tattoo parlor. You need to look like a modern man, not an uncivilized warrior," he said before stepping through the doorway. "You look like a barbarian, Roman."

I followed him and was assaulted by loud buzzing like a million insects flying through the room.

Men and women, their skin all elaborately marked, bent over other men and women, moving some strange device across their skin to create the markings.

"What is making that incessant noise?" I asked Lee.

"Those are the tattoo guns." Lee pushed through a door in the back leading to a room with several men getting their hair cut. "I have a customer for you, Sebastian."

"Oh, hey, Lee!" Sebastian, a swarthy-looking male bearing many symbols, looked up from the man whose hair he was cutting. "Is it that guy?"

He pointed at me.

"Yep. This is Roman Alexander. Roman, meet my friend Sebastian the Great," Lee said.

I stepped forward to shake Sebastian's hand. "You must be a warrior. I am also."

"Uh, sure," Sebastian said, switching the scissors and comb to his free hand and pumping my arm. "Some people think so."

"Doesn't your title designate your greatness?" I blinked in confusion.

"Oh, that. Sebastian the Great means I'm a badass hair barber and a badass tattoo artist."

"Badass?" I said.

Sebastian the Great eyed me suspiciously. "Don't you know what badass means?"

Embarrassed, I shook my head.

"You from another country? You sound like you're from England. I thought they used the term 'badass' over there." Sebastian frowned.

"I, uh, don't get around much. I don't follow trends," I said, using a term Jack had explained to me when he tried to show me something called "social media."

"It's a word that means I do excellent work." Sebastian the Great proceeded to comb the fat man's hair between his fingers and slice it off at the ends. "My work has helped me recover from the brutality of war."

Clouds and shadows flitted across his face.

"Roman fought in warrior games overseas," Lee said.

"Oh, you're a military man, too," Sebastian said, glancing at Lee.

I looked to Lee for guidance.

"That's right. Roman is a military man," Lee said.

I simply nodded.

"I served in Afghanistan. Brutal. Where did you serve?" Sebastian set his hair-cutting tools down and brushed the fat man's neck with a small brush.

"He served in special forces," Lee interjected. "Top secret. He can't speak of them."

"That's right," I said, following Lee's lead. "They were very special and very secret."

And under the emperor's domain.

"My brother is a spy, too. He comes home for Thanksgiving, and we can't get a word out of him." Sebastian shook his head before turning to his customer. "Okay, Frank, we're done. Lisa will check you out at the front desk."

"Does Lisa verify that you've done an excellent job?" I said, scrutinizing Frank. "Frank's haircut seems to have been done well."

"Thanks, but—" Sebastian began.

Lee cut him off. "English is not Roman's first language."

"I see," Sebastian said, removing the fabric cape from Frank's neck.

"Wait, yes, it is," I said to Lee. "I grew up in…"

"It's a phrase," Lee interjected. "It means you didn't learn all the subtleties of English in the Americas when you grew up in your tiny village in Europe."

He inclined his head forward as if to say, *Just follow along.*

"Ah! Right. I didn't master the subtleties. I have been gone for a long time."

"I understand." Sebastian grabbed a broom and swept the trimmings of Frank's white hair into a pile next to his area. "Let's get you spruced up."

"Spruced up?"

"Looking good, my man. Looking good!" Sebastian patted the black leather chair, and I sat down.

Sebastian wet my hair with a misting device. Then, he picked up a tool with a long cord and flipped a button. The tool buzzed and hummed like the tattoo guns. "Head down. We're going to give you a fade."

A fade?

I surrendered to Sebastian's ministrations, not wanting to annoy him with my endless questions.

Lee and Sebastian continued to chat as if they were long-time friends.

Sebastian pressed the device to my head. It vibrated against my skin, and long, thick waves and curls fell from my skull.

Panic surged through my chest at the sight of my hair falling all around me. I wasn't vain, but I knew my hair was a glorious asset. What would Olivia think when she saw me again?

Olivia, my love... I hope to be with you soon. Once we find this Tristan fellow...

Sebastian laid the buzzing device down.

Long hanks hung in my eyes.

He lifted up pieces of hair and cut them, continuing his conversation with Lee. Then, satisfied, he picked up the buzzing device, fit something over the tip, and brought it to my jaw.

I yanked my head away, and Sebastian jerked the device away from me, appearing alarmed.

"What did I do?" Sebastian said. "PTSD? I've got it, too."

"That's right. Roman suffers from PTSD." Lee turned to me and said, "Easy, Roman. He's only going to spruce up your beard. Tidy you up. It's not going to hurt."

I stared at the device in Sebastian's hand and then at Sebastian. "Please proceed. I'm sorry I reacted."

"Don't worry about it, man. I understand. The weirdest things can trigger it, and then, bam! You're right back on the battlefield." Sebastian the Great's eyes glazed, and he whispered, "My children's laughter can echo through the house. Then, a siren wails and a dog barks. Somewhere a mother cries. I live with a constant hum and buzz in my ears from loud explosions, gunfire, and screams. I hear the cries and death rattle of the men I failed to save. I hear the screams of…" He shook his head and his eyes cleared. "Shit, man, I'm sorry. This fucking PTSD can sneak up on you at any moment."

I didn't know what he was talking about, but I nodded.

"Bam," I repeated.

After he was done, Sebastian stepped back and whistled. "Damn, you do look good if I say so myself. Lisa!"

He gestured to a young woman who sat behind a counter.

Lisa looked up and said, "Damn, baby, you look hot."

She rounded the corner, sauntering toward us wearing short pants and a tight shirt. Her pink hair had been pulled into two ponytails high on her head, making her appear young. Even she was covered with symbols.

Did Olivia wear such inappropriate attire when she lived here?

Intense heat crept up my neck and face as Lisa approached.

Lisa took my jaw in her hand and turned my face from side to side.

"Fuck me, you outdid yourself, Sebastian. Are you single?" she said to me. "I'd be down."

"Down what?" I said, blinking.

"He's married," Lee said.

"Pity." Lisa pursed her lips which were covered with a glossy pink stain. "Well, give me a shout if your wife ever leaves you."

She grinned.

"A shout?" I tried to imagine shouting at Lisa.

Why would I do this?

"Roman's from a tiny village in Europe. He doesn't know our vernacular," Sebastian explained.

"I see. You know what I mean," Lisa said, putting her hand next to her face with her thumb and pinky finger outstretched. "Call me."

"He's happily married," Lee said, saving me. "There's no chance he and his wife will ever part. They've already endured more than most couples could ever imagine encountering."

"The good ones are always taken." She spun on her heel and sashayed back to her seat behind the counter.

Sebastian brushed off my neck and removed the cape. "You do look hot, my man."

"I am a bit flushed, yes," I replied.

Sebastian laughed. "I meant you look fantastic. You're a handsome dude."

I didn't know what a dude was and didn't want to ask.

Sebastian glanced at the brand marking my arm. "Who did your tattoo?"

"After a battle. The slave owner in Ro—"

"Roman was a POW for a time," Lee quickly said. "He served beneath a brutal warlord."

"Oh, man, that's harsh," Sebastian said, grabbing his broom and sweeping the trimmings of my long hair into a flat tool. He dumped the pile in a trashcan unceremoniously.

"Do you want any other ink? Your right arm is bare." He inclined his head toward me. "I mean, I don't have any other hair appointments for the day. I'd be honored to inscribe something meaningful on your skin. Badass to badass."

His expression grew somber.

I glanced at Lee, who nodded. When I looked at Sebastian, I said, "I would be honored, too." I pulled my dagger from the sheath on my belt. "Could you replicate this knife on my forearm?"

Sebastian let out another whistle. "Holy fuck, dude. I'd be so honored. That looks fucking ancient, man."

We proceeded back to the tattoo room, and Sebastian led me to his "station." There, he sketched the dagger to my satisfaction. He was indeed a "badass" artist.

When he was ready to brand me, he said, "I prefer not to chitty chat when I work. Are you cool with that? I might put on my headphones and get into the zone. Don't worry. I'll keep checking in with you to see how you're doing, but do you mind?"

I sat baffled at the words "headphones," "chitty chat," and "cool."

Lee helped me out again, saying, "That's fine."

"Yes, I have something to ask Lee while you are working," I added.

Lee arched his eyebrows but said nothing.

I lay back on Sebastian's comfortable tattoo chair covered with paper.

Sebastian poured ink into tiny cups, dabbed at my skin with ointments and tonics, and pressed a paper "transfer" against my forearm. When he removed it, the outline of his illustration marked my skin. "Ready?"

"Yes," I said solemnly.

"I'm right here with you," he said, fitting something over his ears. Then, he turned on his gun, dipped it in ink, and began to apply it to my skin.

I simply endured the sensation. It was nothing compared to a tiger's sharp teeth ripping my skin or a short scimitar blade carving apart my chest.

"What did you want to talk to me about?" Lee asked, perched on a nearby stool.

I glanced at Sebastian.

"He can't hear us. He's got his headphones in place." Lee cupped his hands around his ears.

"After you time traveled me to find my brother, I always wanted to know what happened to my mother. Was anyone informed of what happened to me? I'm sure she was worried. I thought you might know."

Lee's expression drooped. "Ah. Elizabeth. I wondered if you might ask me someday."

"After I left her in England, I never saw her again," I said.

With a sigh, Lee began. "When you left, I wanted to return to her and leave everything behind. The day I was supposed to go on the boat, Alina came to the tribe looking for me and asking me for help to defeat Balthazar. My father, the Great Chief, said I had to follow my destiny and help Alina defeat the darkness. So instead of leaving the tribe, I wrote your mother a letter and told her everything that had happened. I loved your mother so much. She was my light in my dark life. She never wrote back to me, but I knew it was my duty to go back to her one day and explain everything to her in person."

A wistful light appeared in his eyes, speaking to his love and longing for my mother.

"What about my father? Balthazar told me he was darkness." I shuddered as I said this. "Is that true?"

"Yes," Lee said simply, his cheeks reddening. He sighed and looked at me through haunted eyes. "When Olivia was born, I told Alina we had to keep a low profile and stay away from time traveling completely. I told Jack and Alina that I needed to spend time with my people, but in truth, I time traveled back to your mother to the 1700s. I was with her for about eight years. I was so in love with her. We got married and lived very happily together. Those were the best years of my life, being with her and having her by my side.

"When we were together, she told me that your father was the darkness, and that Balthazar wouldn't allow your father to be with her. So she stayed away from everything. That's why she didn't want the blades when you were born. She didn't want your father or Balthazar to find you or you to be connected with them."

Lee stared off into the distance. "Elizabeth was funny. She was smart, and she was beautiful. She appeared pleased when I told her you time traveled to Rome and reunited with your brother. She tried to be strong, but I know she ached to see you again. And especially to see your brother."

His cheeks puffed with air, and he blew it out. "Yet, when she died, there was peace in her heart. She was safe and unharmed. I buried her and returned. I had been gone for eight years when I returned to the future. When I came back, I knew Alina was up to something. She betrayed me and time traveled herself several times, risking her life and making Balthazar one step closer to finding us."

We sat surrounded by the cacophony of noisy machines.

Sebastian continued to apply ink and wipe.

I studied his artistic mastery and then turned back to Lee. "Why do you think this Malik fellow saved me? And if he's with Olivia, will he seduce her?"

Lee blinked in surprise. "You don't have to worry about Olivia being seduced by Malik. The blood you carry is dark, too."

That wasn't reassuring in the least. "What do you mean?"

"You were born of darkness, Roman. And even if Olivia fell in love with Malik, she'd only be falling in love with the darkness—she wouldn't be able to tell the difference between you two. You both are one and the same blood and dark ways."

I frowned. "This doesn't comfort me. It makes me feel expendable, like, 'oh, Olivia could be with you; she could be with Malik… It's all the same.'"

"I'm probably not explaining it correctly," Lee said. "You're not a demon. Malik is. You're a Timeborne. But you have the same blood. And Malik stays away from love. He will not seduce your beloved Olivia."

That still didn't reassure me, but I accepted it for now. "Why would Malik need Tristan?"

"Now that I don't know," Lee said.

We lapsed into amiable silence until Sebastian removed his headphones and said, "I'm done. She's a beauty, don't you think?"

I looked down at the striking image on my arm, coiling my fingers into a fist and turning my arm side to side. "It's wonderful. You did an excellent job."

He grinned.

"That's why I'm Sebastian the Great. I'm honored, man, truly. I can tell this has significance to you. And I know, I know, top secret everything."

He proceeded to tape transparent film over my skin and give me "aftercare instructions."

Then, after Lee paid, we were on our way.

Lee and I sauntered outside in the temperate evening air. The sky was a deep shade of blue-gray, and a wash of pale orange spread across the horizon. As we passed by many shops, I marveled at the goods displayed, cataloging similarities and vast differences.

We wandered past tables set up like a Roman bazaar.

"This is a street fair like the one where I last saw Olivia,"

Lee said, before beelining toward a stand labeled *Adele's Antiques*.

I hurried after him.

"Look, there's a sale going on," Lee said once he stood before the stand filled with trinkets and bric-a-brac.

I smiled at the elderly woman behind the stand. *She must be Adele.*

Adele glowered back at me with her arms crossed over her chest. "Are you two fellows going to buy, or are you lookie-loos? I've had a lot of lookie-loos here today."

I didn't know what "lookie-loos" meant, so I turned to Lee.

"Depends on what you have to sell," Lee said, matching her demeanor. He ran his hand over various objects, pausing when his palm landed on a cheap-looking dagger. He lifted it and stared at it in wonder. "Where'd you get this?"

"Oh, that old thing? It's pretty worthless if you ask me. Some young fella wandered past a short while ago. He said he needed a drink, and could I buy this from him." She shrugged.

Lee leaned in close and whispered to me. "This is the fake dagger I gave Olivia to trick Tristan on the night she time traveled."

My heart began to race.

"What are you two whispering about?" The woman unfolded her arms and wiped her palms on the grimy green apron around her waist.

"I know this knife. What did the person who sold it to you look like?" Lee asked.

Her shoulder rose and fell. "He looked like a guy desperate for a drink, that's what. But he was about six feet tall, with light brown hair, somewhat strongly built...Oh! He had this mole on his neck right here."

She tapped beneath her right ear.

One eyebrow lifted on her wrinkled face. "Are you fixing to buy it or what?"

"Which way did he go?" Lee asked.

The old woman pointed down the street. "There's a bar down that way a few blocks. It's called *O'Donnell's*. I'm sure that's where he was headed. Poor fella looked like he could use a drink."

Lee turned to look at me, his eyes bright. "That's him. I know it is."

"Let's go," I said, already pivoting.

Lee dropped the knife, and we rushed toward the Jeep.

"Damn lookie-loos!" the woman called after us.

A loud engine roar, louder than all the cars and trucks, rumbled down the road as we hurried down the sidewalk.

I turned to stare at a fellow riding a two-wheeled vehicle with shiny silver trimmings, black metal, and a black leather seat.

The fellow was dressed all in charcoal-colored leather with boots on his feet. He leaned back on the two-wheeler and gripped silver bars in front where the steering wheel should be.

"What's that?" I pointed.

"That's a motorcycle, my friend, and are they ever fun to ride." Lee pressed his key thing, and the Jeep chirped. "It's unlocked. Climb on in."

The motorcycle zoomed away, all power and speed.

"Are you thinking you'd like a motorcycle?" Lee glanced at me and smirked.

"Maybe. Maybe I am." I pulled the seatbelt across my chest and watched the motorcycle as it disappeared down the road.

When we pulled up to *O'Donnells*, Lee let me out at the

front, saying, "I'm going to go park around back. Go on in and look around. I'll meet you at the bar. That's the long counter at the back where you order drinks. Ask for two pale ales. You'll like it."

"Okay." I entered the bar. Inside, the light was dim.

Several patrons sat at tables, booths, and the long counter.

I paused, gathering my bearings. I'd never been to a bar to drink. Did one simply sit around and sip alcohol? And why were all these women in here?

These are different times, I told myself and headed toward the back.

A mirror sat on the back wall. Rows of bottles lined the mirror.

I did a double take when I caught sight of myself in the mirror with my side "fade" and short hair. But, I noticed other fellows with similar haircuts and relaxed.

I settled next to a muddy-blond-haired fellow who looked to be my age.

A gruff-looking fellow behind the counter walked toward me and said, "What will it be?"

I searched my mind for an answer to this odd question, feeling my palms grow sweaty.

"What do you want?" he said.

"Two pale ales," I said.

"What kind?"

"What do you suggest?"

"The Dragon's Blood is popular. It's on tap."

Dragon's Blood? On tap? I nodded, hoping Lee would like whatever it was I ordered. "That's fine."

The man retrieved two glass mugs and pulled a lever.

A stream of amber liquid poured into one of the glasses.

The muddy-blond-haired fellow to my left watched me. It made me uneasy about being scrutinized in such a fashion.

"You fresh off the turnip farm?" he said to me.

I studied him. He matched the street vendor's description, even down to the mole. A prickle of alarm danced across my scalp.

This couldn't be Tristan... could it? That would be too easy.

I turned to give him a dismissive glare.

His face reminded me of gladiators nearing their end of life in the arena. There was often a desperate meanness in their demeanor.

I frowned at him, then turned away.

He laughed. "You *are* stupid, aren't you?"

The barkeep placed two frosted mugs filled with the amber liquid in front of me. I lifted one to my lips and took a long swig.

Quite good!

I glanced at a woman to my right who approached the bar. A strange snapping came from her mouth as she loudly chewed on something.

The muddy-blond-haired fellow called out to her. "Hey, Diane. Stop eye fucking the idiot there and give me a blow job like usual."

Whatever "eye-fucking" and "blow job" meant, it didn't sound flattering.

"Don't speak to her like that," I said. "Act like a gentleman."

Muddy-Blond laughed again. "Man, you are a *hoot* getting all up in my business. 'Don't speak to her like that,'" he said in a mocking British accent. "'Act like a gentleman.' Can you believe that guy, Di?"

"Maybe he's right," Diane said, sidling closer to me. A pink bubble emerged from her mouth and popped. She licked it off her lips and continued to chew. "Maybe you shouldn't talk to me that way."

She traced the outline of my ear.

I brushed her hand away. She was like Severus' whores insinuating herself on any man in the vicinity. "Please. I don't wish to partake."

Muddy-Blond guffawed. "Did you hear that? He don't wish to partake, Di." He leaned closer to me and said, "She ain't nuthin' but a slut. You can do whatever you like to her. Only she's spoken for this evening, got it?"

"Even a woman of the night deserves respect," I said, urging him away from me.

He rolled to the left like his body was made of molten wax.

This man smelled foul, like he'd been drinking for days and hadn't washed for weeks.

"Whoa," he said. "I'm more fucked up than I thought."

When he managed to sit tall again, he said, "Hey, cunt. Get over here and crouch between my legs. You can suck on my dick while me and Mr. Fancy Pants are having ourselves a little talk about manners and such."

I'd had enough of this foul little man. I rose and towered over him. "I don't think you heard me the first time. Don't speak to her like that. Act like a gentleman."

Muddy-Blond lurched to his feet, swaying as he stood next to me.

"Hey, now," the barkeep said. "I think you've had enough to drink."

"I've had enough to drink when I say I've had enough to drink. Now fuck off." Muddy-Blond took a swing at me.

I caught his fist in the palm of my hand and pushed it away. I could fight this buffoon with one hand tied behind my back and not break a sweat.

Muddy-Blond charged me, ramming his head into my abdomen.

That was it—I was done with his ridiculous behavior. I hit his jaw with my right fist, then punched him with my left.

He staggered backward, recovered, and charged me again. I brought my knee up, ramming it between his legs. He howled and collapsed to the floor.

Patrons screamed and shouted. This was nothing new to my ears—it was a far cry from a Colosseum crowd. I fell to my knees, straddling this fool, and began to pummel him.

Loud footsteps approached, and Lee called, "Roman! Roman! You can't do that here."

He grabbed my arm as I was about to land another blow.

"Well, well, well. If it isn't Sensei Lee," Muddy-Blond said.

"When will you ever grow up, Tristan?" Lee said. "No wonder Olivia left your ass. You're a weak, pathetic worm of a man."

So this is Tristan.

My rage increased, crashing through me like pounding waves.

"Fuck that shit. Olivia was a cunt. I was glad she disappeared." Tristan spat blood out of his mouth.

It landed on my shirt.

"Don't you dare talk about my wife like that," I roared.

"Your wife?" Tristan said, the whites of his eyes glistening in the dim light.

By now, a crowd surrounded us.

"I've called the cops," the barkeep said. "They'll be here any minute."

"Roman! We've got to go!" Lee said, yanking on my biceps.

I couldn't see straight, couldn't track what he or anyone

was saying. I focused solely on Tristan, the man I swore I would kill for Olivia. I shook off Lee, hauled back my arm, and landed a deadly blow on Tristan's nose, hoping to break his bones and pulverize his brain.

His lips parted, and his eyes closed. He dropped to the floor.

Before I could strike him again, Lee shouted, "Roman! Roman! We've got to get out of here. Grab his torso. I'll get his legs. Let's go!"

My heart pounded like a heavy drum in my ears as I scanned the crowd who watched me with the same eagerness as spectators in the coliseum. Then, I looked down at Tristan. His lifeless figure lay before me, and I felt defeat closing in around me. Had I really expected finding my beloved wife would be easy? The thought seemed absurd now, even if I followed Malik's instructions to the letter.

CHAPTER NINE

OLIVIA

As soon as Malik left the room, I felt a sense of unease settle in the pit of my stomach. This was his private domain, a place where he kept his secrets and conducted his business.

The walls were lined with shelves that held countless books, their spines cracked and worn from years of use. A large mahogany desk dominated the center of the room, its surface littered with papers and files. I couldn't help but wonder what kind of secrets were hidden within those documents.

Outside, a shrieking gale whistled through the rafters, adding to my unease.

As my gaze roamed over the room, I felt a sense of foreboding. There was something off about this place, something that made my skin crawl. Malik was a force of darkness, a complete mystery.

I stared at the journal in my hand. As I turned to Emily, I saw the same fear reflected in her eyes. "Should we really read this in Malik's office? I'm already nervous about reading

Mom's diary. And I feel as if we're violating Malik's space about to be swallowed in his world of secrets."

"I know what you mean," Emily whispered, her eyes wide as she took in our surroundings. "But maybe this is the perfect place in which to unravel mysteries."

"Okay," I said. "Let's do this, then."

Caught in the spell of Malik's surroundings, I crossed to the sage-green velvet sofa with its ornately carved legs.

Emily followed behind me.

Neither of us said a word as we settled at either end of the couch.

As I held the journal in my lap, I was struck by the weight of it. It felt heavier than it should have, as if it was filled with enigmas and clandestine knowledge that were begging to be uncovered. The leather cover was worn and faded, and as I ran my fingers over its surface, I couldn't help but wonder what kind of stories were hidden within its pages. My heartbeat ricocheted inside my ribcage as I cracked open the cover of my mother's journal. I wasn't sure if I wanted to see what lay inside. But I knew I had to. I had to read my mother's thoughts and feelings and the chronicle of her life. Maybe then I would glean understanding.

"Are you all right?" Emily said.

"What?" I said, looking up from my lap.

"You're white as a ghost. Are you sure you want to do this?"

I nodded solemnly. "Yes. I'm ready. And yet I'm uncertain. I'm so glad you're here with me."

I reached out to her.

She squeezed my hand and then released it. "That's right. I'm here for you to lend support or whatever you need."

After taking a deep breath, I began to skim the pages. Some entries were marked by little stars, indicating their

importance. Others were underlined in my mother's neat handwriting.

I flipped back to the beginning and read an entry with no date. A photograph of me on my birthday had been tucked between the pages. I removed it and stared at little me grinning at the table before a white frosted birthday cake with pink and green candied horses galloping across the top.

Dad sat beside me, smiling, and Mother sat next to Dad, a soft expression in her eyes as she studied me.

Olivia, my sweet darling. I'm sorry for everything. I hope you'll understand someday.

I blinked back the tears that pricked the back of my eyes.

"Let me see that," Emily said, plucking the photo from my fingers. She turned it around and around. "What is this? It looks like you as a child, but it's not painted."

"We have something called photography. It's sort of like camera obscura, only it happens with something called film."

"Oh, my!" She studied my likeness. "It's so detailed. You were a pretty little girl."

"Thank you," I said, reaching for the picture. I tucked it back between the pages and flipped the page.

The writing was all in Italian, written in my mother's neat, flowing penmanship.

"You're fluent in Italian, right?" I glanced at Emily.

She nodded.

"And so we proceed," I said somberly, my stomach twisting into a knot as I prepared to mentally translate my mother's words.

The following entry read, *June 1, 1556.*

I had a week of more exciting nights than I'm used to. I was invited to Pietro Costa, the father of Raul Costa's masquerade party. Everyone will be there and it looks like it's going to be quite a night. I'll be wearing an off-white lace dress with straps that fall off my shoulders. It fits snugly around my waist making me look dainty and graceful. When I spin around the skirt billows out in a beautiful way. Tomaso, who is much older than me and very sophisticated, tells me that I should be with boys my age. But I tease him back that sixteen-year-old boys are like baby sharks—they chew off the fins of their lovers! This definitely makes him laugh and he remarks how much fun I am. He invites me to meet him at his place tomorrow and I can hardly wait.

I was slightly repulsed by Mom's rendition of her date with an "older man." How much older were we talking here? Was he eighteen? Twenty-eight? At age sixteen, she would be considered jailbait in my time. But I swallowed back my judgment and kept reading.

June 2, 1556.

Tomaso and I rushed to the Pietro Costa party, energized by our desire for one another. He eyed me hungrily and let out a low growl that made me laugh. I pushed him away playfully. As we entered the masquerade, I felt his intensity growing, until suddenly he gestured for me to follow him. We left the festivities behind and I asked in amusement why he'd brought me to such a smelly barn.

"We are going to christen it with our love," he replied, before crashing his mouth against mine so ferociously that stars appeared behind my eyes.

Before I knew it, Tomaso was inside me, pushing hard against the stone walls of the horse barn as we both moaned with pleasure.

Suddenly, this woman appeared out of the blue. Her hair was wild and messy, her eyes were a strange dark color, and her skin was unnaturally pale. She growled like a feral cat and brandished a knife in her hand. She lunged forward and drove the weapon into Tomaso's back while he was still inside me. I shrieked with terror so loudly that people from the party ran over to us. Tomaso lay motionless on the cold ground surrounded by his own blood, but the woman had already disappeared.

As the revelers tended to Tomaso, carrying his limp form out of the barn, I raced outside. There, I saw the woman again in the distance. She watched everyone disappear into Pietro Costa's house, then ran toward me, wielding her knife. This time I didn't scream—I stood my ground, as frightened as I was. I knew she wanted to kill me, too. I prepared to meet my maker and be with Tomaso, who I was sure was dead.

But suddenly a mysterious man materialized out of thin air, like a ghost, only he was very much alive. He struck down the woman with his own dagger, and she literally transformed into a dry corpse.

I was more intrigued than scared by him. He was mysterious and powerful and moved with nimble grace like an athlete or a dancer. I couldn't help myself—I kissed him for saving my life. The kiss started out as gratitude on my part but turned into a passionate fire. I'd never experienced a man like this—he seemed to burn with fire and lust, and it was all directed at me.

When we disentangled, I stroked my lips with my fingertips, then his. We stared at one another with wonder. At that very moment, I knew I would love him for the rest of my life—no other man would compare.

"Who are you?" he said, running the side of his finger down my cheek.

"I'm Alina." I trembled at his touch. "Are you going to kill me, too?"

"No," he said gently. "She was a bad woman who wanted to harm you. I couldn't let that happen."

He placed his warm fingertip beneath my chin and tipped

my head to face him. "You and I belong with each other now, my lovely Alina. I'm sorry that woman frightened you. You no longer have to worry about her. She is gone. And, I'm sorry I kissed you so wantonly."

I just looked at him and shook my head. It was like we both existed in some other time, disconnected from the reality of Italy and the horror that had just occurred.

"I will take care of you from this day forth," he said, still stroking my cheek.

I nuzzled his finger like a kitten, never wanting to be away from him. In some inexplicable way, I knew he "got me"— that he understood me in a way no one could. It was as if we'd known each other throughout time. I was protected and treasured by this man. And, it was so strange, since we had just met, but I felt like I'd known him forever.

I lifted my gaze and rubbed my forehead. Mom was describing Balthazar. A queasy sensation rocked my insides, like I was back on the ship in Rome, heading for battle in Caledonia under cruel orders by Emperor Severus.

I flipped several pages ahead, not wanting to read any lusty encounters between Balthazar and my mom.

July 17th, 1561. For the last five years, Balthazar and I have been having an affair in secret. We meet after sunset when no one can see us, our love burning bright in the darkness. His presence lingers in my mind throughout the day. My parents have been pushing for me to marry someone of Italian descent. That's why I've said no to marriage proposals from men I don't love. Finally, I decided it was time to tell my father the truth about Balthazar. So, after we'd finished dinner and he had a few glasses of mead, I took a deep breath and told him everything.

"Papa," I said, sitting on the arm of his chair.

"What is it, my sweet?" he said, his happy smile spread across his face. Papa always got jovial after drinking mead.

"I need to tell you something."

Papa frowned and sat up, perhaps sensing the weight of what I was about to say. "You'd better not tell me you've rejected another suitor. The townsfolk are talking. They're saying you're out of control. They've seen you at night with a man, only your mother and I don't know who this man is."

"Oh, Papa. I've been seeing someone since Tomaso was murdered. I didn't think I could tell you about him, but now I must." My heart quivered in my chest, fearing my father's rejection. "He's the only man I want to be with."

Papa's jaw tightened as if he were biting iron. "Who is it? Who is this man?"

His fingers balled into fists by his side.

Anxious by his reaction, I slid from the chair arm and stood before him. "It's Lord Balthazar. He's my true love."

Papa's face grew red, and he looked like he might hit me. "You will not be with Lord Balthazar!" he roared. "He's lived in our village since I can remember, here for lengths of time and gone for equal amounts. Foul deeds happen when he's here. He's a dangerous man!"

I folded my arms across my chest. The room had grown chilly, despite the fire crackling in the fireplace behind me. "He is the most beautiful man I've ever been with—he understands me and adores me, Papa, don't you see?"

"I don't see, amore! Everyone knows Lord Balthazar. He has a horrible reputation and, most importantly, is dangerous. There are whispers of him and the darkness and danger he carries. People say that he is a killer and a murderer."

Could the rumors be true? Balthazar had never shown me anything but passion and love.

My skin rippled with gooseflesh, and I had to look away from the journal.

I turned to Emily and said, "Can you believe this, Emily? How our mother fell for Balthazar and how he ensorcelled her."

I handed the journal to Emily while I gathered my thoughts about what we'd just read. Balthazar had seduced my mom at age sixteen! Intense loathing at the demon ripped through my insides. I wrapped my arms around my midsection and rocked.

Finally, Emily said, "Let's finish reading."

"I need some water first." I glanced at a ceramic pitcher at the edge of Malik's desk. A dainty teacup with tiny painted violets sat next to it. I rose and poured water into the cup which was stained brown from the tea. Then, I gulped it down. "Want some?"

Emily declined.

I set the teacup on the desk and walked to the window. Outside, the wind continued to howl, shrieking around the eaves.

"Olivia, come sit with me again," Emily said.

With a sigh, I joined her on the velvet sofa.

She handed me the journal, and I opened it, flipping to another page.

Once again, we huddled together, reading our mother's tales.

My father stood before me and said, "I'm not your birth father."

I frowned at this and turned the page. *Was Mom really adopted?*

"Why are you telling me this now?" I cried out. "Are you trying to distract me from your fears about Balthazar?"

"Hear me out, child. I'm your adopted father," my papa

said. "Your mother and I couldn't have children, so we adopted you. We were in the park—you know that beautiful park with all the statues of gods?"

I numbly nodded but still stood with my arms crossed. Inside, I was reeling at this new admission, barely tracking his words. Adopted? Me? My legs trembled like they couldn't hold me aloft, so I sat on the sofa across from him.

A cascade of sparks shot above the flames in the fireplace, perhaps in keeping with my mood.

Father continued speaking. "So, we were walking, arm in arm, enjoying the beauty of the park, and we saw a baby in a basket with a note. A baby! Can you believe it?"

His eyes shone as he looked at me, but I could barely meet his gaze. How could I be adopted? What kind of parents would give up their child?

Several small blotches stained the page, slightly smearing the ink.

Had Mom been crying when she wrote this?

I turned the page.

Father spoke again. "There was a handwritten note in the basket. And you were tucked inside a blanket, staying quiet, like someone had told you not to make a sound."

He smiled wistfully as if he was back in the park gazing down at me.

"This is my daughter, Alina. Please take care of her. That's what the note said. Your mother and I felt like it was providence smiling down on us. It was a sign that our prayers had been answered." Father wiped at his eyes with a hand-kerchief he pulled from his pocket. Then, he continued. "There was this dagger in the basket. There was only one man I knew who would know about the knife—Giovanni. Giovanni liked to study ancient antiques, maps, and things out of this world.

"So, we took you home with us, overjoyed to have found you. The next day, I went to Giovanni and showed him the dagger. He paled when his eyes landed on it. He told us that you were a Timeborne, a person who could time travel. But with that, you would unleash the darkness, and that darkness will hunt you and try to kill you."

Now Father looked sorrowful. The skin around his eyes pinched, and he looked like he might cry. "And I won't lose you to Balthazar. I think he is that darkness who wants to destroy you." He clenched his fist and shook it. "There are whispers about Lord Balthazar…They say he is a dark, vicious monster that hunts people and kills them for power. Alina, you must stay away from him. He will eventually grow tired of you and kill you."

I felt so confused, torn between my defiance and refusal to listen to reason and a niggling fear in the back of my mind. What if Father was right?

I shook my head. He was telling tall tales based on fear.

"What about my siblings?" I asked him. "Are they adopted, too?"

"No, amore. After you came to us, your mother got pregnant with your siblings. But that makes you no less precious to us. We love you from the bottom of our hearts."

I just don't know what to think.

I flipped the page, letting it all sink in.

July 18th, 1561. I couldn't stop thinking about what my father had said to me. It bothered and ate at me. How could my father believe that I was a time traveler? How preposterous!

And the foul things he said about Balthazar. I still couldn't understand or believe what he said. My father has been imbibing in the mead too much. I fear he has lost his mind. But I still loved him.

Later in the day, I was out for a stroll through the park, and I saw it with my own eyes—so horrifying—the man I love, Balthazar, killed another woman. I was horrified! He strangled her with his bare hands right there in the park! I don't believe he knew I was there, for why would he want me to see such a thing? But, see it, I did, and, without thinking, I ran away, frightened to death!

Balthazar chased me and caught me. It was awful. We had a huge fight right there next to the dead woman.

Balthazar captured my wrists and drew them behind me, holding me with such force that I couldn't free my hands. I did not know any man was capable of such strength. Then, standing behind me, he leaned close to my ear, so close I could feel his warm breath tickling my neck. He used his other hand to stroke my neck.

Ah, mercy, it was such a torment to have this woman lying there dead while I stood so close to him as he seduced me with his touch. I am a fool for him. And yet, crazier was how I still desired this man, my evil, despicable lover. I craved him with an unearthly desire that scared me. How could this be possible after witnessing such a horrific scene?

I gathered my wits around me and said, "Why did you slaughter that poor woman?"

He said, "She was a bad woman. I saw her kill her children."

I desperately wanted to believe him, but I had not heard such a tale of a woman murdering her kin in our village. But what did I know? Lord Balthazar traveled in different circles than me.

"My father thinks you're dangerous. He thinks you are a bad influence on me," I said, leaning my head against Balthazar, taking solace in his warmth.

"I am nothing of the sort," he said, continuing to caress

my neck and collarbone. "Villagers are afraid of power. I am very powerful."

"And would you kill me just as easily?" I said, wanting to turn around and beat his chest, but my wrists were held in his iron grip.

His soothing voice landed in my ear.

"I will never kill you or hurt you, Alina. You are my love, my life."

I saw the dead woman's blood puddling on the ground. Some of it had seeped near me and stained my shoe. My father might have been right about Balthazar—he was a cruel and dangerous man. But I was obsessed with him and couldn't imagine life without him.

"Let me go," I begged him.

"I can never let you go," he said. At the same time, he released my wrists and turned me so swiftly in his arms I was dizzy. And then he savagely and brutally kissed me, claiming me with his passion.

I could not resist him. I let him take me away, and we made love through the night like two wild savages.

August 10th, 1561

I have not been able to stay away from Balthazar. He is my soulmate, my very heartbeat.

My father surprised me when I sneaked into my home tonight after midnight. He was sitting in the dark next to the hearth, which still burned with embers from an earlier fire.

"Alina," he said, and I nearly jumped out of my skin.

"You frightened me, Papa! I was out getting some night air—I couldn't sleep."

I heard Papa's noisy sigh.

"I am old, but I am not a fool, child. I know where you were. I have been watching you—you were with him, weren't you?"

My father is a good and loving man, but his watchfulness angered me. "I am a grown woman, Papa! How dare you spy on me!"

"And yet you behave like a child! Don't you see? Your mother and I love you very much. You were given to us those many years ago. And I don't want you to end up dead!" His voice shook as he spoke. "Your sister married a good man who treats her right—I want the same for you, Alina!"

My stomach burned with rage at being told what to do. I almost turned and ran.

Yet, through the shadows and gloom of the parlor, I could see him rise from his seat and approach. When he stood before me, I could tell he'd been crying—his cheeks were damp, and his eyelids were puffy. I hated to see him like this on my account. It broke my heart, transforming my fiery anger into sorrowful sympathy.

"You will defy me at every turn, Alina. You're very willful." His hands landed on my shoulders. "But promise me one thing."

"What is it, Papa?" I blinked back the tears threatening to fall.

"Promise me!" He shook my shoulders. "Promise me you'll visit Giovanni. At least talk to him. Then, if you continue to see Lord Balthazar, I will have some peace that you spoke to a trusted adviser."

I leaned my head against the sofa, wiping my eyes. How many times had Papa and Lee warned me of Tristan's treachery? Papa felt concerned about Tristan and didn't trust him and Lee wasn't certain about him either. But had I listened? No. I'd refused to accept their counsel and nearly got my father killed. As hard as it was to admit, I could see similarities between my mother and me.

But then I looked at Emily. She seemed so very different

than me. She didn't have the same willfulness and rebellious spirit. She seemed kind and willing to forgive, whereas I was headstrong and spirited.

Emily smiled. "What are you thinking?"

"I wonder what you think of our mother having read this journal part." I waved the diary before me.

Emily gazed across the room at the elegant bookshelves.

"She was very complex, wasn't she? She got caught up with a bad man, and he seduced her. I suppose it could happen to any of us," she said, her expression darkening.

I reached out and took her hand. "We're very different, you and me. You seem to regard her words with considered reason. I'm more of a hothead."

Emily chuckled and squeezed me back. "I have heard the term hot-brained or hot-mouthed, used to describe someone who is headstrong, ungovernable, or hot-hearted. While I would not use the term hothead to describe you, you have a fiery temperament. Mine is more soothing, like the moon."

"We complement one another," I said, retrieving my hand, and gazing at her fondly. "How far did you get in your reading?"

I tapped the worn leather cover.

"Oh, let's see." Emily rested her fingertip on her mouth. "I got to the part where Alina's papa advised her to seek counsel with Giovanni."

"That's where I just ended, too. Let's read the rest together," I said, scooting closer to her. I opened the diary to where I'd left off, and together, we bent our heads over the journal and quietly read.

August 19th, 1561

I have resisted seeing Giovanni but am more and more suspicious when with Balthazar. I know he keeps secrets from me. There are rooms in his house I am forbidden from enter-

ing. He tells me it is for my own good that I stay out of his private chambers, but what could he guard so closely?

He caught me trying the doorknob in one of the forbidden rooms. I have never seen him so wrathful, so angry. But he could tell he frightened me and took me in his arms like a child to soothe me. His reaction worries me, so I decided to visit my father's friend, Giovanni.

August 20th, 1561

I sneaked at nightfall to Giovanni's like a husbreche, a common burglar. I worried that Balthazar might see me and grow suspicious. Giovanni met me at the door. He poked his head out the door and looked both ways as if he was cautious. Then, he ushered me into his parlor and fed me tea, letting me warm my bones before a blazing fire.

"I know why you're here, child," he said once the pleasantries were out of the way. "Your father is worried. Lord Balthazar is indeed dangerous and cannot be trusted. He is not as he appears."

"What do you mean?" I said as gooseflesh peppered my body. I rubbed my sleeves with my palms, seeking the kind of warmth that didn't come from the sun or a fire in the hearth.

Giovanni sighed. "There is so much to tell you. The dagger that was found in your little basket when your adopted parents discovered you—it appeared at your birth. This is always the way with Timebornes."

I frowned. "I am a Timeborne? That's such a preposterous notion. I heard my father say this, but I thought he was crazy."

"And yet it's true. There are whispers in my circle that Lord Balthazar is not human—he is darkness, a blood-killing demon. I believe he is a darkness, and that darkness only goes after one thing—to kill Timebornes. He is as old as time. And he will hurt you, Alina, as certain as the sun rises."

Giovanni's voice shook with emotion. "You must travel to another time where hopefully he can't find you. Live your life!"

His arms swept into the air. "There are people who want to kill Lord Balthazar. He is a hunted man."

I shivered, overtaken by the thought that someone wanted Balthazar, my beloved, dead. "Even if I believed you about this time travel madness, I don't know what to do! And why should I believe you? How do I know you and Papa aren't conspiring against me with some fantastic tale?"

"I wish it was only a story, dear Alina." Giovanni shook his shaggy head. "The moment your father told me he found you with the dagger, I began to study and learn. I have poured through ancient tomes and documents. Lord Balthazar is real, and he is deadly. Don't be fooled!" His voice bounded off the high ceilings, echoing around the room.

I shot to my feet. "This whole idea is ridiculous!"

"I'm sure it seems unfathomable. But trust me, Alina, I speak the truth. Since your father came to me with that blade, I've spent my life studying Timebornes. You must believe me!" He pounded the side table next to his chair with his fist.

I jerked in surprise. "What would you have me do?"

You must travel to another time and get away from this place. Start over, have a family, but most importantly, get away from Balthazar."

I let out a bitter laugh. "You know how foolish you sound, don't you?

Once again, Giovanni slammed his fist on the side table. "You've got to believe me, child! I speak the truth."

I stared at him, my limbs trembling.

"Balthazar isn't your only problem. There are Time-hunters out there—people who want you dead," he said.

I wrung my hands beneath my chin. "You don't under-

stand, Giovanni! Balthazar would never hurt me—he loves me, and I love him. I could never leave him!"

My mind flitted toward our passionate lovemaking last night, where Balthazar told me he would always love and protect me. That he was sworn to keep me safe. God, how much I love him. Just thinking about him and our passionate lovemaking is driving me mad with desire.

Now Giovanni was telling me Balthazar was a monster. I didn't know who to believe, so I bolted, racing from his home, and stumbling to my house in the dark of night.

To my horror, I found my family dead, lying in crimson pools. I let out a scream and crumpled next to Papa's lifeless body in the dining room archway.

"Oh, Papa! What has happened to you?" I held his head in my lap and rocked him. But his eyes remained vacant, staring at Heaven's gates.

Mother lay in the kitchen face down.

I sat there for the longest time, sobbing, holding my father and willing him back to life. But his body grew cold in my arms.

I heard a disturbance in the back of the house. Numb with grief and shock, I got to my feet and stumbled through the house. Blood splattered the walls in sweeping arcs and hand-prints. I wanted to retch but I had to save the rest of my family if they weren't already dead.

I came upon my brother and two sisters, also slain. I staggered into the back bedroom, where my youngest sister slept with my now-dead middle sister. To my shock and disgust, I witnessed Balthazar plunging a knife into my youngest sister's body.

She let out a blood-curdling scream when she saw me. "Alina! Help me!"

But then her eyes rolled back in her head, and she fell

upon the pillows of her bed, now stained crimson with her life essence.

I lunged toward Balthazar, ready to kill him. "You monster! What have you done?"

He easily caught me in his arms, crushing me to him.

I writhed and squirmed, trying to escape him, but he was too strong.

"I had to do this," he said, kissing my hair. "Your father was poisoning your mind with lies. He's filled your head with poison."

He peppered my cheeks, nose, and eyebrows with kisses, but I tried vainly to resist him.

Now, at last, and too late, I could see him for what he was —a bloodthirsty demon.

"Everything I do is to protect you, my darling," Balthazar said.

I squeezed my eyes shut. His words were starting to get to me, making me believe him over the horror around me. My entire family was slaughtered. Fat tears rolled down my cheeks.

Balthazar slurped them into his mouth.

My dying sister made a hideous gurgling noise like her spirit was slithering from her body.

I wanted to vomit, scream, and murder the man who held me so tightly. I became aware of Balthazar's rigid erection pressing against my belly.

"I want to fuck you, Alina. I need to be inside of you."

"Are you insane? You want to screw me after killing my entire family?" I struggled in his arms.

"I did this all for you, my sweetheart. I would do anything to protect you." His eyes held hints of scarlet at the edges of the blue. "I can make this better. Let me love you."

He lifted me, cradling me in his arms, and strode into my bedroom, which lay unsullied.

There he took me wantonly, savagely, fucking me like an animal.

I put up no resistance. I was too numb.

Afterward, I cried myself to sleep in his arms.

He kept kissing me everywhere, telling me he would make it up to me and that all would be okay. But nothing would ever be okay after what he did tonight to my family.

August 21st, 1561

I awoke at dawn to find Balthazar already gone. I couldn't face the sight of my dead family, so I climbed out the window and hurried to Giovanni's house, keeping to the shadows lest I be seen.

I found Giovanni outside feeding his chickens. He appeared alarmed when he saw me.

"Your skirts!" he said, pointing.

That's when I noticed I was covered in blood. I told him how Balthazar had murdered my entire family.

Giovanni held his head with his hands as if it might fall to the ground if not secured. "Oh, God in Heaven! This is worse than I could have imagined!"

His chickens scurried around his legs, clucking.

"What can I do?" I wrung my hands before me. "I believe you now. I was a fool to not heed your words."

Giovanni scanned his surroundings. "Come, child. We must get you cleaned up and hide you somewhere safe."

Not waiting for my response, he placed his hand on my back and urged me toward his house, where he led me down the stairs to his basement.

"I will bring you clothing and food. You are to stay here until the full moon five days from now. You must hide and not

show yourself to anyone." He grabbed my shoulders and looked sternly at me. "Do you understand me?"

I nodded, unable to speak from the thick lump lodged in my throat. I didn't understand what was so important about the full moon, yet I was overcome with emotion. I was responsible for my family's demise.

Giovanni echoed my thoughts. "Your father's blood is on your hands. Your siblings and mother are all dead because of you."

"I know," I said, tears streaming down my face. "What can I do?"

"You must leave and travel to another time and start your life over. I will teach you the ancient scripture. You must cut your hand with your dagger as the full moon rises over the horizon and repeat the words I will teach you. The dagger will know where to take you. Do you understand me?"

"Yes, yes, Giovanni. I shall heed your warning. You were right." I sobbed. "Balthazar is a monster. I will time travel and escape him."

I lifted my gaze from the page and looked at Emily. We were both crying, and I didn't realize I'd reached for her hand and she for mine.

Our gazes tangled in torment.

"Our poor mother," I whispered.

"Yes," Emily said. "Her entire family, killed by that monster."

I knew in that moment I would do whatever it took to destroy Balthazar, even if it meant my own death in the process.

CHAPTER TEN

OLIVIA

S itting in Malik's office with my mother's journal in my lap, I reeled from this slice of her memory. Mom's life wasn't easy by any stretch of the imagination. She had fallen for a demon—a monster who followed no moral code but his own warped ethics. There was so much information to process I didn't know where to begin.

"We've got to read this to the end, Emily. We can't possibly stop now."

"Of course. I just need to stretch out my arms and legs. I didn't realize how tense Mother's words made me." Emily let out a shaky laugh and stood, stretching side to side.

I walked toward the door, cracked it open, and listened for Rosie. There were no giggles, no child's laughter or cries coming from the rest of the house. Was she okay under the watchful eye of Malik?

I assured myself that she was fine. Malik had been so lovingly attentive to her needs at the dining table. Why would he wish her harm? But then, why would a demon do anything? They had their own ways of justifying their actions.

I closed the door.

Outside, it had grown pitch-black, and the wind had stopped, leaving an eerie silence around us where once were shrieking gales. A bloated gibbous moon lit the sky, lighting the trees and wet ground from the recent rain.

I placed my hands on my back and lifted my face to the ceiling, working out the kinks in my back with my fingertips. Then, I turned to Emily and said, "Ready for more?"

"Yes. I'm ready."

We curled up on the sofa, our shoulders touching, huddled together like two puppies, the journal resting on our laps.

August 24th, 1561

I have memorized the words, the sacred scripture Giovanni taught me. But I am very much afraid. And, to be honest, I miss Balthazar, craving him with a kind of madness reserved for the insane. The effect he has on me is profound and makes no sense. How can I long for this demon, this creature who took the lives of my family? But, hiding in the basement, everything seems surreal. Did I make it all up? Was I having a fever dream and imagining the slaughter of my loved ones?

I pressed my fingertips to my lips. Balthazar had a surreal hold on my mother. But wasn't that what demons were known for? Seducing their victims to get what they wanted?

August 26th, 1561

I can see the top of the moon rising over the horizon. I will sew this journal into a pocket in my skirt. Giovanni says I must be precise and unwavering in my commitment when I say the sacred words. I am still scared but also resolved.

The murders were real. Giovanni, perhaps sensing my wavering spirit, made me watch the funeral procession through the narrow egress windows in the basement. My entire family passed by inside wooden coffins secured in horse-drawn wagons. All dressed in black, the villagers wept as they strode past Giovanni's. I was forced to face Balthazar's deeds. And Giovanni is right—I must flee at once.

Giovanni told me the villagers are outraged by these senseless murders. And with me missing, blame has been cast my way. I am to leave the basement when the world is shrouded by night. He will go with me and see me safely off.

August 31st, or so I think

The time travel was most mysterious—as I said the sacred scripture, with my hand sliced open by my dagger, I felt the world blur. I became quite ill and thought I would vomit. Then, I was surrounded by whirling blackness, as if in a dream. When I opened my eyes, I lay in a tall field of grasses. I am alone and frightened. I have been traveling for days and have seen no one.

Sept. 8th

Balthazar has already found me. He has traveled to this time. As I was famished, I welcomed seeing him. I was so weak I could barely put one foot in front of the other.

Balthazar told me how much he loved me and that he missed me. He has promised to be a better man.

"I have a home here in the Americas," he told me. "I will take you there and keep you safe. I vow I will control the darkness inside of me. You need not fear me, my beloved."

I was too exhausted to protest and collapsed in his arms.

When we arrived at his stone mansion at the top of a mountain, I let him lay me down in a bedroom filled with finery, lit by golden sconces on the walls. Velvet curtains hung from a four-poster bed lined with furs and pillows. A cheery fire blazed in the massive stone fireplace, warming my bones. I had been cold for days but tucked beneath this bedding, I know I shall survive.

Balthazar fed me sweetmeats and candies. He bathed me

with a sponge and held me while I drank water. Gradually, I became stronger from his care.

When I could walk on my own, he ravished me again, coming to me in the middle of the night to lay with me. Our lovemaking was violent and exhausting, leaving me laid bare and vulnerable. Yet, when he would depart, I'd long for him, twisting and writhing beneath the bedding, wishing he were here by my side. I was obsessed with his touch and our frenzied passion.

Two weeks after I arrived here, the killings began again. I'd be gazing out the window and see him carrying a limp body. This happened on several nights. As I had not been allowed to leave the premises, I don't know where he found the people—usually women—to kill. But kill he did.

When I confronted him about it, he tried to justify his actions, telling me he only took the diseased and the sick. But then he confessed that slaughtering sick people left him with the lingering effects of their illness. So, he had to go back to murdering the healthy and hale.

"What do you get out of this behavior?" I asked him, utterly nauseated at the thought of so much destruction.

But he would not answer. Instead, he would leave without a word and lock the door behind him. I made plans to leave him—but I didn't know how I would escape. I was on the second story of his estate and my full strength had not yet returned. I worried that if I started the intonation here in his house, he'd arrive home and interrupt me. I have to get away from here to work the magic of time travel.

Sept. 30th

When I saw him leave tonight, a plan sprang into my mind. I quickly removed the top bedding and stripped off the muslin between the sheets and the feather mattress. I tore it into strips which I shoved into the bottom of the armoire. He never looks there. He only leaves me with clothes he has purchased from town, wherever that is. He spreads them across the bed and tells me to wear them when we dine together. That's the only time I am allowed out of this room.

October 5th

I have been watching the moon, and Balthazar has been watching me. I think he suspects something. I tried to maintain calm and eagerness about his arrival, throwing myself at him when he came home.

But he's taken to dining with me in my room.

I don't question his decision. I compliment him and murmur adoring phrases to him. I do all I can to please him and satisfy his insatiable appetite for sex.

Tonight is the night, however. The moon was full. I pretended to fall asleep by his side, keeping my breathing deep and even. Finally, at midnight, he arose and slipped out of my bedroom. The lock snicked into place when he left.

I listened intently to his footsteps as he trekked down the hall and descended the stairs. The distant sound of the front door let me know he was outside. I lay in bed, too scared to move. I dared to venture out of bed when I heard him calling to the horses, and the clip-clop of hooves sounded below. I tiptoed to the window and peeked through the curtains, watching his retreating form in his fine carriage.

I quickly dressed in warm clothes, tucked my dagger and journal in my pocket, and prepared to leave.

Swiftly, I retrieved the muslin from the armoire I had knotted together. I tied one end to the leg of the bedframe. I had to work the window open with much effort. When I got it open, I clung to the makeshift rope and made my way to the ground.

I ran toward a clearing near the house on trembling legs,

slit my palm, gazed up at the moon, and repeated the sacred words.

And then I was gone.

"Oh, my goodness! Mom had to live like a fugitive!" I said to Emily.

"How awful her life must have been," Emily said, pushing some stray hairs away from her forehead.

We bowed our heads and continued to read.

We have continued this cat-and-mouse game for some time now. I escape, I time travel, and he finds me wherever I go. I don't know how he does it. I almost think he enjoys the chase and the wooing that happens once he finds me. I always end up in his bed. But I honestly crave it and love his dark desires. I don't know how to help myself. He always makes empty promises to change. And then the killings begin.

It is a vicious circle, like being trapped in Dante's Inferno.

Then I landed somewhere different, and something unexpected happened—I met a man named Malik and everything changed.

A chill shot up my spine. "Oh, my god, Emily, this is so exciting. She met Malik!"

"Turn the page so we can keep reading." Emily waved her hand at the diary.

I flipped the brittle paper and immersed myself in the story.

Malik is staying with Balthazar—he's a darkness like Balthazar. I think he is under Balthazar's tutelage. He is intelligent and interesting. And handsome—so very handsome. His eyes are a deep jade, the color found at the edge of a creek. His long lustrous hair hangs to his shoulders. But I think his heart is bound to another's as he looks at me with only the politest interest. We converse when Balthazar is not around. When Balthazar is here, we act like strangers around one another.

Tonight when Malik and I spoke after Balthazar had left the dining table, Malik told me he was in love with a woman named Layla. He said his love for her is helping him control the darkness inside.

"Oh!" I said, surprised by his confession. "So you are a darkness, like Balthazar?"

I took a sip of the heady wine Balthazar served us tonight.

"Yes," he said, but he didn't elaborate. "Layla and I are trying to find a way to help or cure me, so I don't have to kill to survive. "

"Wait, wait, you have to kill humans to survive?"

"Yes," Malik said. "If we don't kill people daily, we lose our strength and weaken. It's a vicious cycle, and I'm trying to find a way with Layla to stop it. I love Layla and want to be with her, so I shall do what I can to control my hunger for killing."

After learning what Malik told me, I understood why Balthazar murdered people. He needed strength to survive, and without killing, he would weaken. I told Malik we would help each other. So we made a pact. But then, many days turned into months with no sign of Malik.

At dinner last night, I innocently asked where Malik was. "I haven't seen your friend, Malik? Is he traveling?"

A fiendish look washed over Balthazar's face.

"I got rid of him," he said coldly. "He became a problem."

I nodded and spoke of other things but inside, I was deeply saddened. Malik had become my only friend; now he was gone, killed by my monster lover.

Since so many years had passed with us playing the same game of "flee and find," Balthazar let me roam his estate. It was as if he dared me to time travel. On one occasion, when Balthazar left to conduct whatever madness suited his whims, I decided to explore. I wandered through the house, trying locked doors, then moving to the next one. It was a way to kill the boredom of this life.

I was tired of wandering the upper floors and took my search to what I thought would be the basement. I descended stone stairs, using only a candle to light my way. The air smelled damp and dank, peppered with foul odors. I nearly stopped and turned around; the house seemed to be haunted. When I stepped off the last stair, I peered through the gloom. This was no basement—it was a dungeon.

A single door constructed of iron and softly glowing, as if infused by magic, lay ahead. I cautiously moved toward it, certain an evil ghost, wraith, or devil would spring out at me. But, as I approached, I only heard rasping, labored breathing coming from the cell.

"Hello?" I said through the small rectangular window to the room. It was so dark in there that I couldn't see a thing. It smelled of human waste and vomit. I held my nose.

"Alina? Is that you?" came Malik's weak reply.

"Malik!" My heart was overjoyed to hear the voice of my friend. I'd thought Balthazar had killed him.

On a wooden post, a set of keys was hanging.

"I found some keys! I can free you!" I seized the keys and fumbled with them to find one that fitted in the lock. As soon as the key touched the keyhole, a severe shock blasted my hand and arm.

The keys flew from my hand and landed with a jingling crash somewhere in the shadows.

"Don't open the door!" Malik rasped. "You'll be killed, and I don't want you to die."

I lifted the candle to the opening, trying to see inside.

Malik sat hunched over his sick. His hair hung in greasy waves, and a sheen of sweat covered his grimy skin.

When he spoke, he couldn't even hold up his head. It looked like it took extreme effort to even get a word out.

"Balthazar is using us. I know you're trying to help him, but he's too dark and evil. He threw me in here because I became a threat to his plans. You need to get away from him." He paused to catch his breath. "Layla is dead. Balthazar killed her. He slaughtered her in front of my eyes. I need you to save yourself.

"Layla and I found a way to help me. You must go and look for a man named John James. Time travel to the 1700s. John James is the only one who can help you." Phlegmy coughs erupted from his throat.

"How can I find John James?" I clutched the candle holder so hard my knuckles were white.

Malik waved his hand at me, still consumed by his coughing fit. "1700s. Americas. John James," was all he managed to say.

I raced up the dungeon stairs and hastened to my bedroom, where I prepared for bed. It took me nearly an hour to gather my composure. But when Balthazar pounded up the stairs, I had calmed my breathing and erratic heartbeat.

Balthazar flung open the bedroom door, where it crashed against the wall.

I jerked in alarm. "What's the matter?"

"You've been talking to him, haven't you? I could smell you in the dungeon." His face was a rictus of malevolence.

"I don't know what you're talking about." I drew the bedding up to my chin as if it could shield me from Balthazar's wrath.

"Whatever he told you—it was all lies!" Balthazar stormed toward me.

I drew away from him when he sat on the bed.

"Look at me!" he bellowed.

I shook my head.

"Look at me!"

Again, I shook my head.

Balthazar took several long, deep breaths, and then his hand landed on my shoulder.

"My beloved, I am sorry I frightened you." He caressed my neck and jaw. "I've missed you so."

He rolled me to face him and started kissing my cheeks, jaw, nose, and eyelids while murmuring sweet, tender phrases to me.

I had to relax and yield to him. He couldn't know I was planning on leaving him tomorrow when the moon was full.

His nimble fingers unlaced the front of my nightgown, and he slid his warm hands beneath the fabric.

I pretended to relax and respond. But inside, I was terrified. I cried out his name when I pretended to orgasm and tore at his back with my fingernails, the way he loved.

He slept with me the entire night, no doubt fearful of letting me out of his sight.

But the next night, I sliced my hand with my dagger, intoned the words from my bedroom, and left him again, praying he wouldn't find me.

December 15th, 1783

I have landed in the Americas. A group of uniformed marauders found me as I was wandering through a forest. They heckled me and taunted me. They tried to force their way inside me, but I beat them off. This angered them, so they struck me repeatedly, shouting things I didn't understand. They left me for dead, galloping away on their horses to let me rot.

Bruised and broken, I managed to find a stream and

quench my thirst, but I was so hungry. A man in a wagon found me staggering across the Plains tired and famished. He took pity on me, helped me into his wagon, and carted me to his home.

"Do you think that's Philip?" I said, looking at Emily.

"It could be. The date is right. Turn the page."

Turning to the next page, I noticed the rough edges where a page had been ripped out. "Oh, no! There's a page missing!"

I thumbed through the diary, hoping to find the missing entry, but it was gone.

"There must have been something important here." I tapped the journal. "We've got to ask Malik about it. Maybe he knows where it is."

I started to rise, but Emily put her hand on my arm.

"Let's finish reading first."

June 5th, 1784

I have been staying with Philip for quite some time. Balthazar has not found me, yet. I suppose it is only a matter of time, but I am lulling myself into a false sense of safety. To simply live an ordinary life is divine!

Our life here is quite peaceful. I have grown affectionate with him, and we share a bed now. Even though he is nothing like Balthazar, I have no choice but to enjoy him.

March 10th, 1785

I have met John James! I left Emily with Philip, determined to find him. He was as eager to speak with me as I was to talk to him. We took off together, heading for his cabin.

Along the way, we were attacked by a group of dark-skinned, shirtless men John James called "Pawnee." John James was able to fend them off with a rifle. After that, we galloped to his cottage, fearful of another attack.

When we arrived at his dwelling, he prepared me some

tea by boiling water over an open flame. Then, he sat me down at his rickety table and told me that men like the Pawnee are always looking for people like me, namely, time travelers. He said I needed to speak to another time traveler who lives in a nearby tribe called "the Sioux."

"I can bring him to speak with you," John James said.

After finishing our tea, we rode toward where the tribe was camped. John James left me with the horses and strode on foot toward a group of dwellings he called "teepees."

He returned nearly an hour later to find me sprawled in the grass, drifting to sleep, drowsy from the sun warming my face. He introduced me to a serious-looking fellow named Dancing Fire.

Dancing Fire was of an average build with long dark hair hanging in braids. His expression seemed ancient, like he had traveled other worlds. He told me he was a Timeborne like me.

I told them of my relationship with Balthazar and both men grew somber.

"You must find the sun and moon daggers," John James said.

"That's the only way you can defeat Balthazar," Dancing Fire added. "You've got to find them. But there are more resources in the future. I will accompany you there."

"All right, Dancing Fire," I said. "We shall leave at the next full moon."

Emily sniffled next to me. "Mother left to protect herself and me and my father."

"So it seems," I said, reaching up to massage my shoulders. "Makes sense if a demon like Balthazar is after you. That's why we're here, in Malik's home, after all. We want to defeat Balthazar as badly as Mom did."

Emily nodded, and we resumed reading.

Dancing Fire and I have time traveled for two years now and have been unable to find the daggers. We have gone into the 1980s and searched. Finally, frustrated with our search, I returned to see John James again. He told me to find a man named Jack James—he assured me, Jack, a future generation, was key to this entire endeavor.

So, I time traveled, returning back to 1987. In 1988, I found Jack James enrolled at a college. I was twenty-eight by then. I registered in the college and started observing him.

He was passionate about the topic of time travel. I didn't find him attractive, but I admired his heart and soul and the conviction he spoke about temporal displacement. I lurked in the audience when he gave his Ph.D. dissertation on temporal journeying. The audience ridiculed him and turned the dissertation into a disaster. He raced from the auditorium, and I later found him in a clock tower, ready to kill himself. I talked him out of it, and we formed a connection which I vowed to use—I needed information to defeat Balthazar. I had to succeed.

Jack seemed very self-conscious and walked with a bumbling gait. I didn't see how I could ever be with him, given his looks and withdrawn mannerisms—not after having been with Balthazar.

My stomach clenched as I read this. Papa was a kind and loving man who gave his all to Mom and me when she was alive. I didn't like hearing how she thought about him.

April 12th, 1992

I married Jack and graduated as an anthropologist. On our honeymoon, I insisted on combining it with excavation to search for the daggers. Jack was visibly disappointed, but he relented.

I managed to find the sun dagger! I was elated. I now wondered if I could perhaps save Balthazar instead of killing him. I missed him terribly all the time I was with Jack. How could Balthazar find me throughout time during my first four years of escape but then not seek me out during these last many years? Had he moved on and found another lover?

This thought breaks my heart.

November 17th, 1994

I have birthed another child, this one in La Cueva del Fuego. I dragged Jack to this cave, hoping it held the moon dagger—I was so determined to find it I barely noticed when I went into labor! The baby seems strong and feisty, like she will be a force to be reckoned with. We have named her Olivia.

But she was born during the eclipse! I tried to delay her birth. I even tried to stop her from entering the world. I didn't want her to have the kind of life I had, on the run from demons, but she was determined to enter the world at this time. So she is a Timeborne.

My time of safety is running out. I haven't seen Balthazar in a long time. I have to protect my child from him. I just have to! I don't want her to suffer as I have suffered these many years. I would rather she grew up safe and ordinary. I will hide the dagger that came into existence when she was born. She will never see it and have to time travel.

I wiped my eyes with my thumb and forefinger. I felt unsettled by what I'd just read. I knew Mom had tried to kill me when she was in labor. Here, she confessed to trying to protect me at all costs.

Several more journal entries described her rocky relationship with my father. When I was seven, Papa begged her to divorce him, saying, "I can take care of our child. You can travel the world and find whatever you are looking for."

Mom vehemently refused, but when I was about to turn

eight, Mom surprised Papa by saying, "I need time and space away from the relationship."

"Okay," Papa said. "Take whatever time you need."

"I'm going to go on another excavation. I might be gone a long time."

"I understand," Papa replied.

With tears sliding down my face, I flipped to the next page.

I have decided to time travel again, even though Lee told me not to go.

"Balthazar will find you," he warned. "He will feel you time travel and he will know where you are."

"I don't care," I said. "I've got to do this and find the second blade. Balthazar has not been hunting me for the last fifteen years. Why would he start now? He no longer wants me."

It saddened me to think this was true. I still loved him, despite his evil ways. I missed him.

I traveled back to Italy to the year 1582, intending to hide the sun dagger there. I returned to the village and sought out Giovanni. The blade would be safe with him.

When he saw me, he peered at me through rheumy old eyes. "Alina? Is that you?"

"Yes, Giovanni, it's really me!" On impulse, I reached out to hug him and he embraced me.

"Come inside," he said, patting my back.

His home looked much the same as before, just more worn. Once we'd settled with a glass of mead wine, I told him of my travels. I left out my obsessive need for Balthazar through the years, but I sensed that he knew without me uttering a word.

"I found the sun dagger, Giovanni," I finally said. "I need you to keep it and protect it with your life. Make sure to

keep it safe. Make sure whoever wants to defeat the darkness gets it."

I retrieved the dagger from my pocket and handed it to him.

He eyed the blade with a mixture of wonder and fear. "I don't know who to give it to. Who would be searching for it?"

"Trust me. When the person arrives looking for this blade, you will know who he or she is."

Giovanni's head bobbed up and down in acknowledgment. "I shall guard it with my life."

"Have you seen Balthazar?" I asked with a mixture of trepidation and unwelcome desire.

Giovanni shook his head. "Not for a while now."

He rubbed his weathered face with his palm.

"Do you know a man named Malik?"

Giovanni frowned and scratched the white stubble on his jaw. "That's a name I don't recognize."

After we exchanged a few pleasantries, I left him. I needed to find Malik.

I strolled down the cobbled walkway, past the hens pecking the dirt, and onto the dirt road leading into town.

A man approached me. When he got within touching distance, he exclaimed, "Alina?"

I squinted at him. "Raul Costa?"

He was much older than when I was sixteen and he was my eighteen-year-old lover but still looked the same, sans the boyish features.

I didn't know whether he would hug me or not, so I stood awkwardly for a moment, waiting for his response.

He glared at me. "What are you doing back here?"

He removed his hat and crumpled it between his hands as if he wished to do that to me.

TIMEBOUND

I took a step back. "I'm looking for a man named Malik. Do you know him?"

"No," he said abruptly. "But I would not be inclined to tell you if I did."

My jaw dropped open for a second. "What did I ever do to you?"

He poked my sternum with his forefinger. "You chose Lord Balthazar over me, that's what."

"I thought you were interested in the Contessa," I lied. I knew Raul had wanted me.

"I was never interested in the Contessa. You were the one I longed for," he said, his eyes growing sorrowful.

I cast my gaze at the ground. "Well, I'm sorry. If it's any consolation, Balthazar broke my heart."

Raul seemed to like this answer. "And I would have made you my queen. You got what you deserved."

I ignored his slight and said, "Does your family still make tonics, potions, and the like?"

Raul squinted. "Why do you ask me this?"

"I need something from you—I need poison." I wanted to use poison on Olivia's blade. If she ever tried to time travel, she would die. It was a better fate. I didn't want Balthazar to find her.

My stomach lurched as I read this. Now I knew why I was so sick when I arrived in Rome. Still, it was hard to digest the knowledge that my mother wanted to kill me to supposedly "save me" from my fate as a time traveler.

"I would grant you your wish, Alina, but I want something in return, and only then will I give you what you need."

"What would you possibly want from me?"

"You know my family makes the best potions and poisons, which you won't find anywhere else."

I believed him because I knew what his family would do to

people—they killed with their poisons. When Raul leaned into my ear and whispered to me what he wanted, I had no choice but to do as he said even though it came with a price and would be a huge risk.

I became his lover again.

Italy 1583

Raul had tricked me. I'd thought I would be his lover and be done. But I was chained to a bed for a whole year and treated as his "experiment." I was tortured, and escaping was almost impossible. When I was finally free, I ran far away from Raul and his cruel men. Raul wasn't the same man I used to know.

I tried to find Malik again, but he had become a ghost. I couldn't find him. John James told me that he had survived and lived, but no one knew his whereabouts.

My time was running out. I knew either Raul or Balthazar would find me again and surely kill me.

As I departed from Raul Costa's house, a man slid from the shadows, wearing a hood and a long cloak. I nearly screamed at him as he rushed toward me, but he clapped his hand over my mouth and dragged me into the trees.

He gripped me with unusual strength and hissed in my ear, "I know you have been looking for Malik. I know where he is."

I stopped struggling and pushed his hand away from my mouth. "You do?"

I whirled to face him.

"Yes. He is in Britannica in the year 1323. Find him there." He gave me the address where I could find Malik and then faded from sight like a spirit.

May 15th, 1323

I have trekked to Britannica and found Malik's address. He lives in an old stone manor house. I hurried up a tree-

lined walkway, past a tumbling creek, and strode up a set of stone stairs to the door. I lifted the metal knocker and let it fall.

A few minutes later, heavy footsteps pounded in my direction.

Malik opened the door and once he saw me, an angry scowl spread across his face.

"What are you doing here, Alina?" he hissed. "Who told you where to find me?"

"I...I..." I stammered, taken aback by his reaction. "I found the sun dagger."

"I don't care. I'm done being the darkness and want nothing to do with the dagger or your life." He started to close the door in my face, but I jammed my foot in the way.

"Wait, Malik. Don't turn me out like this. I'm no longer with Balthazar," I began, but Malik interrupted me.

"Don't you dare say his name here!" Malik hurried out onto the stoop and closed the door behind him.

"What happened to you, Malik?" I said, thoroughly confused. "Why are you so angry with me? Last time I saw you, we were still friends."

"Last time you saw me," he whispered, "I was chained to a dungeon wall being tortured by my former mentor."

I reeled back, stunned. But he was right. Who knew what kinds of atrocities Balthazar committed? I didn't want to know what Malik had to go through to escape.

I reached into my pocket and procured my journal.

"Here," I said, thrusting it toward him.

Malik threw out his palms and backed away. "What are you giving me? I don't want anything from you."

"It's my diary. It's a full account of what I've been through. Please take it. If my daughter survives, which I hope she won't, she will seek it out. I'm certain of that."

A baby's wail came from inside the house.

We both turned to stare at the open window.

"Malik, are you a father?"

He didn't answer me. Instead, he said, "I want you out of my life, Alina. I'm in a very dark place in my life, and if you don't leave this instant, I will kill you and put you out of your misery."

The baby started crying louder and louder.

"Malik, I'm sorry if I have upset you, but please just take my journal and protect my daughter. She is in danger from Balthazar. He will kill her."

Malik shook his head. "Alina, after I barely escaped Balthazar, I vowed to have a normal life. I wanted to disappear from the world. I want nothing to do with Balthazar. I just lost two important people in my life, and I want nothing to do with you or your problems."

The baby began to wail more, and I rushed inside the house. I walked over to her small crib and saw a baby girl with a Timebound necklace around her neck.

Malik grabbed the child and started calming her, and she fell asleep in his arms. "Leave, Alina, and never come back."

I stayed put. "You think you can protect her forever? One day she will grow up and see the monster inside you, and she will despise you."

His eyes blazed with anger.

I took a step back from him, becoming frightened.

"You knew what Balthazar was, but you continued to fuck him and be with him no matter what," he roared. "I will protect my child from Balthazar or anyone that will come near her. I will die for her. But you can't say the same."

He slashed the air before me.

Tears went down my face because he was right. I was weak. I couldn't protect Olivia.

I turned around and left. The same night I went back and left my journal through the window to the baby's room and never looked back.

There was one last entry in the diary with no date.

I left the journal for Malik. I have made many mistakes in my life, but in the end, I wanted to heal and fix Balthazar and make him a better man. I tried to change him, so we could be together and start a life together. But I failed. I couldn't find the other blade, and my time was up.

Malik has changed. Whoever changed him to be better succeeded. I still hold out hope that maybe one day, Balthazar will change. I still love and care about him, and I love Jack. But most importantly, I love my daughters. They are my most prized possessions. One day I hope to make things right. Only time will tell.

I flipped the few remaining pages, but they were all blank. "What did she mean that she would make everything right? And what happened to Malik's child?"

"I don't know," Emily said. "But did reading this journal change your attitude toward our mother? Are you able to forgive her?"

I couldn't answer her question.

CHAPTER ELEVEN
ROMAN

In my twisted, time-traveling life, I had many opportunities to be angry, bitten with the fever of revenge. Yet I'd never been more fueled with rage than when I carried this fool, Tristan, toward Jack's house, cradling his unconscious body in my arms.

I couldn't believe this sniveling idiot had bedded my wife. Olivia was a warrior woman, strong and capable. And this man, this whimpering, whining joke of a man, was nothing more than a worm, a blight upon the existence of humanity.

I stepped onto the porch, stopping to readjust Tristan with a grunt.

Jack had left the door open, as usual. He liked the fresh air circulating through his home when the weather was nice like it was today.

"Where shall we put him?" I called over my shoulder to Lee as I kicked the door wider and crossed the threshold to Jack's home.

"Head for Jack's office," he called back, his feet crunching over the gravel driveway.

As I entered, Jack hurried from the kitchen, a tea towel in his hands. He came to a stop when he saw who I carried.

"Where did you…?" he began.

"Look who we ran into," Lee said, coming close behind me. "Rather, look who got in the way of Roman's fist."

Jack pressed his fingertips to his cheek, eyes wide. "You can fill me in later. Where are you going to put him?"

"Your office," I said, heading down the hall.

"No!" Jack said. "Take him to the basement. I don't want his smarmy ass anywhere near my office."

I made a turnabout and headed toward the stairs off the kitchen. "Can someone get the door?"

"Already on it," Lee said, thundering toward the basement door. He threw it open and reached inside to flip on the light switch.

I almost dropped Tristan when I reached the landing of the basement. I struggled to right him in my arms, then proceeded toward the corner, where folded chairs sat in a row.

"Get me a chair before I drop him," I said.

Tristan stank in my arms, smelling like blood, sweat, and ale, and I was getting sick of his stench.

"On it," Lee said, scrambling around me. He seized a chair and unfolded it, then gestured to me to lower Tristan.

I plunked Tristan on the chair, then grabbed onto his hair to prop him up.

"What do you have to secure him?" I asked Jack as he rushed down the stairs.

"I've got some rope in the cupboard," he said.

"I'll get the rope. You get some ice water," Lee said.

Jack frowned. "Ice water?"

"Just do it," Lee said, swishing his hand in mad circles.

Jack clomped up the stairs, taking two at once.

While Lee and I busied ourselves with tying up Tristan, the slimy bastard groaned in protest.

"Feel the pain, Tristan," I grumbled, "for all the pain you've caused Olivia. This is only a taste."

I yanked on the knot I had just finished, squeezing the life out of his wrists.

Jack returned bearing a stainless-steel pitcher covered with condensation. The ice cubes clinked against the walls of the pitcher, and water sloshed over the edge as he hastened toward us.

"Give it to me," I said, extending my hand.

Jack placed the freezing-cold pitcher in my grip.

"Perfect temperature," I said. "Wake up, asshole."

I poured the entire pitcher over Tristan's head, taking pleasure in his shocked gasps.

Once he'd caught his breath and shook the water off of his head, he looked at Jack and Lee and sneered.

"Well, well, if it isn't the old geezers, Jack and Sensei Lee. Where'd you get this dude?" He inclined his head toward me. "You're such a pussy. You always get people to help you. You're too much of a twat-waffle to get anything done yourself."

While I knew what a waffle was and had been enjoying them of late with bacon, I didn't know what a "twat-waffle" was—but it sounded like a slur.

I yanked on his hair, making him wince. "You son of a bitch, don't talk to Jack that way."

"What are you going to do to me? I've already failed at everything," Tristan said, his jaw jutting out in defiance.

I got in Tristan's face. "You're going to get what you deserve for hurting Olivia!"

Tristan flinched. But then he had the nerve to say, "I don't give a shit. She's worthless."

Without thinking, I backhanded his face, sending his head whipping to the side. "I dare you to say one more word about my wife. I will beat the shit out of you until you beg me to kill you."

He twisted around to face me, blinking madly.

"Fuck," he said, licking the blood leaking down his cheek from where I'd struck him.

I seized both his ears and pulled hard. "You betrayed her and went after her father. I'm going to tear you to pieces."

This time he had the decency to look afraid.

I slugged him in the belly. He collapsed as best he could over his midsection, given the ropes, wheezing.

Lee grabbed my arm.

"No, don't. We need him!" He pinched both of Tristan's cheeks. "What happened to you the day Olivia time traveled? Why did you snap? You behaved perfectly as if you adored Olivia and then simply turned on her. What do you know?"

Tristan struggled, shaking his head to try and free it from Lee's merciless grip.

Lee stretched Tristan's face even tauter.

"I'm not telling you anything." Tristan spat into Lee's face.

As Lee wiped the slime from his face, Tristan smirked, inclining his head toward me. "Who's the hired meat?"

I pulled myself up and said, "I'm no hired meat. I'm Roman Alexander, a warrior, and husband to Olivia. You better start talking and tell me what you know, starting off with who is Eyan Malik and why does he want you?"

Tristan's eyes grew wide, and a sheen of sweat broke out on his lip and forehead. He shook his head.

"You good for nothing asshole," Lee snarled.

I took my knife and began to carve Tristan's face in a

manner I'd used to extract secrets from my enemies when I was a gladiator.

Tristan let out a screeching, garbled cry.

Jack rushed over and seized my arm. "Roman, you can't! There are rules in this country."

My brows drew together. "Rules? What rules?"

"About what you can do to another person." Jack looked at me pleadingly. "We shouldn't even be holding him hostage in my basement!"

Still puzzled, I released Tristan.

"Fine, but you better start talking before I unleash pure hell on you," I said with a snarl. "Who is Malik?"

Tristan pressed his swollen lips together.

I clutched his hair again, twisting the greasy locks. "Why did you want Olivia to time travel? And how do you know about time traveling?"

Tristan's eyes moistened. "I was on a mission to prove to my father that I'm worthy to be by his side. But, now that I've failed, my life is worthless."

Where was this self-pity coming from? At first he was so defiant and arrogant. I backhanded him again.

Tristan spat a wad of bloody saliva at my feet. "I did everything to please my father, only everything wasn't enough for him." He sobbed. "To prove my loyalty to my father, I had to bring Olivia to him. But I failed and now he is right. I am a complete loser."

My forehead furrowed. None of what he said made sense.

The water heater in Jack's basement hissed and rumbled, and the clothes-washing machine kicked to life.

I was startled but remembered Jack telling me something about clothes-washing devices and their "cycles."

"All this time you were with her, you knew Olivia was a

time traveler? How is this possible?" I released my hold of his hair and scratched my stubble-covered cheek.

"My father told me," Tristan said, sounding more like a mewling kitten than a grown man. "He told me about Jack and everything. The only way to prove myself to Father was to time travel Olivia to him. But I failed."

A ripple of fear crawled up my spine as all the puzzle pieces began to fit together.

One lone tear slithered down Tristan's cheek, and his head slumped onto his chest.

This man was pathetic. I reached for his hair again and gave it a yank. "Keep talking. Who's this father of yours?"

Tristan ignored me, shaking his head. "I was trained about Timebornes from a young age," he said, his chin jutting forward. "My whole life was spent making my father proud. I tried to be the best son I could, to always make him happy and do as he said. But, I saw in my father's eyes that nothing would satisfy him, no matter what I did to please him. It was never enough. Then one day, he told me about Olivia and Jack. He demanded that I bring Olivia to him, and only then would I be part of his world and accepted as his son.

"I started spying on Olivia, learning about her and her life. I thought dating her would make her spill her secrets. And then, one month turned into a couple of years, and still, I got nowhere with her. I learned nothing. Instead, I fell in love with her. But my duty to my father was more important than love. I couldn't betray him.

"I started to worry that my father would kill me for taking so long. I needed to make my move. Then Jack called her over for breakfast and spilled the beans. It was a perfect setup for me to make my move, but it failed miserably."

My gut twisted at the thought of him loving Olivia. She was meant for *me.*

I crossed my arms over my chest. "And then what happened between you and your father?"

Tristan tugged at his bindings. "My father disowned me, telling me that I was the worst mistake of his life. He said I was a failure. After that, no matter what I did to please him and earn his love, nothing was enough for him. All he wanted was Olivia. She was my ticket to earn his love and approval."

His voice came out as a whining, mewling bray, much like a donkey.

"The moment she time traveled, I went into hiding, afraid of what my father would do. But nothing has happened, and I haven't seen him in years." He sniffled.

His self-pitying behavior was pathetic. No man worth his salt should stoop so low as to snivel and whine, painting himself as the victim.

I grasped Tristan's bony shoulders and shook him. "Tell me, who is your father that you fear so much?" I suspected I already knew, but I wanted him to say the name.

Tristan said nothing, averting his eyes.

I grabbed him by his hair. "If you won't let me know who your father is, then I will ask again. Who is Eyan Malik?"

Tristan's eyes rolled about in his head like small pebbles kicked across the road. He glanced to his right and said, "Father said he got rid of him."

"Who is your father?" I demanded. I was getting annoyed by his avoiding my questions.

Tristan met my eyes with a cold, lifeless glare. "I'm not at fucking liberty to say."

"Then, I'm not at liberty to let you fucking live." I lunged for him, wrapped my hands around his neck and squeezed.

Lee came behind me and wrestled my grasp away from Tristan's neck. "We need to keep him alive."

None of this made sense to my gladiator mind, but I

heeded Lee's warning. "I'm going to beat your father's name out of you."

Tristan tried to draw up his knees without success—his ankles were bound to the chair. "No! Please spare me. I can't tell you who my father is."

"Can't or won't?" I said, drawing my hand back again to slap him.

"I can't. I just can't," Tristan wailed.

I was baffled at what would work with Tristan to get him to talk. I inclined my head toward Lee. He, Jack, and I stepped into the corner to confer.

"What are the rules for getting information out of someone?" I whispered.

"We'll have to have a long talk," Lee said, crossing his arms, "but Tristan might be lured with an incentive."

"What do you mean?"

"The same way we got him over here for dinner when Olivia was with us—we'd offer him dinner, and suddenly his hectic schedule would clear up," Jack said.

I stroked my jaw, considering. "I see. We need to bribe him."

I returned to Tristan and stalked around him in a slow circle. "How about you tell me who your father is, and I will allow you to time travel with me?"

Tristan offered me a glance but shook his head and looked away.

Was that interest or fear?

I continued to prowl around him. "I will time travel you somewhere you want to go. You can go anywhere." I swept my arm through the air. "Name your place. You can disappear. Or you can see Olivia and apologize."

Tristan stuttered and stammered nonsense, looking as if he might wet himself.

No, that's fear. Tristan's terrified of his father.

I came to a stop in front of him and seized his chin.

"I'm offering you an escape, Tristan," I said in a low, soothing tone best used on a child. "You can go anywhere. You can be free of your father and disappear."

Tristan trembled in my grip as the clothes-washing device shuddered to a stop.

"If you hurt me, my father will kill you," he said in a shaky voice. "He is a dangerous man."

"Really?" I bore down on his jaw. "What does it matter if anything happens to you? You just got through saying your father doesn't care about you. Why would he care if something awful happened to you?"

Lee, who had been hanging back, pressed in close beside me. "Is your father a Timehunter?"

I released Tristan's chin.

He flexed and stretched his jaw.

Olivia had told me, "The Timehunters are going to come after us and kill us." But where did I hear that? Was it in one of those strange nightmares I constantly see at night?

"Answer me!" Lee demanded. "Is your father a Timehunter?"

"No! My father's not a Timehunter." Tristan pulled against his restraints.

"What is he, then?" Lee asked. "Who is he?"

Tristan pursed his lips which were stained with dried blood.

I clasped my hands behind my back and began to circle him again. "I'm a patient man, Tristan. I can wait you out. Sooner or later, you'll feel the urge to eat, drink, or even piss. I can wait it out. We've got nothing but time."

The irony of that last statement didn't escape me. I had nothing but time at my disposal.

SARA SAMUELS

Lee and Jack stayed quiet while I continued to walk. After a few revolutions around him, I stood before him and pulled my dagger out of its sheath. The tip glistened. I tapped the blade against my palm.

"You're going to tell me who your father is, Tristan." I traced the shell of his ear with the tip of my blade.

Lee and Jack exchanged a look.

"Remember there are different rules in this time, Roman," Jack said.

Tristan winced and pulled away from me.

"Did I get the wrong ear?" I grabbed his hair, then carved the swirl inside his opposite ear.

"Roman!" Jack admonished.

Lee put his hand on Jack's arm. "Let him work this out in a way that makes sense to him."

"But we could be arrested!" Jack said.

I ignored them both, focused on Tristan who trembled beneath my hand.

"Better?" I said.

He shook his head back and forth like the rattle of a rattlesnake.

"N-n-no," he stammered.

I stood before him and used the tip of the knife to trace a smile around his lips.

Tristan screamed. "Stop!"

Blood began dripping down his face, dropping from his chin in fat globules.

"Tell me who your father is," I said.

"You'd better tell him," Lee said. "He's not kidding when he says he's patient."

I brought the blade toward his eyebrows, intending to give them a devilish point.

Tristan struggled against his bonds, his desperate cries

punctuating the air. "Alright! Alright! I'll tell you what you want to know!"

I stepped back, unsure of how to proceed. I knew he was in pain, and yet here was the information I'd been seeking.

"My father is Lord Balthazar," Tristan yelled.

A chill ran down my spine as I realized it was true—just as I had assumed all along.

The basement stilled like someone had dropped a bomb, and we were all experiencing the fallout.

I let out a stunned laugh. "You? You're nothing but a pathetic idiot."

"It's true! He's my father!" More tears streamed down his face. "And I've done nothing but disappoint him."

"I can see why," I said. "You're a wimp of a man."

I looked at Lee and Jack.

Lee shrugged as if to say, "Anything's possible."

Jack appeared to have shrunk into himself like a turtle.

I wanted to punish Tristan, both for his behavior as well as his father's. Balthazar was a monster. And now I wanted to torture his son like he'd tortured Olivia and me. I longed to bring him tremendous pain.

"Will you let me go now?" Tristan stammered.

"No way in hell!" I growled. "I think you just earned yourself a harsher punishment."

My eyes flicked to Lee, silently asking if this was okay.

Lee shrugged noncommittally.

Part of me wanted to follow through on my promise, but another part of me was too scared to actually do anything. The rules of this time made no sense to me. I wanted to give Tristan the beating he deserved, but deep down I also wanted to show mercy. My stomach churned with indecision—should I follow my heart or my head?

Frustrated and exasperated, I could think of nothing to do

—no action I could take to make things better. But what help was inaction when so much depended on me?

CHAPTER TWELVE

OLIVIA

Sitting in Malik's office, I stared blankly into space, trying to come to grips with everything I had just read in my mother's journal. My gaze drifted like a leaf, landing on the door, which stood slightly ajar. Malik was out there somewhere in his house, caring for Rosie. And we were in here having our brain cells rearranged.

And somehow, everything and everyone was connected.

The wind howled again, picking up as much speed as my emotions. This vivid snapshot of my mother touched me in countless ways. *With all that pain and fear, she lived a tortured existence.* But her overriding support of Balthazar and her desire to save him still repulsed me.

"What are you thinking?" Emily said quietly, touching my hand.

I stirred from my mental musings, returning to the room.

"I'm thinking Mom's life was a mess. I'm thinking I still don't like or trust her. I'm thinking…" I ran my hand across my forehead. "I'm thinking I don't know what to think."

"How can you still not like her? She was possessed by a madman, by a demon," Emily said. Her face appeared bruised from the shadows in the room. Then, she frowned. "Actually, I don't like her now, either."

She shuddered, her limbs trembling like a dog attempting to shake off water. "Balthazar," she said, her expression crumpling.

She didn't need to say anything else.

"Exactly. Mom, of all people, had the power to kill Balthazar. She knew him intimately. Surely, she knew his weaknesses," I mused. Lee had always taught me to look for a person's weaknesses.

If you know someone's weaknesses, however slight they might be, you have the power to do them harm, he often said. And you have the power to heal them, he would usually add, but I didn't want to think about that part.

Balthazar was a hideous, foul, evil monster who needed to be removed from this planet. No two ways about it. Still, I couldn't help but wonder—why was her goal to save him? What possible redeeming quality could he have possessed that moved her so profoundly? I didn't get it. Not when Balthazar had assaulted me, causing me to lose my unborn child. He threatened me, and nearly cost Roman his life. There wasn't a shred of evidence to support his continued existence.

"Are you wondering what I'm wondering?" Emily asked.

"I don't know. Are you wondering why Mom chose to save a monster? Monsters can't be saved." I twirled a strand of hair around my finger.

"No, darling," Malik said, gliding through the door. "Monsters can be saved."

I jerked at his sudden appearance. I still didn't understand how he moved through this world like a cat.

He leveled his gaze at me. "Even the darkest of the dark can change."

I blinked a few times to orient myself to his presence.

"Are you saying that about you? If you're speaking of Balthazar, I'm afraid we'll have to agree to disagree."

I stood and stretched my back, stiff from sitting so long.

"You must be tired, and I have things to do here. Why don't you two head to bed, hmmm?" Malik said in the manner of a good host, artfully evading my question.

"Oh! We're sorry we took up so much time in your office," Emily said, bolting to her feet.

"Nonsense." Malik swept his hand through the air. "I wanted you to finish the journal. And now I need my office back."

He was so reasonable I didn't trust his mannerisms. But, truthfully, I was fatigued. All my questions could wait.

"Well, good night, then," I said, trying to suppress a yawn.

"Pleasant dreams, you two," he said, smiling broadly. His intense gaze, directed at *me,* didn't match his warm smile. He propped his hands on his hips, waiting for us to leave.

"In the journal, you had a child," I said. "What happened to her?"

Malik gave me a deadly glare, saying nothing.

"Will you tell us what happened?" Emily said kindly.

His expression shuttered, leaving only cold regard. "It's late. I will answer that question another day. Good night."

He reached for the doorknob, his expectations clear.

Emily and I shuffled from his room and out into the hallway, where we separated, heading for our respective bedrooms.

As I walked along the plush carpeting, I couldn't help but recall how his eyes tracked my every move.

The following morning I awoke to soft scratching on the door. I blinked, yawned, and stretched, then said, "Who's out there?"

"It's me. It's Emily. Can I come in?"

"Sure." I pulled myself upright, swung my legs off the bed, and reached for the delicate lace and silk robe left in my armoire. As I tugged it around me, Emily entered the room, looking disheveled and still fatigued.

"What's wrong? Sleepless night?" I crossed the room to hug her.

Embracing me, she nodded into my shoulder. "I tossed and turned all night."

"Me, too. I couldn't stop thinking of everything we learned about our mother in the journal." I kissed the top of her head and released her. "What kept you awake?"

I glanced at the gap in the curtains, finding the sun reasonably high in the sky.

"That missing page." She hugged herself tightly and studied the floor. "I'm convinced it contains vital information. We have to ask Malik about it—what does it say? And where is it? Why was it removed from the journal?"

My mood darkened as last night's journal reading flooded my mind. All that new data to process about Mom...

The sound of tiny feet met my ears, distracting me.

Rosie! I didn't even think to ask about her last night.

Rosie pushed open the door without knocking and jumped into the room like a bunny rabbit.

"I've been having a tea party!" she announced, swirling in a circle.

"A tea party? How fun!" I said, crouching to get on her level. "Isn't it a little early for tea?"

"No, silly!" She tapped me on the nose. "It's high noon."

She raised her hand over her head, standing on her tiptoes. "That's what Malik calls it. He said, 'It's high noon,' and if I stand up tall, I can reach it."

I glanced at Emily with a quizzical expression. *Is Malik playful?*

"Who did you have the tea party with? Cook?"

Rosie clasped her hands before her and pivoted side to side. "Not Cook. Malik! Malik and I had a tea party. And now he said to come to get you for lunch!"

She spun and darted out the door like a baby bird.

I stared at Emily.

"Malik had a tea party with Rosie? Stranger things have happened, I guess," I said with a shake of my head.

"I don't know. This one is pretty strange," Emily said.

We both burst out laughing.

"I'll be right down after I change. And don't worry— we'll ask about the missing page." I crossed to the armoire to pick out today's attire. A long high-waisted day gown in vivid blue called to me.

After I dressed, I swept down the gleaming staircase and headed into the dining room, letting the savory smells guide my way.

As usual, a feast had been placed on the table.

Malik looked up from his plate at me as I entered. He pierced me with his stunning emerald gaze. "Good afternoon, Olivia. How are you?"

Rosie sat by his side, playing with the peas on her plate.

"We don't play with food, sweetheart," Malik said, gently covering her hand with his.

"Okay," she said softly.

He turned his attention back to me, waiting for an answer to his question.

"I'm groggy. I didn't get much sleep last night." A yawn escaped my mouth, underscoring my statement.

"I'm sorry to hear that. Do sit down and restore yourself

with food and beverage." He motioned toward all the dishes filled with provisions on the table.

I sat next to Emily, whose plate was piled high with meat, potatoes, vegetables, and a ramekin of custard.

As I loaded my dish, I said, "There's a page missing from the journal. It was ripped out. Do you know of its whereabouts or what it said?"

I brought a turkey leg to my lips and nibbled at the crispy brown skin and tender flesh, cooked to perfection.

"I'm afraid I don't." Malik looked at Rosie, who sat swinging her feet. "Sweetheart, why don't you see if Cook needs any help?"

She shook her head, making her glossy brown ringlets bounce. "I want to stay with you."

"If you want to stay with me, you'll have to stay rather still, like stodgy old adults." The corners of his mouth lifted in mirth.

"Okay, I'll behave like an old adult," she said solemnly.

Malik chuckled.

I glared at him. "I know you know more than you're letting on, Malik."

I forked some potatoes and gravy and shoved them in my mouth.

Malik frowned. "I honestly don't know what you're talking about. I know nothing about a missing page."

He leaned back in his chair like a contented king.

I swallowed my mouthful and said, "Please don't toy with me, Malik. My nerves are frayed. Neither of us slept well last night…and you insist on keeping secrets."

Like a lightning strike, his demeanor changed to something dark and menacing.

I swore the temperature dropped ten degrees in the dining room. I shivered, drawing into myself.

"Why do you insist on thinking you know my mind?" Malik carefully pulled his napkin from his lap, folded it, and placed it next to his plate.

I stayed mute, realizing I'd triggered his fury.

"Forget the missing page. That is not important right now. What's important is that you have to make a decision. What are you going to do? What's your next move?" He looked into me, through me, and beyond with his penetrating eyes, pinning me to my chair.

Another chill, made of fear, gripped me. I was unable to speak or even move.

Malik drummed his fingers in a slow, deliberate cadence. "What. Are. You. Going. To. Do?"

"I don't know," I said, the words barely audible.

He slammed his fist into the table, and the dishes and silverware clattered and clinked. "That is *not* what I want to hear. You've read your mother's words in the journal. Now you have to decide what you are going to do."

Finally, I snapped, bolting to my feet. "I don't know! It was a lot of information, and I'm still trying to process everything. It's all too much. For now, I need to clear my head. I'm going to take Rosie for a walk."

I blinked, staring at Malik's empty seat.

Then, a low snarl came from behind me. "You'd better figure out what you will do next when you clear your head. If you don't, I will toss you out, leaving you to defeat Balthazar by yourself, and you won't see Roman again."

I whirled around to confront him, but he was gone. Shaking, I fell back into my seat.

Emily busied herself with cleaning up, taking her plate and silverware into the kitchen.

I brought my trembling hands to my face, trying to smooth my features.

Rosie sat across from me, staring at me with wide eyes.

"Do you want to go for a walk, honey-pie?" I said in a tremulous voice.

"Okay," she said, pushing away from her seat. She rounded the table and patted my hair with her tiny hand. "Everything's okay."

I wanted to believe her, but I knew nothing was okay.

Emily, Rosie, and I put on weather gear to face the rain and tromped outside.

While Rosie searched for mushrooms and tree frogs—her idea, not mine—Emily and I discussed our next move.

"Malik's right, you know," Emily said as we trekked beneath the wet trees. "We can't just hide here forever."

Occasional splats of water rolled from the branches, bouncing off our bonnets.

"Oh, how I wish we could," I said, stooping to pick up a sturdy branch perfect as a walking stick. I sighed. "But, you're right. Malik is not obligated to care for us, especially since he is a darkness. For all I know, he can turn on us and kill us. But his hospitality has been more than generous."

"So, should we go to Italy, then? Head for the 1500s?" Emily ran her hand across a tree trunk.

"To find the sun dagger?" I massaged my neck, trying to bring life back into my body. Malik scared the bejesus out of me.

"Exactly. That's exactly what you'd have done before Balthazar got to you," Emily said.

I was sure she was trying to be supportive, but that was the wrong thing to say. It brought up my terror of Balthazar and the utter apathy and fear I had walked with since losing my unborn child. I was no longer courageous. I was a clucking hen in the barnyard and couldn't force myself to be any different.

"Well?" Emily looked at me hopefully.

"I don't know, Em," I said, my booted feet squishing the moist forest floor. "I just can't decide."

A shape blurred into view, and a man dropped from the tree right before us.

Emily and I let out piercing screams.

I flung my walking stick to the ground.

Rosie looked up from her mushroom hunting behind a large oak tree. She stared at us with eyes wide and uncomprehending.

Emily held out her arms, flinging herself at him. "Marcellious!"

He pushed her away, snarling, "Step back, bitch."

Emily paled as her moment of joy was quashed. "What do you mean? Don't you remember who I am? It's me. Emily. Your wife."

Her voice sounded small and far away.

"We thought you *died*. How are you here? How did you find us? What are you doing here?" I said, some of my old defiance rising as I leaned forward, angry that he rejected my sister.

"I'm here for one reason," he said, stalking toward me.

"And what's that?" I hissed.

Marcellious' eyes looked unhinged and wild. "I'm here for the journal on Balthazar's orders."

I stumbled backward as terror gripped my limbs. *Balthazar's orders?*

"Show me where it is, and no one will get hurt. I need to bring it to Lord Balthazar." Marcellious seized the front of my dress with a sneer, bunching it in his hands.

"Let go of me, you asshole." I wrenched his hand away from me as some of my fire returned.

Has Balthazar poisoned Marcellious' mind like he did to me when I tried to kill Roman?

Marcellious lunged at me, reaching for my neck.

I darted out of the way, glancing at Emily. She had fallen to her knees weeping.

"His mind has been poisoned, Em. He doesn't mean it."

She blinked away her tears, seeking hope in my words.

"Don't be ridiculous," Marcellious said. "I need the journal. My master needs the journal, and I will get it."

"What the hell are you talking about, Marcellious? Have you lost your mind? Surely you don't believe in Balthazar as anything other than an evil demon." I scratched my cheek, bewildered.

Marcellious balled up his fists. "I only believe in my master, Lord Balthazar. *Only him*."

Spittle flew from his mouth as he spoke.

My stomach knotted up, and sweat poured from my pores. *He's as insane as Balthazar.*

I contemplated my next move. Rosie still stood behind the tree. Emily still knelt on the forest floor.

There was no way I could gather them up and race toward the house. And where the hell was Malik? He had to know Marcellious was on his property.

"Give me the fucking journal," Marcellious said through clenched teeth.

"We don't have it," I said, trying to catch Emily's attention.

"Yes, you do," Marcellious said, stalking me in a slow circle. "I've been watching you for days. You have it. I want it. Hand it over."

I turned with him, not wanting to take my eyes off him. Finally, I caught Emily's gaze and inclined my head toward Rosie.

Emily nodded, wiped her eyes, and scurried toward her.

"I know it's in the house, bitch. Go get it for me," Marcellious said.

"I'm not your bitch, asshole," I hissed.

An icy chill shook my bones before another shape blurred into form before me.

Oh, my God, It's Balthazar.

He stood before me, leering. "Miss me, my darling? It's been quiet for a while, hasn't it?"

My mind and body became utterly numb, incapable of movement, save for the trembling in my legs and arms. I was so seized by fear that I could barely support my weight. The last time I saw Balthazar, he'd warned us to run for our lives. So we ran to Malik's, where I was sure we'd be safe from this predator. But no—not only were we unsafe, the owner of this estate, Malik, was nowhere to be found. He had to know there was danger in the yard. He was a demon, after all, with supernatural abilities.

Balthazar reached out a finger and dragged his long fingernail across my cheek. "I asked you a question, my love. Did you miss me?"

I shuddered and drew my face away from his despicable touch.

"So, tell me where the journal is. I want it." His teeth unnaturally caught the light, causing them to sparkle and gleam.

I said nothing, still incapable of speech.

"What are you, mute?" A wicked grin formed on Balthazar's face. "Or were you so stunned by the depth of love I shared with your mother that you can't think of a snarky retort? Didn't we have the greatest relationship? It was the true love of a lifetime, full of passion."

I snapped out of my torpor. "My mother *hated* you. She *despised* you. You killed her entire family."

"All lies," Balthazar said with a swish of his hand. "No matter what happened between us, what tragedy and pain she endured, she still loved me and wanted me till the end of her days."

"You really think I'm going to just hand over the journal, so you can see what it contains inside? I won't let you have it. With the knowledge that I have, I will kill you. I don't fear you any longer." I kept my voice low and even, although I shook inside.

Balthazar barked out a chilling laugh.

"You think you don't fear me? Look at you. You are broken inside. I broke your soul. You stand there trembling before me. The strong Olivia I knew once no longer exists." He seized my throat, backing me into a tree. "You think Malik is going to save you and help you? I don't see him anywhere. All I see is fear in your eyes."

"How do you know Malik is even here?" I said as Balthazar pressed my skull into the unyielding bark.

"I know everything. Malik fears me. That is why he's been hiding all these decades from me. Where is he?" Balthazar said evenly.

I side-eyed Rosie, who huddled next to Emily.

Balthazar turned to see what held my attention. "What a beautiful child. Come here, sweetness."

He stepped away from me, and I skittered out of his reach, rubbing my sore neck.

Rosie shook her head as Emily squeezed her tighter.

I looked around frantically. Where's Marcellious? Where did he go?

"Were you trying to hide this lovely child from me?" Balthazar said. "I love children. Come here, sweetness."

He extended his hand.

Rosie recoiled.

"I won't hurt you," he said.

"Don't believe him," Emily said, pressing her palms over Rosie's ears.

Leaves crunched behind me. I whipped my head around.

Marcellious stood before me with the journal in his hands.

What in the goddamned hell happened to Malik? How could he do this to us? Is Balthazar right that Malik fears him, and that's why he's hiding from him?

"I've got the journal, Master. We can leave now." Marcellious waved my mother's diary in the air.

I became outraged. So, Malik just let Marcellious waltz into his house? Did he stand there in the doorway, journal in hand, and give it to Marcellious?

Emily stood, still clutching Rosie to her legs. "Please, don't do this! If you love me, you won't do this. We can be a family together."

Marcellious spat into the damp ground. "I never loved you. It was an act from the day I met you."

"You never loved me?" Emily repeated, her chin quivering.

Marcellious sneered. "Not one bit. It was all a ruse. You don't even know how to please a man. I had to sneak away to get some satisfaction."

Red spots of shame bloomed on Emily's cheeks.

I clenched my fists, wanting to destroy both men.

Balthazar let out a hideous laugh.

"Oh, yes, let's tell them the truth about everything. It's the perfect time for sharing." He rubbed his hands in glee. "Did you know Marcellious has been working with me since you landed in the Americas? How do you think I knew all the things I knew? Marcellious was my spy."

Marcellious stepped next to Balthazar; his chest puffed with pride.

"How else would I know about John James, when you got married, and when Emily and Marcellious got married? Or, how I came to your campsite and destroyed the village. I broke you and ensured Roman was injured enough to have him die. It was all Marcellious' doing, telling me about your whereabouts and reporting to me daily. You were all blinded by him." Balthazar gazed fondly at Marcellious.

Anger flared in my chest. Marcellious had betrayed us all. He was responsible for Roman being injured on the battlefield. He was as evil as Balthazar, carrying the same dark blood inside. I was disgusted by him.

If only Roman knew…

I snatched the walking stick from the ground. Holding it like a bat, I ran toward Marcellious.

Balthazar laughed as he waved his arm, and the stick flew from my hands.

Emily howled her despair. "You're a barbarian…a savage. You're nothing but evil, Marcellious! I hate you!"

Marcellious joined Balthazar in laughter.

"What would Roman say about you?" I shouted at Marcellious.

Marcellious sobered, shooting a vicious glare at me.

I backed away.

"I don't give a *fuck* what Roman thinks about *anything.*" Marcellious' arms flew about as he spoke. "I was supposed to kill him on the battlefield in Rome, but then *you* happened."

"So, you lied to Roman, me, everyone," I said. "You didn't mean any of the things you said. I knew you were evil. I knew the bastard that you are would never change. Monsters can never change. Emily, he's been lying to us, deceiving us all along. He is his father's son. A monster born out of darkness will die a monster."

Emily continued to sob while clutching Rosie.

I lunged for the walking stick again. A hand seized my wrist, and a female voice cooed, "Don't hurt my lover."

I jerked my hand away, staring into Dahlia's eyes.

"Why did I have to endure your pathetic attempts at sexual pleasure when I could be pleased by the darkness?" Marcellious said to Emily, before his gaze slid toward Dahlia.

Dahlia strutted toward him and snaked her arm around his shoulders.

Marcellious grasped her jaw and lowered his mouth to hers, kissing her deliberately and loudly.

Dahlia moaned.

Emily wailed. "Don't do this to me, Marcellious. I loved you!"

"You two are despicable." I grabbed the stick and swung it at Marcellious and Dahlia.

Balthazar's hand whipped out to seize the stick.

"You're a fucking monster!" I screamed as he wrenched the branch from my hands.

"I don't give a damn what you think about me," Balthazar said. "Now that I have the journal, I no longer need you. I will end your misery and give you a painful death, so I can be with my beloved Alina."

"Emily, run! Run!" I yelled.

Emily grasped Rosie's hand and took off.

I faced the three demons, ready to fight. This would be my final battle, but I would give it everything I had. I tugged up my skirts and retrieved my dagger, slashing the air in front of Dahlia and Marcellious.

Balthazar stood there, appearing amused.

With a thunderous roar, I drove my heel into Marcellious'

thigh with all my might. The sickening crack of his leg bone shattering and grating against one another echoed in the air as he collapsed beneath me in agony. His piercing screams reverberated all around me, sending shivers down my spine.

"Do something!" Marcellious called to Balthazar.

I held my dagger up to the sun and repeated the sacred words. The blade began to glow, lighting up with dark magic. I pointed it at Dahlia, who shrank away from me. *As long as she's in human form, I can kill her.* I was weak and sloppy, but I vowed to die with honor.

I could feel Dahlia's heart racing beneath my grip, as I held her head in my hand and slowly inched my knife toward her chest. I had no choice—if I wanted to survive, she had to be stopped. She let out a sorrowful whimper as the blade pierced through her, and Marcellious' howl of anguish filled the air.

His wails were deafening. "No! You've killed my lover!" Yet I had done what must be done.

Emily screamed from a distance away.

I spun around.

Balthazar held her in his arms and squeezed her.

Tiny flames licked her dress and her hair, and smoke billowed around her neck.

"Oh, God!" I cried out. "He's burning her alive!"

I willed my legs to run and sprinted toward her.

"Help me, Olivia! Help!" Emily shrieked, breaking my heart.

I would never reach her in time. The flames were growing, consuming her while his body stayed untouched by the fire. My legs seemed to turn to lead as I ran, becoming heavier and heavier. It was useless. I would be too late.

A shimmering ball of energy descended, and I pulled up

short. Some strange dark force pulled Emily away from Balthazar.

Malik suddenly materialized several yards away and clasped Rosie's hand tightly, with his other arm embracing Emily. He drew them both near, encircling them in a protective hug.

Balthazar's face grew crimson. "Well, well, well, look who decides to be the hero now. You have been hiding from me all these years, Malik."

Malik disappeared and reappeared before Balthazar. "Here I am in the flesh, Balthazar. I must say it's been quite some time. You haven't changed much except you have become uglier."

The whites of Balthazar's eyes shone. "I don't know how you escaped the belladonna I poisoned you with. You were dead. Your body became a dried-up corpse."

Malik smiled, appearing unperturbed. "Let's just say I had an excellent savior who didn't just save me from death."

"Who saved you?" Balthazar demanded.

When Malik didn't answer, he said, "You know, Malik, I don't care who saved you. I will recreate Layla's death, and you will watch how I drain the life out of Olivia. I can see in your eyes how much you desire her. Too bad you can't be with her either."

Balthazar blurred out of view and reappeared before me.

I let out a screech and fell to my knees. This was it—this was the point at which I would perish.

I'm sorry, Roman. I'm so sorry.

I squeezed my eyes shut, ready to die.

A horrifying, strangled cry filled the air.

My eyes flew open in time to see Malik plunge a blade into Balthazar's chest.

"What have you done?" Balthazar screamed. "What have you done to me?"

"What I should have done a long time ago," Malik said, tossing the bloody blade into the underbrush.

"You…you…you've poisoned me!" Balthazar fell to the ground, writhing and gasping.

He let out a deafening roar, staggered to his feet, and stormed toward Marcellious. Clutching the journal in one hand and Marcellious' arm in the other, he blurred out of view.

Unable to comprehend anything, I fell to the ground and fainted.

CHAPTER THIRTEEN
ROMAN

We had to form a plan to deal with Tristan. Currently, he lolled on a chair in the basement, unable to support his weight.

I wanted to kill him in revenge for betraying Olivia and harming her father.

Lee had other ideas. So, Lee and I retreated upstairs to explore options. Jack had gone into the kitchen to finish cleaning up.

We stood in the hall, leaning against the wall.

"The letter from Malik said we need to take Tristan to Italy, but how can that be possible?" I said, rubbing my jaw. "Besides, spending any amount of time in his presence is pure torture."

"I know, I know," Lee said, pumping his hands up and down. "He's a sniveling idiot. But he's a *useful* sniveling idiot, and he can be controlled by his weaknesses."

His gaze shifted away from me as if he had something to

"What aren't you telling me?" I said, eyes narrowing.

Lee let out a long sigh. "Tristan can time travel."

"He what? How? Is he a Timeborne?" I pushed away from the wall.

"No, no, nothing like that." Lee rolled so his back leaned against the wall. "He's what is known as a Timebound."

"Explain."

Lee offered me a side-eyed gaze before continuing. "A Timebound is a person who can time travel with the help of a Timeborne. If the darkness or a Timeborne has a child, the child is automatically a Timebound. Unless, of course, the child is born during the solar eclipse. Then it's a Timeborne. Every Timebound has a necklace they are born with that is unique to him or her. It looks like a sword and is a key of sorts. It fits into the hilt of the Timeborne's dagger and opens it."

My brow furrowed as I listened to him. "I didn't see any necklace on Tristan."

"I have it. I took it from him when he was unconscious." Lee pushed away from the wall and fished in his pocket. He procured a charm dangling from a gold chain.

I pointed at it. "Emily has a necklace just like that."

Lee nodded. "She, too, is a Timebound." He extended his hand, palm up. "Where is your dagger? I can show you how it works."

I retrieved the dagger from its sheath and handed it to Lee.

He took my dagger and gently tugged the hilt. It opened, revealing a small keyhole inside. He inserted the pendant, and the blade started to glow.

"For the necklace to work, the Timebound must cut their hand, draw blood, spread it on the pendant, and insert the charm. Then, the time traveler will cut their hand, say the ancient words, and travel," Lee said.

"Bloody hell," I said, staring in wonder.

Lee removed the charm and handed me back my knife. "There's a catch, though. Any Timebound that loses their time traveler will be bound in that time, possibly forever."

"That would serve him right. Maybe he'd end up as some lord's scullery maid." I laughed.

"I doubt that. Women were only employed as such. But he'd make an excellent stable hand, sleeping in barns with the pigs for warmth."

We both enjoyed a mirthful moment at that image.

Then Lee sobered. "So, you've got to do it. You've got to take Tristan with you to Italy."

"Bloody hell," I said with a sneer.

"If Malik isn't there yet, once you get to Italy, find a man named Giovanni Zampa. Giovanni has the sun dagger Alina gave him. She told me this right before her death. When you find Malik, you must do as he says." Lee pierced me with his gaze. "Promise me you'll do as you're told."

I squinted at him. "What choice do I have? But how do you know all of this?"

"I can't tell you," he said, shifting his gaze away from mine. "As of right now, we all have parts to play."

My shoulders tensed. "How can you hide information from me? I need to know as much as I can to successfully fulfill this request."

Lee shook his head. "I can only tell you the pieces you need to know. It's part of an ultimate plan to defeat Balthazar and all the other darknesses out there."

A faraway expression appeared on his face.

I snapped my fingers in front of his face. "I hate when I'm in the dark about a plan. Tell me what you are hiding from me, Lee!"

He started to walk away.

"Where are you going?" I said, following him.

"To my house." He lifted his hand over his shoulder as he walked. "All you need to know is that this is part of a plan. If you can't find Malik, you must find Giovanni to get the blade. Ask around."

He reached for the doorknob to the front door and stepped outside.

"Fuck," I said, right behind him.

Lee whirled around, his eyes blazing. "That's all you need to know at this time."

I held up both my hands and backed away. If that was how it was, I had to follow orders. If I'd learned anything in this strange lifetime, it was how to obey commands.

I stormed into the house and sought Jack for advice.

Jack stood at the sink, washing dishes.

"I'm so angry at Lee right now," I said, heading for the coffee maker to pour myself a cup.

Jack picked up a mug from the dish drainer and handed it to me.

I slammed it on the counter with a noisy thwack.

"Welcome to the club." Jack leaned his back against the counter, hooking his hands over the edge. "I've known Lee a long time. Since before Olivia was born. He's a secretive man, that's for sure. I would get frustrated with him when I went through difficult moments with Alina. Both of them would grow silent when I approached and when I asked them what they were discussing, they said vague things like, 'Nothing that concerns you,' or, 'Nothing meaningful.' I could press, argue, but no more information would ever leave their lips."

His shoulders rose and fell in a sigh.

I crossed to the kitchen table, coffee in hand. I sat down, poured sugar and creamer into the beverage, and then took a welcome swallow.

"Lee's doing the best he can to protect you." Jack sat across from me and smiled warmly at me.

"I wish I had a father like you," I said before taking another sip of coffee. "You're truly kind."

"That's one way to look at it. I've been called worse." He straightened the blue and gold placemat before him. "So, what do you plan to do?"

I shrugged. "I must do as I'm told. The full moon is in three days. Tristan's coming with."

I explained the whole thing about the Timebound bit, and Jack listened intently.

When I'd finished, he said, "So you're going back to Olivia. Goodness, how much I miss my strong, beautiful girl. Tell me, when you married my daughter, did you get rings to symbolize your marriage?"

I lifted my left hand and shook my head. "I don't have one. We married in haste at a tribal encampment. All we cared about was declaring our love and making our relationship official in the eyes of God."

Jack's eyes moistened, and he wiped them with his thumb and forefinger. "I'd like to take you into town to buy rings to exchange. I think she'd like that."

It was my turn to tear up. I always wanted to do right by my beloved, and Jack's idea touched my heart. "Thank you."

Jack wiped his nose and stood up. I guzzled the rest of my coffee and joined him. We put on our coats and went outside to Olivia's Jeep.

As we zipped across the road, the trees and houses blurring by, I said, "I'm still not used to traveling so fast."

"Wait until you fly in an airplane," Jack said with a grin.

"A what?"

"An airplane." He peered out his windshield and pointed. "Look up there."

I jerked when I saw the sizeable bird-shaped contraption in the sky. "What is that? A mechanical bird?"

"Sort of," Jack said, flipping on his turn signal. "It's an airplane filled with people traveling 460-575 miles per hour."

I whistled. "That's fast. Isn't it disorientating?"

"You would think, but no. It's a comfortable way to travel. Didn't you ever travel by train in your time?"

"No," I said simply.

We stopped at a "jewelry store." Glass counters were filled with jewelry of every kind, sparkling and glistening in the overhead lights. I picked out two gold bands—one for Olivia and one for me.

The slight, mustachioed cashier, a friend of Jack's, turned to me and said, "Would you like a saying engraved inside the bands?"

I looked at Jack—the thought had never crossed my mind.

"It's your choice," Jack said. "Rodrigo is an outstanding jeweler. And I would love to send you off on your long journey with two rings of the finest quality and crafts-manship."

I felt deeply moved by Jack's generosity.

Jack's palms pressed against the glass counter, his eyes boring holes into me as he asked, "Is there any phrase of meaning you would like to have inscribed?"

My mind raced as I struggled to come up with the perfect words. Suddenly, it hit me—"Forever yours, Olivia, my beau-tiful flame."

Rodrigo snatched a pen and paper, scribbling down the phrase with feverish intensity. But then he asked about the other ring—the one to be placed on my finger.

Heat rushed to my face, and I turned to Jack for help. He stepped in smoothly, saying, "I'm sure Olivia would want yours to say, 'Forever yours, Roman.'"

With a satisfied grin, Rodrigo scribbled down this new inscription as well. "Excellent! We're not too busy at the moment, so I can have them for you later this afternoon." His eagerness was palpable.

"Wonderful," Jack said. "Roman's leaving on his trip soon."

"Where will your travels take you?" Rodrigo said, beaming. The overhead lighting made the top of his bald head shine.

I glanced at Jack, who chuckled. "Italy. I'm going to Italy."

Rodrigo's smile broadened. "Declaring your love in Italy is a beautiful thing." He kissed his fingertips. "I'm honored to send you on your way."

After Jack and I left the jewelry store, we wandered along the sidewalk of this downtown area in a section of Seattle known as Wallingford. We passed many colorful shops selling a variety of goods and services. It was a warm day, and the sun beating overhead was welcome. I would miss the brilliant sun and all the waterways in this region. I would also long for coffee, bacon, waffles, and indoor plumbing. But I wouldn't miss the rain when I time traveled to Italy. Seattle had a lot of rain.

We passed something called a "hardware store," and several rifles were displayed in the window. I paused to look at them. A couple of handguns similar to Olivia's were on display as well. "Is this where Olivia purchased her gun?"

Jack's eyes widened. "Olivia still has her Glock?"

"Yes. Same as that one." I pointed at the display.

"Has she fired it?" Jack said, his face white with alarm.

"A couple of times, yes," I said, my forehead scrunching. "Why?"

"She could alter history!" Jack's arms shot overhead. "This is terrible!"

I patted his shoulder. "It's not as terrible as you think. She uses her weapon judiciously, I can assure you." I glanced back at the window. "But I'm sure she would appreciate more ammunition. Do you think they sell gunpowder here?"

Jack chuckled. "Gunpowder? No, Roman, now we use something called bullets."

"Bullets." I tossed the word over and over in my mind. "Do you know what kind of bullets she would need for her gun?"

Jack nodded. "Let's head in here to purchase some. You can take those with you as well."

After our shopping day, we arrived back at Jack's house as the sun painted colors in the sky, signaling its departure. I appreciated being back at Jack's home in the forest. The noise of town was daunting.

I headed to my bedroom to deposit the rings and bullets. When I returned to the kitchen, Lee stood there, appearing apologetic.

"I apologize for not being able to offer you any more information," he said. "Jack told me how distressed you are."

"A bit, yes." I sat at the kitchen table.

"Beer?" Jack said.

"Yes, thank you." I drummed my fingers on the table. "Jack explained to me how you are only trying to protect us. I can live with that for now."

I nodded when Jack sat an icy cold beer in front of me. I twisted off the top and took a long swig.

"I've come to ask you a favor," Lee said.

"What is it?" I arched an eyebrow at him.

Lee sat across from me and pulled an envelope from his jacket pocket. "This is a letter for Marcellious. The little boy I raised and cared for has been gone so long that I yearn to see and talk with him. This letter explains everything."

I rested the envelope on the blue and gold placemat. "I don't know if he's alive, Lee."

Lee winced. "I pray that he is. Find him and give him this letter."

His face looked like it was carved from granite.

I tapped the envelope. "I'll take it, but there are no guarantees I'll find him."

"That's all I ask," Lee said.

"Have you checked on our prisoner?" I said, turning to Jack.

Jack sat beside Lee. "Oh, yes. He was bellowing for food and drink, so I fed him a peanut butter sandwich and bottled water. He doesn't look so good, Roman. He looks ghastly."

"I wish he looked worse," I said, rolling the beer bottle between my hands.

Jack cringed. "We've learned to be kinder in this century. We don't take matters into our own hands."

"That's ridiculous. That makes you dependent on others to secure your land and property and protect your family." I picked at the beer label with my fingernails.

"Yes, it does. I'm sorry we won't have time for me to share all the rules and customs of this land." A wan smile tipped the corners of his lips upward. "Perhaps when you return."

A wistfulness filled my heart, making it heavy. I was going to miss both Lee and Jack. I hoped to return here with Olivia by my side when the time was right.

∾

On the morning of the full moon, after breakfast, I secured my packages, made my bed, and tried to leave my room neat. Then, I wandered downstairs to the basement.

Tristan's face was all black and blue, but his gashes had mended somewhat, covered with a crust of scabbed skin.

"Hey, asshole," I said.

He glowered at me.

"Are you ready for our time travel? We're heading to Italy."

He frowned but stayed mute.

I gripped his cheeks between my fingers. "And you're going to do everything I say, or I'm going to kill you."

He tried to pull away, but I didn't let him.

"I don't care if your daddy comes after me. You're to move when I say move and swallow when I say swallow, got it?"

He still said nothing, so I shook him hard.

"I'm talking to you. You will follow my orders, or else you're dead. They may have rules around here involving 'kindness' and dependency, but I guarantee those rules don't exist in 16th century Italy." I dug my blunt fingernails into his skin.

He winced and closed his eyes.

"I still haven't heard you acknowledge my orders, Tristan. I can screw with you all day if needed. We have hours before our departure."

His eyes flew open, and he blurted, "I understand you. I'm to follow your command and nothing else."

"Good." I flung his head to the side. "And if you contemplate escape, you're even deader, understood?"

Tristan opened his jaw wide and then wiggled it side to side. "I understand."

"Good," I said again. "I'll be back."

I tromped up the stairs and found Lee again in the kitchen, chatting with Jack.

"So, how can I get to a specific time?" I said as I sat across from them. "I've always just landed in places."

"The dagger is powerful, Roman," Lee said. "You hold the place and the year in your mind, and it will take you there."

"Okay."

Jack pushed away from the table. "And you can't show up dressed like that. I've bought you and Tristan period pieces."

"You have?" I said, surprised. "How did you manage that?"

"eBay. I bought them from an antique dealer. They're not from that period, but they'll look more convincing than jeans and a sweatshirt." He let out a snort as he hurried away to fetch them.

I remembered meeting Olivia for the first time in Rome when she wore strange clothes. That felt like it was many lifetimes ago.

The rest of the day was spent practicing the sacred scripture, and he taught me the translation, as well.

"Moon protector of night, I call upon you to unleash the light and guide me through the dark. Allow the great sun to dance around you with love and passion. Together open your gates and grant me to travel through time and space like the shadows of the night."

The words were beautiful, like a hidden message within.

As I repeated the words to Lee, I had odd flashbacks of conversations with Olivia and memories with Malik that came from my recurring dreams.

"Lee," I finally said at midday. "You never said anything to me about my recurring dreams. I've had glimpses of the dreams all day in my mind."

Clouds of emotion flitted across his face. "I cannot offer you the answers you seek, but I am sure that Italy can."

I didn't bother arguing. I knew enough about Lee at this point to know he wouldn't say more.

Finally, as the sun slid from the sky, I was ready to depart. I hauled Tristan's ass upstairs. For extra security, I tied our wrists together with some of the rope used to secure him to the chair. I didn't trust him to not make a run for it.

Jack met me at the top of the stairs. His face looked pinched with concern. "Do you have everything?"

I patted the shoulder strap of my rucksack, another one of Jack's "period pieces" purchased on eBay.

"Well," I said, looking at Jack as my throat clotted with emotion.

"Well," he said, his eyes filling with tears. "Godspeed to you."

I nodded and wiped my damp eyes.

Jack threw his arms around me and gave me a fierce hug. "I'm so glad Olivia is with you, Roman. You're a good, good man." He slid something into my pocket and patted my jacket. "Make sure Olivia sees this. And take good care of her, all right?"

Tristan snorted.

I backhanded him.

"What?" he said once he'd recovered. "I was only thinking how I had a gun to the old man's head the last time I was in this situation."

"And this time, you're under my command. Do you honestly think I'm done punishing you for your actions?" I flashed him a cold smile.

Tristan paled and shut his mouth.

"Goodbye, Jack," I said. "We'll see each other again, I hope."

Jack smiled sadly and lifted his hand in farewell.

I crossed the wooded yard and headed for a clearing I'd seen earlier. Then, with the moon rising above the clouds, I slashed Tristan's hand, smeared his blood on the pendant, and inserted it inside my blade. I cut my palm, repeated the scripture, and disappeared from 21st-century Seattle.

Confusion clouded my every thought as I hurtled through the ages, jumping from one era to another. I felt my reality slip away, no longer sure of what was real, or who I had been before this all began. I was filled with a mix of wonder and dread as I knew that whatever I found there would irrevocably change my life forever.

CHAPTER FOURTEEN

OLIVIA

There was something to be said about waking up in the arms of a sexy monster. As I came to, I savored the warmth of powerful arms holding me close. The musky smells emanating from the man next to me were so familiar, like I *knew* whoever was holding me.

When my eyelids fluttered open, I stared into the emerald pools of Eyan Malik regarding me so tenderly I thought I'd melt into a puddle.

Malik brushed a strand of hair from my eyes.

"You're alive," he whispered. "I thought I'd lost you again."

He kissed my forehead.

The warm press of his lips to my skin made me swoon. But what did he mean he'd almost lost me *again*? I didn't want to speak; I didn't want to ask him questions. Instead, I longed to float away in his arms, away from all the madness of this world with demons tracking me.

But I forced myself to speak. "What do you mean? You never lost me before. You saved me instead, and I'm truly grateful."

A knowing smile curved his lips, and he leaned forward and kissed both my eyelids.

"How did you manage to hurt Balthazar? I didn't think anyone could hurt him," I said, eyes closed beneath his tender ministrations.

"I told you," he said in a low, throaty whisper. "I told you I'd protect you, Olivia."

Even the way he said my name sent me soaring. I opened my eyes and traced the lines and planes of his face.

He closed his eyes and nuzzled his head into my touch.

I felt spellbound as if we were in a different plane of existence altogether—not anywhere I'd ever been, only here with Malik in some magical dimension. "I'm so grateful that you saved us. Even though you're the darkness and you can kill us instantly, you protected us from Balthazar."

The energy humming between us was thick and heady, some strange elixir of arousal.

He pushed himself up on one elbow. "Olivia. My beautiful Olivia. I'd move heaven and earth to save you. I would never allow anything to happen to you or Roman."

He lowered his mouth as if to kiss me.

I turned my head into the soft bedding before our lips could touch.

What was happening to me? Why was I losing myself in Malik's embrace?

I tried to pull away, but he kissed my neck. Each place he touched with his lips grew warm with desire for him.

He drew his tongue up my neck, and I groaned, hooking my leg over him, and pulling him close.

"Malik," I whispered, and his name sent a thrill down my throat. "Why am I drawn to you? Why does my soul have this connection with you?"

He let out a low chuckle of satisfaction. "You ask too many questions."

I was so wild with passion. I wanted nothing more than to melt into Malik, have him sink into me, and writhe together in bliss.

But this nagging thought, like a fly, flew into my brain. *I'm married.* I frowned, wondering where that thought came from. *I'm married to Roman Alexander.*

I stopped breathing at the memory of my husband's name. *Roman!*

I snapped out of my trance and shoved away from Malik. "I'm a married woman! Roman is my husband and I love him. I can't betray him. Whatever this is, Malik, it stops now. Roman is the man I want, and I will forever love him."

Malik rolled on his back and smiled. "Roman is lucky to have you."

I sat up and stared at him. "I can't do this…this…" I waggled my finger between us. "Whatever *this* is between us. I can't explain it, but I also can't submit to it. I love my husband. I miss him, but I would never betray him."

Malik swept the tip of his tongue across his upper lip. Then, he closed his eyes and smiled as if savoring a delicious meal.

This massive tractor beam of attraction pulled me toward him again. The bond between Malik and me was intense—but I had to ignore it. I couldn't—I *wouldn't*—submit to it.

With a groan, I rolled from the bed and fled Malik's room.

"Emily," I muttered as I raced down the carpeted hallway. "I've got to see Emily and check on her wounds."

I barged into her room without knocking and stopped abruptly at the sight of Rosie's sleeping form and Emily crying next to her on the bed. I raced across the room and knelt by her side.

Stroking my sister's face, I said, "Emily, you're all healed! It's a miracle! What happened? And why are you crying?"

"Malik healed me before heading back to where he took you. For that, I'm truly grateful. But Marcellious…" A fresh wave of tears burst from her eyes. "What an *evil* man. I never should have fallen for him. I should have listened to you and now Balthazar has the journal! Marcellious has been betraying us this whole time!"

I crawled onto the bed and drew her close to me. "Shhh, Em, you'll wake Rosie."

"I can't stop crying," Emily wailed. "I'm carrying his child. What a fool I've been. There's no way he would ever want a child with me. He told me in plain words—I mean *nothing* to him. Nothing! Can you believe it, Olivia? I gave him my heart and soul. I tried to change him for the better, but I failed. And now he hates me. It was all a charade for him. I'm so stupid."

Her chest rose and fell as shuddering sobs escaped her throat.

I held her tight and smoothed her hair. "Emily, you are not stupid. He didn't deserve you. Dark, broken men can't be changed. Marcellious was broken long ago. We will raise this child together and stick by each other. Don't worry."

She eased back from me and studied me, her lashes wet with tears. "What would I do without you, Olivia? You give me hope. And now that Marcellious and Balthazar have the journal, we need to ask Malik what to do next. He can advise us and help us."

Arousal swirled through my body as Emily said his name.

"No!" I spoke with too much force. "We can't ask him for help."

I squeezed my eyes shut. I didn't want to tell her of my connection to Malik. Roman was the love of my life, my happiness. But the longer I stayed in Malik's presence, the more temptation clawed me. I was as pathetic as my mother.

"What's wrong?" Emily whispered.

I shook my head.

She caressed my cheek. "Tell me what's wrong, Olivia. That's what we do for one another."

"I can't tell you, Em." Now I was starting to cry. *Great.* We were a couple of blubbering idiots, in a twist over men.

"Yes, you can. You know you can trust me."

I rolled on my back and swore. "I am starting to have feelings for Malik. I have this connection with him I can't explain. I woke up in his arms, and it felt so right to be there. It was like Roman didn't even exist. I don't understand what's going on. Do I have some sort of death wish to be attracted to a monster and deny my true love?"

"You're just our mother's daughter. You love the darkness, too," Emily said in a light, teasing tone, but it struck me like a hammer.

"Ugh!" I pressed my palms to my face. "I don't want to be like our mother. I haven't yet forgiven her. How could I possibly forgive myself if I ended up a whore like her?"

"Olivia! I don't think our mother's a whore. Look at me." She grabbed my wrist and pried my hand from my face.

I squinted at her.

"Mom was a complicated individual. You know that. She had to make difficult choices with her life—they went against the grain of society's dictates. You have to do that, too. You'll never be ordinary, Olivia. Deal with it." Her eyes blazed with intensity.

She might be right. Still, I didn't want to betray the love and trust I put in my marriage. Why did Roman and I have to get separated? God, I missed him so damn much. I *needed* him.

"Maybe Malik cast some sort of spell over me?"

"Maybe he did. He's the darkness, after all. We don't yet know what he's capable of. I'm glad he rescued us both and healed me from my awful burns." Emily shuddered. "That was a horrible experience. It feels like a dream now, but at the time, it was wretched."

We both grew quiet, steeped in our own thoughts.

Finally, Emily said, "We must figure out what to do, Olivia. If Balthazar has the journal, he will go to Italy and get the dagger. We need to somehow get there before he does." She let out a long sigh. "If only I could time travel and help you with this."

"Right," I said, rolling to face her again. "Neither you nor Rosie can time travel. And I don't want to do this alone."

I scrunched up my face.

"We have to ask Malik for answers," Emily said. "You mustn't be scared of him. He's our only choice."

Sadly, I realized she was right.

We exchanged a solemn nod and then climbed off the bed. Wordlessly, we trekked down the dark corridor, heading to see Malik.

He wasn't in his bedroom, but a soft light escaped the bottom of his office door. The door was ajar a bit, so I eased it open.

He stood staring out the window at the darkness.

"Lord Malik," Emily said timidly. "May we speak with you?"

He whirled, eyes blazing, and said, "Don't call me that."

Emily's hands flew out to ward off an attack. "Forgive me. I didn't mean…"

"What do you want from me now?" Malik snarled. His eyes caught mine and pinned me in place. A torrent of energy swirled between us.

I closed my eyes to break the spell. When I opened them, I didn't meet his gaze as I said, "We need to time travel to Italy and retrieve the dagger. Balthazar has the journal now and his next move would be to go to Italy and get the sun dagger."

Malik said nothing, coolly regarding me.

I was tired of his games of intrigue and snapped out of my insecurity. "How could you let Marcellious waltz into your house and take the journal?"

Malik waved his hand. "The journal is worthless."

He crossed the room and settled on his small sofa, placing his ankle on his knee, and spreading his arms along the sofa's back.

"No, it's not," I snapped, some of my fire returning. "Did you allow him to come into your house and retrieve it? I know you can sense intruders. You're anything but stupid."

My body shook with anger.

Malik smirked. "Is that a compliment, Olivia?"

He said my name in a voice as smooth as silk, laced with seduction.

"No! I'm just…" I shook my head. He was toying with me. And I wasn't in the mood for being teased.

"We need to time travel. We can't just stay here like sitting ducks," I said.

"Like sitting ducks," he said, smiling. "You and Emily are anything but ducks, my love."

He stroked the stubble on his jaw.

The phrase "my love" snaked inside me, coiling through my insides, giving me thrills.

"Malik," I said in a warning tone. "Don't—"

He put up his palms to silence me. "I don't want to fight with you."

"I don't want to fight, either," I said, glancing at Emily, who stood to the side, watching our exchange like a game of tennis.

"Who's this 'we' you want to time travel with? Is it me? Emily? Rosie? Do you think I will drop everything and babysit Emily and Rosie while you go to Italy? His tone had turned sharp and mocking.

Emily interrupted our exchange. "Please, sir. You were about to explain what a Timebound is. That could possibly be the solution we're looking for."

"Ah, yes." He strode across his office and settled at his desk. "Do have a seat, won't you?"

He gestured toward the couch.

I gravitated to the place he'd just occupied like a cat seeking her owner's warmth. Emily sat next to me.

"A Timebound can travel with a Timeborne," Malik said in a matter-of-fact tone.

"What?" I glanced at Emily's eager gaze. Then, the seeds of anger seized my belly. "How is this possible?"

He gave me a "come hither" gesture with his hand. "Hand me your dagger."

"My dagger? Why?"

He pressed his lips together and made that same gesture again.

"I'll show you how the Timebound works." He turned to Emily. "Hand me your necklace."

Emily and I exchanged a quizzical look and shrugged.

I hiked up my skirt and retrieved my dagger from my

thigh. When I turned around, Malik's gaze was fixed on me, and a wicked glint shone in his eye. I narrowed my eyes as I met his gaze.

He let out a low laugh like everything was funny.

Emily and I handed him our individual items.

Malik placed the necklace charm on his polished desk and turned the knife around to show us the hilt. He picked it open with his fingernail and revealed the inside. "See this little slot in here?"

"Yes," I said. "I never knew it opened."

He picked up Emily's necklace in his free hand. "This fits here." He inserted the gold tip of the charm into the slot. "See?"

I peered at the knife hilt and met his gaze. "Wow. That's cool, but how does it help Emily time travel?"

Malik set the blade down and leaned back in his chair. The chair creaked from his weight.

"Let's say you time travel, Olivia, and Emily wants to go, too. You slice your hand with your dagger. Emily draws blood using her necklace charm, ensuring the tip is covered. You insert the bloody tip into the knife, and voila! You both time travel, with you saying the ancient scriptures." He grinned.

My mouth gaped. "How could I not have known that? I had no idea."

He flashed me a secretive look. "There's much you don't know about your dagger. It's quite powerful."

"Don't you think it would be useful to know things like this?" I said, pulling myself upright.

"All in good time."

I scoffed at his haughty retort.

"How does a Timebound come into existence?" Emily

asked, leaning over the dagger, her hands propped on Malik's desk.

Malik turned his attention to me with that same smirking smile. "A Timebound comes into existence when one of the parents is a Timeborne, a Timebound, or the darkness. Since Alina was your mother Emily, you automatically become a Timebound. And if you, Olivia, were to have a child, that child would be a Timebound. It's that simple."

A cascade of elation washed through me, replacing the anger, and I reached for Emily and hugged her. "This is incredible news, Em!"

"Yes, it is! We get to time travel together!" Her eyes glistened as she eased away from me. Then her gaze darkened, and she glanced away.

Is she worried about time-traveling with her baby?

"There's a catch, ladies."

"What is it?" I said, pivoting back to face Malik.

"If you, Olivia, die wherever it is you've time traveled, Emily is stuck in that time."

I reared back slightly. "Just like that?"

"Just like that. Unless, of course, another Timeborne lands in that period and meets the Timebound. This is quite rare, since no Timeborne ever reveals its identity. But that's where the name Timebound comes from, being stuck at a certain time and place." He drummed his fingers on the desk. "So, what about Rosie? Have you thought your plan through? You can't assume I'm on childcare duty while you two are galivanting around through time."

"Oh!" Emily's hand flew to her mouth. "Oh! We forgot about Rosie. I'll stay behind and stay with her Olivia. You must go and find the dagger yourself."

Another secretive smile spread across Malik's face.

I wanted to roll my eyes. Malik and his damn mysteries.

"Rosie will time travel with me," he said. "I am the darkness, and I can time travel one person. I have that kind of power."

My heart raced as I looked up at him, my gaze cold as ice. If it wasn't for Emily standing there by my side, would I finally have the courage to tell him how much his secretive attitude and manner of treating information like a precious prize bothered me? But deep down I knew it wouldn't make the slightest difference—he was so powerful that no matter what I said, I could never change him or his behavior.

"What if Rosie gets sick from time travel? What if she freaks out? Will you have a clue what to do?" I propped my hands on my hips.

He lifted his gaze to mine with equal frostiness. "I think I can manage." He glanced toward the door. "Now, if you don't mind, I have things to do. Go get some rest and collect the things you want to take. There's much to be done before we time travel tomorrow."

The moon was a perfect circle in the sky, its light spilling through the window like liquid silver. I zipped up my coat and followed Emily out of Malik's office, excitement and dread contending in my chest. The time had come to set off on our journey back in time—this time with Emily, Rosie, and Malik.

We made our way to our rooms in anticipation of the morning. A shiver ran through me—part thrill, part terror—as I imagined what we might find in Italy when we arrived.

The following morning, at breakfast, I told Rosie we would be going on another trip today.

She looked up from pushing peas around her plate, a pout on her pretty little face. "What kind of trip?"

"Oh, it will be a fun trip. We're going far, far away." I tried to enthuse my words with positivity.

"Will it be like the last trip, where we were always hungry and tired? Will you and Emily be crying?" she asked.

"It will be nothing like that," I said in reassurance. In truth, I had no idea.

But she seemed to accept the idea, picked up a pea in her tiny fingers, and popped it in her mouth. "Yum! Peas are good!"

Emily and I had dedicated the day to getting ready for our journey, as thoroughly as one could prepare for the unknown. We both knew that what lay ahead of us would require more than just the essential supplies and standard equipment. We had to prepare ourselves psychologically and emotionally, and steel our minds for whatever awaited us. We spoke little as we made our final preparations, both of us lost in thought and uncertain of what lay ahead.

As darkness fell, we found ourselves standing side by side in the middle of my bedroom. A heavy silence settled around us, and I felt the weight of Emily's gaze as she turned to face me. We stood there for what felt like an eternity, our eyes locked and neither of us saying a word. Then, with a nod, Emily finally broke the silence.

"We're ready," she said, her voice clear and determined.

I watched her carefully, her normally bright eyes now filled with uncertainty. Despite the fear that we both shared, I could see strength and courage in her expression. I smiled back at her, a silent expression of understanding. "We're ready," I echoed.

Desperate to know where Malik had gone, I scoured the house for any sign of him. He was nowhere to be found.

Racing upstairs, I burst into his office, then his bedroom, but nothing. With a chill of dread, I crossed the room and stepped out onto his balcony—only to find it empty and cold.

The balcony provided a sweeping view of the mountainside and the valley below. Today had been cloudy but no rain, so I could see for miles.

I placed my hands on the railing and stared at the trees. Many hosted mistletoe between their branches. The distant hills were the color of winter, blue-gray. The sky stretched for miles, awash with orange, peach, pink, and purple. A fresh scent lingered in the air from yesterday's storm. I breathed deeply, thankful for Malik's care since our arrival.

He truly lived in a place of beauty. He was like a king, high atop his mountain home, where he could survey the land below and feel safe in his dominion.

Still, I wondered—why had he allowed Marcellious to enter his home and retrieve the journal? Was it as unimportant as he said it was? Or had Marcellious entered on some blind spot of Malik's? I just couldn't fathom Malik being unaware of anything, let alone someone as lowly and devious as Marcellious.

I felt Malik's presence when he entered the room, the way one senses a blast of air billowing from the furnace. I shivered as he approached.

He placed his warm hands on my upper arms. "There's nothing to worry about when you go to Italy."

I spun around to face him. "How can you be certain of that?"

We were inches apart, but I didn't feel the same compulsion to fall into him.

He smiled at me. "Stay by my side, and all will be well."

"Easy for you to say." I trembled inside at the thought of

catapulting into ancient Italy. Would it be as brutal as the gladiator times?

He kept on smiling at me, radiating nothing but warmth. "All you have to do, love, is follow my instructions. Soon you'll be reunited with Roman."

His smile faded.

I hesitated before saying, "Malik, about what happened yesterday between us…"

"It will *never* happen again," he said, cutting me off, clasping his hands behind his back. "I do not want to hurt you or Roman again. Roman is your husband and I have to honor that. If I were to have a wife and the darkness was trying to seduce her, I would be angry. I sometimes lose myself and forget that I can't ever have you, Olivia. You and Roman belong with each other and I will never make the same mistake again."

I have no idea what Malik is talking about it, but his apology sounded sincere, and he seems to care about me and Roman in some strange way.

I canted my head to the side as I looked at him. I felt both relieved and a little bit disappointed. I was torn between my love and loyalty to my husband and my fleeting lust for Malik. It was like being caught between a furnace and a bonfire.

I huffed out a breath. "Thank you."

"I do know one thing," he said as his finger traced down my cheek. "When you get to Italy, your life will never be the same."

A swirl of emotions filled me, and I felt like a storm was raging inside me. We were standing there in silence, each stuck in our own thoughts, neither of us willing to let go of this moment.

Malik cut our eye contact with a harsh jerk of his head,

his eyes now locking onto something out the window. "She's here," he muttered in warning, as the full moon emerged menacingly on the horizon.

I stared up at him with a mix of fear and excitement—was I truly ready to travel through time? But before I could question it further, a faint smile crept onto my face and I managed to blurt out, "Yes, Malik. Let's go."

CHAPTER FIFTEEN

ROMAN

We landed with a crash in a vast field, presumably in Italy, surrounded by verdant hills and stunning wildflowers. A few pheasants blasted into the air, disturbed by our sudden arrival. I threw my arm over my face to avoid their flapping wings. Then, standing, I took a moment to orient to my surroundings, pivoting in a circle.

Did we land in the right place? How would I know?

"Christ on a cracker, but that landing hurt." Tristan clambered to his feet and began rubbing his butt. The restraints binding our wrists had disappeared.

"Christ on a cracker?" I said, frowning.

"It's a modern phrase." He put his hand over his eyes and scanned our surroundings. "Fuck. We're in the middle of fucking *nowhere.*"

"Shut the fuck up," I said. "I'm already sick of you. Don't make me any sicker."

I headed downhill, lured by the sound of a distant, trickling stream. Civilizations often placed roads near waterways,

"Do you have a plan?" Tristan said, breaking a wildflower off its stem.

"Not yet," I said as my footfalls sunk into the rich loam beneath my feet.

"Are you going to make a plan?" Tristan stuck the flower behind his ear, lending a touch of femininity to his appearance.

I scoffed, shaking my head. *What an idiot.* "Of course, I'm going to make a plan."

"Will you tell me when you make it?" Tristan's eyes flicked side to side.

"Probably not." I tipped back my head and sniffed, smelling water.

He started to say something else.

"Shut up, Tristan!" I interrupted. "Stop with all the questions. I'm trying to find a road, got it? Then, we'll head along the road and see if we can find someone who knows something. That's the best I've got now, got it?"

"Thank you," he said, his cheeks growing crimson.

He stayed silent as we tromped down the hill.

Relief washed through me at the sight of a rustic road ahead flanked by a trickling stream. It was a dirt road, nothing fancy, but it looked well-used, as evidenced by the grooves from wagon wheels and the horse hoof prints.

I paused at the edge of the road and glanced at Tristan's scowling face. "Do you speak Italian?"

"Let's see." Tristan rubbed his forehead. "*Parlo*…uh… *parlo un pah*…no, wait. Is it *po*? Yeah. *Parlo un po d'italiano.*"

"That's perfect. You speak a little shit Italian. I speak Italian fluently, thanks to my mother. From now on, you'll do well to keep your mouth shut. Your role is that of my manservant. You'll speak when spoken to, do what to do when told, and nothing more, understood?" I glared at him.

"Why do *you* get to be Prince Charming?" he spat back.

"Prince what?" I said with a shake of my head.

"Prince Charming. He got the girl and all the glory in the movie." Tristan scowled.

I knew what movies were now, having watched a few with Jack in the 21st century, but I'd never heard of this Prince Charming fellow. I ignored Tristan and took up a brisk pace on the road.

The sun overhead was scorching, beating down on our heads. I stopped several times to scoop water out of the cold creek, and Tristan did the same.

"You can get so many diseases from drinking contaminated water. Giardia, cholera, diarrhea, dysentery, hepatitis A, typhoid, and polio are all waterborne illnesses." He wiped water droplets from his face.

"Good. Maybe you'll get one and die. But wait until you've fulfilled your purpose here in Italy, okay?" I squinted, spying something of interest in the distance.

Tristan glared at me. "What's my purpose?"

I didn't know either, but I didn't feel like telling Tristan that. "That's on a need-to-know basis, and you don't need to know."

I smiled at the memory of Jack, who'd told me that phrase, referring to Lee.

Tristan's scowl deepened, but he kept his mouth shut.

I shielded my eyes to keep the sun out. "Look." I pointed. "It looks to be a carriage in distress."

Tristan gave a grunt. "Huh."

The elegant carriage, made of polished dark wood with red-painted wheels canted perilously to its side. One of its wheels was stuck in the mud. The two horses attached to the wagon via harnesses stood in the stream, their heads lowered, slurping water.

On the other side of the wagon, out of sight, the sounds of splashing and muttering could be heard.

"Hello, friend," I called in Italian. "How can we help?"

A man's face popped up, and he peered at us, unblinking, through the footwell in front of the driver's seat. He said nothing.

"Parli italiano?" I said.

"Sì, Sì. Ovviamente parlo italiano. Questa è l'Italia, no?" He grinned.

Of course, I speak Italian. This is Italy, no?

My shoulders relaxed; my face said it all.

His face looked much like a rabbit's with bright brown round eyes. He splashed his way around the horses and came to stand in front of us, hand extended. Mud covered his hands and his velvet, leather, and silk attire. His face was smudged with grime. He glanced at his palm and wiped it on his leather trousers before extending it again. "I'm Count Mathias Montego, and I seem to have gotten into quite a fix."

I shook his hand. "I'm Roman Alexander. We saw your carriage stuck, and I thought you might need some help." I glanced at Tristan. "This is my manservant, Tristan. He doesn't speak much. He's a little simple," I said, hoping Tristan didn't understand my Italian.

Count Montego nodded. "I have one like that. In fact, I sent him off to get help, and he hasn't returned yet. I don't know where he might have gotten off to." He propped his hands on his slender hips and stared at his wagon. "But since you're here, offering to help, I accept your offer and shall repay you in kind."

He grinned, revealing perfectly white teeth, which was odd for this century. His tousled salt and pepper-colored hair framed his bearded face. His indulgent expression made me think he was used to fawning attention and getting his way with people.

I spoke to Tristan in English, ordering him to find a slender log to put beneath the wagon wheel.

"Why should I do that?" he countered, pouting.

"Because you don't want to be left on the side of the road to fend for yourself," I said, glowering at him.

"Fine." He flung his hand over his head and stomped off into the trees.

"He's new at this job," I said in Italian to the count.

"I can see that. He seems a bit hot-tempered," the count replied.

"A bit, yes, but I'll have him heeled soon enough."

Tristan dragged a sturdy branch toward us. When he got closer, he said, "Will this do?"

"Good enough," I said, eying the branch.

Together, we positioned the branch in front of the stuck wheel. I climbed into the driver's seat and picked up the reins.

The horses lifted their heads and assumed a ready position.

I clucked and whistled at them as they heaved the wagon over the log. Soon the carriage was back on dry land.

"Splendid! You, gentlemen, are wonderful," Count Montego exclaimed. "Now, how can I help you? Where would you like to go? I must repay you for your services."

Though his finery suggested he could provide payment in return, I never liked to lean on others. I shook my head and held out my palms. "No need, Count Montego. We were happy to assist a fellow traveler. I'm afraid we can't accept your help."

I pivoted as if to leave, but Tristan seized my upper arm.

"What are you doing? Of course, we can accept his help. Are you out of your mind?"

"What, you suddenly understand Italian?" I pried his fingers off me.

"I know enough to understand 'can't accept help.' Don't be an ass. You don't even know where we are!" He flung out his arms in a dramatic gesture. "Look around. There could be nothing for miles, and this kind guy is offering assistance!"

I side-eyed the count, who watched us as if we were the day's entertainment.

I sighed and said, "Act like a manservant."

"I'll be your hired help if you agree to take this man's offer. Do *you* want to traipse all day in the hot sun?"

"I used to run all day with armor on, you measly little worm. I can do it easily," I said in a low, deadly whisper, crossing my arms over my chest. But the costumes Jack had provided us were more like winter wear, and here in Italy, we seemed to be in midsummer. Already, I was drenched in sweat.

Tristan's face blanched. "Okay, I see your point. But I've never done that. I'll only slow you down."

He had an excellent point. He was already slowing me down with his incessant whining.

I faced Count Montego and said, "If it's no trouble to you, might you drop us off at an address if it's on your way?"

"Most certainly!" the count gushed. "Where are you headed?"

I stuck my hand in the pocket of my pleated overcoat, which was far too warm for this kind of weather. I handed the count the damp piece of paper, and he stared at it.

"Yes, I can take you there. It won't be any trouble at all."

The count and I climbed into the seat, and Tristan heaved

himself into the carriage. Knowing him, he'd probably take a nap. Tristan was a weak, pathetic excuse for a man.

On the slow, plodding journey to the address I had for Malik, the count and I conversed. He gave me a steady stream of information about this region and regaled me with stories of his lavish dinner parties. Count Montego seemed to live at the center of everything.

Eventually, he pulled up in front of an opulent villa surrounded by olive trees and hills.

He reined the horses to a stop. "I'll wait to ensure the party you're looking for is here."

He flashed me a generous smile.

"Thank you." I hopped off the driver's seat and poked my head in the curtained window of the carriage.

Sure enough, Tristan was curled on the seat, fast asleep.

I trekked up the stone walkway and passed an enormous fountain with carved Italian maidens pouring water from their clay jugs. Ascending the stone staircase flanked by two sculpted lions, I reached the front door. I lifted an iron door knocker and rapped it several times against the iron plate affixed to the wood.

A diminutive young woman with dark hair and intense eyes the color of coal opened the door.

"Yes, may I help you?" she said in cultured Italian.

"How do you do? I'm here to see Eyan Malik." I stood stiffly at attention as if I was still in the military.

"*Mi dispiace, signore*," she said politely. "Signore Malik is not at home at this time. He sent a letter informing us of his arrival in two days. Who shall I say stopped by?"

My heart sank. *Two days!*

I gave her my name and said I'd return.

She nodded and shut the door.

Disheartened, I dragged my feet down the stairs and headed back to the carriage.

"Why the glum face, Roman?" Count Montego asked.

"My friend, Eyan Malik, isn't home yet. He'll return in two days." *And I have no place to sleep for those same two nights.*

"Eyan Malik lives here? I haven't seen him in such a long time! I wonder when he purchased this place," the count said. "You must stay with me. I have rooms galore, no children—no one but my servants to keep me company. An old man like me gets lonely if not surrounded by friends."

"No, we can't accept your help," I said, but Tristan crawled from the carriage.

"I don't want to sleep on the ground for two nights," he whined. "Let's stay with him."

"And how do you intend to repay his generosity?" I hissed at Tristan.

"It sounds like he won't ask for anything. He just wants the company," Tristan said.

I glanced at the count. In my experience, people always seemed to want something for their kindness. But, the thought of sleeping on the ground at night listening to Tristan bitch and moan held little appeal.

"All right," I said to Count Montego. "We'll stay."

"Excellent! I assure you, it won't be any trouble at all." He waited for me to climb back in the seat and for Tristan to crawl in the carriage, and then he clucked the horses forward.

I fell into a moody fret about Malik not being here. I hadn't expected this. What if something had held him up? I was eager to find the dagger and, more importantly, find my beautiful wife. I missed Olivia so much. The last time I saw her physically was the day I went to battle with the Kiowas. It seemed a lifetime ago.

Lee's voice came into my head. If something happens, seek out Giovanni Zampa.

Of course! Find Giovanni Zampa! Satisfied with my plan, my mood improved.

Half an hour later, we arrived at Count Montego's impressive villa. As we passed through the iron gates surrounding the estates, the horses increased speed, probably eager to get the harnesses off their backs.

Two groomsmen met us at the entrance to the grand house, ready to take the horses and carriage to their respective places.

The count gestured for us to follow him into his house, and we did, stepping over the threshold with trepidation. Inside, it was much grander than I had expected, with high ceilings and ornate furnishings. The walls were adorned with paintings, and the floors were lined with polished tiles.

We made our way down the hallway toward the back of the house, where the count opened a door and ushered us into a large room filled with dark wood furniture and bookshelves.

The count waved his hand around the room, indicating the various treasures within. He pointed out a leather-bound edition of Francis Bacon's "Essays" on one of the bookshelves and a painting of a woman playing a guitar on the wall. He then proceeded to tell us the story of the woman in the portrait, revealing her to be a distant relative of his who had left her native Spain to seek her fortune in Paris.

I was captivated by the tale, and it seemed like a fitting introduction to the count's home.

"Please feel welcome in my home," he said to us. "You can do as you like here. You want whores; I'll get you whores. Exquisite food and drinks, prostitutes, wild entertainment…whatever your heart's desire will be my pleasure to provide."

The years seemed to fall from his shoulders as he spoke.

"Thank you, Count Montego, but I shall require none of those," I said politely.

An elegantly suited man stepped through a doorway in the rear of the house and approached us.

"Antonio, please show Signore Alexander's manservant to the servant guest quarters," the count said, nodding at Tristan. "And I shall show Signore Alexander to his room upstairs."

Antonio nodded and asked Tristan to follow him in Italian.

"He doesn't speak much Italian," I said, looking at Tristan's perplexed expression.

"He's simple," the count added.

"Ah," Antonio said in understanding. "Come."

He grabbed Tristan's arm.

Tristan yanked his arm away, eyes wide with alarm. "Where is he taking me?"

"Relax, Tristan. He's showing you to your room," I said.

Tristan followed Antonio as they headed toward the back.

"And I suppose you'll be somewhere palatial," he called over his shoulder.

I ignored him and proceeded up the stairs with Count Montego.

My room was indeed palatial, but it was nothing new—I'd been inside the emperor's palace in ancient Rome. Still, each era held its own opinions on what qualified as opulent. In this case, I stood in a room with dark wood Italian furniture carved in elaborate patterns. Rich tapestries lined the walls like downstairs, and heavy velvet curtains lined the windows. The four-poster bed was framed by more velvet and covered in pillows.

"We'll only be here for two nights at the most," I said.

Count Montego waved his hand. "Stay as long as you like. It is a most welcome surprise to have guests so soon after my return from France. It will be no trouble at all to accommodate you, I assure you."

"Thank you." I crossed the room and sat on an ornately padded chair.

"Can I get you anything before I depart?" the count said. "We'll share a meal in about an hour."

I thought a minute about my plan and said, "Yes. I'm looking for a man by the name of Giovanni Zampa. Do you know him?"

The count's face brightened. "Yes, yes! Giovanni Zampa lives just fifteen minutes from here. After our repast, you and your manservant may take my horses and head to his home."

I held up my hands. "No, no, we can walk."

"Nonsense! No guest of Count Montego shall refuse my hospitality. I am an exemplary host, *Signore*." He gave a modest bow. Then, when upright, he smiled. "It gives me pleasure to share my wealth. Any man worth his salt does not hoard his wealth—he shares it freely."

"Well, thank you again, Count Montego. I'm honored by your generosity." I nodded, fatigued.

"You are most welcome, Signore Alexander." He spun on his heel and left the room.

I lay back on the lush pillows and closed my eyes, falling into a doze.

The count and I dined alone in his well-appointed dining room during lunch. His chef had prepared various Italian dishes, including wild game stew, Erbolata cheese pie with herbs, and hemp seed soup. And wine. Lots and lots of wine.

By the time I was ready to depart, my belly was full, and I was a wee bit tipsy.

A groomsman handed me the reins of a fine black steed

reminiscent of Tempestas, my horse in Rome, and brought a mule for Tristan.

Tristan joined me in the stables, a sour expression on his face. "You probably got to eat the good food. I had to suffer a servant's meal."

"And yet you were fed," I said, not wanting to spoil my good mood as I secured the saddle.

"Where's my horse?" Tristan placed his hands on his hips and looked around.

"See that mule? That's yours." I smirked.

"Fuck. Why don't I get a horse like yours?"

"This is a stallion. Can you ride a stallion?" I said, moving my hand over Fury's glistening coat.

"Sure. It can't be any different than riding any other horse." Tristan puffed out his chest.

"Tell you what. If you can ride this horse, we'll switch."

"Easy peasy. Watch me." Tristan swaggered over to Fury.

Fury backed away from him.

"Hold him still for me," Tristan said, fear evident in his wide eyes.

"I'm trying," I said, holding the reins lightly.

"Doesn't look like it to me. Looks like you want him to buck. You need to hold the reins tighter," Tristan said.

"That's where you're wrong. Riding a horse is a partnership, not a means of control." I flashed him a grim smile.

"Whatever." Tristan lifted his foot into the stirrup.

Fury reared and squealed, flinging Tristan to the ground.

"Fuck!" He got up, brushed himself off, and said, "Show me how you can ride, Lone Ranger."

"Lone Ranger?" I said, furrowing my brow.

"Forget about it. Get on your damn horse, and let's go."

I mounted Fury, and Tristan got on the back of his mule.

As we trotted down the road, heading for Giovanni's

house, I completely ignored Tristan and his whining. I enjoyed the beautiful Italian countryside too much. Florence was different than where I'd lived in Rome, with rolling green hills, Magnolia and olive trees, and goats and sheep dotting the land.

We arrived at a plain, white-washed house surrounded by clucking hens pecking in the dirt and grass. A few goats grazed beneath olive trees in the distance.

A hound dog raced toward us, barking as he announced our arrival.

"Hello, pup," I said once I'd dismounted. I patted the dog's head. "You stay here, Tristan."

I looped the reins of my horse over a nearby tree branch.

"Yeah, yeah," he said with a scowl, waving me away. "Go do your important things while I stay outside doing nothing."

Continuing to ignore him, I strode up the dirt walkway and knocked on the door.

A young maid answered the door, looking furtively right and left before greeting me. "Yes? Can I help you?"

"I hope so," I said, standing at attention. "I'm looking for Giovanni Zampa. Is he here?"

"*Mio Dio*," she said, making the sign of the cross. "He's not here."

She peered past me, craning her head to look this way and that.

My heart sank with disappointment. I was getting nowhere to find the dagger, my wife, or Malik.

"Livia!" a male said sharply from deeper in the house. "Who's at the door?"

Maybe it's Giovanni, I thought as hope surged through my chest. Maybe she lied about his whereabouts.

"I don't know, *Signore*," Livia said, turning to look over her shoulder.

A man in his late forties stormed through the small room cluttered with mismatched furniture. He clutched Livia's shoulders and urged her away from the door, whispering something in her ear.

She nodded and scurried away.

"Who are you?" he demanded as he stood before me. The hair on top of his head was missing, leaving a brownish fringe circling his skull. A huge bulbous nose sitting above thin, cracked lips captured my attention.

"I'm Roman Alexander. I'm here to see Giovanni Zampa."

He pointed past me. "Is that man with you?"

I glanced behind me and said, "Yes, he's my manservant."

The man directed his attention at me again. "And who are you?"

"I already told you. I'm Roman Alexander, here to see Giovanni Zampa."

He narrowed his eyes. "My father is dead. He was murdered six months ago. What do you want?"

I clutched my hands before me, unsure what to say next. It was evident these people were frightened by the murder. "Might I ask your name?"

"My name is Vincenzo. Vincenzo Zampa," he said, with a scowl, continuing to scan past my shoulder.

"It's a pleasure to meet you, Vincenzo." I extended my hand.

He stared at it before shaking it. "What do you want with my father?"

I wasn't sure if I should tell him about the dagger or time travel. Then, I relented. I had to gain information. Maybe Vincenzo knew *something*.

"It was my understanding your father studied time travel."

Vincenzo's face drained of color. "Don't ever say such

things!" He seized my sleeve and dragged me into the house, slamming the door behind me. "Such thoughts are treasonous."

"Treasonous to whom? To you?"

"No," he hissed, brushing his hand across his bald pate. "To the people who killed my father."

Standing on dark red tiles in the tiny foyer, I blinked, trying to piece together his story. "Do you know anything of the whereabouts of the sun dagger? I was told to collect it from Giovanni. That he would be happy to hand it over to me."

I was improvising the story but figured what could it hurt to embellish the truth?

"They already took it," he whispered. "It's gone."

I seized his lapels. "Who took it? I must find it. There's a demon hunting my wife, and we need the dagger to vanquish him."

Vincenzo twisted his head to the side, trying to escape my grip. "Are you one of Costa's men?"

He wriggled his hands between us and attempted to shove me.

I shook my head, releasing him. "I don't know anyone named Costa. Who is he, and what does he have to do with the sun blade?"

"Raul Costa. He's a Timehunter. He sent his men here to attack my father. I couldn't save him," he said, his voice thick with regret.

"A Timehunter?" I scratched my cheek. "What's that?"

Vincenzo continued as if he hadn't heard me. "They attacked Livia and me, too." He pushed back his sleeve, revealing several wicked-looking scars. Then, he lifted the hem of his shirt, showing me more jagged pink lines across his abdomen. "We played dead, waiting for them to leave.

They ransacked the house and found the sun dagger's hiding place. Only then would they leave us alone."

He fell to his knees, dropping his head in his hands. "My father was a gentle scholar. He wasn't evil. He tried to guard that blasted knife all these years, but in the end, his oath to protect it cost him his life."

He let out a horrible sob, fraught with grief. "They robbed us. Costa's men. They tried to kill us. And now, he wants me dead for the same reason he killed my father—he thinks I know something. Raul Costa is a dangerous, despicable man."

I crouched next to him, placing a hand on his shaking shoulder. "I can help you."

Vincenzo lifted his face, his eyes blazing with anger. "I don't want your help. I want nothing to do with you or anyone regarding time travel." He bolted to his feet, dragging me to mine. "Get out! Get out and stay away! Don't ever darken my door again!"

He hustled me to the door with surprising strength and shoved me outside. I managed to stay upright. He slammed the door so hard the entire house seemed to shudder.

"Didn't go as well as you thought?" Tristan said as I headed toward my horse.

I shook my head at him, freed the reins, and mounted Fury. We headed back to the Count's estate. I disregarded all of Tristan's pleas and demands for information.

So, what's a Timehunter? And who is this Raul Costa, and where can I find him? Why did he want the dagger so badly?

My mind continued to whirl like a wagon wheel in the mud, not coming up with any answers.

Upon our return to Count Montego's stables, I dismounted, and a groomsman stepped forward to take care of the horse.

I patted Fury's sweaty neck and left Tristan to deal with his mule. Somehow I needed to get ahead of the game here in Italy. I was meeting dead end after dead end.

As I strode across the marble foyer, heading for the stairs, the count emerged from a door on my right.

"Did you find Giovanni? How is he?"

"I'm afraid he's dead, count. He was killed six months ago." I reached for the swirling wooden railing that flanked the stairs.

Count Montego's face fell.

"Dead! How is this possible?" Without waiting for an answer, he said, "I need a drink. Come. Join me in my study and tell me everything."

I followed him into his office, which was as large as Vincenzo's front room. A gigantic desk sat squarely in the center of the room, surrounded by bookshelves with leather-bound books. Exquisite oil paintings hung between the bookshelves, and small, finely detailed marble statues sat on the shelves between books.

I padded across the thick carpet as Count Montego headed to a dresser with several bottles of liquor and crystal glasses sitting atop it.

"This calls for my best liquor," he said, uncapping a bottle of amber liquid.

He poured a healthy slug into both glasses and handed one to me.

"To Giovanni," he said, lifting his tumbler in the air.

"To Giovanni." I tossed the liquid down my throat, letting it burn a pathway to my stomach.

Count Montego retrieved the bottle, refilled our glasses, and said, "Please, sit," gesturing to a high-backed, over-stuffed chair.

I sat in it while the count headed for his desk, drink in hand.

"So, Giovanni was killed. Who told you this?" He took another swallow of his drink.

"His son, Vincenzo," I said, lifting my glass to my lips.

"Oh, Vincenzo." The count scoffed and flicked his fingers.

I didn't know what he meant by that, so I stayed silent.

"Does he know who killed him?" The count swirled the amber liquid in his glass.

"Yes. Vincenzo said something about Costa's men."

"Ah. I see. He's referring to Raul Costa, is he not?" The count stroked his full beard.

"Yes, that's the one," I said, hoping the count had more to say about Raul.

"Costa is well-loved by society. His family is well respected. His father had passed some time ago, and Raul took over the family business. They are quite wealthy, and usually, when people have a lot of power, they start to over-power people and not follow society's rules. I don't know why Costa's men would come after Giovanni and kill him, but maybe he has changed into a criminal. I have been gone for some time." He bowed his head. "It is regrettable to hear that Giovanni is dead. He was my friend and a scholar that I looked up to."

His face melted into sorrow. "So, now what? You can't find Malik. Giovanni is dead. God rest his soul."

He made the sign of the cross on his chest, the same as Livia, the maid.

"So much happened here while I was away," he said as an afterthought.

"It seems that Raul Costa has something I'm looking for.

And I don't know where to find him." My shoulders slumped slightly.

"Ah!" The count seemed to brighten. He drummed his fingertips together, a glint of delight sparkling in his eyes. "I know how I can help you, Roman."

"You do?" I sat forward.

"I do, indeed. In two days, there will be a masquerade ball. It's an annual event around here. Extremely elegant. People covet invitations to the ball, but few are chosen. My closest friends and I are always welcome since we come from money and power." A secretive smile curved his lips.

My heart pounded. "You can introduce me to Raul Costa?"

"Of course," he said. "You'll love it. You'll have the grandest of times—it's a wonderful event. The wealthiest of the wealthy attend. And the filthiest things happen there. It is a party like no other."

"So, Raul Costa—does he flaunt his wealth? Use it to give him status?" I said.

"He likes to think he's the richest man around. I have more money than him, but who's counting?" The count sniffed. "It's all his father's money. He left everything to Raul when he died with the clause that he should care for his mother as long as she lived. Poor old dear is still kicking, although I doubt Raul lifts a finger on her behalf. That man is wicked. So…will you join me?"

I had attended so many gala events when in attendance of Emperor Severus, only I was usually part of the entertainment as a gladiator fighting against another gladiator to the death.

"I accept your invitation," I said formally.

"Good." The count drained his glass. "Then we shall prepare your disguise. No one shows up at the ball as who they are. Hopefully, you can get what you need from Raul."

I hoped so too. Otherwise, I had no idea how I would ever be reunited with my lovely wife.

CHAPTER SIXTEEN

OLIVIA

Utterly disoriented, I bolted upright as if emerging from a coma, my heart hammering, and looked wildly about. Gilded wallpaper in a fleur-de-lis pattern covered the walls of wherever I was. The four posters of the bed I was in were covered with gold. I was immersed in royal blue velvet, from the bedding to the pulled-back curtains hanging from the bedframe. Heavy, ornately carved furniture stood directly across from the bed, flanking a window concealed by more velvet curtains.

It was like I was in some sort of palace. And I had no memory, absolutely none, of how I got here.

I rose from the bed, finding a long white muslin night-gown covering me. *Holy hell, who dressed me?* My feet were bare, and there was no sign of the garments I'd dressed in yesterday when I woke up—if that moment even existed.

Had I lost my mind in some time travel time warp? This was surreal. I put my hand out to steady myself on one of the carved columns of the bedframe. My gaze fell to the immense paws carved into the base of the column, which looked like lion feet.

I staggered across the white tile covered with blue squares lined in gold, each inscribed with an elegant "M." Did I dare open the door? I felt like Alice in Wonderland. What lay beyond that massive carved door with the golden doorknob?

I hesitated before my fingers curled around the cold brass handle, bracing myself for what I might find. When I opened the door, I was met with a long hallway lined with intricate wallpaper and ancient paintings. An expensive-looking rug ran along its length, and at the end of it was an ornate staircase.

A young woman dressed in a constrictive corset over a long-sleeved striped shirt, a long light-blue skirt with a bustle in the back, and a shiny striped scarf draped over her shoulders hurried toward me. She curtsied when she stood before me, then asked, "*Parli Italiano?*"

"*Sì, lo parlo bene*," I said in a rush, answering her inquiry of whether I spoke Italian.

"Oh good," she said in Italian, pressing her hand to her bosom. "The Master indicated you only spoke English which I'm afraid I do not."

"Where am I?" I said, glancing around.

Her eyebrows drew together. "You are in the Master's home, of course."

Hoping "the Master" was Malik, I said, "Is my sister Emily here?"

Her expression grew mournful, and she lowered her gaze to the floor. "Poor Emily is so ill. She can't keep anything down."

"Can you please take me to her?"

The maid gave me a critical look. "Where is your dressing gown? You can't traipse through the corridors looking like *that*. What if the Master were to see you like that?"

The Master, if it was Malik, had seen me in various versions of dress and undress. Still, I wanted to respect the household customs. "Can you please show me to my armoire?"

The maid curtsied again and said, "Of course. My name is Giulia, by the way."

"Olivia," I said, pressing my hand to my sternum.

"*Lo so,*" Giulia murmured as she scurried past me.

She already knew? I followed her to an armoire filled with dresses and dressing gowns, all appearing to be my size.

After donning a pale gray dress, I followed Giulia to Emily's room.

My sweet sister lay in bed huddled over a pan of sick. "Oh, God, Olivia. This is awful."

"I'm so sorry, Emily." I crossed to sit by her side, and smoothed her tangled hair away from her face. "Please get her a clean pan," I said to Giulia, who hovered nearby.

She nodded, retrieved the metal pot, and hurried away.

"I had the most disorienting experience," I said. "I awoke in a bedroom with no memory of how I got there."

"You're lucky," Emily said, her pallor greenish. "I was conscious of my heaving stomach the entire time."

Footsteps sounded outside the door, followed by a polite knock. Then, Malik entered, hand in hand with Rosie.

"'livia!" Rosie exclaimed. "Emily! Malik gave me new, pretty dresses!"

She romped into the room, stood before me, and twirled in a circle. Her off-white, flared petticoat dress, festooned with pink ribbons, fluttered around her like a flag. "Isn't it pretty?"

"So pretty!" I said, clapping my hands.

I met Malik's piercing gaze. All sorts of intense, pleasurable sensations swirled through my lower abdomen. I averted my eyes to stop the swirl and looked back at Emily.

"I think I'm going to throw up again," she said, clutching her abdomen.

"Rosie, sweetness," Malik said, stooping in front of her. "Why don't you go play with the new toys I got you?"

"I want to stay with you, Olivia, and Emily," she said with a pout.

"And we want to be with you, too. But please give us a moment." He kissed the top of her shiny curls, and she smiled and skipped away.

I shook my head in wonder. Malik had such a sweet and loving connection with Rosie.

Emily groaned again.

"Where's Giulia?" I said, hoping Emily didn't vomit all over her bedding.

Giulia returned with a fresh basin, shoving it before Emily.

As Emily threw up into the pan, Malik's brow creased in concern.

"Giulia, fetch me the doctor at once." He snapped his fingers.

Giulia hurried from the room, moving like a busy bird.

"Oh, no, not a doctor," Emily groaned.

I searched for something to wipe her face and finally found a small towel that had fallen to the floor. I dabbed at her mouth.

"I insist. The matter is decided," Malik said. "He should be here shortly."

He stood regarding us both, his hands on his hips, looking anything but comforting.

Many uncomfortable minutes later, the clatter of hooves sounded outside the window.

I strutted across the room and pulled back the curtains. An elegant black carriage pulled around a sweeping circular driveway. The manicured, well-tended grounds surrounding the house spread far. Malik's place here in Italy was like a palace.

A slender, bespectacled man stepped from the carriage carrying a black satchel. He disappeared from sight, ducking beneath the awning, as he headed toward the house.

Malik exited the room, his footfalls treading confidently toward his destination.

Shortly, Malik and the bespectacled man appeared in the doorway.

"So, you are the patient, my dear?" he said, crossing toward the bed and directing his attention at Emily.

"Yes," she said weakly.

He bowed slightly, then said, "I am Dr. Tarantino."

He sat his satchel down and placed the basin full of putrid vomit near the bed.

"I'm Emily," she croaked.

"What seems to be the problem?" He perched by her side. "Are you perhaps with child?"

Emily glanced at me and back at the doctor. She shrugged. "That's for you to determine."

"Well, let's see if we can find out the cause of your ailments," he said with a smile. Glancing over his shoulder, he said, "Might we have some privacy?"

I hesitated until Malik said, "Well? We must do as the doctor decrees."

Placing his hand on my back, he guided me from the room. Out in the hallway, he scrutinized me like an eagle.

"What?" I said, glancing at him, then at the lush carpet lining the hall.

"You tell me," he said.

"I don't know what you're talking about or inferring." I nibbled on my nail.

A secretive smile formed on his face. "You know exactly what I'm talking about."

I shook my head dismissively and leaned against the wall, my hands behind my back.

We remained in the hall without speaking until the doctor called us in.

"Shall I prove that you already know what's ailing Emily?" Malik said, with an imperious smile on his face.

"If you knew I knew, why did you summon a doctor?" I retorted, my face ablaze.

That lofty, arrogant smile remained as he turned to follow me into the room.

"I have splendid news!" the doctor said, beaming at us. "Miss Emily is with child!"

"What a surprise," Malik said, staring at me. "Aren't you surprised, Olivia?"

"I'm delighted is what I am," I said, skirting his accusation. I'd suspected Emily might be pregnant, but I hadn't wanted to say anything lest Malik refuse to let her time travel.

Dr. Tarantino held up a small glass container full of golden liquid. "Her urine told the tale."

"You performed a urinalysis?" I said, skepticism informing my gaze.

"I'm not so lofty to call it that," he said, swirling the pee in the jar. "I'm what's called a 'piss prophet.'"

"A *piss prophet*? What on Earth is that?" I said.

"Here. Look." He thrust the jar at me.

I recoiled.

"Note the color," he said, holding it under my nose. "It is a clear pale-lemon color leaning toward eggshell white, with a distinctive cloud on its surface."

"I believe you." I put out my hand, pushing the foul-smelling urine away.

Malik, who stood behind me, leaned forward and whispered, "It's because you already knew."

I brushed him and his intoxicating smell away from me.

Malik moved toward the end of the bed and smiled warmly at Emily. "This is wonderful news! Rosie needs a playmate and a friend."

"You'll need rest, Miss Emily. Rest and good nutrition." Dr. Tarantino pulled back the covers and palpated her abdomen. "I suspect you're three months along. May I ask where is the father?"

Emily's eyes welled with tears.

"He's not the man I thought he was." She rolled away from his touch, landing on her side with her back to us all. "Can you all please leave? I need to be alone."

Malik flashed me a concerned look.

I reflected the same look back to him. I was worried about Emily. I was also angry that Marcellious had gone to the dark side. I still found it bewildering that we'd been so fooled by him.

Dr. Tarantino, Malik, and I left the room and traipsed down the curving staircase.

I lingered in the foyer as Malik stepped outside and bade goodbye to the doctor.

When Malik returned, I stepped toward him.

But Giulia hurried toward him.

"Master, if I may," she said, curtsying when she stood before him.

"What is it?" he snapped.

"A gentleman came to greet you yesterday," she said, staring at the tiled floor.

Malik's nostrils flared. "What gentleman? Who was it?"

"He said his name was Roman Alexander, sir," Giulia said, still staring at the floor.

I was so overwhelmed with excitement, I nearly crumpled to the floor. It had been so long since I'd seen my beloved husband that I had to prop myself against the wall. He was finally here in Italy at the same time as I was.

"Where is he?" Malik's eyes blazed with excitement.

"He's gone, sir. I told him you'd return in two days," the maid said.

"You *what?*" The veins in Malik's neck bulged. "Why didn't you put him up? That's what I told you to do! Where did he go?"

I fell back against the wall, too stunned to speak. *Giulia sent Roman away?*

Giulia's voice quavered. "He was with another man. They both rode fine horses. When I told him you weren't here and wouldn't return for two days, he said he would return and departed. He didn't seem upset."

"Whether he seemed upset or not is missing the point. You had one job, Giulia—to greet the man I told you was coming and offer him your hospitality."

"B-b-but, sir," Giulia stuttered. "I didn't think you'd want a stranger…"

"I don't pay you to think! I hired you because you follow orders, and if you don't like it, there are plenty of fresh road apples for you to plow." Malik pointed toward the door. "Get out! You're no longer under my employment!"

Giulia's head popped up in surprise, her cheeks ruddy and mottled. "B-b-but, sir. My family…"

"*Out!*" Malik roared. "*Get out!*"

Giulia rushed from the foyer, slamming the door behind her.

That was harsh.

"Was that really necessary, Malik? It was an honest mistake."

Malik glowered at me like a scorching fire, burning everything around it.

I slid down the wall to the floor and dropped my face in my hands. My husband is finally here, after long months without him. But where is "here"?

"What will we do now?" I asked.

Footsteps approached, and a hand gently seized my wrist.

"Olivia, look at me," Malik said as he crouched next to me.

My hand slowly drifted down and my eyes found his. My despair was palpable in the silence between us.

"Sweetheart," he said, cupping my cheek with his palm. "Don't worry. I know you miss Roman, and you will see him soon. Right now, let's get in my carriage and retrieve the sun blade, shall we?"

I scrambled to my feet, nearly knocking Malik over. "What are you waiting for? Let's go!"

As we rolled through the streets, I marveled at the breathtaking green hills and farms. Wherever we were in Italy was so different than Rome.

Rome was a teeming city. This distant town nestled in the hills was small but beautiful.

"What part of Italy are we in?" I asked Malik.

He clucked to the sleek onyx-colored horses pulling the carriage. "My home is in Sicily, at the southern tip of Italy.

The township has everything—gossip, intrigue, political scandal, and all the rest."

He appeared relaxed as he guided the horses along the dirt road with the high sun overhead.

I smiled, enjoying the easy camaraderie between us. It seemed like nothing could go wrong today. We would get the dagger and be one step closer in my quest to destroy Balthazar.

Malik guided the horses up a winding, leaf-strewn drive to an old Italian villa. He reined them in at the end of the path and leaped from his driver's seat to help me out of the carriage.

I took his hand and sprang from my seat, as a raucous pack of red hens squawked and clawed in the brush around the house. A great hulking hound bounded around the corner, baying with ferocity.

A scraggly man, bald on top, scrambled after it, screeching, "Lupo, Lupo what is it?" His face immediately went pale upon seeing Malik's cold glare.

"Vincenzo," Malik spat, his voice slicing through the air like a razor.

Vincenzo stumbled backward as if shoved. Then, remembering he had manners, he pulled himself upright and bowed.

"My Lord," he said once he stood again. "How may I serve you?"

Malik's eyes bore down on the disheveled man. "I'm here for the sun dagger. Alina said that she left it here with your father, Giovanni."

"I...I...I..." Vincenzo stammered, his gaze darting all around him.

Malik's voice rumbled like thunder, shaking the very ground beneath them. His face a mask of rage and his eyes burning like coals. "You *what*?!" He snarled, enunciating each word with a vicious bite.

Vincenzo quivered in fear, sweat dripping from his forehead as he stammered out an answer. "I-I told your friend y-yesterday I no longer have it!"

Malik's anger erupted and in an instant he was on Vincenzo, gripping his shirt so tight it threatened to tear. "What friend is this?!!"

"R-R-Roman Alexander," Vincenzo stuttered. "His name was Roman Alexander."

Roman! My heart swooned. Where is he now?

Malik shook Vincenzo. "What do you mean you no longer have the sun dagger? You and your father were told to guard it with your life."

He curled his hand around Vincenzo's neck.

"My father was killed six months ago," Vincenzo wheezed, grappling with Malik's arm. "Raul Costa attacked us, took the dagger, and murdered my father."

Malik bared his teeth. "You imbecile. You were supposed to protect the dagger at all costs. Where is Roman Alexander?"

"I don't know," Vincenzo choked out. He clutched Malik's wrist with both hands.

Malik seemed to tower over us, his presence growing more oppressive with each passing moment as he unleashed his darkness.

Fear seemed to radiate off me like a mist, causing my knees to tremble and my heart to race in terror.

"I'm going to kill you," he hissed in a voice that reverberated.

"Malik!" I yelled, lunging at him. "Stop!"

Malik seized my neck with his other hand. He turned his face to me, his eyes deadly and dark.

I felt like I was looking straight into the mouth of hell. I shook in his grip.

"Do not meddle in my affairs. This does not concern you."

His fingers squeezed, and tiny stars clouded my vision.

"Malik, you're hurting me. I know you don't mean this. The darkness inside of you is controlling you. Please stop hurting me," I said, appealing to the human inside of the monster. "We have this inexplicable bond."

It was beginning to get hard to breathe.

Malik's eyes turned to an inky abyss, and he seemed a million miles away from me. His hand tightened on my neck like an iron vice, crushing the life out of me with a grip that threatened to never let go.

"Malik, stop," I wheezed. "This isn't you. It's the monster inside of you controlling you. I know you can feel me and my pain."

His stormy gaze began to clear, and he looked at me as if remembering who I was.

"Olivia?" His grip on my neck lessened.

"That's right. It's me. Olivia."

Malik frowned, letting me go, then turned toward Vincenzo. He released a frantic, deranged stare that swept across the room, his eyes bulging wide with hysteria and insanity.

What's happening to Malik?

"You!" Malik roared with a ferocity beyond comprehension, pouncing like a wild panther leaping from the shadows and taking Vincenzo to the ground. With both hands clenched around his throat, he pinned him beneath his full weight and bore down.

Vincenzo made a horrible gasping sound before Malik eased up on his chokehold. "How can I find Costa?"

Vincenzo coughed, rubbing his neck. "He is hosting his annual masquerade, my lord. You can find him there. He'll probably have the blade on his person."

Malik lowered himself so his face was inches from Vincenzo's. He grasped Vincenzo's jaw, his fingernails digging into Vincenzo's skin. "If you ever speak of this incident, you won't live to see another day."

Vincenzo tried without success to turn away from Malik.

"I won't ever speak of it," he croaked.

"Good," Malik said, shaking the man's jaw.

In a flash, he was beside me, ushering me toward the carriage.

I gasped. Malik's ability to jump through time and space unnerved me.

I clambered into the carriage seat beside Malik and sat in uneasy silence. I was angry with him, and how he'd almost lost control and killed me. Whatever connection I'd felt with him, I was now disgusted. When it came down to it, he was the darkness, and he could kill me without a second thought.

He clucked to the horses, and we were headed away.

I waited for my anger to simmer down and until we were well away from Vincenzo's house before speaking.

"Who is this Raul Costa?" I struggled with Giovanni's death, the sun dagger's disappearance, and Malik nearly choking me to death. The only thing keeping me going, and not raging at Malik, was the fact that my beautiful husband was somewhere nearby, and I would see him soon.

I caught Malik's gaze, and his face transformed into a tempest of dangerous emotion.

"He's not someone you want to mess with; he's a Time-hunter. His society is the one who held me prisoner for years."

He flicked the reins, urging the horses into a trot.

"How is that possible? Nothing can hurt you, weaken you, or kill you. Only the blades that we are looking for can but…" I gripped the seat as the carriage bumped down the road.

"There is still much you don't know, Olivia." Malik stared straight ahead. His features were grim. "But know this —Raul Costa is a Timehunter and he will want to kill you."

I shivered. Danger was all around me.

"And that fool Vincenzo speaks of the masquerade, confronting Raul, and getting back the blade as if it were easy. Ha! That fucker." His lip curled in a sneer.

I studied his profile. I didn't think he was scared, but something was wrong. I stayed silent the rest of the ride, the world around me blurring into nothingness. I was too tense, too uptight to notice anything.

When we pulled to his palatial home, a groomsman stood waiting to take the horses.

Malik jumped from the driver's seat and stalked into the house, not helping me down or waiting for me.

I followed him into the house and hesitated. Should I go see Emily? Disappear into my own room?

As I stood at the foot of the stairs, Malik whirled and appeared before me.

"I don't understand why your husband isn't following the orders I gave him," he growled.

"What? When did you talk to Roman?"

He waved his hand, dismissing me. "There is something you should know about Timehunters."

I stepped back, away from his intensity.

"What are you talking about?" I gasped, my voice barely audible.

His gaze hardened, his eyes turning a menacing black. "They are the most wicked of all creatures, the embodiment of death and destruction. Their touch can take away your breath, twist your mind and soul, damage your body beyond repair. But they also have the power to weaken the darkness itself."

He stared at me a moment longer before turning away, leaving me with a whirlwind of emotions: fear, confusion, anger, and uncertainty all vying for dominance.

CHAPTER SEVENTEEN

MARCELLIOUS

The chittering, incessant sound of cockroaches grated against my eardrum as Balthazar and I landed in a dank, dusty room. I let out a howl of anguish, feeling the sharp pain radiating from my shattered leg. I stared with horror at the grotesque shape it had taken; my bones twisted and bent like broken twigs.

Wisps of spiderwebs hung from the ceiling and walls, rippling from the hot breeze blowing through the cracks in the floor. Light from perpetually burning torches cast an eerie glow on the webs.

I threw my hand over my nose and mouth. The stench of decay wafting from the room below, where the cockroaches lived, was overwhelming.

I knew this place; we were in Balthazar's dungeon. He must be in worse shape than I'd thought—he always brought us to his opulent lair.

I searched for him in the shadows, my gaze tracking the old baby buggies littered around the room filled with sightless dolls. The dolls had been placed here by Balthazar once in an attempt to torture Olivia.

A shape writhed in the corner.

I made a three-limbed crawl toward Balthazar. I nearly recoiled from the smell of scorched, burning flesh.

Steam issued from a bloody, gaping slash in his abdomen. I drew my elbow over my mouth and nose.

"What are you gawking at?" Balthazar hissed. His face was a mixture of shadows and ghostly pale skin. "Go get me my healing tonic. It's in the room off of the dungeon."

"Shouldn't we get you to cleaner quarters?" I said, spying a fat cockroach trying to wriggle through a crack in the floor.

"Do I look like I can move?" Balthazar wheezed. "Go! Get me my Calabar tonic. The one I used to heal you."

"What if the cockroaches get to you before I return?" I lurched to stand, balancing on my one good leg.

"I'll bite off their heads. I don't know. Can you stop asking me so many fucking questions and just do as you are told? Just *go!*"

I hopped into the next room, a much tidier space, and found a tonic labeled *Calabar* sitting on the mantel of a fireplace. The putrid liquid in front of me gleamed like fresh blood spilled on the pavement. And as I stared at it, my mind started to spiral out of control with searing flashbacks of the same vile substance that was used to heal me when he shot me. The memories were so vivid that I could almost feel the sticky, acidic goo dripping upon my abdomen, searing my flesh.

When I returned, several cockroaches had escaped and swarmed toward Balthazar. I stomped on the ones closest to him, feeling their bodies snap and squish beneath my feet. Their brethren scurried toward the dead and began eating them, their mandibles popping and cracking as they dissected their fallen friends.

Balthazar waved his hand over his belly. "Pour it over the wound. Then, pour some over your mangled leg."

Sweat poured from his face and neck and dampened his linen shirt.

I clamped down on the cap with my teeth and twisted it off with ease. The putrid mixture inside smelled like burnt hair, mold, and spoiled milk. My stomach turned as I took a whiff of the foul odor. Finally, I poured some of the liquid onto Balthazar's open wound, hoping it would help disinfect it.

Balthazar let out a scream that sent the cockroaches scurrying for shelter.

"More!" he cried in a raspy voice.

I let another drizzle fall from the glass bottle.

Balthazar screamed again, louder this time. "Pour it on your leg. Do it before infection takes over."

I hesitated. I'd already experienced the wrath of this so-called "healing elixir."

"Do it!" Balthazar screamed.

My hand shook so hard I nearly spilled the tonic everywhere, but I managed to pour some over my misshapen bones. I howled like a dying dog when the liquid hit my skin. Then, I must have blacked out because I came to, draped across Balthazar, the tonic bottle still clutched upright in my hand.

I pushed away from him, eying his wound. It looked like a nasty injury, with angry red flesh surrounding a pus-filled hole, but no more steam and stench arose from it.

I lifted my leg, and it, too, appeared slightly healed.

"Help me up," Balthazar gasped.

With effort, I stumbled to my feet and got Balthazar upright. Then, arms around each other for support, we staggered into the next room.

I guided Balthazar to a red velvet sofa.

He fell onto it, landing on his back.

I made my way to an oversized, overstuffed chair in the same color.

We both lay gasping for a few long moments.

Balthazar spoke first. "That son of a bitch. How dare he do that to me? He poisoned me with the belladonna! How did he come across it?"

"Who are we talking about?" My eyelids were too heavy to open.

"Malik, that's who! How did he escape and survive? I saw his damn body steaming, burning, covered in scorch marks and fistulas. Who the hell helped him? No one is stronger than me." He struggled to sit up, then gave up and collapsed.

I couldn't think of a thing to say. I continued to lay back, my eyelids refusing to open. I sank into a merciless sleep where I experienced falling, endlessly falling through space and dark shadowy places.

I awoke to someone's tender ministrations and the feel of a warm, wet cloth on my forehead. My eyelids fluttered open.

Balthazar crouched before me, dipping a thick cloth into a basin, and dabbing my skin. He smiled at me like a doting father.

What the hell changed in him? It stirred a strange feeling inside me that I couldn't quite discern.

"You made me proud today, Marcellious," he said in a tone I'd never heard before. It sounded…fatherly.

I blinked, wondering what had happened to the demon known as Balthazar.

"Thanks to you, we now have the journal," he said, squeezing the rag over the basin to remove excess liquid.

It trickled into the pan with a noisy splash.

He wiped at my brow and neck. "I'm so very proud. You've been a good soldier."

I glanced around the room at the crackling fire in the fireplace. The pleasant scent of beeswax candles contrasted with the decay and filth in the next room.

"I'm glad to hear it, master," I said.

"You're like my son now. You're an ally I can count on." He gazed down at me with the softest expression on his face.

His kindness made my heart ache. "Thank you for saying that. You have no idea what it means to me."

"It's true." He caressed my cheek with his rough, callused hand. "It doesn't matter that Dahlia is dead. You served her well and made her end days a blessing instead of a curse."

He dropped the rag into the basin and strode across the room, then returned with the journal in his hand.

"Sit up and read it to me." He slid his hand behind me and helped me out of my slumping shape into an upright position.

I took the worn book and flipped through the pages. "I'm afraid I can't read it. It's in a language I don't know."

"Let me take a look." Balthazar took the book from my hands and settled on the sofa. He flipped a few pages. "It's in Italian. That's where I met her, you know—Italy."

Then, smoothing open the book, he began to read aloud.

"July 17th, 1561. Balthazar has been my secret lover for nearly five years now. We meet in the cover of nightfall, coming together in the shadows with lusty abandon. Thoughts of him consume me. My parents have been on me for some time now to get married."

"Ah, yes," he uttered, bowing his head in reverence. "This is the place where she spills her heart to her father about how important I was to her." His voice held a pain and longing that betrayed the strength of their bond and the depth of his agony.

A mask of serene awe descended upon Balthazar's features as he embraced the journal, his eyes tightly shut. His arms pressed against it with all his strength, as if this embrace could save him from a torturous fate that awaited him. "Oh, my dear sweet Alina. My one and only true love."

I studied him, unable to make sense of his demeanor. *Had the injury inflicted by Malik twisted his behavior to something less evil?* His sudden kindness, no matter how welcome, unnerved me.

He continued to read passage after passage, sometimes in English or Italian. And as he read, his countenance changed, becoming more and more familiar as the obsessed monster emerged. His head fell back on a swoon, and he groaned. "Oh, my beloved Alina! How I miss you. I long to see you, feel you, and taste you again. Ours was the love of the ages, unsurpassed in all its glory."

He angrily flipped through the pages, his brow furrowing. His mouth twisted into an irritated scowl, and his eyes flashed like two fierce hawk's eyes surveying the terrain.

"No!" His voice echoed, bouncing off the walls as he frantically flipped through the journal. "It can't be gone..." His hands shook violently, nearly ripping the pages in their haste to find the missing page. Sweat dripped from his forehead and his voice took on a panicked edge.

When he handed it over, I turned the book round and round, opening it and closing it.

"Look there." I pointed to a ragged place on the spine. "It's been taken apart. There are stitches like someone has put something in there."

"Open it." Balthazar sat forward. "Quickly. Open it now. We must see if the missing page is in there."

I patted my waist. "I don't have my knife."

"There's a letter opener over there on my desk." He pointed to an oak desk in the corner.

I crossed retrieved the sharp gold opener and fit the tip into the spine. I had to maneuver it back and forth until I could pry it open. Then, I wiggled a finger into the tight opening. I could feel a tiny lump but couldn't get it out. With the letter opened, I sliced either side of the spine to pry it open.

A small piece of folded paper fell onto the floor.

Balthazar's hand shot out to snatch it up. He unfolded the delicate paper and read silently. Then, he began to weep.

"What does it say? Tell me!" I said, standing next to him.

In a tremulous voice, he said, "Oh, Alina! She says, 'I'm carrying Balthazar's child. I'm in so much danger I don't know what to do. He's going to come and take my baby from me. I must deceive Philip and tell him that the child is his.'"

Anguished sobs erupted from his throat.

"Alina," he wailed. "You gave me the greatest gift I could ever hope for, and you hid it from me."

Tears slid down his face and landed on his linen shirt in damp blotches.

I swayed where I stood. *Balthazar, a father?*

"This means Emily is my *daughter*. I'm such a fool," he raged.

I looked into his eyes, realizing he was right. His eyes were the same color as Emily's, and his facial structure bore a remarkable resemblance. But Emily was nothing like her father. She was an angel with a beautiful soul.

I am so fucked.

Balthazar dropped the piece of paper, and it fluttered to the floor. He bolted to his feet. "I must return and find her— no matter the cost. I will do whatever it takes to show her my sincerity and demonstrate my unwavering loyalty. She'd be the best daughter any father could hope for, far more than my fool of a son ever could be. I'll make it right—one way or another.

"I'm so angry that I didn't know. I nearly *burned* her to death and caused her so much pain." He waved his fisted hands. "Damn you, Alina, for not telling me!"

I stood reeling in my own revelations. *I was married to the daughter of the most potent darkness on Earth.* Only, now, she wanted nothing to do with me. If only I could tell her the truth.

When Balthazar passed by the sofa, he snatched up the journal and began to read again.

"What's this? Alina found the sun dagger and gave it to that fool of a scholar, Giovanni Zampa." He turned a few more pages with his thumb. "And Malik had a child? Good god, the secrets that are in here…I must find a way to use this information against Malik."

He turned to look at me, and his eyes glinted red.

Oh, yes—the demon was back.

"Do you have a plan?"

"Yes," Balthazar snapped. He rushed from the room.

I had to hurry to catch up with him. "Where are you going?"

"We are going to Italy. I must find the dagger, my daughter, and win back control before it is too late." We raced down the stairs, two at a time.

I followed him, my right arm still weak. His stomach couldn't have healed completely either. But a demon with a mission was a monster on the move.

We stepped outside beneath the full moon, each of us holding our daggers. Minutes later, our palms dripping blood, the scripture lingering on our lips, we were hurtling into another dimension.

We emerged at midday in what looked like Italy from my recollection of the Roman countryside.

When we landed, Balthazar leaped about the vast field, his arms flung wide. "Oh, we're in Sicily! The place where my love and I first met. Come, Marcellious. My villa is right over there."

He pointed to a sweeping structure down the hill. He moved like a galloping stallion.

We rushed down the hill and clambered up the stone steps to his home.

I tried to catch my breath. It was like an invisible wind buffeted his every step.

Twisted, monstrous statues lined the walkway to his home. Gargoyles perched at every corner of his house, their eyes tracking our movements as if they were alive.

Balthazar burst into the foyer. "Ginevra! Giorgia! I would like a bath at once!"

The house exploded in activity as servants scurried toward us.

"Master!" one of them cried out. "Welcome home!"

Balthazar bounded up the steps ahead of me, and I shouted his name as I tried to keep up with him.

"What shall I do, master?" I wheezed.

Balthazar whirled and steadied his hand on the ornate banister. "You will go and get the dagger from Giovanni."

"What? Where?"

Balthazar ignored me.

A plump maid waddled up the stairs, gasping and groaning with each step. "Master, wait. I shall prepare your bath."

"Fine, fine, Ginevra, but hurry! We have much to do." He sprinted up the stairs with me in hot pursuit.

He entered a large room off the hall.

SARA SAMUELS

Inside stood a copper tub on carved metal legs in the shape of deer hooves.

I hesitated in the doorway.

"Come, come." Balthazar gestured with his hand.

Devilish-looking plants with wicked thorns hung from the ceiling. A stained-glass window provided colorful light.

Balthazar stripped, tossing his clothes in every direction.

I glanced at the red, angry-looking wound on his abdomen. My gaze drifted lower. I couldn't help but notice his impressive cock hanging between his legs. Embarrassed, I averted my gaze.

Except for that nasty gash, Balthazar was a fine specimen of a man with a well-muscled physique.

Ginevra lifted a copper lever and began pumping water into the tub.

Balthazar simply stood in place, hands on his naked hips.

Several men and women servants lumbered into the room, carrying wooden buckets laden with steaming water. They poured most of the buckets into the deep basin and set the others nearby.

Ginevra stopped the pump and dipped her hand into the water.

"It's the perfect temperature, my lord," she said, keeping her gaze away from his bare body.

Balthazar propped one hand on the edge of the tub and entered the water. He let out a satisfied groan, lowering himself to prone. "All of you, leave! But remain close by for reheating the water."

Each servant bowed or curtsied and backed out of the room. As they progressed, they ducked to keep from getting snagged by the thorny tendrils of the overhead plants.

"Shall I depart, master?" I said, disturbed at the thought of watching the man bathe.

Balthazar lay with his head back, eyes closed. "Reach into my trousers and get Alina's blade. You must place it on my trophy wall."

"Your trophy wall, my lord?" I said, canting my head to the side.

"You know—where I store all my prized possessions, like the many blades of Timebornes I have killed."

His eyes met mine.

"I know I can trust you, Marcellious," he said in that same soft voice of earlier when he cared for me. "Now, once you place Alina's dagger on the trophy wall, you will go to Giovanni's house and retrieve the sun dagger from him. He is a weak man, so it should be easy for you to get it. Then return at once to me."

"I shall make you proud, master," I said, crouching to rummage through his pants. I found the sheathed blade.

"My trophy wall is downstairs in my office. Ask Ginevra to take you there, but don't let her see you reveal my possessions." His gaze pinned me in place.

"Of course not, master." I inclined my head in servitude.

He looked away from me. "It will be so splendid to reunite with my daughter. Shall I bring her flowers? Fine chocolates? Jewels?"

"I'm sure she will appreciate your every gesture and deed," I lied. I couldn't imagine Emily's horror at learning who her father was. "Will there be anything else, master?"

Balthazar waved his hand and rested his head on the tub's lip once more.

I bowed and backed out of the bathroom, Alina's blade in hand.

In the hall, Ginevra and a couple of others hovered a short distance away.

"Ginevra, can you please take me to Balthazar's office?" I said.

"*Certo*, *maestro*," she replied, taking off at a brisk gait. She unlocked the door with a key from a keyring around her ample waist. Then, she opened the door and stepped aside. "I shall lock up after you are finished."

"Thank you," I said with a curt nod. I entered the room, closed the door, and fell against it. My heart was heavy with the uncertainty of my predicament. But placing the dagger inside Balthazar's trophy wall was not in my best interest—I needed to get it away from Balthazar's possession.

I remained in his office for what I felt was an appropriate amount of time before hiding the sheathed dagger inside my waistband. Then, I exited, told Ginevra to lock up, and hurried out of the house.

I marched into the stables, burning with a raging fire. I demanded a horse from the groomsman and set off on my quest for Zampa's house. The horse galloped through an endless sea of olive trees, its hooves pounding against the dirt like thunder. As I neared my destination, fury boiled inside me—Balthazar wanted me to steal the sun dagger, but I had had enough of his sinister games. No longer would I bow down to him; I was determined to take back what was rightfully mine—my dignity.

I urged my steed to a trot and headed toward a tavern. I had something different in mind other than going to the Zampa residence. I needed a drink.

I dismounted my horse, tied it to the hitching post next to another horse, and stepped inside the tavern.

The interior was dark, and I had to blink a few times to clear my vision. A hooded figure sat at a table in the corner.

I crossed the room and settled in the seat opposite him. "I can't do this anymore. I want out."

The man pushed back his hood, revealing his face.

"I just can't do this, Malik. I'm done being your spy. I can't do this anymore," I said.

Malik nodded. "Did you retrieve the dagger from Balthazar?"

I patted my waistband. "Yes, I have it. I want out. I want to go back to my wife and my life. This is getting out of control. I have been gutted, almost killed, tortured. I don't know how long I can survive. Yet Balthazar trusts me now, just like you said he would. I did everything you told me and now I want out completely. No more secrets and we tell the truth to Emily and Olivia."

Exhausted, I wiped my face with my palm.

Malik sat across from me, unmoving.

"You told me it wouldn't take this long. I want my life back," I pleaded. "Emily and Olivia hate me. They think I turned against them."

Malik nodded. "I know it's been difficult, but I'm proud of you for staying the course. Things just got out of control."

I gaped at him. "Is that what you call it? Out of control? My wife *hates* me. She's disgusted by my actions. I had to tell her all these lies. I had to pretend to love Dahlia." I waved my arms around as I spoke. "It broke my heart to see Emily's face when she saw me with Dahlia."

My insides burned with disgust.

"I understand you, but you know that the plan was to bring me Balthazar and Alina's dagger. Not just Alina's. I need his too," Malik said, dismissing my protests.

I screamed in desperation, my throat raw with the force of it. "How can you expect me to get Balthazar's blade?! I would be a fool to even attempt it! I'm not sure if I'll make it out alive this time!"

I pounded the table with both fists.

Malik tamped the air before him. "Patience. We are dealing with forces far greater than you can imagine. Now you must bring me Balthazar's dagger."

A chill rippled up my spine. "How do you expect me to do that?"

"Find out where he stores it and take it." Malik shrugged, pulling the hood up over his head again. He leaned as if about to get up.

My hand shot across the table to seize his wrist. "Wait! Did you know Emily is Balthazar's daughter?"

An expression of shadows and secrets fell across Malik's face.

I blinked in surprise. "You knew! You were the one who ripped the page from the journal!"

Malik didn't confirm or deny my accusation. "It's better that she doesn't know. And you're going to keep it that way. She doesn't need any more pain or surprises. Neither does Olivia."

My head pulled back. "But Balthazar has all these plans to reunite with his daughter. He was overjoyed to find out Alina gave him a child."

"Emily will not find out," Malik said. "And you will keep your mouth shut about it. Balthazar doesn't even know what is coming to him yet."

"How can you be so sure? She already despises me. You convinced me to agree to your plan, telling me everything would be okay. Everything is a fucking mess!" I flicked my hand his way. "Balthazar will find out who I am and destroy me before I can explain anything to Emily!"

Malik rose from his chair, looming over me. "Don't worry. Balthazar will not kill you. I am your ally, and I am standing by your side and will protect you. Now listen to me very carefully—Giovanni is dead. I just found out. Raul

Costa is in possession of the sun dagger and will be at his annual masquerade ball. Tell Balthazar to go to the masquerade ball, and all will be well. I will take care of everything from there. Trust me—everything will work out."

I huffed out a long sigh. "Okay, if you say so. I will go…"

"You are a good man, Marcellious. Even the darkest monsters can change with a woman's love. You have done well, and once Emily and Olivia learn the truth they will be proud of you. You only have to bring me Balthazar's dagger and then you may return to your wife."

"I don't know if she will take me back after everything I did. I am a terrible person, a monster," I said, getting to my feet. "Emily will always hate me."

Malik stopped, his breath shallow and eyes widening. "You should know... Emily isn't just carrying your child, but your legacy. She will find it within her to forgive you, no matter the cost. I swear it," he said with a solemn determination. "I promise you that I will explain everything to them. Bring me Balthazar's blade and meet me back at my home once you have it." He slid a folded piece of paper to me.

And then, like a ghost, he was gone, leaving me to fall back into my chair, stunned.

CHAPTER EIGHTEEN

OLIVIA

Malik's demeanor toward me had been cold to the point of frostbite since returning from Vincenzo Zampa's house. I was still struggling to control my anger toward him for unleashing his darkness against me. My thoughts raced a mile a minute as I attempted to come up with ways to get back at him, but I knew that wasn't the answer.

Despite my seething anger toward Malik, there were moments when all I could think about was my husband. The turmoil inside me was a cacophony of emotions I couldn't ignore—love and hate, devotion and betrayal all clashed together in a dizzying whirlwind of conflicting thoughts.

When Malik returned from his mysterious "monster business," this afternoon, I scurried away from the front room, not wanting to see him.

He appeared directly in front of me in the infuriating way.

"Olivia." He took my chin in his hand and tipped it up.

I ground my teeth together, refusing to speak.

"I understand that you're mad at me. I apologize for letting my dark side come out."

His hypnotizing emerald gaze shimmered, pushing its way past my defenses.

"It doesn't matter if you meant it or not—the fact is, you did it. I no longer feel safe around you," I said.

Malik let out a pained sigh. "It will never happen again. We must be allies. Tonight is important."

"How can I be your ally if I don't trust you?" I tried to pull away from his iron grip without success.

He released me and stroked my cheek with the side of his finger.

"I told you I'd never do it again and I meant it." His gaze pierced me. "You have to trust me. Now, come—talk with me."

Could I trust him? It seemed I had no choice.

I took his hand and let him lead me toward his front room.

We settled on opposite sides of his silk-covered sofa.

The decor in this room didn't match the monster who lived there. In every corner of the room, exquisite paintings adorned the walls and tables. Hand-painted vases and fans sat on the tables and on the bookshelves. Even a serene statue of the Buddha rested in the corner on a stand. The room was a masterpiece.

I perched on my side of the couch, barely breathing, waiting for him to speak.

"Tonight's ball is a regional event. There will be people from all over. To attend, they travel from surrounding cities even as far away as Rome." His face revealed nothing—no kindness, warmth, or disgust.

"Okay," I said, nodding to encourage him to keep talking.

"Your mother met Balthazar at this event," he said evenly. "The gathering is debauchery at its basest level."

I frowned.

"You, Olivia, will be expected to partake." He pointed at me.

I shook my head. "I only care about Roman. I won't be tempted to do anything other than find my husband."

"Ah, but you're wrong, love." His gaze grew stern. "The atmosphere is so highly charged you'll be filled with cravings."

"I'm a grown woman," I said. "I can control my impulses."

Malik smirked. "Oh, I see. You are an expert in orgies and parties of this nature."

My face reddened. "No, I didn't say that."

"I'm warning you, Olivia. You must heed my warning. Trust me, you *will* be tempted to partake." His eyes closed briefly as if remembering something. "It's an intoxicating environment. Lust, in all its shapes and forms, will be the star of this event."

An unexpected shiver cascaded through me.

Looking out his window, Malik stroked his jaw, drawing my attention to his strong neck.

I gulped, forcing myself to look away. Remember Roman. Roman is the man for you.

And he *was* the man for me. I loved Roman, heart and soul. I just couldn't explain Malik's effect on me.

Malik's icy stare bore into me with a warning. "The thing you need to remember most about Raul Costa, the host of this ball, is that he is not just menacing and dangerous, he's downright malevolent."

"You already told me that," I said.

He pursed his lips. "I don't think you understand the gravity of the situation. You think the darkness, Balthazar, and I are dangerous."

"You are."

"Timehunters are more dangerous than all of us combined." Malik's probing gaze seemed to peel me apart to a place of extreme vulnerability.

I suddenly felt cold.

"H-h-how is that possible?" I stammered.

Malik's expression transformed into something somber, adding weight to the room. "Ever since Timebornes were created, a secret society came into existence concurrently. They called themselves the Timehunters. They thought time travelers were a threat to society. They got crazy ideas about Timebornes and Timebounds and made it their mission to kill us all. They made it their passion."

I rubbed my arms now covered with gooseflesh.

"They are the Maestri del Veleno—the masters of poison. They combine their knowledge of poisonous substances with a unique alchemy to produce fatal substances with no known antidote. Well, I should say there is an antidote, but it's very hard to come across it. Their poisons can weaken the darkness."

I sucked in a breath.

He smoothed back his long hair. "Here's how they work. They trap the time traveler and experiment on you to find the perfect poison or combination of poisons that will work on you." Shadows fell over his eyes, making him appear haunted. "They secure you in a room and poison you, torture you, finding out the best methods and poisons to cause you pain and weaken you. They'll flood the room you are in with poison which causes you to hallucinate, sweat, and gag. Your mind will eventually go. Then, they'll drain your blood and kill you."

I pressed my hand to my mouth. "This is what you experienced, isn't it?"

He didn't answer me. "Raul Costa is the head of the

society here in Italy. Your mother trusted him. He used her and tortured her. Somehow, she survived the torture and escaped."

"I know—she had it written in her journal."

"Oh, yes she did," Malik said, nodding. "Every year Costa finds two Timebornes or Timebounds to torture. I don't know how he finds them, but he makes a show of it. There will be an exhibit at the masquerade ball. People love it. They think it's theater—an act, nothing more. Other Timehunters will become aroused as they watch. The thrill of torture, the burning pleasure of inflicting pain, and deafening screams; they revel in it all with sadistic glee. Every moan, every scream that escapes from their victims' mouths tastes like honey to them. Afterward, they'll find ways to slake their desire at the ball."

He snorted. "Meanwhile, a real-life person is suffering acute and prolonged torture."

My stomach lurched, threatening to expel its contents. "This is so sick. I didn't know any of this. I thought there was no weakness in the darkness. All I knew was that you kill daily to survive, in order to keep your strength. As well, your original time traveler dagger can control you. But I didn't know that certain poisons can weaken you."

I leaned forward, picking at my fingernails, unable to relax.

Malik shrugged.

"So, did Balthazar put you in prison and grant access to a Timehunter to torture and weaken you?"

Malik turned cold, dead eyes on me.

"Yes," he said simply.

My mind moved sluggishly, connecting everything Malik had just told me with what I was about to do. "So you want me to attend this masquerade ball, put on a mask, try not to get seduced, and just waltz around as if all is well?"

Malik laughed.

It was the first laugh I'd heard since we'd headed toward Zampa's house, giving me a—minimal—measure of comfort.

"Don't worry," he said, a broad smile stretched across his face. "It's hard for a Timehunter to determine who is a Timeborne since your dagger is always hidden. You don't wear anything obvious like a necklace, like the Timebounds do."

He reached between us and tapped my collarbone. "Your job tonight is to find the sun dagger and leave Costa's ball like a shadow unknown."

"Piece of cake," I said, with an accompanying eye roll.

"Piece of what? Are you hungry?" Malik said, one eyebrow lifted.

"It's a phrase common in my time. It means 'how easy,' which we both know it won't be."

"Ah," he said. "Sarcasm."

"Yes," I said.

"In this case, it might well be. The party will be held at Costa's. The dagger should be in his study. We only have a couple of hours there. We don't want to see who he's torturing this year." Malik placed his palms on his knees as if ready to stand.

I shot out my hand to stop his movement. "I'm a little frightened. It sounds dangerous."

"It *is* dangerous, especially for me, love. If he finds out I am there, he will kill everyone with a special concoction of the belladonna."

"Oh, my God, Malik! This is a lot to take in. Don't you think I could have been let in on all this danger sooner rather than last minute?"

Malik got to his feet, looming over me. "If I'd told you

everything when we learned about the ball, you'd have obsessed and worried until you made yourself as sick as Emily." He shook his head. "You think if you kill Balthazar, all your troubles will be vanquished, and you can live a fairy-tale life somewhere with Roman. Nothing could be further from the truth. You will still have the Timehunters to worry about. They're far more deadly."

He started to stride away.

I bolted to my feet and lunged for his arm. "You don't get to drop this news bomb at my feet and then walk away from me."

"Oh? What should I do instead?" He slowly licked his upper lip.

"God! This is like a joke to you, isn't it?" I threw out my arms in exasperation.

His expression became stony. "I assure you, it's no joke."

"Why am I learning about this now? Why didn't I know about it when I was catapulted into ancient Rome or the Wild West? Why didn't my time-traveling savvy mother mention anything?

Malik gently tapped my temple. "You know the answer as well as I do. In Rome, you never talked to anyone except Roman and his housekeeper Amara. Who would tell you there? In what you call the Wild West, the Native Americans were consumed with their own culture and livelihood. Your father protected you after your mother was killed."

My head jerked back. "Were there Timehunters in Seattle?"

"Yes," he said. "They are everywhere."

"Was I in danger then? Was my mother in danger?"

"Probably, and yes," he said, heading down the hallway, presumably for his office; I followed his long-legged stride.

"You were being watched. The nexus that started in Italy has become strong. Their network has expanded."

He paused at the doorway to his office, blocking the entrance. "Tonight, you must get back the dagger. They took the dagger from Zampa for a reason. They obviously have something planned for it. We must be extremely cautious. If Raul finds out who you are or realizes I am there, it will be horrible for both of us. No matter how quick I am, the smell of the poison can weaken my ability and slow me down."

I steadied myself against the wall for support. Could I do this? I'd never regained my strength and confidence following the death of my child, but I simply had to summon courage, restoring it in whatever measure I could manage.

Malik took my chin in his hand. He held me with tenderness like I was made of fine-spun glass. "Follow my lead tonight. I will do my best to protect you, but I can't always be there."

His glittering emerald eyes became soft pools lit by some inner light.

I fell under his spell, leaning into his touch until he said, "It's getting late. Let's start preparing for the masquerade ball."

He ducked into his office and closed the door, leaving me quaking in the corridor, uncertain about everything.

CHAPTER NINETEEN

OLIVIA

I stood before the full-length mirror in my dressing room, turning side to side to study my reflection.

I wore a rich blue silk gown with cream-colored sleeves. Tiny golden hooks held the bodice together down to the waist. A slit down the entire front of the dress revealed the golden petticoat. A matching golden placket had been sewn at cleavage level, making the dress stunning yet modest. Golden thread had been used to embroider embellishments down the front seams and sides of the gown.

A new staff member, Florentine, had piled my hair atop my head and placed tiny blue flowers throughout. She'd tugged a few strands of hair free from the numerous hairpins used to fix my updo in place.

"You look beautiful, no?" Florentine said to me as she eyed me.

"I barely recognize myself," I said.

"All heads will turn when you enter the room, that is for certain." She fussed with the gown and my hair, clucking and tutting like a mother hen. "There. The master will be most pleased."

"*Grazie*," I said, making a small curtsy.

"You are most welcome. You'll have to tell me all about the masquerade when you return. I've heard the stories, but I'll never be of a caste to be invited." A wistful look played upon her features. She brushed at the imaginary lint on my shoulder and then said, "I will fetch the master for you."

"*Grazie*," I repeated.

After she left the room, my nerves began to fray.

Florentine looked at the ball as a lavish affair only the privileged attended.

I was only going to retrieve the dagger and get out with my life intact. I feared being apprehended and tortured to satisfy the whims of the partygoers. When Malik had told me how Raul "played" with his Timebound or Timeborne victims, tormenting them onstage for sport, I'd been sickened. I couldn't let my Timeborne abilities be discovered.

A gentle knock rapped on the door, and then Malik entered.

I gasped at the same time he sucked in a breath.

He looked devilishly handsome in a gold doublet and trousers, with no shirt underneath. An enormous codpiece bulged at his groin.

"That's provocative attire," I said, lowering my gaze to the tile floor.

"And you, my love, look exquisite," he said, stepping toward me. "Except for one thing…"

"What's that?" I said, lifting my eyes to see him approaching.

He fingered the golden placket at my chest, moving slowly across my skin back and forth, back and forth.

I shivered at the touch of his warm finger.

He ripped the placket from my gown with a knowing

smirk, and I gasped. His hands clamped down on my shoulders, spinning me to face the mirror.

"Look," he whispered in my ear, his hot breath caressing my skin like tendrils of silk.

My reflection showed a much different woman than before—far more daring and seductive.

He reached over my shoulder and traced the line of my cleavage with his finger, sending sparks racing through me.

"This is perfect," he purred.

I jerked away, taking a step back as I glared at him. "You said I wouldn't partake in any of the 'festivities,'" I spat.

"Oh no," he chuckled darkly. "But you must look the part." His eyes were laced with lust as he gazed at my reflection. He retrieved from his pocket a diamond necklace. When he fitted it around my neck, the huge diamond pendant dangled between my breasts like an invitation. "Are you ready?"

A flash of fear shot through me like a lightning bolt.

Malik must have noticed because he squeezed my shoulders.

"Don't worry, *amore mio*," he breathed into my ear. "I shall be with you every step of the way."

I took comfort in his assertive gaze and nodded. "All right, then. Let us depart."

Two elaborate masks lay on a table near the front exit.

Malik picked them up.

"Allow me." He stood behind me and tied one of the ornate lacy masks in place.

One side of the mask covered my left cheek, and the other coiled toward my forehead like a snake. The eye covering had tiny sparkling stars embroidered on it that seemed to twinkle in the moonlight. It felt soft and luxurious against my skin, almost as if it were trying to protect me from the world.

Malik gestured to a mirror hanging on the wall and said, "Look how beautiful you are."

I gazed at myself, stunned at my own reflection. Who was this person staring back at me?

Malik handed me his gold mask and said, "Would you please tie mine in place?"

I stood on tiptoes behind him and secured the silken cord.

We stood side by side in the mirror, connected through a searing, scorching gaze.

I could feel the cool night air blowing through the window, sweet with a summer's day and touched by magic. I was ready to face Raul, no matter how much my hand shook as I reached out to reposition my mask.

Footsteps clattered down the stairs. I turned to see Rosie running toward us, wearing one of her pretty new dresses.

"Livia!" she exclaimed. "You look like a princess!"

"Thank you, sweetie. You look like a princess, too."

Malik crouched and tapped her nose. "Don't stay up past bedtime, okay?"

"I won't, Eyan."

Eyan? No one called Malik by his first name. It was so sweet. Their connection continued to baffle me.

We hugged her goodbye and made our way to the carriage waiting for us outside.

Butterflies soared in my stomach as we approached Raul's lavish villa equally impressive as Malik's.

Malik guided the trotting horses up a stone-strewn path and through a sculpted opening. Carved marble couples engaged in passionate embraces on either side.

The carriage veered down a circular driveway surrounding a fountain entirely made of copulating couples. Water poured from their mouths, from jugs they held, or from their hands. Males even spewed water from their penises over the bodies of female forms.

The whole thing was so naughty, I blushed.

Malik glanced at me and smirked as he pulled the horses to a halt behind the carriage ahead of us. "That's nothing, my love. Wait until we get inside."

My nerves jangled and jolted.

We moved forward at a snail's pace until we reached the entrance, where masked groomsmen took control of the horses and helped me from the carriage.

Unapologetically, they watched me until Malik rounded the carriage and grasped my hand.

As Malik and I climbed the stone stairs leading to the mansion, he leaned over and whispered in my ear. "Be prepared to be eye-fucked throughout the night. Remember to be strong and avoid all advances. You're here for one thing and one thing alone."

A shiver coursed through my spine. The sun dagger. I had to find it.

"I understand," I breathed. I became aware of the absence of my Glock strapped between my thighs. I'd only brought my blade.

Would that be enough to defend me if needed?

With a lavish, wiggling swish of my hips, I sashayed through the door held open by a besuited butler.

"*Sei mozzafiato, bellezza mia,*" he murmured, reaching for my hand, and pressing it to his lips.

Malik ushered me away.

"He's right, you know. You are breathtaking. But you are not his or any other man's beauty." Nuzzling my ear, he whispered, "We shall pretend to be a couple. I'll be watching for Costa. Remember—you'll be in danger if he finds out you're a Timeborne."

He nibbled my earlobe, sending a thrill coursing through my abdomen.

"Find the dagger. Let nothing else stop you. Don't be tempted by anyone or anything," he said softly, running his nose around the shell of my ear.

The foyer opened to a vast space with chandeliers dangling from the ceiling and marble floors.

Beautiful people stood in small groups talking, clad in fur, silk, and leather. The women's cleavages were fully displayed, and men's codpieces advertised what lay between their legs. Some men were already bare-chested, like Malik, and a few women wore no tops, their breasts bouncing against their ribcages, jewels dripping from their necks.

Several naked women undulated through the crowd holding snakes that looped around their shoulders and waists. Naked men cavorted through the gathering bearing torches. They would sip from a flagon, bring the torch to their lips, and breathe fire.

Musicians sat in the corner playing hand drums, sitars, and flutes. The music added a sultry ambiance to the room.

The scent of musk, amber, and sandalwood incense drifted through the air as Malik guided me through the crowd.

Both men and women gazed at me, their eyes hooded behind their masks. Hands reached out and stroked me until my skin crawled.

Malik draped his arm around my shoulders, letting his hand slide beneath my bodice.

I wanted to push him away but felt I must play my part and pretend to enjoy his attention.

At times, he stroked my collarbones while nuzzling my

ear and murmuring things like, "*Tu sei bellissimo amore mio.*"

I became wet with arousal, and my steps grew languid, hips undulating in time with the music playing. I felt immersed in a dream, an erotic fantasy of epic proportions. This party was intoxicating.

A loud horn blared, and sexy young bare-breasted women drifted into the room wielding trays with drink and food.

The partygoers helped themselves and began feeding one another grapes, and drizzling honey across body parts and licking it off.

I closed my eyes briefly and tried to quash the excitement coursing through my body.

Malik continued touching and caressing me and then whispered in my ear. "I'm going to go find Raul, sweetness. I will distract him while you search for the blade."

A jolt of energy shook me out of my amorous impulses.

Malik drew his fingers up and down my neck, "You can do this, *amore*. Pretend to observe everything, as if deciding what to partake in."

I brought my lips close to Malik's ear, savoring his warmth. "Where do you suggest I look?"

He planted a trail of soft kisses along my jaw. "Look for an office or a study. Don't be afraid. If anything happens, get out at once."

I shivered, either from the kisses or the danger I would soon face.

He brushed his lips against mine. "You are strong, Olivia. You can do this. I trust you."

I withdrew from him, and we exchanged one long searing gaze. Then, I pivoted and sauntered away.

I wandered up a staircase covered with a rich burgundy carpet. Beautiful paintings hung from the walls, depicting naked women draped across love seats, a man between their legs fucking them or eating their pussies. One picture showed a man with an enormous cock tied to a gilded pole. Several women surrounded him, holding feather wands or pouring oil from a carafe down his muscled body.

As I made my way up the stairs, an unmistakable symphony of pleasure grew louder and more passionate. At each landing, couples in various states of undress walked past me, their eyes smoldering with heat and desire.

A couple paused before me, and the woman said, "*Vorresti unirti a noi?*"

She brought her palm up to my cheek and cupped my face.

"No," I answered in Italian. "I don't want to join you. Someone is waiting for me."

The woman glanced at her partner. "Can we watch?"

My mouth grew dry as I contemplated a convincing answer.

I was spared, however, when another man seized her arm and said, "Alexia! Allesandro! You must accompany Gianna and me."

Alexia cooed, "We'd love to, but we're trying to woo this beauty."

She gestured to me, but I slipped away and darted between a throng of approaching partiers.

That was close. As I continued down the hall, I noticed two costumed males guarding each door. I sauntered past them, letting my hand brush across their codpieces. If they were truly guards, they wouldn't be allowed to engage in the festivities while on duty.

The men's gazes focused on me, eye-fucking me, making me feel dirty inside. But I had to keep up my pretense.

A young man staggered down the hall, inebriated. When he saw me, his eyes glittered behind his dark mask.

"*Amore*, I've been looking for you," he slurred.

I turned to look over my shoulder, thinking he meant someone behind me.

"I meant you, my beauty." He fondled one of my breasts.

I batted his hand away, looking right and left for onlookers. It probably wasn't good form to deny someone's advances.

"Playing hard to get, eh?" He hooked his hand behind my neck and brought his boozy-breathed mouth toward my lips.

On instinct, I shoved my knee into his groin, and he doubled over, shouting, "*Puttana! Puttana!*"

I raised his head, seized his jaw, and growled at him. "There's this thing called consent, asshole."

I pushed his head away, and he crumpled to the floor, groaning.

I hurried down the hall.

Below me, women writhed in cages suspended from the ceiling. Men with greasy hair and beady eyes milled around them like carrion crows, drunkenly pawing at their breasts, slipping fingers between their legs, and committing other acts of blatant depravity.

I hastened my steps down the hall.

At the end of the corridor, I skittered into a room and closed the door behind me.

Welcome silence greeted my ears.

I pressed my back to the door and panted, catching my breath. This party was beautiful and terrible. I'd never been in such an environment, surrounded by people engaged in copulation, fellatio, threesomes, foursomes, and every act of depravity you could ask for. I didn't consider myself a prude, but this was over the top.

When my eyes adjusted to the dim light, I scanned the room. Vivid reds, oranges, and greens on a blue-black background rippled down the walls like marbled paper. Nothing stood out or seemed out of place. Thick curtains trimmed in black brocade hung from the ceiling to an unseen floor below. An ordinary-looking mirror, decorated with scrollwork, was poised above the mantel—black frames and beveled mirrors hiding anything beyond them.

I pressed my ear against the door to listen for anyone approaching. *Nothing.* I tiptoed through the room, investigating.

The room was lined with stone bookcases, the dark recesses between them filled with ancient skulls and bones. The ceiling was painted a deep red, as if an apocalypse had stained the heavens. Carvings in the stone depicted scenes of torture and death. This was not just Raul's library but his throne room and church, where he displayed his trophies.

I picked up a leering skull and shuddered. *Had this been a Timeborne or a Timebound?* I set the head back on the shelf, my stomach roiling with disgust.

A table sat pushed against the back wall.

Across it lay documents containing finely sketched plant illustrations. I picked one of them up and read *Atropa belladonna* next to a lifelike drawing of the plant. The picture was so detailed even the fine hairs on the buds were depicted.

I set this drawing down and picked up another labeled *Poison Hemlock*. This one showed tiny white flowers arranged in umbrella-shaped clusters atop branched stems. It appeared so lifelike I thought I could pluck it from the stem.

Next to the plant illustrations sat a stack of parchments. The top one showed an elaborate drawing of a dagger. I sifted through the pages below, finding more knives. My heart clattered about in my ribcage when I saw a blade like mine.

I pressed my fingertips to my mouth.

Yet another stack held hand-drawn Timebound necklaces.

"Oh my God," I whispered. "This is a detailed database, drawn by hand, of Timebornes and Timebounds knives worldwide, I'll bet. Holy hell! There's even a drawing of my dagger. I'll bet they've even cataloged Emily's necklace."

A sense of panic pushed through me, making me feel weak. I had to find the sun dagger and get the hell out of here, fast.

Where could it be?

I hurried toward the massive desk and began opening drawers and shuffling through the contents. *Nothing! Damn it! Maybe it's hidden inside the books?*

I took out book after book, opening each one and riffling through the pages in search of a secret hiding place. Then, I'd slide the book back into place.

Many of these leather-bound volumes were scientific tomes on poisonous plants, on creating tinctures from the leaves and roots. Everything a mad scientist hell-bent on ridding the Earth of Timebounds and Timebornes would need to exact punishment.

My stomach lurched and churned from both the contents held in the pages and my quest for the sun dagger.

Where is it, where is it, where is it?

I was so engrossed in my search for the knife that I paid no attention to the footsteps approaching the door—until the door opened.

I stiffened, slowly sliding the tome in my hands back in place. Shit. How could I explain my actions? I was in trouble, big time.

"This isn't what you think," I stammered, not daring to turn around.

"Isn't it?" a deep male voice said. "I'm afraid you're

mistaken. It's obvious to me you're in a room where you don't belong. There's a penalty for spying around."

"Is there?" I clutched my hands together to keep them from shaking. "What is it?"

"Twenty lashes."

My mind raced for a way out. I couldn't find one—there was no plausible reason for my presence in this room.

There was only one thing I could do now, and that was to fight.

Slowly, I turned around.

CHAPTER TWENTY

ROMAN

If Raul Costa thought his parties were unique, he had best borrow a page from history. As a Timeborne, I'd seen a lot of depraved activities, mainly when serving under Emperor Severus in ancient Rome. The emperor's parties transformed into orgies in which every act, from the sacred to the profane, was freely exchanged.

When I stepped into Raul Costa's villa, it felt like a paltry reenactment of what had taken place in Severus' palace. I'd seen it all before: naked people, half-naked people, fire swallowers, snake dancers. It only tormented me and served to stir my longing for Olivia.

"Looks to be a grand evening," the count said as we crossed the foyer.

I forced a smile and responded, "Doesn't it?" not sure if I wanted the night to end in success or failure.

The count had provided costumes for all of us, even Tristan.

I turned to look at Tristan, who gawked like a schoolboy. He'd never been to a sex party if his stunned expression was any indication. "You don't get to partake, Tristan, sorry."

His mouth snapped shut, and he pivoted his head to look at me. "What did you say?"

"All of this," I said, gesturing to the ballroom facing us, "is off-limits to you, do you understand?"

Tristan rolled his eyes and flashed a smirk. "Off-limits. Yes, master," he spat out mockingly. He crossed his arms over his chest and challenged me with an arched eyebrow. "I suppose you get to do whatever you feel like?"

"I have no interest in whores, or the kind of sexual proclivities found here." Ice dripped from my words. "Nor should you be—you'll likely catch a disease. Do you think sixteenth-century Italians were immune to STDs?"

He scowled, but I sensed he was still intrigued.

"We'll all have a good time. There are whores aplenty." The count's eyes gleamed as he surveyed the crowd. "Do what you like. Drink freely! Enjoy!"

"I don't get to do anything," Tristan whined in English. "You two get to have all the fun."

"What is your manservant saying?" the count asked.

"Complaining as usual," I said.

"Pity," the count said. "Hand him a drink and tell him to enjoy himself. I'm about to do the same. I'm hoping to find Raul and catch up with him."

He strode away, disappearing into the crowd.

"You're to find a quiet place in the corner and sit, Tristan. That's it," I said.

His sour expression stared at me through the mask on his face. "Like a good boy."

"Yes, like a good boy. Can you just do what you're told for once?"

"Yes, my lord," Tristan said, shuffling toward a chair shoved against the wall. He plunked down with a thud. "How's this? Satisfied?"

"It's perfect. Have a good time." I smiled and then headed into the ballroom.

When I caught a glimpse of the woman's red hair, my heart thundered. Everything about her—her curvy shape, the breathtaking beauty obscured by the mask—could only mean one thing: Olivia was here. Yet, even though my heart raced with excitement, I couldn't help but feel a twinge of nervousness as I wondered what would happen if she recognized me.

Each cell in my body craved to touch and hold her, and my heartbeat became a soaring staccato. I wanted to run to her, grab her, and kiss her wantonly—until I saw the man by her side.

He looked strangely familiar, but I couldn't place where I'd seen him before. But I felt like I knew him.

Whoever he was, he nuzzled her neck and kissed her jawline.

An intense stab of jealousy twisted my gut.

As I watched, Olivia appeared to be playing along but not really interested.

Of course, she's not interested. Her heart belongs to me… *We are forever soulmates.*

Then she laughed and brushed her fingers along his neck.

Insecurity pinned me in place. Did she like his attention? Had she given up on me?

The male couldn't keep his hands or mouth from her. How could any man? Wherever she walked, hungry wolfish leers devoured her. She left a wake of desire wherever she went.

But this dark-haired man by her side. I *knew* this man. I'd seen him before…but where?

He brought his mouth to Olivia's lips and brushed hers. They seemed so…intimate with one another.

A low growl emerged from my throat. Whatever claim he thought he had over my wife would have to end—now.

I pushed past the crowd, intending to confront this stranger and claim my wife.

But the pair separated, and Olivia headed toward the stairs.

I tracked her, staying a distance behind.

Men and women continued their lame seduction acts with Olivia, but she rebuffed them.

A woman draped her arms around my neck and cooed, "Well, hello there. You look like you could use some company. I'm available."

Her gilded gown fell well below her full breasts. Rubies dangled between her cleavage and dripped from her ears.

"I can see that," I said in Italian. "But I'm *not* available."

I pushed her away from me and craned my neck past the woman to find Olivia, but she'd disappeared. My heart sank. I had to find her. I skirted around the woman, ignoring her pleas and protests, and headed in the direction I'd last seen Olivia.

I nodded to the guards at each door along the long hallway and said, "Sto cercando il mio compagno di giochi. I suoi capelli sono del colore delle fiamme. L'hai vista?"

"*Si*," they each replied. "You are looking for your play-mate. Your flame-haired lover is that way."

The last guard smirked. "Save some for us, friend."

He and his fellow guard laughed.

"Si, si," I said, smiling, thinking, no way in hell will I share her. I've already shared her enough tonight with a stranger. Once I claim her again, she'll know who she belongs to.

I hurried past them to find a man doubled over, writhing,

and moaning on the carpeted floor. "Did a woman with hair the color of flames do this to you?"

"*Sì, è una puttana*," he said with an effort.

I gave him a swift kick with my boot. "My wife is no whore, I can assure you. You probably put your hands where they don't belong."

There was no one in the corridor ahead. I tiptoed across the plush carpet, putting my ear to each door. *Nothing.* When I reached the last entrance, faint scraping sounds echoed within, as if someone was quietly moving furniture across a wooden floor.

This is where Olivia is. She's looking for something. Perhaps she's on a quest for the sun dagger, too.

I slowly turned the polished brass knob and eased the door open.

Olivia braced, holding her beautiful back stiff.

"This isn't what you think," she said in Italian, facing the bookshelf.

Oh, Olivia. How I've missed the sound of your voice.

"Isn't it?" I replied, also in Italian, disguising my voice. "I'm afraid you're mistaken. It's obvious to me you're in a room where you don't belong. There's a penalty for spying around."

"Is there?" Her shoulders tensed. "What is it?"

"Twenty lashes."

Slowly, she turned around. Her brow furrowed when she saw me, but she gave no signs she recognized me.

My hair had been cut short, and my jaw shaved. Then, there was this fine costume Count Montego had given me to wear tonight.

Deep blue leather breeches hugged me like a second skin. A close-fitting, waisted, padded doublet in the same rich blue covered my torso. Sleeves had been sewn into the armholes of the high-necked jacket. Ermine fur and gold embroidery served as accents.

The count had urged the seamstress to forego the sleeves.

"He'll want to take it off soon after our arrival," he'd said with a chuckle.

"No, please, sew them on," I'd said to her, resisting the count's suggestion, not wanting to engage with any woman other than Olivia.

"At least open up the jacket." The count had stood before me, fussing with the doublet until it hung open. "You must give something to tease the women. They'll all have eyes for you."

I'd relented to that, at least until I'd arrived. Then, I'd fastened the hooks and eyes, securing the doublet.

My mask was the same striking blue as the doublet, shielding my cheeks, nose, and eyes from view. I was sure that my short haircut and fine clothes served to baffle Olivia and make her think I was a wealthy Italian.

Olivia's gaze fell to the floor. "I'm sorry. I lost my way. I didn't realize this was someone's office."

"I don't believe you," I said, speaking in Italian with a slightly lower pitch than my normal voice.

"Oh, but you must believe me, good sir. I had far too much to drink and lost my way." Her gaze flickered between me and the floor.

I stalked toward her. "I think you're a spy and up to something."

Olivia gasped. "No, I'm not a spy. I simply stumbled my way here into this room."

Before I could back her into the bookcase, she scurried to the right, away from my reach.

She lifted the volume of skirts cascading around her body, revealing her shapely legs.

My eyes glittered.

"Yes, please," I said. "I'll have some of the silk beneath your skirts."

Olivia whirled away from me, reaching beneath her gown. When her hand returned, she held her dagger. She bared her teeth and thrust the knife at me. "I'm going to kill you."

I leaped away from her, pivoted, and seized the hand holding the blade.

"Drop it," I hissed.

"No!"

My fingers bore down on her wrist. "*Drop it!*"

She cried out and released the dagger where it clattered to the floor.

"I'll find another way to kill you," she hissed. "I'm a trained fighter."

I kicked her blade out of the way, then backed her into the bookshelf. I took both wrists and pinned them over her head against the wood frame of the bookshelf. "I'd like to see you try."

I leaned forward and nuzzled her nose like that stranger had.

She yielded to me, then resisted. "Stop, *please.*"

I gripped both wrists in one hand and then used the other knuckles to stroke her soft cheek. "Why should I? I saw you doing the same thing with a man downstairs. It was most arousing. It stirred the fire of desire for you, so I followed you up here."

"That man meant nothing to me. He is a friend. That's all."

Is she telling the truth?

"He's a friend, you say. If that's how you behave, I'd like

to be your friend, too," I whispered. I brought my nose to her ear and nuzzled the shell of her ear.

Her eyes closed, and her head fell back.

"*Mio Dio*," she breathed.

"See? You are interested in me."

"No!" She writhed and squirmed. One of her breasts popped free from the bodice.

I dropped my hand and circled the pigment surrounding her nipple. "You're a breathtaking woman. I'm afraid I must claim you as my own."

Her chest heaved with deep, gasping breaths.

"I'm not going to hurt you, my love," I murmured, then licked a lazy line down her neck.

"*Mio Dio*," she breathed again.

"I want to have my way with you." I thrust my hips against her soft belly, letting her feel my rigid erection. "But only if you consent."

Oh, what torture it had been to be away from Olivia. Now that I had her, I would never let her go.

"You can't," she said, grinding her hips against me.

"Can't I? Tell me, why not?" I brushed my lips against her mouth the way the stranger had.

These lips are mine.

Olivia's mouth grew soft and pliant, and for a second, I thought she might kiss me back. But then she wrenched her face to the side. "I have a husband. I love him with all my heart and refuse to betray him."

"At this party, anything goes. I will give you all the plea-sure in the world, and your husband will be none the wiser." I kissed and nibbled her neck, sensing the throbbing pulse beneath the skin.

"Please stop this!" she cried. "My husband…"

"Where is this so-called husband of yours?" I said. "He's

not here. But I am."

I bit down on the juncture between her neck and shoulder, then sucked.

"Oh, God," Olivia said in English, her head falling back. "What are you doing to me?"

"What any loving husband would do to his wife had they been apart for far too long," I said in my normal voice.

Olivia stiffened. "Roman?"

I released her and ripped the mask from my face.

A myriad of emotions flashed across her face, from shock to elation, to anger.

Then she drew back her hand and slapped my face. "Roman! You bastard! I thought you were going to have your way with me."

I caressed my stinging face. The tip of my tongue darted across my lips as a wicked smile curved my lips. "You want to play rough? I can play that way."

Olivia just studied me as if considering my offer. Then her mouth formed an O, and she embraced me, kissing my face everywhere. "Roman! I'm so sorry! It's just that I was terrified, thinking I would be thrown into a dungeon and tormented with poisons in someone's sick experiment. And then, when you kept teasing me, I became confused. I thought I knew you…even disguising your voice, you sounded familiar. And your touch…good God, your touch intoxicated me. I felt betrayed by my own body."

I eased her away from me and stroked her cheek with my knuckles. "I'm sorry to have played with you, my love. I knew it was you behind that mask."

I gently lifted the feathered ornament from her face.

We simply stared at one another.

I drank in the sight of her beautiful face. A few tiny lines framed her eyes, adding to the overall picture of a life marred by tragedy. The weight of those experiences was written in the lines on her face, but it never dragged her beauty down.

I knew I must look older, too, ravaged by the impossible circumstances we found ourselves in.

I cupped her jaw with my hands. "Olivia," I breathed. "How long has it been?"

"Far too long. At times I feared never seeing you again. When we arrived in Italy, I knew you were close, but I didn't know where to look to find you. But you found me."

"And now I'm going to claim you," I said. "You're mine, all mine. No one else's. I'm going to erase all traces of that other man from your skin, from your soul."

I dropped my mouth to hers in a savage, consuming kiss.

Her lips felt like medicine long denied to my soul.

The music from downstairs vibrated against the floor, against the bookshelf, in time with my beating heart. The loud drumbeats thrummed into my legs.

Trickles of distant laughter rippled into my awareness as Olivia and I ground our lips together. My heart leaped about in my ribcage like a wild stallion, exultant. It beat in a manner at once excited and terrified. I had located her— indeed, I had truly found her.

Downstairs, upstairs, everywhere, there was depravity and debauchery. Eroticism pounded against the walls and beat against the floor. Wanton displays of coupling were freely engaged in, creating a thick atmosphere of lust.

Here, inside this shadowed space, we indulged in the sacred; two lovers joined again, touching stars as we familiar- ized ourselves with each other's mouths.

She fumbled with my doublet, tearing it apart to reveal my chest.

Once again, our gazes tangled.

She swept her hands over my chest as she said, "The last

time I saw you, we were in the teepee, and you were about to go to war."

"That bloody war is a distant memory," I said, letting my fingers trail across her collarbone and around the pendulous breast that had escaped her bodice.

"I thought you died," she breathed, her words laced with pain.

"I thought I died, too. But enough talking—I need to show you how I feel." I thrust my hips against her.

The bookshelf gave slightly.

We both tensed.

"Did you feel that?" Olivia whispered.

"Yes." I lowered my mouth to hers again, sucking her sweet lips for nourishment. As I kissed her, I fingered her nipple, tugging it and teasing it into a tight bud.

She moaned into my mouth, the humming vibration snaking down my throat.

I let out a groan and slammed against her, driving my hips hard.

The bookshelf shuddered again.

I couldn't stop—I shoved my hips against her once more.

The bookshelf gave way, opening like a door.

Olivia screamed as we both fell backward.

I caught her and cradled her head in my hands as we tumbled to the floor. I winced as my knees struck the unforgiving wood.

But nothing mattered now but the woman in my arms. I had to have her. I palmed her freed breast while I fumbled with her voluminous skirt. "Good Lord, where are you beneath all these fabrics?"

Olivia laughed, helping me in my quest.

It seemed there were layers and layers of clothing preventing me from touching her skin.

My desperation increased as I clawed through her attire, the bone stays, the hooks, the miles of cloth, finally landing on short muslin undergarments. I seized the flimsy fabric with my teeth, tearing it away from her hips.

Olivia's musky scent filled my nose. "Christ, woman, I've missed the way you smell."

I took a long, deep inhale, filling my lungs with her signature fragrance.

The skirt still ballooned around her waist, but at least I could access her creamy, beautiful skin.

I got comfortable between her legs and drew my finger up her slick opening.

"Mine," I growled.

I pushed two fingers inside her wet silk and flicked her clit with my thumb.

"All yours," Olivia murmured.

I circled her pearl with the flat of my finger.

Olivia moaned and writhed beneath my touch.

"Do you know what this is sometimes called in Italian?"

"Tell me," she breathed.

"*Amor Veneris, vel dulcedo*. It is the love or sweetness of Venus." I lowered my mouth between her legs and licked her silken folds.

Olivia cried out. "Roman!"

"Yes, my love. Who owns this *amor Veneris*?"

"You do," she gasped.

I continued to lathe and stroke as the driving beat from the drums beat against the floorboards. My cock pulsed between my thighs, eager to enter her wet canal.

Her core milked my hand as her arousal built. But I wouldn't let her come around my fingers. She must climax around my cock.

The drums below grew frenzied, stirred by all the fucking,

sucking, and coupling people. Fueled by lust, drugs, and alcohol, they couldn't match the intensity of the lovemaking Olivia and I shared in this secret room. And yet we were held, all of us, in this throbbing vibration.

Frantic to enter Olivia, I shoved my breeches from my legs, grasped my erection, and fit it inside.

"Oh, God, Olivia," I said through clenched teeth.

"Fuck me, Roman." She clawed my ass. "Fuck me hard."

I reared back and plunged inside her. "Mine!"

"Yours," she whispered.

I thrust again. "Mine!"

An image of her and the stranger below flashed through my mind. I pictured him as grotesque, sneaking glances at me, his eyes glowing red like some monster as he took advantage of my wife. He taunted me as he kissed Olivia's neck, her shoulders, and her collarbone. His tongue danced across her skin.

My jealousy grew like a bonfire as I ravished my wife. *She's mine, not yours,* I silently growled to the stranger. *She's always been mine.*

Manic jealousy shot through my limbs. Whoever that man was, he would never have her. I would mark her, claim her, make her mine from this day forth. My hips bucked in rhythm with the driving beat shaking the walls. Each time I thrust into Olivia, I repeated my claim on her. *Mine, mine, mine, mine, mine.* I grunted and groaned in time with Olivia's sweet, guttural moans.

Lacing my fingers with hers, I drew her arms over her head and dropped my mouth to hers. *Mine, mine, mine, you're mine.* I kissed her with an all-consuming need, an intensity I'd never experienced.

Our bodies crashed together over and over, undulating,

craving, seeking. I was utterly out of my mind by my desire for Olivia.

Lightning bolts cascaded through my limbs, and I wrenched my mouth away from hers. "Oh, God, Olivia. I can't last much longer."

"Come inside me, Roman." Her sharp nails raked my back.

The pain collided with the pleasure, stoking my arousal.

I felt her tense around my cock, and the look on her face grew rapturous.

"Who do you belong to?" I roared.

"To you—only to you," she gasped, and then her head rolled from side to side, and she came with such force I had to let go, too.

I drove inside her, spilling my seed as she cried out my name, writhing in the throes of rhapsody.

Our moans and cries filled the air, joining the others until it felt like the entire house was in a state of orgasm.

Our euphoria sent us soaring like two shooting stars streaking through the heavens.

I held onto this feeling as long as I could.

But eventually, we fell back into the darkness of this secret room. I stroked Olivia's damp, disheveled hair away from her face.

"Olivia," I breathed. No other words were needed—not after what we'd just shared.

She tensed and stared past me at the room beyond the open bookcase. "Roman, we're in danger. We shouldn't linger. I'm here to find the sun dagger, and then we must get far away from this place. Do you know who Raul Costa is?"

"He is the host."

"He's a dangerous man. If he finds us, finds out that we're

Timebornes, he'll try and destroy us." She glanced at the new tattoo of the dagger on my arm.

My doublet had come off during our frenzied lovemaking.

"When did you get this? It's beautiful."

"I had it inked in Seattle when you and I were apart," I said.

"You must cover it up!" She urged me off her and scrambled to find the jacket.

When she saw it, she thrust it at me.

"Put this on. If anyone here sees your tattoo, they'll apprehend you, torture you, and ultimately kill you. That's what the Timehunters do. Raul is one of them."

"How do you know this?" I said, feeling around for my breeches.

"I have learned many things while we've been apart."

I stopped listening to her as something caught my eye.

"Olivia, look." I pointed toward an arched opening at the other end of this dark room.

She whirled around. "What?"

"That archway… Where do you think that goes?" I pointed toward the opening.

"Let's find out. We need a light of some kind." She pushed to stand and righted the skirt and petticoats.

The undergarment was useless as I'd ripped it in two.

We searched the office until we found a beeswax candle, a pewter candle holder, and a tinder box. Inside the box lay a sliver of wood coated with brimstone, a flint, a steel striker, and charred rags used for tinder.

I fiddled with the flint, steel striker, and tinder until tiny flames formed. Then, I lit the brimstone. I took the makeshift match and held it to the candle wick.

"I've got light—let's go," I said.

We both hurried toward the bookshelf and slid into the space behind it.

This room would never be the same—we'd purified and christened it with our love. It almost seemed to glow, or maybe it was just me.

I lifted the candle, and we peered into the gloom ahead.

"It looks like a staircase over there," I said, pointing to the archway.

"Maybe the dagger is down there!" Olivia clutched my arm. She pushed the bookshelf back into position until we were trapped.

"Why did you do that?" I said.

"If Costa finds we've breached this secret corridor, we'll be in peril. Let's see what's down there."

I held the candle high, sending dim light and shadows falling down the stairs. Then, I took the first step.

CHAPTER TWENTY-ONE
OLIVIA

My body felt sated from our lovemaking as we descended into the depths of Raul's house. I was so overjoyed, I grabbed the back of Roman's doublet before he took another step down the dark stairs. When he turned to see what I wanted, I kissed him unapologetically, running my hands across his back. We lingered in the kiss, tasting, teasing one another with our tongues and lips.

I wanted to stay here, immersed in the feel of his mouth against mine. I'd missed him with every cell in my body. Every breath I'd taken in his absence had been filled with longing. Now, he and I were together again.

Roman's eyes glistened as he looked at me. "I love you, Olivia, my beautiful flaming fire. I'm so happy to have found you again."

"I love you, too, Roman, my handsome warrior. With all my heart." I squeezed his hand.

Then, we descended the stone stairs. I pressed my palm to Roman's back as I followed him. Our single candle provided dim light in this cavernous corridor.

"Stop for a moment, please, and lift your light."

Roman did as requested, and the candle flame flickered across the rough polygonal masonry wall.

Plants were carved into the walls with the same care as the illustrations in the room above. I brushed my fingers against them, tracing the leaves, stems, and flowers.

"Look," I said. "The Timehunters are obsessed with cataloging and understanding poisonous plants. There are similar illustrations upstairs. They're so detailed; they look like photographs taken in my time."

A strange mustiness met my nose, growing stronger with each step.

"I wonder if it's safe to go down here. What if it's poison-filled?"

"Then, we'll soon be dead," Roman said. "But why would they set a trap if this place is supposed to be a secret?"

"You're probably right," I said.

Still, growing anxiety pulsed in my stomach.

We resumed our journey down the stairs.

Our footfalls echoed in the high-ceilinged corridor. Each step sounded like a thudding anvil.

I hoped the sound didn't carry to the rooms upstairs.

At the landing, we found ourselves in a skull-lined catacomb. Skulls had been stacked against the walls in neat, tidy rows.

A violent shudder swept my spine, and my hand flew to my sternum. "Oh, God. Roman, these bones were probably once Timebornes or Timebounds. And the Timehunters kept them as some sort of trophy. They're *so* sick."

An archway stood at the back of the room, past all the leering heads.

We trod across the calacatta marble floor and peeked into the circular room beyond.

The candlelight provided a shadowed glimpse of the vast round table filling the center of the space. On the walls hung paintings of plants, much like the ones upstairs, only these were in color.

"My God," I said. "They're like the modern-day scientists of my time, only with evil intent."

"Indeed." Roman approached the table.

Daggers had been arranged in a sunbeam pattern along the shiny surface. There were spaces where no blade rested. Perhaps those knives were on the Timehunters' "wish list."

The thought made my insides boil.

"One of these must be the sun dagger," I said. "Hold the candle over the table so I can see more clearly."

As Roman lifted the light, I brushed my fingers across the hilt of each knife.

The blades pointed toward the center, where a few cryptic symbols had been painted.

If this had been the 21st century, I would have whipped out my cell phone and documented the symbols. But this was 16th-century Italy, and I could only commit them to memory —not that I would be able to Google "cryptic symbols and their meaning" or anything.

At the far end, I spied a blade with a sun carved in the hilt. Tingles spread through my fingers as I looked at it.

"I think this is it! We've found the sun dagger! It looks like my knife, but bigger. And the script carved in the blade is different."

I picked it up and turned it back and forth in my hand.

"It looks so ancient—so powerful. And this sun…" I brushed my fingertips over the finely carved sun on the handle. "Exquisite…"

"Let's examine it later," Roman said. "We need to leave."

A loud scraping sound came from the walls.

Alarmed, I turned my head to see where it came from.

The wall panels were pivoting.

I let out a yelp and scooted around the table, ready to flee.

Three shadowy shapes, clad in black with black masks covering their faces, emerged from between the panels.

"The blade is not yours," one of them said. "It does not belong to you."

"Nor does it belong to you. You stole it." I tossed the sun dagger to Roman. "Here."

He shoved it inside his leather boot.

The cloaked figures moved in closer, surrounding us.

Roman and I crawled on top of the table. We snatched up the blades so fast they clanged in our hands as we took our fighting stances. With a snarl on my lips, I watched as one of the attackers lunged at me. Without breaking my gaze, I raised my foot and smashed my heel down into his hand with punishing force. Satisfaction surged through me as I heard the sickening crunch of bones shattering beneath my shoe.

He roared and scrambled onto the table, scattering daggers as his boots landed on the surface. He grabbed my arms and whipped them behind my back.

I tried to connect the back of my head with his nose without success.

Roman moved in close, snarling with contempt. He tipped the candle holder until molten wax began to flow like red-hot tears down the man's face. The wax engulfed his eyes, searing and blinding as it solidified into an ivory mask on his cheeks.

He screamed and batted the candle away. It clattered against the wall and fell to the floor, extinguishing. We were plunged into darkness.

I heard a knife swish through the air, Roman's grunt, and a thud.

"What happened?" I said, hoping Roman was still okay.

The man screamed and toppled to the floor.

"I slit his throat," Roman said.

"Raul is going to find you," the dying man wheezed. "He'll torture you and then kill you with the poison." And then he fell silent.

I felt utterly disoriented in the darkness. "Where are you, Roman?"

"I'm here." His hand landed on my cheek.

"Let's get back-to-back," I said.

Roman pressed his back to mine.

I slashed my blade viciously in front of me, a silent prayer on my lips that I'd strike down at least one of the guards. Triumph surged through me as a bellow of agony and rage rang out from my target, letting me know that I'd made the hit.

Now there was only one guard left.

Grappling sounds came from behind me. Roman moved away from me. Shouts, more cursing, and screams met my ears. I couldn't see a thing.

"Roman!" I cried.

"Let's get out of here. *Now*, Olivia!" He latched onto my fingers with an icy grip. "The last one is dead. Get out *now*!"

We scrambled out of the dark cavern and clawed our way to the door. I trembled as we inched through the room filled with glistening skulls. The bones lining the walls seemed to reach for me in desperation.

"Oh, God! My stomach is churning!" I gasped as nausea rose up in my throat.

Roman's grip on my arm tightened to a vice as he tugged me toward safety. My fingers were met with the cold, hard surface of an endless array of skulls, and I fought against my panic-induced tremors. When my foot finally found purchase on the steps, I could barely contain the wave of relief that washed over me.

Roman gave a triumphant shout, his voice echoing off the walls of our macabre surroundings.

Still hand in hand, we moved as quickly as we could up the dark staircase.

"How will we get out of here? You closed the bookshelf," Roman said when we reached the top landing.

"There's got to be a way to open it from the inside. You start at that end, and I'll start at this end," I said.

"Olivia, we're in total darkness—which end are you referring to?" Roman said.

I seized his shoulders and turned him to face opposite me. "You go that way. I'll go the other way. If you find a lever, a pull string, anything that feels like it should be pulled, cranked, or tugged, have at it."

"On it," Roman said.

I felt along the wall, crouching low and stretching high. Finally, my hand landed on some sort of protrusion. I pushed it, and a loud click came from the wall.

The bookshelf eased open a crack, revealing a sliver of light.

Roman and I rushed through the opening and closed the passageway behind us.

The office was illuminated by moonlight.

"What should we do now? We both look a mess." I glanced at Roman's fine doublet, now stained with blood. "But if you remove the soiled clothes, you'll reveal your tattoo."

"There's nothing I can do—not if my tattoo will flag me as a Timeborne. I can say it's wine." Then, he looked at me and said, "Take off your bodice."

"What? No!" I clutched the fabric to my chest.

"Olivia, you're as bloody as I am. Bloodier, in fact. Take it off. At least one of us has to look like we weren't in a fight to the death with Raul's henchmen. You'll blend in and provide a distraction," he said, smirking.

"Damn it!" I slid off my top and shoved it into a drawer.

I hoped we would be long gone when Raul discovered my crimson-stained garment and the bodies below.

Roman cracked the door and peered into the hallway. "It's time to get out. The only way this will work is if we act like we're completely inebriated, swaying, and slurring our words. Let's go now and make sure everyone sees us leaving. We have to be convincing!"

"Wait! Our masks!" I retrieved them from the floor, then strode toward Roman and affixed his mask to his head.

He tied mine on and gave me a quick kiss. "Ready?"

I nodded.

When we reached the part of the corridor previously filled with revelers, we found it mostly empty.

A black-clad guard stepped free of one of the rooms, fastening his fly. He paused when he saw us. "Why aren't you downstairs with the others?"

Roman and I glanced at one another.

Roman fondled one of my breasts and said, "I wasn't finished with her."

"No," I said, dropping my hand to his groin. "We haven't had enough of one another."

The guard scowled at us. "You were to head downstairs as soon as the bell tolled. No one is allowed to miss the big event."

"We were actually going to leave," Roman said. "But thank you for the invitation."

The guard blocked our egress. "No one leaves before the show is over. *No one.*"

He drew a sword from the scabbard by his side and held the tip at Roman's chest.

Roman put his hands up in surrender. "Of course. We understand. We'll head to the event straight away."

The guard's eyes narrowed behind his mask. "I'll accompany you to ensure you find your place in the audience."

"As you wish," Roman said smoothly.

The guard stared at Roman's jacket.

"It's wine," Roman said, grinning. "I'm so drunk I missed my mouth."

The guard shook his head and said, "Get moving."

We proceeded down the hall and descended the stairs.

I exchanged a worried look with Roman.

"Do you know what this show is?" he whispered in English.

"I'm afraid so. We're about to witness a Timebound or a Timeborne being mercilessly tormented. Malik told me about this. He said it's part of the annual event. The crowd thinks it's all an act, but it's not—the pain and suffering will be real."

Roman growled through clenched teeth. "You know I have questions about the nature of your relationship with Malik, don't you?"

"With Malik? Why?" I said cringing as I recalled the blurred lines between us.

"Because you belong to *me,* not him. I hope I made that clear upstairs."

I felt truly, maddingly, joyously possessed by Roman. "You have nothing to worry about."

When we reached downstairs, the guard jabbed Roman's back with the tip of his sword.

Roman winced.

"We're doing as told," he hissed to the guard.

"Just making sure. Go to the right and head toward the crowd in the back. The stage is the largest ballroom." The guard waved his blade about.

"We're going. Wouldn't miss it for the world," Roman said, sneering.

I turned to look at Roman's back.

Blood seeped through his doublet.

Roman caught my eye. "Don't worry about it, *amore*."

We picked our way through the scattered clothes and fallen food. I felt so vulnerable with no covering on my torso, as if I were part of the entertainment. I reached down and scooped up a woman's top, which I tugged on, fastening the tiny buttons.

We headed through a set of French doors.

I leaned over and whispered in Roman's ear, "We've got to find Malik and get out of here."

"Keep an eye out," Roman said. "I need to find Tristan."

I came to an abrupt stop. "Tristan? The guy I used to date? What's he doing here?"

A queasy feeling rocked my belly.

Roman sighed. "It's a long story. Let me just say he's Balthazar's son."

My eyebrows shot up. "You mean I was dating a demon's son?"

Someone behind me pushed me, and I stumbled forward.

Roman took my hand. "Come, Olivia. There is much to discuss, but it must wait. For now, our primary objective is to escape this hellhole."

He guided us through the crowd toward the edge where we could make a hasty escape.

We were surrounded by an eager crowd, their anticipation palpable in the air. The stage before us was a blank canvas and had yet to be graced with any performers.

Roman stood behind me and drew me close, wrapping his arms around my shoulders.

I welcomed the feeling of being cocooned by him as if we stood in our own private world. I couldn't get enough of him and longed to be somewhere remote where we could revel in one another.

My mind also reeled with the news I'd just learned about Tristan. Had Balthazar put him up to dating me? How long was I tracked by that foul demon? My entire life? I shivered.

Roman gently rocked me from side to side and whispered in my ear, "Olivia, my love, I've been having these recurring dreams ever since we separated from one another."

"Have you?" I pushed my cheek back and forth against his jaw. "Tell me about them."

"They're always about you, me, and Malik. When I saw you with him earlier, I was both insanely jealous and strangely comforted to see you with him. I didn't know who he was, but I did. Does that make sense?" His gaze bore into me.

"Yes, like when you found me upstairs. My mind said you were the enemy—but my heart kept saying, 'he's here; Roman is back.'"

"Exactly." He kissed my cheek. "So, in the dreams, I'm usually on horseback, galloping through a field side by side with Malik. We seem to be great friends, or brothers, out hunting, returning home. I'm always eager to get home to my wife and children—and you are, of course, the person I'm eager to see."

"Then what happens?" I frowned, wondering if these matched my horrific dreams.

"As we approach my home, I see flames. The entire village is burning in some of the dreams. But *my* house is always on fire. And you and the children have burned to death. It's awful. I usually wake up sobbing or in a cold sweat, with my heart beating erratically."

I turned in his arms to face him. "I keep having similar dreams. They're horrific and painful. I hope it doesn't portend the future."

Roman kissed my nose. "God help us, so do I. But they seem to carry a feeling of something that has already happened. And they also speak to some inexplicable connection with Malik I can't for the life of me comprehend."

I squirmed in his arms, thinking of how Malik had tried to seduce me—and how I had nearly succumbed to his seduction.

How can I tell Roman this?

"What could they mean? And why are we both having the same kind of nightmare?"

"I don't know. But look." Roman pointed behind me.

I pivoted back around and leaned against him, letting him envelop me again.

A handsome man strutted onstage, his arms lifted, a big grin spread across his face. He was dressed in black and blood-red with a crimson mask covering his eyes.

The crowd let out cheers and applause.

The man shushed the crowd. "Welcome, welcome, everyone. Most of you know me, but I am Count Raul Costa for those first-timers to my grand event."

The cheers increased, many of the partygoers calling, "Raul! Raul!"

"Thank you. Thank you, one and all." He bowed several times, then quieted the crowd again. "As you know, only the best of the best are invited to this masquerade ball. I hope it has been to your liking and has satisfied your hunger." He waggled his eyebrows.

Many people laughed.

"I'm still hungry," a man called out.

More laughter.

Raul grinned. "You shall have time to slake your hunger. But first, I have a show for you all to help stir your desires."

A woman let out a long moan.

"Exactly," Raul said, strutting back and forth before us.

Again, laughter broke out.

"As you know," Raul bellowed, "the society I belong to is committed to finding the people who threaten our world—the Timebounds and the Timebornes."

Gooseflesh peppered my skin, and sweat moistened my forehead.

"Shit," I whispered.

Raul pumped his fist in the air. "We will destroy them! We will protect you!"

The audience rejoiced, whooping and hollering.

"Bring in the entertainment," Raul shouted, cupping his hands around his mouth.

Several fire dancers pranced onto the stage, twirling batons engulfed in flames at each end. They stayed to the back, providing a backdrop of pyrotechnics.

Two guards dragged in two people, a man and a woman.

They both had black bags over their heads and had been stripped naked. Their hands had been lashed together behind their backs.

Bile shot into the back of my throat.

"Remember, everyone. These two are actors. This is all to show you how we keep you safe." Raul beamed as the guards pulled the resistant couple toward him, then released them with a shove.

The woman fell to her knees, and the man lurched forward, managing to keep his balance.

Raul whipped the bag from the woman's head.

A rag had been secured to her mouth, and her mask was slightly skewed. But the terror in her eyes was evident.

"They're not actors," I whispered to Roman, who hugged me tightly. "This is as real as it gets."

I felt dizzy, like I might collapse at any moment.

The woman let out a keening sound.

Raul nodded to the guard who sliced the bindings around her mouth and those cinching her wrists together.

She let out an ear-piercing scream.

At the same time, the fire dancers breathed a stream of fire from their mouths.

"Wonderful performance," Raul exclaimed. "Isn't she wonderful?"

The onlookers applauded, shouting, "Brava, Brava!"

Raul ripped off her mask.

Tears streamed from her eyes as she continued to wail. "Don't hurt me! I'll do whatever you want, but please don't hurt me!"

"Child, this is just for fun," Raul said, lifting her arm and petting her skin like a cat. He produced a small knife, like a switchblade, and sliced her wrist in one swift move.

"We have to help her!" Roman hissed into my ear.

"No, no! If we try to help, we'll both be up there, too." I began to cry, too, repulsed by this horror show.

Raul gestured to the guard who procured a gold goblet. Once the goblet was in his despicable hands, Raul held it beneath the woman's wrist, and the blood dripped into it.

"What marvelous sleight of hand!" a man yelled.

"It looks so real!" a woman exclaimed.

Raul raised the chalice to his lips and drained it. He gave a satisfied groan and wiped his mouth with the back of his hand.

I pressed my hand to my mouth as the urge to vomit overtook me.

The fire dancers seized the batons between their teeth and performed cartwheels across the stage.

Raul tossed the grail into the crowd.

People screamed and scrambled to catch it.

"Oh, God, I can't stand this. I think I'm going to be sick." My mouth filled with saliva.

As Raul stood behind the woman, he stroked the hair that drooped on her neck. Then, he seized a hank of her glistening locks, lifted her head, and slashed her throat.

Blood gurgled from the wound and her mouth, and she slumped to the ground.

The audience roared its approval.

The fire dancers tossed their flaming batons into the air and deftly caught them.

I leaned over my knees and dry-heaved. Nothing came out but strings of spit.

When I righted myself, Roman said, "Let's go. I don't care what the rules are. We've got to get out of here."

As the guards dragged the woman offstage, Raul sauntered toward the man. "Let's have some more fun, shall we?"

The din of noise was deafening.

Roman began sidling through the crowd, clutching my hand.

Raul whipped off the man's hood. Roman halted, staring at the stage.

"Oh, fuck. It's Tristan. I told that damn fool to stay put."

Raul sliced through Tristan's gag and wrist restraints.

With his mask still in place, Tristan began screaming and waving his arms. "I'm not who you think I am. You have the wrong person! Let me go!"

Raul beamed. "Oh, we have the right person, all right.

Just look at the necklace dangling on your neck. It's a Time-bound necklace. Your kind is dangerous and a threat to society."

He captured Tristan's arm and held it high as if Tristan had won a prize fight, and slashed his inner arm with the switchblade.

Another guard handed him a goblet which Raul held beneath Tristan's bleeding wrist.

Unintelligible, garbled words streamed from Tristan's mouth.

Raul brought the chalice to his mouth again and drank Tristan's blood.

"This is better than the last," he said, tossing the goblet toward the crowd.

We were all plunged into darkness.

The fine hairs over my body stood as fear swept through me. I bore down on Roman's hand.

Screams and shouts came from the crowd.

When the blackness cleared, Balthazar stalked toward the stage, his expression one of fury.

"What the fuck are you doing, Raul?" he bellowed, his voice making the ground tremble. "Why is my son on stage with you drinking his blood?"

Raul cringed and stepped back. Then, he pulled himself together and clapped. "Well, well, well. Look who's back in Italy. It's been a long time, Lord Balthazar."

"I see you're the same bloodthirsty vermin as always," Balthazar said, seizing the collar of Raul's crimson doublet.

Raul shook him off.

Sensing this new danger, the crowd stood silent.

"How is it that I caught your son? This must be destiny," Raul said, but beads of sweat lined his upper lip, belying his boasting confidence. "I didn't even know you had a son."

"I'm going to burn your house down and kill every last Timehunter here," Balthazar said, his voice echoing all around us.

"Who gave birth to this spawn?" Raul said. "Was it that bitch Alina?"

"I killed Alina," Balthazar stated flatly.

Raul jerked as if surprised by Balthazar's admission.

Raul's mouth gaped. "I thought you were in love? Yet you killed her?" He backed away, moving behind Tristan. Then, he grasped Tristan's hair. "If you come closer, I will release the belladonna, and then all of you will suffer."

Balthazar waved his hands. "Childish threats. How about I save you the bloodbath, and you and your friends can live? Just hand over my son."

A wicked sneer curled Raul's lips. "Why should I? I have your son—you killed mine long ago, and I will destroy yours. An eye for an eye and a tooth for a tooth."

As if to illustrate his words, he deftly carved around Tristan's eye.

Tristan shrieked.

A thunderous roar flew from Balthazar's throat, and his hands shot into the air.

The entire villa trembled like an earthquake making the marble columns crack and shatter. Flames exploded from the demon's palm, devouring the walls, and spreading to the audience with a ferocity that their screams could not match. The blaze spread quickly through the velvet curtains and silk fabrics of the furniture, leaving nothing but charred ruin in its wake.

Balthazar disappeared into thin air with Tristan.

Roman yanked me toward the exit.

I kicked off my shoes which hindered my progress and raced behind him.

A man sat in the driver's seat of an elegant carriage.

"Roman! Over here!" another man called from inside the coach.

Roman sprinted toward the carriage, yanked open the door, and practically threw me inside. Then, he leaped in next to me.

I glanced at the handsome, elegant-looking man who studied me from his seat opposite me.

"Hi-yah, hi-yah!" the driver called, flicking a whip to the horses' flanks.

The carriage lurched, and the horses reared.

I screamed and clung to Roman.

We hurtled down the driveway like a wild stampede, the screams of the horses drowning out cries of anguish from the burning ruins. Choking smoke obscured the carnage, but we felt its weight clinging to us inescapably as ghostly screams lingered in our ears and souls. The specter of the fire seemed to follow us, its destruction etched into our memories forever. It seemed impossible that we could recover after the events of this night. We'd left behind nothing but pain and sorrow.

Everyone had been affected by what happened and I felt powerless to do anything about it.

CHAPTER TWENTY-TWO

ROMAN

Tearing my gaze away from the macabre sight of Costa's burning estate, I tucked Olivia in my arm in the back of the carriage. My eyes desperately searching for solace, but all that remained was the memory of crimson blood dripping from the walls and gut-wrenching screams piercing the air. Even as we pulled away, I could still feel disgust coursing through my body — not even my years as a gladiator had prepared me for such a monstrous scene.

The horses' hooves thundered along the road, rounded the corner, and the burning estate came into view once more.

Costa's elegant villa burned like a hellish nightmare. Screams and cries of anguish filled the air as the partygoers, immersed in the throes of pleasure a mere hour ago, were now burned to death.

Even with my ability to witness and withstand horrible acts of torture and violence, I could not stomach the agony all around me.

"Oh, God," Olivia sobbed, pressing into my side.

I wrapped her in my embrace. "Shh, my love, we're safe."

"Are we?" she wailed. "Are we ever safe when that madman is around?"

I pulled her shaking body close.

Count Montego sat across from us in the back of the coach. His face appeared pale, and the corners of his eyes creased in concern. He stared out the window at the night sky, seeming like he was in shock. "Such a tragedy! I'm appalled such a thing has occurred."

"Indeed," I said, wondering how much the count knew about Balthazar. Raul seemed to have regarded Balthazar as a known acquaintance.

"Do you think the fire dancers could have started the blaze through their careless actions? The way they were tossing around their batons…" The count shook his head. "Anything could have happened."

And there's my answer—he knows nothing about the kind of treachery Balthazar is capable of.

"Perhaps. Whatever it is, it's a horrifying tragedy." I rubbed my palm up and down Olivia's arm to soothe her.

Olivia buried her face in my shoulder. Her cries were unrelenting.

The three of us grew silent, save for Olivia's sobs.

"Your manservant, where is he? Did the flames consume him in a torturous death?" The count's body was rigid, and his shoulders tensed up to his ears. "What a horrific fate."

"You didn't see the show?" I asked him.

"No," the count replied with a strained voice. "I had other matters to attend to."

Other matters? Knowing the count, those matters were probably between the legs of a lusty woman. I gave Olivia a side-eye. "No, he left with someone. I'm sure he's all right."

The count nodded.

"Good. That's good." He studied Olivia, his expression

somber; his head canted to one side. "And where did this beauty come from? I've never seen her before."

"This is my wife," I said, holding her close.

"Ah, splendid! Your wife! Such a shame she had to witness the horror tonight. Our town will mourn and grieve this for ages, I fear." He trained his gaze out the window.

I, too, turned to see the villa, engulfed in smoke and flames, receding into the distance.

Olivia let out one last sniffle and straightened. "I apologize for my manners." She thrust her hand toward the count. "I'm Olivia Alexander, wife to this wonderful man by my side, like he told you. We've been apart for a long time. I was overjoyed to be with him tonight, but the party ended in a way none of us could have envisioned."

She took a shuddering breath.

Count Montego leaned forward, as did Olivia. He drew her hand to his mouth and kissed her knuckles. Releasing her, his gaze landed on a bunch of crumpled news sheets on the seat next to him. He seized the news sheets like a life preserver in a raging sea, clutching them to his chest as if they were all that stood between him and a howling void. He opened the paper with trembling hands, anxiously skimming the headlines as if they held his salvation from the tragedies of the night.

I spun around to face Olivia and our eyes met like lightning. With a heartbeat like thunder racing through me, I leaned in and gently kissed the top of her head. "It's so good to be back with you, *amore mio*," I declared as my lips moved over her cheek in hungry desperation. A soft sigh escaped her lips and sent shivers down my spine as she melted into the crook of my arm, placing a delicate hand on my chest. I breathed in the scent of her, letting it fill me up until I thought I would burst.

"I'm so thankful to have found you," she whispered back. "I didn't realize how empty I'd become without you."

"I'm the same. I coped but couldn't thrive." I kissed her eyelids, sucking away the tears that lingered.

She made a small moan.

As I continued to kiss her face and neck, my ardor grew. Ignoring the count's presence in the coach, I dropped my mouth to hers. All the longing and unrequited desire I'd experienced during our time apart came rushing to the forefront. The sex we'd shared upstairs had been a tease to my passion. I was on fire for Olivia emotionally, physically, and spiritually.

She climbed into my lap and pressed herself against my stiff erection.

Our kisses grew more frantic until it seemed we would devour one another. I knew she had no knickers on; I'd ripped them apart with my teeth. And the feeling of her pressing her bare core against my breeches made me wild with desire.

The carriage lurched and bumped along the road, caught in the horses' galloping gait. The entire coach lifted off the ground and landed with a thud, causing Olivia's body to slam on top of me.

"Oh, God, Roman!" Olivia moaned into my mouth. She threaded her fingers through my hair.

My hands were around her hips, urging her up and down my stiff length.

I was just about to thrust my tongue into her mouth the way I longed to slide my cock inside when a vision flooded my mind. As clear as day, I pictured us in a dark cave, sated from lovemaking, curled around one another. Our bodies were slick with sweat, and Olivia's hair hung wildly about her head. Her eyes glistened with adoration as she traced the contours of my torso.

I stiffened and pulled away from the kiss.

"Roman! What is it?"

"I…I don't exactly know." I dismissed the vision as mental folly, caught sight of the count watching us, and urged Olivia off my hips.

"Pardon us, Count Montego, for our unchecked ardor. We have been apart for an eternity."

A raging inferno blazed within me, and a rosy redness painted Olivia's cheeks.

"Yes, please forgive our behavior—we were terrified that Roman could be lost in the fire. Our love for one another was too much to contain."

Olivia wrung her hands together nervously in her lap.

"No need to apologize," the count affirmed with a flourish of his hand. A wistful smile spread across his lined face. "I, too, experienced youthful love. My fingertips can still recall her soft skin, and my lips remember her sweet kiss. The raw passion of our connection was undeniable."

"What happened to her?" I said.

The count simply shook his head and resumed reading his news sheet.

Olivia and I exchanged a silent understanding before she spoke.

"I'm so sorry for your loss," she said, reaching out her hands to offer comfort.

He clasped them as his eyes moistened. "Thank you, my dear. My beautiful wife passed away a long time ago, and a part of me always holds on to her."

Olivia's grip on the count's hands looked like iron before she pulled away, settling back beside me. "I lost my unborn child a few months ago, and the grief I feel floods over me every time something bad happens. Roman and I were apart for too long; each day of separation felt like an eternity in hell."

Our eyes locked, my gaze intense and understanding of what had occurred. I reached out to grasp her hand tightly, my voice wavering with emotion as I spoke, "I cannot begin to fathom the sorrow you must be feeling, my love."

"Tragic," the count murmured, shaking his head. "I'm so sorry for your loss."

We all grew silent, rocked in the carriage by the horses.

The count eventually broke the silence. "I've assumed you'll be coming home with me. Am I correct in my assumption?"

His kindness sometimes overwhelmed me, like right at this moment. "Oh, no, Count Montego. I don't want to over-stay my welcome. Besides, I must find Malik. That's where you're staying, isn't it, my love?"

I gazed with fondness at my wife.

"Nonsense! I insist that you stay with me!"

Olivia and I exchanged another glance.

I turned back to the count and said, "I need to speak with Malik."

"I shall escort you there; you can have your conversation, and then you can join me at my home." The count beamed, picked up his news piece, and resumed reading, as if we had agreed to his declaration.

Olivia looked at me and shrugged. Then, she whispered, "What do you think will happen to Tristan?"

"Who can say? His father is a madman."

The wagon lurched over another rough road patch, and we bounced on the seat.

Olivia whispered, "In the movies in my time, this always looks so smooth—traveling by carriage or wagon. In truth, it's a bumpy ride."

I snorted. My gaze darted toward Count Montego to see if he was paying us any mind.

He didn't seem to be, so I said, "I got to ride in one of your automobiles. In fact, I rode in your Jeep. It was very smooth."

A wistful expression flitted across her face. "Oh, my Jeep! I loved that vehicle."

"I want to get a motorcycle," I said.

Olivia laughed. "Of course you do! A badass bike for my badass husband." Then, she grew serious. "I still can't believe I fell for the son of my worst enemy. It makes me feel so dirty to have been intimate with him."

"That's not an image I cherish, either," I said, as prickles of jealousy shot up my spine. My voice rose as I said, "I'd rather not discuss Balthazar or his evil spawn."

The count lowered the news to his lap. "Did you say the name Balthazar?"

"Yes, do you know him?"

The count visibly shuddered. "Do I. He's known as the Monster of Darkness. Was he at the party?"

"You mean you didn't see him? He yelled at Costa," I said. "At the show."

"I've seen that show too many times. I was otherwise engaged with a few lovely women."

He grinned.

"I thought all must attend that spectacle," Olivia said, her eyebrows creased together. "One of the guards forced us to watch."

"Oh, they try to enforce that, but we old-timers can get away with bending the rules." He swished his hand before him again. "I've been coming here a long time."

"How do you know Balthazar?" I said.

"He lives around here. He's been traveling a lot, or so I

heard. But if he's back, something's afoot. He brings trouble wherever he goes." Dark clouds of emotion flitted across the count's face. "He changed after Alina died. He was never the same."

"You met Alina?" Olivia said. She grabbed my hand and squeezed it.

"Yes, poor girl. She was all caught up with Balthazar, and everyone knew he wasn't good for her." The count tsked.

"What do you know about her death?" Olivia said.

"Only what the gossip mongers said in town. Apparently, she died a tragic death. And, like I said, Balthazar fell into despair. I never understood their relationship. She was such a bright soul, a free spirit. And Balthazar was nothing but a wind-sucker."

"A wind-sucker?" Olivia's eyebrows rose.

"A jealous cad. He practically kept her under lock and key. Such beauty cannot be captured." The count tipped his head to the side and studied Olivia. "You resemble her. You carry that same ephemeral beauty that she possessed."

"Thank you, count," Olivia said, divulging nothing more.

"So what kept you two apart for so long?" the count said, moving the conversation in another direction.

"Our travels," I said and took in the sea of stars floating in the heavens outside the window.

"Yes, Roman and I had to part for a time," Olivia added.

"And where did you return from?" The count directed this question to Olivia.

"I was staying east of here," she said, keeping her answer vague. "And now I'm staying with Malik. Do you know him?"

"Of course! Lord Malik is well known. He keeps to himself, though."

"Malik was supposed to wait for me at the party. I hope he's okay." Olivia frowned.

"Oh, Malik can take care of himself, I assure you. As a matter of fact, I saw him leave the festivities earlier." The count smiled.

"Did you?" Olivia's frown deepened.

"Yes. He can tell you himself where he went—we're here." The count gestured toward the window as we headed up a driveway to a villa as impressive as the count's and Costa's. When the carriage pulled to a stop, Count Montego said, "I can send the carriage for you later if you like."

"No, thank you. We can arrange transportation," I said, unsure if that was true.

"Nonsense," the count said. "I'll send the carriage. You two must be extremely fatigued. It's far past midnight. I'll send my driver over, and he'll pick you up and take you safely to my home, where you can rest. Sleep all day tomorrow if you must. I don't mind."

"Thank you, Count Montego, but we can find our own way," I said.

"As you wish," he said, leaning forward to open the coach door. "I can admit defeat as long as I get my way in the end."

He flashed a twinkling gaze at me, and I laughed.

"I will expect you at my home in the morning," he said as I climbed out.

"As *you* wish," I said, adding a formal bow. I reached to help Olivia out of the coach and closed the door.

The driver slapped the reins on the horses' rumps, getting them moving again.

As Olivia and I approached Malik's house, I said, "We have much to discuss, my love. There is so much I need to fill you in on."

"Same here. Wait until you hear about Marcellious."

I raised my eyebrows but didn't inquire further as we ascended the steps to Malik's fine home.

Overhead, the sky held a milky tone, a quietude caught in that stasis of deep night.

Olivia opened the door and tiptoed into the house.

I followed her, creeping. My nerves were heightened, partially from the last few hours' events and partly in anticipation of seeing Malik.

A soft clatter sounded from the far recesses of the upstairs.

Olivia and I climbed the stairs, and headed to the right at the top of the landing.

A beam of light shone through one of the doors, illuminating the deep red rug covering the floor of the hallway. "That's Malik's room," Olivia whispered.

We moved with stealth down the corridor and paused before the door.

My heart thumped wildly. I was about to meet the man I'd dreamed of so many times. And the man who had saved me on countless occasions.

A man's voice, presumably Malik's, crooned, singing some lullaby.

Olivia glanced at me, her eyebrows creased.

"How odd to hear a man of darkness singing a lullaby," she whispered. She turned toward the door and said softly, "Malik?"

"Olivia?" Malik said, his voice a rich timbre. "Come in. I'm soothing Rosie after a bad dream."

Olivia pushed open the door. There stood a bare-chested man with a small child pressed to his torso. The girl's head lay on his muscled shoulder as if she were asleep.

A smile fell from Malik's face.

Stunned, I found myself tongue-tied, blinking wildly. A

waterfall of images flooded my brain. This was the man with Olivia at Costa's party—although he wore a mask there was no mistaking. This was the man in my nightmares. And I knew in my soul we had hunted together—if not in this lifetime, then, in another—it wasn't just a dream.

Malik lowered the child to the bed and settled her in the middle, pulling a blanket over her.

The child was utterly beautiful. For a moment, my attention was caught on her innocent beauty.

Then I was drawn back to Malik, who stood across from me, transfixed.

"You may have been born a monster," I said as the words bubbled from my mind's recesses.

"But I will never die a monster," Malik said, finishing the phrase.

"What the hell is going on?" Olivia said, her gaze pinging between Malik and me.

"You remember," Malik said, his unearthly green eyes nearly glowing.

"I remember. But I don't understand how. I only have fragments of memory falling into place, but I can't put them together."

"Will somebody please fill me in? What's going on between you two?" Olivia said. "Why did you abandon me at the party, Malik? You said you'd stay and keep me safe."

"I knew you were safe. I could hear you fucking in Costa's office." A smirk curved his lips.

Olivia's mouth gaped. "So you just left me?"

Malik shrugged. "Well…you and Roman were fucking. I was no longer needed."

"Did you see us?" Olivia's hands landed on her hips.

Malik chuckled. "The noise carried to the hallway when I searched for you."

Spikes of jealousy stiffened my backbone. "I know you tried to seduce my wife when we were apart."

Malik shrugged with indifference. "It seemed like the natural thing to do given our pasts."

I frowned as new insights fell into place.

"If it wasn't for the darkness in my veins, Olivia would have given up on me and gone to you, Malik." My arms hung limply by my sides. "Olivia is attracted to the darkness."

I stared at Malik, dumbfounded.

Olivia snapped her fingers. "Hello, Olivia is standing here, and neither of you is making any sense now."

She stood there in her disheveled gown, which was covered in dried droplets of blood that formed a sweeping pattern across the fabric. Her vibrant red hair hung in a tangled mess around her face. Dark circles loomed beneath her eyes and yet somehow, to me, she was still the most beautiful woman I had ever seen. And yet as memories jostled in my brain, she reminded me of someone from my past, from an age long gone.

"I don't want what we had in the past." I dragged my knuckle down her soft cheek. "I won't share you—you know that."

"Roman," Olivia said, her eyes creased with concern. "I appreciate the sentiment, but I don't understand where this is coming from. What past are you talking about?"

"You know the dreams? The fires? The loss of my whole family?"

"Your nightmares, yes. The ones matching my own," Olivia said.

"They're not just dreams. They were real, my love." I caught her hand and kissed it. "You died in a fire along with our children. Malik was there."

A bolt of anger yanked me around to face him. "And if you hadn't had an affair with my wife..."

The words stopped as my throat clotted with rage.

Malik staggered back, clutching his heart. "Roman, please forgive me. I have made many mistakes in the past. But my biggest regret, which haunts me the most, was losing you two." His eyes filled with tears. "Forgive me. I think of what you always told me. I might have been born a monster..."

"You will never die a monster," I said woodenly, stepping closer to him.

Olivia rushed toward us and put her hands between us. "Would someone tell me what the hell is going on? You're acting like you know Malik—like you've long known him."

I turned to Olivia and cupped her cheek. I'd loved her through the centuries. I knew it in my soul. "We met in another lifetime. You and I will *always* find one another—we are soulmates."

"We what?" Olivia said, looking from me to Malik.

"Roman's right. We have all met before, in another lifetime, in the year 1359 A.D. in Britannia. You were known as Isabelle. Roman was known as Armand Farcourt. You were one of the only two women I have loved."

CHAPTER TWENTY-THREE

MARCELLIOUS

I don't know how I did it, but I managed to beg off the masquerade, telling Balthazar I was feeling poorly.

"Stay then," he had said to me. "See if I care."

He'd removed all his clothes as I stood there, trying hard not to look at his impossibly muscled body. Then, he'd donned his costume, including the mask.

The malevolence radiating from his face through the mask nearly made me fall to my knees and retch. But I kept my composure, allowing my feelings of disgust for the man before me to feed my lie about feeling ill.

Now, as I combed Balthazar's house, meticulously replacing each object I removed from a bookcase or slid from a shelf, I grew more and more frantic.

Balthazar had been gone for a couple of hours, and I still hadn't found his dagger. This was perhaps my only opportunity to find it.

I finally slumped on the bed in one of his guest rooms. Black and silver-striped wallpaper adorned the walls. The floor had been tiled in ebony granite, and even the bed coverings were dark gray. This room was more of a tomb than a welcoming place for guests.

It spoke volumes about the number of friends Balthazar had—that number was a big, fat zero. The demon had only supplicants. He probably hadn't used this room in centuries, if ever.

My gaze landed on a box sitting on a bookshelf packed with leather-bound books with the names like *Defunctis Corporibus Conservandis*. I shivered as the translation floated through my brain.

Preserving Dead Bodies. Why on Earth would he need to preserve them?

I crossed to the box and picked it up, turning it around and around. I tried to pry it open, but it wouldn't budge.

The box was crafted from dull iron and coated with a layer of rust that flaked away at the slightest touch. Its lid was sealed shut, secured through lock and key, some sort of spell, or maybe both. The metal rings around the chest were cool to the touch. There was no telling what might be inside—only that it was valuable enough to require such an elaborate system of safeguards.

While I didn't know anything about the ways and means of demonic spellbinding, I had learned a fair bit about picking a lock. Emperor Severus had occasionally employed my services as a thief who picked his way into the homes of his enemy.

I brought the box downstairs into Balthazar's cavernous front room and set it on a table in front of his overstuffed sofa. Then, from the kitchen, I retrieved a sharp knife and a pewter fork consisting of two long, pointy tines.

I sat on the plush gold sofa, working the utensils in and around the lock, until I heard a satisfying snap.

"Victory!"

I pried open the lid.

Inside sat Balthazar's sacred dagger, glistening like the treacherous tool it was.

I was almost afraid to pick it up. What if it was bonded with its owner? Would it attempt to harm me?

I chided myself on my fearful thoughts and picked up the blade. Nothing happened except for the exultation running through my body. I'd done it—I'd found the bastard's knife.

I slid it into the sheath at my waist, forcing it next to my knife. Then, I hurried upstairs and replaced the box in the exact position where I'd found it. With luck, it would be a while until the monster discovered his sacred knife was long gone, and so was I.

The only thing I could think about at this moment was getting to Malik's and restoring my life.

As I headed down the stairs, the front door burst open.

Fuck. He's back. My heart thundered wildly. I shrank back, not wanting to be seen, and tiptoed up the stairs to watch from the shadows.

Balthazar hauled in a younger man by the ear and shoved him onto the sofa I'd just vacated. He placed his hand on the man's wrist and muttered a strange language as if casting some sort of spell or healing incantation.

When Balthazar removed his hands, the young man lifted his arm and stared at it in wonder. Then, he blubbered, "Dad, you saved me. And now you've healed me! Thank you! All these years, I thought you didn't care."

"Shut the fuck up, you idiot," Balthazar roared. "You are the biggest imbecile, but I will always care for you. It's my *job.* Marcellious! Get down here!"

"Fuck, fuck, fuck," I muttered through clenched teeth.

How will I be able to escape him? If he catches me with his dagger, I'm a dead man.

"Marcellious!" the monster screamed.

I stealthily retreated farther down the hallway toward my room and made sure my footsteps were loud when I moved forward.

"I'm coming, I'm coming." I ruffled my hair and pulled one end of my shirt from my pants, trying to make it appear I'd been sleeping.

I tromped down the stairs noisily as if offended to have been awakened. When I stood near both men, I faked a colossal yawn.

"What is it, my lord?"

Balthazar said nothing. He simply glared at me.

"Who's this?" I said, pointing to the young man. "Is this the pathetic son you've spoken of from time to time?"

Balthazar darted toward me like a snake and seized my throat. "You son of a bitch, don't ever talk to my offspring this way."

"I'm sorry, master. I apologize." I could barely breathe.

"You're going to pay for your mistakes. You've *failed* me." Balthazar's nostrils flared, and his eyes glowed crimson.

I grabbed Balthazar's hand, trying to pry his fingers from my neck.

"Failed you?" I wheezed. "How could I fail you?"

Balthazar shoved me backward, and I fell beside the young man huddled on the couch. My right side—the side with the dagger at my waist—lay exposed. I quickly righted myself, hoping he hadn't seen the hilt of his blade.

"You could have saved me," Balthazar snarled.

"Saved you? Saved you from what?" I said, rubbing my bruised neck.

Balthazar turned to his son. "How did you get here, Tristan? You had to arrive with a Timeborne."

Tristan cowered on the sofa, drawing up his arms and knees for protection. "I came with Roman Alexander."

"Roman? He lives?" The demon picked up a vase from the table next to the sofa and pitched it across the room.

It exploded, sending porcelain shards flying.

Some of them landed in my hair, but I didn't dare move to pick them out.

"Yes, Dad. Alexander lives. He grabbed me in a 21st-century bar and beat the shit out of me based on what some old hag told him about me," Tristan said, still cowering. "Then he said I had to time travel with him. We traveled here and stayed at some count's home. His name is Count Montego."

"That's impossible. I left Roman for dead. No one can destroy me!" He picked up another priceless object, a marble carving from the mantel behind him, and hurled it.

This time the wall shattered, leaving a gaping hole.

"Where's my maid? Bartolomea, get in here!"

A woman scurried out of the back of the house, wringing her hands together. She curtsied and bowed her head. "How may I serve you, my lord?"

Balthazar pointed at the porcelain shards and wood pieces from the wall. "Clean up that mess. And clean up the blood from my son. He's a disgrace. I can hardly stand to look at him."

"At once, my lord." The maid bowed her head and fluttered away like a small, scared bird. She returned with cleaning supplies and dabbed at Tristan's face before turning her attention to the other side of the room.

"No one stands a chance against me. I am the most powerful man in the world! I will get the sun dagger back and bring Alina to life. She will be my queen!" Balthazar threw back his head and lifted his arms into the air. "We will rule the world together!"

My lip curled in disgust. He's fucking crazy! He is a total lunatic to think he can bring someone back from the dead.

Porcelain fragments clattered into the wooden bucket the maid used to clean the floor. When she was done, she stood and said, "Will that be all, my lord?"

Balthazar's head snapped toward her. "What did you say?"

Her eyes widened.

"Will that be all?" she stuttered.

In a flash, he appeared before her, grasping her neck, and twisting it.

As she slumped to the ground, a silvery cloud of smoke coiled from the top of her head.

Balthazar tipped back his nose and inhaled deeply; the silver stream shot up his nose. He let out a satisfied "Ahh."

I looked on in horror.

"That Malik," he muttered, clasping his hands behind his back, "he's the one plotting and scheming. He has Emily, Olivia, and Roman, and he thinks he's winning. Well, guess what? He hasn't won. He'll never win. I shall reign victorious!"

"What do we do now?" Tristan asked.

I glanced at him.

The poor lad shivered where he sat.

"Why do you think I have the answer?" I hissed. I didn't know Tristan, but he seemed like a weak excuse for a man.

Balthazar appeared before us.

I jerked and blinked. A second ago, he was behind us.

"What are you whispering about," he snarled. "Are you plotting and scheming, too?"

An evil leer stretched across his face. He seized my lapels and hauled me into the air.

I hung there, terrified, trying to keep my wits about me.

"You've disappointed me, my boy. You should have come to the masquerade ball and found the sun dagger. Instead, you stayed home like a wailing, whimpering bitch." Balthazar shook me, and my head lolled about.

"Now I don't even know if the dagger is still trapped in the rubble," Balthazar continued.

Rubble? What happened tonight?

He dropped me, and I fell backward like a lump.

"I hope you're loyal. Otherwise, you'll see the worst of me," Balthazar hissed. "Here's what you're going to do for me."

"Anything, my lord. Name it, and I'll do it." I righted myself and tugged down my crumpled shirt. "I'm eternally loyal to you, master."

"Good, good." He circled the front room, muttering and mumbling something I couldn't catch. Then, in a loud, clear voice, he said, "You will bring me Roman and Malik. Find them. I shall kill them, and you shall watch."

Fuck that idea.

"Of course, my lord. I live to serve," I said.

"Why can't you find them yourself, Dad? You can find anyone?" Tristan said in a quivery voice.

"Shut the fuck up!" Balthazar bellowed.

"But Roman's at this Count Montego fellow's home. You can find him there," Tristan said.

"The count will know nothing about Malik. Malik hides from everyone," Balthazar said with a wave of his hand.

"He might," I said, exhausted by Balthazar's tirade. "You can find them and bring them here, Tristan, and we can play catch up."

Balthazar hauled me up and slammed me against the wall.

"I will not tolerate your ill regard toward my son." He shook me, rattling my bones. With his face inches from mine, he said, "Go. Get them. And bring them to me. Do you understand me?"

I couldn't help but tremble. "Yes, master. I apologize. I will go and find them at once."

Balthazar released me, and I slid down the wall, landing on my booted feet with a thud.

I scrambled out the door, panting, breathless, and scared for my life. I had to get away from Balthazar—I just had to.

But he would hunt me down, find me, and kill me.

I grabbed a horse from the stables and kicked him into a gallop. We raced through the darkness until we arrived at Malik's villa. My plan was to explain everything to Emily and beg her forgiveness. I would get down on my knees if I had to. I had no intentions other than reconciling with Emily. But where could we go to escape Balthazar's wrath?

At Malik's door, I pounded on the wood.

A maid answered, and I started to push past her, but she stood in my way.

"Good sir, where do you think you're going?"

"I'm here to see Emily. It's a matter of urgency," I said, trying to sidle past her.

The damnable woman held her ground, not letting me pass.

"I'm sorry, but it's late, and Lady Emily is asleep. You can return in the morning if you like." She started to close the door in my face, but I blocked it with my boot.

"Where's Malik, then? I must speak with him."

"He's not here," she said.

"You're lying. Where is he?"

A shocked expression flitted across her face, followed by

a clenched jaw. "I'm sorry, sir, but you'll have to leave. You can return in the morning."

She placed both palms on the door and shoved my boot and pride out of the way.

The door slammed shut.

I tugged a hank of my hair. I couldn't believe this was happening. I had to find Emily.

I scurried around the house, craning my neck to see upstairs.

A window glowed with golden light and a tall man, presumably Malik, walked back and forth in front of the window, holding a child. His head turned toward me, and I ducked into the shadows of a large tree.

So, that's not her bedroom. Where would she be sleeping?

I searched the house, finding two rooms with balconies in the back.

Sturdy dormer windows stood beneath the balconies.

I could grab the dormer if I got a running start. I walked back a distance, studied the height I had to jump, and sprinted toward the house. I got enough purchase to propel me to the dormer, where I caught the top.

I hung there, trying to catch my breath. Then, I pulled my legs up and over the roofed structure and contemplated my next move.

The balcony was several feet up the wall. From here, I couldn't run, leap, grab the balcony railing, or do jack shit.

I continued to stare at the balcony. *Maybe I could leap and grasp the iron railings.* I looked down. If I missed, it would be a messy fall, likely resulting in my death. I had no choice but to try.

I crouched and jumped but slid down the wall, barely managing to catch the dormer roof.

"Shit. That was close."

I looked up, recalculating the distance. This time when I leaped, I managed to curl my fingers around one of the railings. I pulled up my other arm and grasped both iron bars. Then, I swung my body forward and back, getting enough momentum to power my legs onto the landing and grab the top bar. I pulled my trembling legs over the railing and gasped, securely on the balcony. It took a few minutes for me to catch my breath. Whoever was in this room had to have heard the clatter outside.

I reached for the brass doorknob and twisted it open. Relief flooded me when it turned. I crept inside to find my beautiful angel, Emily, asleep in bed.

I lowered myself to the edge of the bed and caressed her silken hair that lay tangled around her face.

Oh, my beautiful wife. How I've missed you. How will I be able to redeem myself with you, given the way I had to treat you the last time we met?

I shook my head, thinking how Balthazar was her father. How could that despicable demon have fathered such wonder and grace?

I climbed next to Emily and planted feathery kisses all over her cheeks and neck.

God, how I love you.

Emily woke up, her eyelids wide and fearful. She opened her mouth to scream.

I slapped my palm over her lips. "Shh, shh. I'm here to tell you everything."

She screamed into my hand and writhed against me. Then, she bit my palm.

I yanked my hand away. "Ouch!"

"You're a monster! You've betrayed my unborn child and me. How dare you come into my room!"

I clapped my hand over her mouth again and straddled

her. "You must listen to me! Everything I did was for Malik. It was all part of a plan."

The whites of Emily's eyes shone as she screamed against my skin, struggling to free herself.

"If I let you go, you have to promise not to yell. Can you do that?"

She nodded as best she could.

"I mean it. If you scream, I'm going to restrain you again."

Once more, she nodded.

"Okay. I'm going to slowly release you, and you're not going to holler, got it?"

Her head bobbed up and down.

I removed my palm.

She slapped me with so much force my head flew to the side. "You're a liar. I don't believe you! You broke my heart!" She started to sob.

I grasped both wrists and pinned them over her head. "You have to believe me, sweetheart. Everything I did was for you."

She kicked and wriggled beneath me like a wildcat. "I don't believe you! You destroyed my heart. This marriage is *over.*"

The words stung more than the slap did. "You can't mean it."

"I can, and I do. You betrayed me, Marcellious! You slept with Dahlia, and you cast our love aside." Fat tears streamed into her hair.

My eyes moistened, too. "I never slept with Dahlia, I swear. I know you don't believe me, but I love you with all my heart. Everything I did was for you."

"Get out of here! I never want to see your face again." Her mouth bunched up, and she spat at me.

A small blob of spit landed on my face. I wiped it off with my forearm. "I deserve all of this and more, my love. I have made many mistakes, too many to count. But I want to prove to you that I'm a good man. I will show you I'm not a coward and a cheat. Let's start fresh. I want to make passionate love to you, my beautiful wife. You can ride me all night long and scream my name."

I nuzzled her nose.

"What, now that Dahlia is dead, you need a woman?" Her face crumpled in anguish.

My heart knotted into a tight ball. I understood the pain I'd caused, but that didn't mean it didn't wreck me to see it all over her face. "Look, I can prove it to you. And once you believe me, I will show you how much you mean to me with every muscle in my body. I'm going to ravish you, woman, until you can barely stand."

I thrust my hips against her, driving home my point.

Emily blushed and looked away.

At least she'd stopped yelling.

I dropped my head and slowly licked her neck from shoulder to jaw.

She trembled beneath me.

I brought my lips close to her ear and whispered, "Let's find Malik so he can verify I'm not lying. After that, I'll leave if you still don't believe me. But I think you want me as much as I want you."

She squeezed her eyes shut.

"That's what I thought. Let's go find Malik." I swung my leg off her and lowered off the bed. I held out my hand.

She eyed it like it was a raptor.

A long moment stretched between us.

"Come on. I can prove it to you, my darling," I said. "I won't hurt you, I swear. I'm done playing games."

With a sigh, she took my hand and rolled off the mattress.

The thin fabric of her nightgown revealed the gentle curve of her growing stomach. The sight of her pregnant silhouette sent a wave of emotion through me, and I had to bite my lip to keep from crying.

That's my child. I'm going to be a father! I've got to prove to her that I'm not a liar and am worthy of being in my child's life.

When we emerged into the corridor, voices floated out of a room further down the hall. *That's Malik's voice. And it sounds like Roman and Olivia are with him.*

We strode down the hallway and stood before the open door to Malik's room.

"Why, what a lovely family reunion!" I said.

Olivia whipped around to face me. "You bastard! Why are you here? Get the hell out of here, or I'll—"

"Why are you here?" Malik said, interrupting her. He glanced at the sleeping child on the bed and urged everyone out of the room. "We don't want to wake Rosie. You can explain yourself downstairs."

We all tromped down the sweeping staircase to his front room.

Malik lit the lamps, and the room became awash in a golden glow.

Roman and Olivia sat on the sofa while I stood beside Emily, clutching her hand.

Malik faced me, standing. "You're not supposed to be here."

"And yet, here I am. I'm done with that demon, Balthazar. He's a madman. He's become completely unhinged." Shaking my arms, I unleashed the tension that was coursing through my body to emphasize my words. "I adore my spouse and have really felt her absence. I had to betray her in order to fulfill your goals."

"What the fuck are you saying?" Olivia said. She turned to Roman. "He's been Balthazar's minion all this time. That's one of the things I needed to tell you."

Roman's face grew beet-red. "What? So you've gone dark on us all, have you?"

He started to stand, but Olivia held him back.

"Don't. You don't know what he's capable of. Emily and I have witnessed his treachery with our own eyes." She glared at me.

I got in Malik's face, standing nose-to-nose. "It's time they knew the truth. I brought you Alina's dagger. I did everything you asked. And now I want to be out. No more lies, no more games, no more spying. I'm done."

Olivia's mouth formed a round O. "What is he saying, Malik? Is he telling the truth? He's been working for you all this time? Playing some double agent?"

Malik's face hardened, his eyes blazing with rage. "You've failed me, Marcellious," he said through clenched teeth. "I told you to return only once you've secured Balthazar's dagger. Do you have it?"

"I've risked my life and limb," I growled, my voice trembling with anger. "My marriage, everything! But I'm done, do you hear me? Done!"

Olivia looked stunned, her mouth hanging open in disbelief. "Balthazar has a dagger?" she said in disbelief.

Malik raised an eyebrow in acknowledgment. "Yes, the darkness possesses their dagger from their original time traveler," he said calmly. He looked at me expectantly before asking again, more firmly this time. "Well? Do you have it?"

My hand shot out as I unsheathed the knife with a furious clatter. I thrust it forward, staring Malik down as I uttered, "Here it is." With a dramatic flourish, I presented Balthazar's dagger as if it were my own heart on a platter.

Malik's lips curved in a slight smile. He reached for the blade's hilt and hefted it up and down. "I'm impressed, Marcellious. So, you've done everything according to plan. This is excellent news."

Olivia bolted to her feet, and Roman followed.

"This is outrageous! Do you know what we went through tonight? Hundreds died! Was this all part of the plan, too?" she shouted.

"Yes, I knew Balthazar would try and save Tristan." Malik's smile turned secretive. "Please don't be upset."

"Are you fucking kidding me? I'm beyond a mere 'upset,'" Olivia said. "I'm outraged! And traumatized. How could you have known Roman and I would be spared in the blaze tonight?"

"Blaze?" I said. "What blaze?"

Olivia spun to face me. "Balthazar arrived at the party tonight. The Timehunters had his son and were going to torture and kill him. Balthazar intervened and lit the entire villa on fire. Roman and I escaped to the sound of anguished screams. And you're going to tell me this was all part of some sick plan?"

She whipped her head toward Malik again.

The smile fell from his face. "Most of those who died tonight were killers. They were Timehunters or minions of the Timehunters. I knew you'd be able to take care of yourselves." His expression darkened into something menacing. "You should be thankful."

Olivia drew back.

"Timehunters?" Emily asked. "What are Timehunters?"

Malik ignored her. "Where's Balthazar?"

"He's healing his son," I said, bile rising in my throat. "God, I despise that man."

I turned toward my wife, who looked at me with glistening eyes. "Come, my love. I need to explain everything to you."

I extended my hand.

She batted it away.

"No! I need to hear from Malik if this is true." She turned toward him and clasped her hands beneath her chin. "Please, I beg of you. If this is all true, please tell me. I've endured such agony and need to hear the truth."

Malik sighed. "Yes, dear Emily, it's true. Marcellious has been working with me since Roman and Olivia were held captive in Balthazar's lair."

I pivoted to face Emily. "Emily, my love, you've got to believe me. Balthazar poisoned my mind before I met Malik. I hated Roman and Olivia. But when Malik found me, he healed my damaged mind. He saved me. And then I started to get closer to you." I seized both her hands, and she didn't pull away. "I didn't know I would fall in love with you, but I did. You saw something human in me and convinced me I was a good man. Emily, please forgive me. It was the only way to get the things we needed from Balthazar. I had to be a spy and tell you treacherous lies. I never slept with Dahlia, ever. I never loved her. In fact, I loathed her."

Tears fell down Emily's cheeks, but she made no move toward me.

It was okay—I wasn't done speaking yet. "And, Olivia… I'm so sorry for my actions. I had to gain Balthazar's trust to steal his dagger and get your mother's blade. It's all part of a greater plan."

Olivia eyed me with suspicion but said nothing.

I dropped to one knee and pressed my face to Emily's thighs, wrapping my arms around her legs. "I'm begging you to forgive me, Emily. Begging you. I worship you. I've been in agony at what I had to do to convince Balthazar I was loyal to him. Your wounded expression has haunted me for months. Every night I go to bed and beg you to one day forgive me. Let today be that day."

A long beat of silence mantled the room as I clung to my wife.

At last, her hand fell on my head.

"I forgive you, Marcellious," Emily sobbed.

Standing, I took her in my arms and let her cry against my shoulder. "Oh, my sweet, sweet Emily."

"So, you've been helping Malik?" Roman said.

"Yes, brother. I could tell no one." I couldn't release Emily. I finally had her in my arms where she belonged.

"I'll tell you more," Malik said, but I ignored him.

Instead, I cupped my wife's face between my hands and kissed her tenderly. When we came up for air, I whispered, "Let me take you to bed, wife, and show you how much I cherish you."

I carefully scooped her up in my arms and walked toward the stairs. She tightly held onto my neck and gazed up at me with a look of complete affection in her bright blue eyes. "I hope our connection lasts forever," I whispered as we made our way up the steps.

"I want that, too," she murmured.

I also prayed she would never know who her father was. It would crush her.

But for now, I fervently hoped to mend the gaping rift I'd created.

In the back of my mind, I knew there would be trouble

and chaos down the road. No one escaped a demon as evil as Balthazar and lived to tell about it.

And I could be that dead man soon.

CHAPTER TWENTY-FOUR

MALIK

he pounding of Marcellious and Emily's reunion resonated through the walls, vibrating with each beat like a drum. The thump, thump, thump grew louder, as if two hearts were beating in perfect harmony. I smiled, captivated by the music that spoke of their passionate love for one another.

Roman and Olivia intertwined their fingers as they walked toward the settee. They settled down on either side of the plush material. After that, I crossed my hands at my waist and stood in front of the flames I'd ignited a bit earlier.

"I'm sure you, Roman, have gleaned parts of this story— but what I'm about to tell you is the truth of who and what I am, and the history we all share together."

The turret clock on the mantel steadily ticked. Expertly crafted, its gold brass casing held the inner workings of the timepiece that would ring out with a pleasant melody at each hour. I enjoyed collecting exquisite works of art from each century. They spoke of human potential instead of the foul depravity in which much of my life had been spent.

I glanced at Roman and Olivia, who pinned their gazes on

me, rapt. With a sigh, I began my story. "I am a man of many things—a father…a guardian…a demon, a lover, and a friend. I am of Romany descendant, that which is called the gypsy. That's why I look the way I do.

"When my Timeborne created me, I was five years old. I didn't understand anything save for the need to kill. All I wanted to do was kill and consume souls. I had no guidance until I met Balthazar. He took me under his wing, told me he'd be a father to me, raise me, and treat me right." I turned to face Roman and Olivia. "I was a child. How could I know anything different?"

Olivia nodded as if she understood.

"Balthazar had a big impact on me. I worshipped him, and killing felt so natural to me. It wasn't wrong; it was the way I kept myself fed." I paused and scrunched my nose up in thought. "He'd even bring back trophies from his missions. These barely alive bodies would be tossed at my feet and Balthazar would urge me to finish the job so I could partake of their life essence."

I stopped at the mantel and ran my fingertip across the smooth edge of the turret clock. Then, I picked up the iron poker and poked at the burning logs in the fireplace.

They sparked, and flames once more consumed them.

Satisfied, I crossed to my high-backed chair and sat on it. "Balthazar told me our goal was to kill Timebornes. We had the best life together, or so I thought. The years passed without incident, save for the relentless killing."

I canted my head and studied Olivia.

"What?" she finally said.

My gaze softened. "I was just thinking about your mother, Alina. Balthazar was obsessed with her…utterly besotted."

The same way I once loved you. And still do. I sighed.

There are things in this life I shall never be able to have. Olivia will always belong to Roman.

"I stayed out of his romantic life. I had become a young man when he met Alina, even though many centuries had passed. The darkness—we age differently than humans." A wan smile curved my lips, then fell away. "When Balthazar met Alina, I had my own lusts and longings. I traveled obsessively. I was eager to learn different languages and cultures. I had an unquenchable thirst for learning."

I leaned forward, resting my forearms on my legs. "I traveled to Anatolia and met a pasha—a Turkish officer of high rank, in case you don't know. The pasha admired my intelligence and liked having me around. He put me up in his home. That's when I met Layla. She was his beautiful daughter. She was my first love. She was amazing, intelligent, glorious, kind, and sweet."

I grew silent as my heart filled with wistful longing.

Olivia's soft voice brought me out of my reverie. "You must have loved her very much."

I met her gaze. The searing passion I carried in my heart for Olivia rushed through my soul. I had to look away.

"Yes," I said simply, my thoughts tangled in the past. "Very much."

I licked my parched lips.

"Of course, when I was in Anatolia, the same as wherever I traveled, I had to maintain my lifestyle—which meant killing to survive." A deep frown furrowed my face, and my jaw cocked to the side. I sat back in my chair. "Layla saw me kill one night. She was frightened and ran away. I chased after her and told her I'd never hurt her—I was too deeply in love with her. But she didn't believe me. I was desperate. I couldn't let her go, so I told her everything."

Olivia gasped. "She must have been horrified."

Roman said, "How did she take that news?"

I shrugged, feigning indifference I did not feel. "She was, as you said, horrified. Thank God I didn't tell her that my life quest had been eradicating Timebornes. I nearly swallowed my tongue when she told me she was a Timeborne."

"She what?" Roman said.

"Oh, my God! You're kidding!" Olivia exclaimed.

"I'm not. I loved Layla so much that I vowed to never kill again. I did my best, but it was hard. I grew weak. Layla and I had successfully kept everything from her parents, but they somehow found out. They wanted to kill me." I cast a wary glance at Olivia and Roman. "You see, her father was a Timehunter. Layla had been born on a solar eclipse."

"If he was a Timehunter and Layla was born on a solar eclipse, how did he spare his own child from his murderous rampages?" She said.

"Perhaps he loved her too much," I said, shrugging. "I don't know the answer."

Another gasp escaped Olivia's lips. "Malik…this story!"

"Yes, this story," I said ruefully. "So, our lives were in danger once Layla's Timehunter father found out what I was. He'd managed to hold back his rage toward his daughter, yet I did not feel so fortunate: there was no reason why he should have spared me. We ran. God, how we ran. We traveled by boat to the Papal States, what is now referred to as Italy. And then made our way by horseback to Britannia, what you call England. And there we set up a home. We were always looking over our shoulder, living in fear of discovery."

Olivia reached out and patted my knee.

"While we lived in Britannia, Layla explored everything she could get her hands on about Timebornes, Timebounds, Timehunters, and the darkness. She discovered the existence of scholars who could teach me a different way of life. I became hopeful for the first time in my life. I'd managed to kill when Layla was asleep, just enough to maintain my health and energy. But, I desperately wanted it to stop." I glanced at Olivia and Roman. "The killing, I mean."

They both nodded.

"The scholars spoke of the original blades during the first solar eclipse and how they could cure the thirst for killing. Layla and I resumed our travels in quest of these mysterious blades. I grew so inspired and hopeful that I sought out Balthazar. I found him here in England. 'We can change,' I told him. 'Our lives do not have to be about constant murder.'

"But Balthazar was obsessed with power. He was greedy for it. It's all he wanted. So when I told him about the blades, he wanted to find them. He kept the daggers of those he killed as trophies. But if he possessed the sun and the moon dagger blades he could rule the world with his darkness." I shook my head. "I rue the day I told him about the knives."

I fell silent, captured by the dark nightmares of memory flooding my brain.

"What happened next?" Olivia prompted.

I felt dead inside when I looked at her. "Balthazar captured Layla. He tortured her and drained the life out of her. He imprisoned me and turned loose the Timehunters on me. I was trapped between bars, forced to ingest poison. I lived a life of torture, caught in a web of hallucinations and craziness. I lost count of the days, weeks, months, and perhaps years. Nothing made sense anymore. I lost my power and became weak as a newborn kitten. I suffered constant headaches and constant torture. My grasp on reality faded into a world of the bizarre. It was hellish."

I turned my haunted gaze toward Olivia. "Our daggers can weaken us and control us. The sun and moon daggers can cure our hunger, make us live for eternity, or end our lives forever. But the Timehunters' poison is so potent yet gradual that we eventually waste away to nothing. We can't kill, can't move, and are utterly immobilized. And so we die from the pain. It's utterly brutal. Healing from the poison is its own suffering process, and it damages a part of you forever."

"Malik…" was all Olivia said. She rolled her lips between her teeth.

I looked away, once more caught by my nightmares. "I thought I was done for. That's when Layla was brought to me. She was so skeletal. She looked like the walking dead. But for a few moments, hope bloomed in my heart, and I thought we could make it. I naively thought our love was so potent we could find a way out." My eyes narrowed to slits. "That's when Balthazar plunged his blade through her heart. He killed her. I couldn't even catch her when she fell to the ground. I was bound by chains and too weak to move. The pain was unbearable. I was in agony."

My vision blurred from the retelling. "The ringing in my ears…My eyes stung… Every bone in my body seared like I was burning alive. I lay there and watched her die, then watched her decay as the days rolled by. I became a madman. I spoke to her incessantly. I murmured words of love to her, and then I railed against her, shouting, 'Why can't you get up and free me?' I lost my mind in grief and torment."

Olivia had tears in her eyes.

Roman gripped her tightly, with one arm around her shoulder.

"Alina came to me at that time." The words emerged in a barely audible whisper. "I told her to go find John James. He was one of the scholars who knew the secrets of Timebornes. And then I bid her goodbye, hoping death would soon claim me. I had nothing to live for any longer."

My face furrowed as the next recollection surfaced. "But

then a remarkable thing happened. A man sneaked into the dungeon of Balthazar's home. He rescued me from imprisonment. I don't know how he did it. I was far too weak to comprehend anything. But somehow, he managed to burn the Timehunters who held me captive, and then he whisked me away. He took me to his place and helped me regain my strength."

"Who is this man?" Olivia blurted, leaning forward.

I cocked my head and eyed them, considering how much to say. "The only thing I shall tell you is his name—Alastair. That's all you need to know."

"Come on, Malik! Tell us more," Olivia said. "Is he still alive? Where is he? Do you still have contact with him?"

"I'm not going to tell you, Olivia, so stop trying. I will forever be grateful to Alastair for saving me. When I grew stronger, all I could do was kill. I was back to my old insatiable ways. I hated everyone and everything and was angry at life. I became this ruthless monster, a monster like Balthazar.

"But then Alastair found me again and taught me that the darkness didn't have to be bad. I could serve a better purpose in this world—to kill the bad, the villains, the rapists, the sadists, the murderers. In short, I could cleanse the world of evil."

"Is Alastair the darkness?" Olivia said.

"It's not important." I glanced at the fire, noting only glowing embers remaining. A chill hung in the air, so I picked up a log from the iron log holder and placed it in the fireplace. Then, I stoked it with the poker until it burst into flame.

I rested my elbow on the mantel and leaned against the wall.

The turret clock chimed the hour, and I closed my eyes, listening to the soothing tones.

Three in the morning.

When I opened my eyes, I said, "Just know this. Alastair cured me of the urge to kill indiscriminately. He told me my sole purpose was to time travel to another place, heal and grow strong. And then I must kill Balthazar and destroy him forever. That has been my focus ever since I was rescued. I wanted my vengeance on Balthazar, so I time traveled to another time, but the traveling weakened me. I hadn't fully recovered. I couldn't keep track of time or place, but I knew I was in 1359 AD in Britannia. That's where you lived—I met both of you."

I smiled tenderly. "You had a wonderful life, with two girls and a boy. We became fast friends, and you brought me into your world. Because of you, I regained all my strength and healed. You found me in a field, Roman."

Roman nodded. "I can almost recall it."

"And you, Olivia, were a healer. You fed me herbs and good food harvested by your own hands. Rabbit stews. Roasted venison. Vegetables from the garden."

Olivia frowned as if she struggled to remember these things.

"Roman, you and I hunted together. Life was good." I pushed away from the wall and settled in my chair once more. "But I still had to kill. I sought out those I deemed unsavory, people who had harmed others or lived depraved lives. I sneaked out of your home—*our* home—and stalked them for days to discern their worthiness. And then, when I decided, I'd kill them and consume their souls for strength."

I regarded Roman. "You saw me kill once. You didn't judge me. Instead, you promised to help me—that's where the phrase, 'I was born a monster but won't die a monster' came from."

Roman snapped his fingers. "Yes! I can recall that moment as clearly as if it were yesterday."

I nodded. "We returned home, and I noticed the two daggers mounted over the headboard in your bedroom. I asked if you were Timebornes. You both told me you'd been born with the blades but knew nothing about them. The villagers found out about the daggers and assumed it was Christ's intervention and you were meant to be together, so they married you."

I blew out a lungful of breath. "I brought trouble into your lives because I knew what the daggers meant. Everything was normal until I arrived. I shared my story with you, informed you of your time-traveling abilities, and let you know I needed help to defeat Balthazar. At first, you refused to believe me. But then, you conferred with one another and decided to give me the benefit of the doubt. You agreed to help me defeat Balthazar. You took on the quest with pride and honor."

"We left our home," Roman said, "took the children, and searched for the sun and moon daggers."

"Yes, we traveled the surrounding areas in quest of the knives. We were a family. Your children loved me, and I loved them. I felt content for the first time in my life. But then, traveling with three young children became burdensome. You said you'd find the moon dagger by yourself, Roman, and I should stay home and take care of Isabelle and the children." I lapsed into silence. I couldn't bring myself to say more.

Roman shattered the lull in conversation. "You're telling us about the cycle of reincarnation and our past lives and how Olivia and I were once part of a different life with you. Do you live on forever, while the rest of us are reborn again and again?"

"Yes and no," I said. "The darkness ages ever so slowly and it takes time."

"And if I remembered parts of our past, why didn't Olivia seem to?" he asked.

"I can't answer that except to say perhaps Olivia is resistant to knowing," I said.

"What would happen if we ended up in a place and time where another one of our past selves existed?" Roman shuddered as if the thought filled him with dread.

"I can't answer that. As far as I know, that has never happened. The dagger, it seems, possesses a wisdom all its own." There was so much more to say beyond explanations of the hows and whys of time travel and reincarnation. I felt my voice falter, struggling between the desire to keep my thoughts hidden and the need to express something that had been weighing on me for days. I desperately wanted to forget it all, but a part of me knew that the truth had to be said even though it was tearing me apart.

"What aren't you telling us, Malik? Spill it." Olivia pressed her lips into a fierce line.

I looked directly at her. "With Armand gone, well…that's when I became obsessed with *you*, leading you and Armand to your death."

CHAPTER TWENTY-FIVE
MALIK

The look of anger on Olivia's face would have crushed a man lesser than me. Despite my strength and power and centuries of existence, it felt as if I was immobilized.

I rubbed my jaw, considering how much more to say.

"Keep going, Malik," she said, fierce determination drawing lines across her face. "Don't you dare leave out any details."

I almost smiled—almost. Of course, Olivia would say this. Like it or not, the connection between us had always been strong. I couldn't leave her in the dark any longer.

I met her gaze, well aware of Roman's possessive stare boring into me. "It all started when I became obsessed with you, Isabelle."

"I'm not Isabelle. I'm Olivia," she said, grinding out the words.

I nodded. "Please forgive me. I became obsessed with Isabelle."

I glanced at Roman.

The set of his jaw and his flinty-eyed glare let me know he was incensed, too.

I looked at him unblinking. I had betrayed him, yes…I had betrayed both of them. But I refused to show weakness to either of them. My confession had to mean *something* to them.

"You left to find the moon dagger. You trusted me and knew I'd look after Isabelle and the children." I continued to regard him with unwavering attention. "Isabelle and I fell into a most enjoyable rhythm. We shared chores and took turns watching over and playing with the children. We both maintained our roles with one another, but it became increasingly difficult—for me, at least. I began to fool myself into thinking I could finally have the life I deserved." My gaze faltered, and I looked away. "I fooled myself into thinking I could have the love I so desperately craved. Because I fell in love with Isabelle."

I turned to face the fire that crackled in the hearth. My mind drifted into the past, buoyed by the memory of keeping house with Isabelle. Those had been some of the happiest days of my tortured existence.

Still staring into the flames, with my back to Roman and Olivia, I said, "Isabelle was devoted to her husband and children. She was independent and strong, much as you are today, Olivia."

Turning to face them, I clasped my hands behind my back, letting the warmth from the hearth soothe me.

"You didn't take my advances." A wan smile curved my lips. "But I tried. God help me how I tried." I drifted into my memories that tumbled through my mind like storm clouds. "I couldn't control myself. My craving for you grew enormous. It burned so bright."

I held out my hand as if I could cup the memories there

and keep them safe. Finally, I pursed my lips and blew my palm as if scattering the past to the winds.

"You have been who you always were, Olivia. But the longing I held for you so many centuries ago is still with me today," I murmured as our eyes met. I took an uncertain step closer to Olivia, and kneeled before her, taking her hands in mine. Every atom of my being yearned for her, but all I could say was, "I knew I could never have you. We could never be together. Still, nothing would stop me from trying back then."

Our gazes tangled, caught between the prison of the past and my unmet need in the present.

It was excruciating to let myself be this vulnerable, this open. I'd never been this way before. I released Olivia's hands and stepped away.

"I backed off, realizing my attempts at seduction were in vain. Isabelle was too loyal to Armand. She was too in love with him to betray him. But then she let it slip that she and Armand were trying to have another child. I became outraged. 'This is pure foolishness,' I told Isabelle. 'You're both Timebornes. That puts your entire family in danger but especially your innocent children. Your children are Timebounds—they are the targets of Timehunters.'

"We argued through the night, neither one of us backing down. Isabelle accused me of being selfish, of warning her of danger out of jealousy. She thought I wanted to drive a wedge between her and Armand by fabricating lies about Timehunters."

I whirled to face them both.

"Nothing could have been further from the truth," I said, my insides blazing.

Olivia drew her head back, and Roman looked like I had punched him in the gut.

"Having a family was important to Isabelle. But finally,

she heeded my message and grew scared. She cried herself to sleep on many occasions. I consoled her as best I could, doing nothing more but holding you…" I studied Olivia as the past and the present blurred. "Holding Isabelle, I mean."

"And then you…Isabelle…became weak from fear, from shedding too many tears." I rubbed the corners of my mouth. "My desire for Isabelle had grown. It became unquenchable. So did my darkness."

I stared past the sofa at the stone wall, seeing nothing but ghosts of the past. Then, I directed my cold, dead stare at Olivia. "Then one night, Isabelle became so vulnerable that I was able to seduce her."

Roman's nostrils flared, and the blood vessels in his neck bulged. It was a wonder he didn't leap from the couch and assault me.

"Isabelle responded to the darkness inside of me—my potent desires. But her devotion to Armand caused her to rip away from me, to leave me frozen and wanting in her bed chamber. I scrambled out of bed to follow her. She was sobbing, crying, 'What have I done?' She was furious with me. I caught her outside in the moonlight, pacing in wild circles while pulling her hair.

"'Stay away from me,' she growled when I got closer. But, fool that I am, I couldn't stay away from her. I begged for her forgiveness. I said I would not deny Armand my love —I would love you both." I turned toward Olivia, tears in my eyes. "You said *no*."

The ache of rejection roared to the surface as if I were standing in the moonlight with Isabelle.

I couldn't let Roman and Olivia witness my vulnerability. I swiped away my tears with anger and faced Olivia with defiance.

"You swore me to secrecy. You told me you would cast

me out if I even breathed a word of this to Armand. And then you *left* me." My lip curled. "I became nothing but childcare for you both. You and Armand went in search of the dagger."

"Stop talking to me as if I am that same woman!" Olivia said hotly.

"Oh, but you still are. We are *still* in the same situation. I continue to be deeply in love with both of you, but I have sworn to remain on the outside. I shall never have what you both share so freely with one another." The pain in my chest grew unbearable.

I stalked to the fireplace, picked up the iron poker, and stabbed the logs into sparking flames. I was too emotional to speak. *Me*, the man who always remained impassive. The woman who sat before me had an uncanny way of getting under my skin, whether she was Olivia or Isabelle.

I took my time, staring into the flames, schooling my emotions into submission. When I felt they were under control, I rose and turned to face Roman and Olivia again. "I was in agony with you both gone. I missed you terribly. You would return from time to time to check on the children, but *you* ignored me."

I couldn't keep the venom from my words as I gazed at Olivia. "Armand knew nothing. I kept our shared secret. He treated me as a brother, enjoying my company like before I seduced you. But *you*…" My gaze lanced through Olivia. "You wanted to keep away from me.

"Then, one day, you returned bearing the moon dagger. I was too angry to care anymore. For months I endured your refusal to engage with me."

"Quit talking about me as if I am still that woman, Malik!" Sparks flew from Olivia's gaze.

I clasped my hands behind my back and faced her. In a calm, practiced voice, void of emotion, I said, "It does not matter what incarnation you are in, dear Olivia. The spirit is the same. You both have declared your undying devotion to one another throughout incarnations, saying things like, 'I'll always find you.' How can you deny me the truth that you are still the same woman?"

Both Olivia and Roman lowered their gazes to their laps.

"Isabelle," I said. "Isabelle gave me the dagger. I told her I didn't want it. I insisted that she and Armand keep it. I no longer cared about it. *Isabelle…*"

I cast a cold, unforgiving glare at Olivia, who lifted her gaze to meet my eyes.

She shrank back, huddling into Roman.

"Isabelle said to me, 'What's next now that we have found the dagger?' I told her to forget about the dagger. My heart was too crushed to care about anything. I said I wanted to find a way to be with them both. I wanted to freely love Armand and Isabelle. *They* looked at me with derision. Roman—excuse me, *Armand*—said, 'There's no way we can be with you. The village would object.'

"His face flushed as if embarrassed, and he could not look me in the eye. I said it would be our secret. The village wouldn't know. Armand continued to stare away from me and said, 'Not in this lifetime, Malik. Not in this lifetime.'"

I looked directly at Roman, considering his expression. Was it regret? Determination? Sorrow? Intrigue? A combination of the above?

Finally, Roman broke eye contact with me.

"Armand ordered me out. He said, 'We brought you in and cared about you. We made you a part of our family, but you betrayed me. You stole my wife's affection.'" I struggled to mask the emotion that threatened to send me to my knees. "Armand continued, telling me, 'Now I know why Isabelle was so distant on our travels. It took us months to repair our relationship.' I told him I couldn't control the darkness. If I want something, I take it."

Roman squeezed the back of his neck.

Olivia directed her attention at him, her eyes filled with remorse for loving me at one time.

I didn't think my heart could bear the pain.

"I'll be right back," I said and left the room, walking outside to clear my head.

Overhead, the sky was beginning to pale in that telltale way when transitioning to dawn. I regarded the heavens, letting thoughts of a sea of stars that stretched forever soothe my mind. All of this human drama was only temporary. I could endure the pain of never being able to find love— couldn't I?

With a sigh, I reentered the house.

Roman and Olivia were cuddled together in a clear display of "us against him." Roman had his arm around his wife, and she rested her hand on his leg.

Whatever. They needed to hear the rest of the story. I needed to share it and clear the air of secrets. "I'm through cloaking the past. I shall continue this story referring to each of you as you are, not your past names."

Roman gave a slight nod as if in consent.

"When you kicked me out, I told you that you were in danger. You would have to move. The darkness would find you. You put your foot down, Roman, and said, 'We found the dagger, and then you decided to tell me you had an affair. What other option do we have but to cast you aside?'

"I begged you both to let me stay. I promised to keep my hands off your wife if you let me stay and protect you. I wanted to keep you safe—you and the children. But you wouldn't relent. So I left."

I released a heavy and sorrowful sigh. "Those of us who

live in the shadows must accept a different set of rules when it comes to relationships. Haven't you figured that out yet?" My voice rumbled low and deep, full of solemnity. I didn't know if I was telling Olivia and Roman this or reminding myself.

"After you cast me out of your home, I stayed in the shadows. I hid in the woods, in caves, behind copse of trees and boulders—wherever I needed to be to protect and watch over you.

"You realized you weren't safe when you, Roman, went to the village one day and heard rumors of your Timeborne abilities. Some villagers whispered to another about turning you over to the Timehunters. You rushed home, packed up your belongings, threw everything into a wagon, and left with Isabelle and the children. I followed you." I raked my hair with my hand and slumped onto my chair.

"You had to keep moving, though. The rumors of your Timeborne abilities followed you as relentlessly as I did. Whenever a neighbor would find out a Timeborne moved near them, they would tell the Timehunters. Once, you barely escaped before the Timehunters came, ransacked your home, and burned it to the ground." I turned toward Olivia. "I overheard you once telling your husband to find me. You said, 'We should have believed in him. We shouldn't have cast him out.' And you agreed, Roman. But I couldn't allow you to find me. All the time I stayed hidden in the shadows, Olivia, my love for you both grew. It became a terrible burden to carry, this craving to possess you both."

I rested my elbows on my knees and dropped my head into my hands. Dark memories, too horrible to relive, flooded my brain.

I finally lifted my heavy head to regard Olivia. "You became pregnant against my advice. You both thought you were clever enough to escape the Timehunters. All you had to do was keep moving, as difficult as it was. When birth was imminent, you were unable to pack up and go. You had to remain in the house you were in. Travel would prove too challenging for you and your unborn child.

"That's when the Timehunters struck again. It's like they knew your weakness. They galloped through the village with torches, setting fire to everything. They wanted to spare nothing and no one. Your house was to be last. You had given birth that morning and were inside, asleep, when they arrived."

"I rushed outside to stop them," Roman blurted. "But I was killed instantly."

He glared at me. "If you were sworn to watch over and protect us, why didn't you intervene?"

I looked at him for a long time. "I'd given up on you both. I'd finally moved on. I reasoned that I had caused enough damage to your lives and hoped you'd be better off without my presence. That was probably the worst decision I ever made. Because as I was leaving, something kept urging me to turn around and return. I resisted that voice for a long time, before finally heeding it. But I was too late. When I arrived, your home was engulfed by flames and you, Olivia, were outside screaming, cradling your dead husband."

Our eyes met and the air seemed to thicken with an invisible tension. Olivia's voice was heavy with sorrow as she spoke, "I can almost remember that moment. I was screeching, thrashing against an unknown force, desperate to protect my child. I yelled at you to save her, urging you to do whatever it takes to keep her safe."

I nodded. "I so wanted to help you, but I hesitated, thinking, wishing I had never come to your home in the first place. All I brought with me was misery and destruction. Finally, your pleas got to me. I raced inside, through the flames, and snatched the baby out of the arms of the Timehunters, but not before killing each one first."

A long stretch of silence filled the room.

The clock chimed, sending its lilting song through the air.

At long last, I broke the silence. "When I emerged from the house, you were dead, Olivia. Lying next to your husband, forever committed to him throughout time. Your other three children were close by. Even in death, your love for one another was evident."

Olivia's eyes filled with tears, and she seized Roman's hand.

The rejection of being an outsider, a mere witness to their love, still stung. "I raised your child. I was miserable, bereft, and without comfort… but I protected the child.

"Seasons passed, and Alina came to visit me. She said she had given birth to a child. She had birthed you, Olivia." I pushed to stand and crossed to the fireplace to add another log. "But I did not yet know you were Isabelle incarnate."

I propped my hands on my hips, staring into the fire. "Alina also told me she had found a way to destroy Balthazar. She brought me the sun dagger. But I no longer cared about killing Balthazar. I didn't care about anything but nourishing the child. I was despondent over losing everything. Alina wanted to give me her journal, but I wanted no part. I only wanted her to leave."

Olivia and Roman gazed at me in what seemed to be sympathetic pity, their eyes full of condescending compassion. I could feel my blood begin to boil with rage and humiliation, hating their glances as if they were a knife piercing through my fragile skin. To make matters worse, the more I looked into their pitying faces, the deeper I felt engulfed by my own despair.

"When I saw that Alina left the journal behind, I threw it against the wall. I didn't want it." My gaze softened. "But a picture of you fluttered to the ground, Olivia. I looked at it and stared into the eyes of Isabelle."

I bit my lip, savoring the hope the picture had given me.

"I thought I must be hallucinating. I shoved the image back between the pages of the journal and tucked it in the side stand drawer."

I crossed to my chair again and sat down. A curious peace mantled my shoulders as I let the moment sink in. I had shared my truth with Roman and Olivia. I had crept out of the shadows and bared my soul.

I leaned back, somewhat contented.

"What happened to this child?" Olivia said, gripping Roman's hand.

I shrugged. "You have already met her. She's upstairs sleeping."

Olivia gasped.

"What?" Roman exclaimed, leaning forward.

"The child I have cared for ever since you both died is Rosie." A satisfied, cat-like smile spread across my face.

"That's not possible!" Olivia said. "I found her near a stream where a broken carriage lay. The occupants…I assumed they were her parents, were dead."

"Who do you think left her there?" I tapped my chest. "I came across the wagon with the deceased couple. It was the perfect setup. Rosie is brilliant. I told her that 'Two young women are traveling and that they will take care of you and bring you back to me, but you cannot share with them that you know me, that we are playing a game.' Rosie is an extremely bright child and she loves to play games of intrigue."

Olivia pressed her hand to her mouth.

"I raised her as my own for five years. I taught her every-thing. I've been the only one to care for her, to keep her safe. I taught her how to walk, talk—everything. I soothed her during her nightmares, calming her when she screamed at night. I fed her and clothed her. I must have lost countless hours of sleep caring for her, but I didn't mind. When the Black Plague hit, we traveled to the 1800s. I still held guilt over the loss of her parents—of you both—assuming respon-sibility for your deaths. But she's been a gift to me all this time. Through caring for Rosie, I have learned the true meaning of love and sacrifice."

"I don't know what to say," Olivia said, her eyes glistening.

"Nor do I," Roman said.

"There's nothing to say." I glanced out the window at the sky.

A blush of pale apricot and pink peeked over the horizon.

"When Rosie and I arrived in the 1800s, I found you all together, sitting around a campfire. I knew you both the instant I laid eyes on you. I nearly wept with joy. I knew I had been given a second chance, an opportunity to make it all up to you." I clasped my hands at my thighs. "I started watching you, protecting you. Since I had done it before, it came easy to me to do this for you again. My soul was restored as I watched over all of you. I felt a purpose in my life."

I wondered what to say next. "I started plotting and plan-ning, trying to find a way to bring us all together. It felt like destiny to have found you again. I carried you from Balthaz-ar's lair, Roman. I time-traveled you to Olivia's place of origin when you were dying on the battlefield. I knew they had the kind of medical care that could save you."

I allowed Roman and Olivia time to absorb this information, leaning back in my comfortable chair. Deep frowns carved their faces.

"I'm surprised you have remembered so much, Roman." I nodded at him. "And, you, Olivia—I think you push the truth from your mind. You fear it. But you no longer need to be afraid. I know the nightmares that you saw one night, and I came to you. You asked me if we met before."

My gaze fell toward my lap. "I lied and said no. But truthfully, I was shocked that your dreams were showing you memories of your past life. I wasn't ready to share with you then. I needed Roman to be here to explain everything." I rested my palms on the arms of my chair. "I will prove my intentions to you both. You will remember."

I nodded encouragingly. "I want to make things right for you both this time. I give you my word I shall do this."

I brought my clenched fist to my chest.

Olivia stared at me with an indecipherable gaze. "I'm stunned, Malik. I don't know what to say. My mind is in a muddle over everything you shared. I think I'll need time to process it."

I bowed my head. "Of course. But you wanted the truth, Olivia, and I have shared it with you. I love you to the depths of my soul. Even though I will never have you, I promise you —I will die for you to protect you and keep you safe." I turned to Roman. "And, you, Roman. You are my true brother. I will always stand by your side to protect those we love."

"I, too, am shocked, Malik. What happens now? Where do we go from here?" Roman said.

I smiled. "Now we must find where you hid the moon dagger."

CHAPTER TWENTY-SIX

OLIVIA

I sat stunned in Malik's front room, reeling from the news he had shared with us. He had been caring for a child I birthed in another lifetime all this time? First, said caregiver was a demon of darkness. And second, I didn't even remember giving birth to Rosie since it was in a different incarnation. I'd only had dreams of giving birth to *someone*, a beloved child I never got to know. But the story Malik shared seemed real and truthful. The dreams were so vivid, but I was afraid to accept them.

The very thought didn't make sense. I felt like an utter moron as I stared blankly into space, trying without success to let this situation sink in.

The miscarriage of Roman's and my child during this lifetime grieved me. I felt deeply connected to my unborn baby. I still mourned the loss. But Rosie, this very much alive child who supposedly carried my genes, didn't feel like *mine*. How was this possible?

"So a child we bore in another lifetime is alive today," Roman said, stating my thoughts.

"Yes, that's correct. It's one of those things I don't expect you to understand with your human minds," Malik said matter-of-factly.

"Good, because I'm having trouble wrapping my brain around the idea," I said. "I *should* have maternal regard toward Rosie—but I don't. And that messes with my sense of motherly morality."

I reached out to take Roman's hand. He laced his fingers with mine, appearing as confused as me.

"Nothing needs to change. Rosie is brilliant. She thinks of you as her good friends, not her biological parents. But, as far as she and I are concerned, she is my child, and I am her father. I don't expect that to change." Malik nodded as if the case were closed.

"Of course, I expect you to develop a relationship with her," he said. "But the bonds we share run deep. Although she is only five, we have helped one another through tragic times."

His expression shifted to one of tenderness as he looked off into the distance. "Through her, I learned how to love without any strings attached." His eyes returned to me. "You don't want to take that away from me, do you?"

"No, no," I said in a rush. "It makes perfect sense for you to continue with Rosie's care if that's what you want, Malik."

I turned to Roman. "Don't you agree, my love?"

"Absolutely." Roman nodded vigorously.

What didn't make sense was how a child born in a completely different lifetime, many years ago, was now only five years old. The only way I could reconcile this was by remembering that I had jumped backward in time and Malik had time traveled Rosie into the future.

My heart flooded with love for both Roman and Malik.

Malik had lived a difficult life. He'd lost his first love, Layla, having to witness Balthazar kill her. *How horrible that must have been.* And then he had the misfortune of falling in love with "me." My heart was and always would be committed to Roman. And, at that time, he had witnessed the death of Isabelle and Armand, two people he loved dearly. How tragic and utterly heartless it would be to wrench Rosie from his life in some possessive claim.

I simply wouldn't do that. The mere fact that Malik had lovingly cared for a child all this time was proof that monsters could evolve.

I released Roman's hand, leaned forward, and took Malik's. "I'm so very grateful to you."

Malik's eyes shone as they met mine.

"I don't know why I didn't see it all along. Rosie looks so much like Roman. You'd think I'd see the connection, but I didn't. You took her during a moment of tragedy and raised her as your own. How could we not be grateful to you?" I gripped his hand, then settled next to my husband, curling my feet on the sofa, and leaning into Roman's warmth.

Malik smiled softly. "The minute I laid eyes on Rosie, I knew she was mine. I couldn't hand her off to another. It was a sacrifice and a gift to receive your child and care for her how I imagined you would want her cared for. Rosie has wanted for nothing. She gets love, companionship, friendship, and warmth from me. I'll stop at nothing to protect her and keep her safe."

"Our gratitude knows no limits," Roman said, his eyes glittering. He placed his arm around me and pulled me close. "You not only saved our child in our last lifetime but also saved *me* in this lifetime. Not once but twice. You rescued me from Balthazar's lair. Then you transported me to another time when I lay dying on the battlefield. Were it not for you, I would surely have perished in both instances."

Malik swiped a tear away from his cheek. In a gravel-filed voice, he said, "I love you both. I want to make amends for my mistakes and not repeat the past. Taking care of Rosie has given me a heart, a reason to live. It's one small thing I could do for you, but it's a tremendous gift to me."

He crossed to the fire and poked it with the iron as if not wanting us to witness his vulnerability.

Roman and I exchanged a glance.

I said, "Malik, we're thankful for all you've done for us. You're not a monster."

Malik kept his back to us, continuing to crouch before the fire. "I'm here for both of you. I want to beg your forgiveness in any way for the anger, sadness, and issues I've caused." He rose and pivoted, his face an unreadable mask. "Everything I've done was the ultimate do-over for me. Each time I look at you, I see Isabelle and Armand, and it fills me with remorse and drives me to make amends."

His handsome face appeared carved from marble. Only his eyes revealed the depth of his emotion.

Roman cleared his throat and pushed to stand. He crossed to where Malik stood by the fire. "Even though we might have lived before, I'm different now. I was a gladiator in this lifetime. I fought for my existence in the Colosseum. But once I left Rome, you saved my life."

He placed his hand on Malik's shoulders.

The two men's eyes met, regarding one another somberly.

"That's serious to me," Roman said. "We had an honor code when I was a gladiator. If someone saved us from death, we were bound to that person for life. You're the darkness— you could have killed me at any time. You're good in your own way. You took care of my wife when I was gone. When your heart is on the line—with Olivia, I mean—it must be hard for you."

They nodded at one another.

I wanted to cry over the sincerity in Roman's voice and the regard Malik displayed toward my husband.

"As long as we don't repeat history, I trust you," Roman said. "I'm willing to move on and start fresh in this lifetime. We are truly brothers."

He extended his arms, and he and Malik embraced.

I sniffled. It was a beautiful exchange to behold.

Roman and Malik deeply loved each other.

When they broke apart from the embrace, Malik met Roman's eyes. "Everything I do is to protect you and destroy the evil that exists."

He put his hand on Roman's back and guided him back to me.

They each took their seats, and Malik continued talking. "I vow to destroy Balthazar and the Timehunters. And you must know…" He clenched his hand into a fist. "Taking Marcellious into my confidence was vital. I had to be able to spy on Balthazar, and Marcellious was the perfect candidate. He had already been influenced by Balthazar, so I knew Balthazar wouldn't be suspect. No one would notice Marcellious playing a role like this."

His hand unfurled, and he stared at his palm.

Perhaps he was gathering his thoughts.

Then, he said, "I recruited Marcellious when you were headed to find Philip's estate to find the journal. While you were sleeping around the campfire, I compelled Marcellious into the woods and told him my plan."

Malik frowned. "At first, Marcellious was suspicious of me. 'Why should I believe you over Balthazar? Why should I trust you?' I told him, 'Balthazar is only interested in one thing—his own interests. He's using you for his own gain. Everything he does is for his own selfish purposes. But what I do will benefit you, Olivia, Roman, and Emily. If you care even the slightest for any of them, you'll join me in my plan.'"

He looked at me, then Roman, and leaned over his knees, hands clasped. "It was hard on him, but he turned out to be a strong soldier. He was the perfect man to gain Balthazar's confidence and retrieve his dagger. Both his and Alina's knives," he amended.

He sat up and rolled his shoulders as if their tightness was unbearable.

"Why did you need those daggers in particular?" I asked.

Malik's eyes glinted, and a secretive smile stretched across his face.

Oh, boy, I thought. He's still Malik, a man of secrets.

"Your mother's prized possession is mine, now!" Malik spat out the words as his emerald gaze pierced my soul. "You see, when I took away something that Balthazar loved, he was rendered powerless. His dagger is in my possession, and he can no longer time travel anywhere. We control him; we have taken away his freedom of movement and time manipulation. Our daggers are our gateway to any place and era, but with them being confiscated by me, Balthazar is without a means of escape."

The full force of his words hit me like a ten-thousand-ton explosive, sending shivers down my spine. Malik had taken away Balthazar's only form of power—his ability to time travel—which meant that no matter where his enemy would go, he could never run away or hide from him again.

Well played, my friend.

"Why did you bring Tristan here?" I asked.

"Why, to keep the demon distracted. Tristan, as you must know, isn't too smart or too fast. Balthazar is on babysitting duty." A hearty laugh erupted from Malik's throat.

What a clever, clever man. Malik thought of everything to the most exacting detail.

Roman and I smiled, caught up in Malik's moment of mirth.

Malik stood. With his hands clasped behind his back, he said, "Everything I'm doing is to destroy Balthazar. You two will become the most powerful people when you find the moon dagger. And then you will take the two daggers, learn how to use them, and kill me."

"What?" His words lanced me like an arrow to the chest. "You can't be serious. Kill you? No! I refuse to do that!"

Roman stood and grabbed Malik by the shoulders. "You may be the darkness, but you won't die as one. I respect you for all you did. Let yourself be transformed and continue to live on this planet with us."

Malik shook his head, prying Roman's fingers from his shoulders. "I won't have a purpose to live once Balthazar is destroyed."

"We're a family," I said, joining Roman in front of Malik. "We're an unstoppable team now. We can *never* destroy you. You're a good person."

"I'm no saint," Malik said, casting his gaze at the floor. "I do many bad things. But being in your life has taught me to be a good person."

"Think about Rosie," I said. "If you love her as much as you do, how can you leave her? She should be your reason to live."

A tortured, anguished expression flashed through Malik's eyes.

I placed my palm on his stubble-covered cheek.

He placed his palm over my hand and squeezed his eyes shut. Then, he tore his face away and started pacing. "I've lived a long time—too long. I will do what I must."

SARA SAMUELS

I glanced at Roman, tears in my eyes.

He shook his head as if to say, I don't know what to do either.

"I feel your pain after hearing your story, Malik. It's evident you have love inside. When you told us how you offered to be lovers with both of us, well…" I pushed my hair away from my face. "Being a bisexual man through centuries of bigotry, homophobia, and mistrust must be difficult. It must be hard getting your needs met."

Malik stopped before me and met my gaze. His expression was one of a wounded lion.

I took both his hands. "Look, Malik. We love one another but don't want to destroy our friendship. I want to continue loving you. I don't think you'll object to that, will you, Roman?"

I turned to look at my husband.

Tears spilled down Roman's cheeks. "I love you, too, Malik. Just not that way."

He clasped Malik's shoulder.

I began to sob. "Thank you for taking care of me when I lost my child. Thank you for always being on the lookout for us. Maybe because of you, we're one step closer to destroying Balthazar. Yes, you had Marcellious betray us, but how you pulled all the threads together is incredible. We're all a family—Marcellious, Roman, Emily, Rosie, me, and *you*, Malik. You can't ask us to kill you. You just can't," I blubbered. "I know now not all darknesses are bad. You taught me that. You're a good, good person."

I threw my arms around him and sobbed into his shoulder.

Malik held his arms out as if resisting temptation.

Roman moved behind him and hugged him, too.

That seemed to be the permission he needed as Malik

finally wrapped me in his embrace. We hugged that way, with Malik sandwiched between us.

When we broke apart, we all had wet, bloodshot eyes.

I kissed Malik's cheek. "You're so much more than a friend, Malik. We'll work together to destroy Balthazar. Then, maybe we can find peace one day."

Malik looked at the ceiling.

"Maybe," he said, his voice thick with emotion.

Both Roman and Malik wiped the tears from their faces.

Witnessing these two strong men, these warriors cry was almost too much to bear.

"So, how can we find the moon dagger?" I asked.

Something like relief flooded Malik's gaze. "I'll show you. We must take one step at a time."

He headed toward the stairs. Roman and I followed him as he led us to his office.

A new bond thrummed between us, born out of tenderness, vulnerability, and sharing.

When we entered his office, Malik crossed to a cupboard built into the wall. He opened it with a flourish, revealing a wall of daggers similar to the ones in Balthazar's house.

I sucked in a lungful of air. Most of these knives, if not all, represented the lives of Timebornes Malik had taken.

With his back to us, Malik scanned the wall. When he pivoted, he held two knives that almost looked familiar. "These were your blades in your past incarnation—Armand's and Isabelle's."

Roman held out his hand.

When Malik placed a knife in his hand, Roman said, "You kept these after the fire?"

"I did. I didn't want your daggers to get into the wrong hands." Malik nodded gravely. "And now I shall prove the existence of your past lives to you. Here, Olivia, take your knife."

I wrapped my fingers around the hilt. It felt comfortable and natural to hold, but no memories surfaced. I strained my brain to remember.

"I wish I could recall *something*."

"One moment, and you will. Please, take a seat." Malik searched for something in the cupboard as Roman and I settled on the green velvet sofa.

Malik spun around, a small glass vial in his hands that was filled with what appeared to be blood. "This is Rosie's blood," he said softly. "You will hold your knives like so, one on top of the other. I shall pour the contents of this vial onto the metal so that it covers each blade. By doing this, you will be able to view past memories and come into contact with your former selves."

I met Roman's eyes, and we sank into the depth of our connection.

Malik said, "Ready?"

Roman and I nodded and positioned our daggers.

Malik recited the sacred scripture. The room seemed to expand as the words were spoken.

Then, he carefully poured out a minuscule amount of crimson liquid.

An image of a cottage in the English countryside appeared as soon as the red droplets hit the blades.

Startled, I let out a gasp.

A woman who looked just like me, only with raven black hair, stood toiling in a garden. Three children scampered around her, chasing butterflies.

I smiled as I looked at her. She seemed so content.

The woman—Isabelle—rose and stretched her back as the sound of galloping horse hooves rang out.

Armand and Malik charged over the hill, appearing to race one another.

"I win!" Armand shouted.

"You did not!" Malik shouted. "It was a tie."

Malik and Armand leaped from their horses and shoved one another, laughing.

Armand crossed to where Isabelle stood smiling and embraced her, kissing her soundly. He looked like Roman—same eyes, same hair, same everything.

A much thinner Malik watched Isabelle and Armand, longing evident in his gaze.

"Look!" he said, interrupting Armand and Isabelle. "We killed a deer."

Isabelle gazed at him, smiling. "Bring it into the shed, and I shall skin it and salt and pickle the meat."

Armand and Isabelle's love for each other was as strong as Roman's and my love.

The scene changed to where Armand and Isabelle were sated from having sex, wrapped in each other's arms somewhere dark and dank.

"Why this image?" I exclaimed. "Where are we?"

"I don't know," Malik said.

"Any memories coming up for you, Roman?"

He shook his head. "Not one."

Many scenes flashed before our eyes, but the dank-smelling space held my attention.

In all of the visions, the love Armand and Isabelle experienced was evident. We loved each other deeply, just as we did now. Yet we cared a lot for Malik, too. It felt natural to include him in our family.

Then the vision turned dark and foreboding.

The acrid smell of smoke assaulted my nose. I knew I was inside the cabin, sleeping, my new baby by Isabelle's side.

The wicked glow of orange flames shone through the window.

Armand fought with a knife outside the cottage, slashing at several men who surrounded him. They overpowered him, and one of them slit Armand's throat.

Shouts and screams came from outside, awakening Isabelle. Terrified, she raced into the yard to find Armand dead. She dropped to her knees and cradled Armand's head. She screamed and cried as Malik came into view. She yelled at him to save the baby. In her haste to get to Armand, she had left her newborn child inside a burning building.

What kind of mother had I been to have left my child?

"Please, Malik. Save my baby!" Isabelle pleaded.

A Timehunter burst around the corner, flaming torch in hand. He barreled toward Isabelle. A knife was in his hand, and he plunged it into her chest.

I sat quietly sobbing, tears rolling down my face.

Abruptly, Isabelle and Armand stepped from the vision, standing before us. They appeared transparent. They looked at each other and then at Roman and me, smiling.

"You've been given another chance," Armand said.

"You must defeat the darkness and Timehunters," Isabelle said. "Don't make the same mistakes we did."

"Don't repeat history," Armand said.

I bolted to my feet and held out my hands. "Help us remember. Where did you hide the moon dagger?"

Armand and Isabelle looked at one another as if sharing a secret.

"Please," I begged them. "You're the people who hid it. Surely you remember where you put it."

The couple continued to smile at one another, content in their secrecy.

"You don't want us to make the same mistakes," I said,

my stomach bound in frustration. "Please help us. I'm begging you. Please show us where the moon dagger is hidden."

"It's in the same place where it all started for you—somewhere deep and dark, like where you were born." Isabelle's smile broadened. "It's in a cave in Wales. La Caverne de la Viergueux."

Isabelle and Armand faded from sight, leaving behind the chill of a cold, damp place.

"Roman!" I turned to look at him, rubbing my arms for warmth.

"I feel it too, my beloved," he said. "The dagger is in within our grasp. Only how can we find it?"

CHAPTER TWENTY-SEVEN

OLIVIA

"We've got to find the cave!" I said, buoyed by a surge of adrenaline. I was ready to depart at once.

Malik slid in my way, placing his hands on my upper arms. "Olivia. Do you really think you can find anything in this condition? You're exhausted. You look a wreck."

I glanced at my reflection in the window. My once elaborate updo hung in limp, ragged strands around my face. My skirt bore a blood spray, and the hem had been torn. The blouse I'd grabbed and donned at Costa's party was a garish reddish-yellow that didn't even go with the expensive blue silk costume I'd started the night in.

I looked like a bombed Cinderella.

I sagged against Roman. "We can rest, sure, but then we must depart at once."

Roman put his arm around me. "My love, we must sleep, eat, and restore, not run off half-cocked. Count Montego is awaiting us. Let's head to his estate, sleep, then make a plan."

My eyelids became too heavy to hold up and fluttered closed.

"All right," I said as I snuggled into Roman's shoulder. "But we must leave soon."

"We will, my fierce warrior. We will." He kissed the top of my head.

"My carriage driver can drop you off. I'll let him know." Malik spun on his heel and left the room.

"God, I'm tired," I said to Roman, stating the obvious.

"Me, too. Let's get outside to the carriage. The sooner we depart, the sooner we can lay our heads on pillows."

The trek to Count Montego's estate was nothing but a blur. The lurch and sway of the coach proved hypnotic as if we were in a cradle. I kept falling asleep on Roman's shoulder and waking up startled. I didn't want to yield to sleep until we were indoors.

A bright sun climbed through the sky, painting the landscape in every rainbow hue. This part of Italy was gorgeous.

When we arrived at the count's estate, Roman helped me from the carriage and bade the driver farewell.

Bleary-eyed, I struggled to take in my surroundings. We trekked across a terracotta courtyard with a fountain of dancing maiden statues pouring water from jugs at their hips. Brilliant pink and red bougainvillea tumbled over the stone fences surrounding the enclosure. Green hedges and grasses had been artfully placed throughout.

I stumbled up the front stairs, clinging to Roman like a vine. I didn't think my legs could hold me up.

A pretty maid let us in the front door. She exclaimed, "Mr. Alexander! Oh! Sembrate entrambi esausti! Lascia che ti prepari un bagno e poi devi dormire. Il conte Montego ha dato ordine di provvedere a ogni tua esigenza finché non si alza."

My weary brain managed to translate. You both look exhausted! Let me prepare you a bath, and then you must sleep. Count Montego has given orders to fulfill your every need until he arises.

She hesitated and said to me, *"Dove sono le mie buone maniere? Buon giorno. Sono Beatrice."*

Where are my manners? Good morning. I am Beatrice. She pronounced her name as beh-a-TREE-cheh, and I nodded, smiling.

Roman said, *"Questa è mia moglie, Olivia."*

This is my wife, Olivia.

Beatrice curtsied and walked away, waving for us to follow.

We trailed behind her down the hall, exited the back of the house, and meandered toward a small stone building.

Past an archway, we entered a large room smelling of minerals. Steam wafted from a pool in the center, with stone benches lining the walls. Water trickled from a pipe at the far end of the pool.

"We are fortunate to have hot springs on this property. Please indulge yourselves," Beatrice said in her native tongue.

She approached the rim of the pool, crouched, then said, "Perfect. I shall fetch you linens to wear after you bathe."

As soon as she departed, Roman captured me in his arms and hugged me. I melted into his embrace.

We stood there for a long moment, caressing one another's backs, familiarizing ourselves with the feel of one another.

Then, he eased back and began unbuttoning the tiny buttons on my bodice. "Allow me, my beautiful wife."

His eyes glittered as the blouse fell open. He swept it from my shoulders with warm, strong hands, stroking my arms. I placed my hands on his shoulders as he tenderly kissed my collarbones and worked his way up my neck. My head fell back as he planted soft kisses on my jaw and cheeks. Then, his mouth met mine in a series of feather-light kisses.

"I missed you more than the moon and stars combined, *amore mio*," he murmured against my lips. "Each day without you was like torture. At night, I dreamed about holding you in my arms. But waking each day to an empty bed made me howl."

I fell into a swoon, utterly intoxicated by his loving regard.

As he continued with his kiss and tell, he urged the remaining clothes from my body.

When I stood there, naked, Roman stepped back and hissed. "Così fottutamente bello, amore mio."

So fucking beautiful, my love.

His blue-eyed gaze was like liquid heat, deep as a sea cave's quiet inlet. With hooded eyes, he stalked around me, letting his fingers trail across my bare flesh.

I shivered at the contact.

Roman drew me back against his clothing-covered body.

"Would you deny me the touch of your flesh to mine?" I said, dropping my head against his shoulder.

Roman eased me away and removed his clothes. When he drew me back, I met warm, naked skin.

I brushed my palms against his muscular thighs, feeling the press of his swollen erection against my ass.

"Let's get wet, shall we?" he whispered. He lifted me into his arms.

"Oh!" I exclaimed, hooking my arms around his neck.

He descended the stone steps and lowered us both into the water.

I was weightless, warm, and languid. I spread out my

arms and floated in the mineral-rich water. Roman placed his hands beneath me and urged me in a lazy circle through the water.

I closed my eyes, savoring the healing touch of water.

"Let me wash you, my goddess," he said before cradling my head in his palm and kissing me tenderly.

We moaned into one another's mouths.

When Roman drew back from the kiss, he gazed at me lovingly. "I never want to be apart from you again."

"I don't either. It was hell." I lowered my legs and stood to face him.

The water lapped against my ribcage. With my hands on Roman's shoulders, I kissed him savagely, relentlessly, letting him know how much I treasured being back with him.

We were both breathless when we came up for air.

"Oh, my wicked beauty," he said, his eyes heavy with lust. "I'm going to give you every orgasm you deserve. But for now, let me wash you and take you upstairs to bed."

Our eyes locked in a torrid gaze.

"What if I can't wait?" I said.

Roman chuckled. "Olivia, you look like you'll faint once we step out of here. Allow me to help you. Let me make sure all your needs are taken care of."

We both looked down at his throbbing cock bobbing between us.

I curled my fingers around it.

Roman smiled, pried my fingers from his shaft, and said, "Not yet."

He led me to the stone bench lining the pool and had me sit between his legs. Then, he reached outside the water and retrieved a soap bar.

"The count told me all about this luxury soap he gets from Florence." He rubbed the creamy, fragrant bar along my skin.

"He said it's made by virgins, but I think that's what he tells himself."

His low chuckle vibrated against my back. "It's made with olive oil, not lye, and scented with sage, marjoram, chamomile, rosemary, and orange peel."

"It smells fantastic," I said, pressed against his torso.

Roman continued his ministrations, washing my entire body and even my hair. When he was done, he placed the soap behind him and let his hand caress my belly.

"I discovered new ways to please you in the twenty-first century," he said with a teasing lilt.

"Did you? What did you do? Go to a strip club?"

"A what?"

"It's a place where men go to watch women undress onstage," I said, kneading his legs. I swear I could *feel* Roman's blush behind me.

"No, amore, nothing like that. Why would I want to lay eyes on anyone beside you?" he said, melting my heart. "No, I read a book in your…at your…beneath your bed in your old apartment."

Now it was my turn to blush. It had to be the Dirty Little Secrets book I'd purchased to try and spice up Tristan's and my sex life.

Either way, I didn't want to know. "That's too much information, Roman. Show me. Don't tell me."

He lowered his hand between my legs. "Gladly. I'm inspired to try new things."

He parted my folds with his fingers and began stroking my silk.

"I read about different positions. Things like Butterfly and Reverse Cowgirl, although I wonder how a woman who tends to cows is sexy." The tips of his fingers quivered as their paths traced circles and swirls over my body. Every nerve in my body was alight with electricity, aching to be touched.

He whispered words of pleasure in my ear, leaving traces of warmth as his fingertips brushed across my skin. His lips found mine hungrily, hard and eager as if trying to draw out every bit of desire from within me.

"Uncloaking the Clitoris," he murmured, his hands finding their way down to the source of my pleasure. I shuddered at the sensation of his fingers tracing patterns over the hood of tissue concealing my clit beneath it. His hands moved with a gentle precision as they revealed my hidden nubbin of flesh.

I closed my eyes in blissful anticipation as I felt his touch becoming increasingly more intense with each passing minute, stirring up a bedlam of pleasure within me that threatened to consume us both. I gripped his thighs as his skilled fingers took me closer to orgasm. I arched into his touch, creating a cacophony of splashes and ecstatic cries.

He let out a throaty laugh. "You are so fucking beautiful when you come, my love."

"And you are a master at 'uncloaking my clit,'" I said.

As I came down, Roman kissed me deeply. At the same time, he scooped me into his arms again and carried me from the pool. Releasing my lips, he said, "That was just a warm-up exercise."

"I'm feeling quite excited to dive into the knowledge you have acquired."

We found rough muslin cloths near the doorway to dry with and soft linen dressing gowns to don. Once dry and dressed, we exited the stone room and trekked into the house. We tiptoed up the stairs, not wanting to wake the count.

Roman led me into a generously sized, well-appointed room.

Beatrice had turned down the wine-colored velvet covers. Sighing, I slid between the coverings and lay my head on the feather pillow.

Roman slid next to me.

I thought we might continue what we started in the pool, but the lure of sleep proved too much to resist.

Wrapped in one another's arms, I fell into a deep, dreamless sleep.

I awoke hours later to the feel of a fingertip coating my mouth with something sweet and sticky. I licked my lips, tasting honey.

My eyelids fluttered open to see Roman, propped on his elbow, with a plate of meat, fruit, loaves of bread, cheeses, and honey between us.

"Wake up, sleepyhead," he said with a smile. "Beatrice brought us food."

I yawned and stretched my arms. "What time is it? How long did we sleep?"

"All day. A stunning sunset is just outside those curtains." He gestured toward the window lined with thick curtains the same color as the bedding. He propped his torso on the pillows and rested the platter in his lap. He popped a grape in his mouth. "I'm famished. You?"

"Not quite awake yet." I wriggled into a similar position as Roman, propped against the headboard. I shifted my leg over him, savoring the warmth.

Roman tore a piece of chicken from the bones and held it before my mouth. "Try this. It's delicious."

I opened my mouth, and he slid the poultry between my

teeth. My stomach growled in glee. "Mmm, so delicious. It tastes like it was seasoned with bacon."

"I think it was," he said, tearing off a drumstick.

I ripped a piece of bread from a fresh-baked loaf.

"Oh, my God," I said through the mouthful. "So good."

"Speaking of bacon," Roman said, giving me a side-eye. "I loved your twenty-first bacon. And coffee! The coffee was divine. That's one of the things I miss."

"Coffee and bacon," I said, tearing a chunk of breast meat and chomping down. "I was fond of it, too. What else did you like to eat?"

Roman licked the chicken juices from his fingers. "Let's see. Waffles." He nodded. "Waffles and maple syrup. That was delicious." He handed me a piece of cheese smeared with honey, then picked up a bit for himself.

The taste of tangy cheese and sweet honey exploded in my mouth.

I fingered the tattoo on his forearm. "I love this tattoo. Where did you get it?"

"Lee took me to a tattoo shop in Fremont. A man named Sebastian the Great did the honors." Roman leaned over and retrieved a carafe. He poured some down his throat and then handed it to me.

"What's this?" I tipped the bottle to my lips and took a welcome sip.

"It's mead. Wine is ghastly in this period. I was spoiled by the wine in your times." He reached for the carafe and took another swallow.

I devoured the sight of his thick neck, bulging with veins.

Roman was a delight to behold.

I took the mead back and drank my fill. Handing it back to Roman, I said, "I do worry about that tattoo, Roman."

"Worry? Why?" He rested the mead bottle on the floor by his side.

"Isn't it obvious? It's a *dagger*. If a Timehunter sees that marking, you'll instantly be suspect." A ripple of fear rolled up my backbone.

Roman frowned. "I see your point." He tapped his full lips with his fingertip. "I'll keep it covered when we're out. And if a Timehunter accosts us, we'll say we are Timehunters, too. We can say we're searching for the man who owns this dagger—he's dangerous and a threat to society."

I sighed. "Don't you think the Timehunters know who's in the network?"

Roman glanced at me. "The technology you have in your time hasn't been created yet, *amore*. Yes, they have detailed drawings of poisonous plants, but do you think they have detailed drawings of members, too?"

"I don't know." I idly stroked the hairs on his leg. "I'd rather we didn't find out. Keep it covered."

We lay in silence, continuing to eat.

The mead made my head swim pleasantly. I snuggled closer to Roman.

"Oh!" I said. "Did you know Marcellious and Emily got married? And Emily is pregnant. That was hard for her when she thought Marcellious had gone to the dark side and joined forces with Balthazar. He was convincing, parading Dahlia around as if she were his lover."

"Dahlia?" Roman gave me a wide-eyed stare.

"Yes, Dahlia. I killed her."

"You killed Dahlia?"

I nodded.

Roman leaned over and hugged me hard. "I'm so proud of you, my warrior woman."

A surge of pride rocked through me at his compliment. I

recalled feeling weak, not powerful. I was a broken woman. But he was right—I'd found the strength to defeat my darkness. "Thank you, Roman."

Roman smiled. Then, a frown darkened his face. "I saw you through my dagger when you lost our child. I watched Balthazar throw you against the ground."

His expression contorted into a rage.

A searing bolt of pain tore at my heart. I squeezed Roman's hand for comfort.

"It was so awful, Roman. And, coupled with your absence, I don't know how I made it through that time." My eyebrows drew together. "Actually, I do know. I wouldn't have made it had Malik not rescued me."

Roman urged me forward and placed his arm behind me, pulling me close. "We have much to thank Malik for. He has saved us each. And, he saved and cared for our daughter, Rosie."

"Yes." I let my fingers slide into the crease in Roman's leg, stroking.

His cock stirred next to my hand. I wrapped my hand around his shaft and gently squeezed.

"We'll make another baby again, *amore*, I promise," Roman said. He drew my hand up to his lips and kissed my knuckles. "We can have as many children as you desire. After we do away with Balthazar."

"Yes," I breathed.

"Speaking of Balthazar and his twat of a son…" Roman laced our fingers together. "I have no idea how you endured being with Tristan. He's a blithe idiot—a complete pain in the ass. What did you possibly see in him?"

My cheeks flushed with heat. "I think Tristan hid his true colors. His mannerisms were often forced. They seemed calculating, almost too perfect. But I can only see that in retrospect." I squeezed Roman's hand. "I hope you don't think less of me for being with Tristan."

"I could never think less of you, *amore*." He kissed the top of my head. "You are the keeper of my heart. I almost forgot! I brought gifts from the twenty-first century for you."

"Gifts? What did you bring?" My heart thumped with excitement.

"Let me show you." He traipsed across the room and opened the armoire. When he returned, he held several items wrapped in silk. "Your father suggested we buy these."

He handed me the first parcel.

"My father! I can't believe he is alive! All this time I thought he was dead and killed by Tristan. But when I saw him through my dagger, I was shocked."

"Yes, *amore*, he's very much alive and misses you dearly."

With shaking fingers, I peeled apart the red silk and found a box of bullets for my Glock.

"Oh! What a great gift! I'm nearly out of bullets!" I rested the box by my side. "What else do you have?"

The sparkle in his eyes was evident as he handed me the next package. "Extend your hand," he instructed.

I did.

He placed the tiny object in my hand and curled my fingers around it. "This was also your father's suggestion. He's such a lovely, caring man. I enjoyed him greatly."

Tears filled my eyes at the thought of Roman meeting my father. I held the bundle to my chest. "Whatever it is, I already love it."

"Open it," Roman said.

I unclasped my hand and gently removed the silk wrapping.

Two gold bands, one larger and one smaller, rested on the fabric.

A tear fell from my cheek and landed on the silk.

"What are these?" I whispered.

"They're our wedding bands. Jack bought them. He insisted." Roman plucked the smaller one from my hand and said, "Read the inscription."

He held it close to my eyes.

Forever yours, Roman. Forever yours, Olivia, my beautiful flame. I blinked back the onslaught of happy tears. "Oh, Roman. It's so beautiful."

"We're destined to find one another, my love. In this life and the next." Roman's eyes shone as he took my left hand and slid the ring on my finger.

I took the other ring, picked up Roman's hand, and slid the gold band into place. "You mellow my hot temper. You are my sexy gladiator in this lifetime. Yes, we shall always find one another."

We crashed together with a desperate intensity, our mouths meeting hungrily. Our kiss was like a supernova, and I felt my soul splitting open as we connected. Tiny filaments of energy swirled around us, creating an inextricable binding between us that seemed to overflow from some otherworldly source, unleashing a power that shook me to my core.

We broke apart and regarded one another.

I smiled. "Forever yours, Roman."

He returned the smile. "Forever yours, Olivia, my beautiful flame." He glanced at the final parcel that lay on the bed. "Here is your last gift. It's a letter from your father."

I reached for the silk and pressed it to my chest. I swore I could feel Papa through time and space. We hugged in some ethereal realm, and my heart felt full and nourished.

I held onto that sensation until curiosity got the best of

me. Then, I carefully pried apart the layers, finding several sheets of paper folded into a square. I smoothed the paper with my hand and began to read.

Dear Olivia,

First and foremost, I'm sorry for not telling you who you are sooner. I kept you in the dark. I wanted to shelter you, but I went about it all wrong. I should have protected you by telling you the truth so you could be ready for the challenges ahead.

A circular water stain blurred the words. Had Papa been crying when he wrote this? The thought broke my heart.

Your mother and I weren't compatible. We were seldom happy. I loved her, but she wasn't as in love with me as I was with her. I tried so hard to please her. To make her happy, but it was never enough.

More tear stains marred the writing.

Your mother kept secrets from me. Those secrets grew like a poisonous weed, tearing us apart. Yet, she saved me from killing myself when I was most vulnerable. I will always be grateful to her.

Only, when your mother was murdered, I wanted to kill myself again. I was in a dark place. I was alone, had a child to care for, and had too many questions. I couldn't feed you or take care of you. I was always crying.

I told Lee to take care of you. He said, "No, you have to keep going. You have a daughter, and she needs you very much."

Then he told me the truth. "Alina was a time traveler," he said.

I was shocked.

I vowed to find your mother's killer. I dedicated my life to destroying the darkness.

I wiped away the tears falling down my cheeks.

Papa has been working to kill the darkness!

A protective surge rocked through me. *He's too frail to deal with Balthazar.*

Roman caressed my shoulder. "Are you okay?"

I couldn't speak with the logjam of emotions in my throat, so I nodded, shaking more tears free, and resumed reading.

Lee told me Alina had an affair with a madman. I wish she had told me the truth.

Now I want to be part of this whole plan. I believe we all have a role to play.

I let out a sob and pressed the back of my hand to my mouth.

When I met Roman, I was stunned. Imagine my shock when this giant gladiator of a man appeared in my home.

I could picture Papa's smile when he said this. He must have been utterly surprised.

I'm so glad you're with Roman. You're well matched now…with a man worthy of your affection. I enjoyed him. Knowing you're with a good person who has your back lets me know you will be okay.

I love you, sweetheart, and know you're strong. Even though your mother couldn't defeat Balthazar, I know you can. You're stronger than Alina, more fiercer and bolder.

I don't know when I'll see you again, but my door is always open. Forgive me for not being the best father I could be. I was in the dark all these years. All I wanted to do was protect you. I fell into despair when I found out Balthazar was trying to kill you. Be strong. Stay vigilant. Never give up.

I love you forever, my little moon,

Papa

Now I was ugly crying. Huge sobs wracked my ribcage.

Roman wrapped me in his arms and pulled me close. He stroked my hair and murmured soothing sounds into my ear.

When my sobs subsided, I eased away from Roman. "I read Mom's journal."

He wiped away my tears with his thumbs. "Did you? What did you learn?"

"How much she loved Balthazar, and how she wanted to save him." I frowned. "I don't get it."

"Well, think of Malik and how close we are to him now."

I shook my head. "They are not the same. Balthazar is a monster."

"That's true," Roman said, in his "reasonable" tone. "But how do you know the journal is telling the truth?"

My frown deepened. "You're right. Mom was devious. But she's long dead. Only time will tell the truth of her words."

Roman nodded.

I folded the letter and tucked it in the silk, resting it on the box of bullets. But then, a horrible thought crashed through my brain. "Roman!"

"What?" he said, alarmed.

"Where is my dagger?"

"What do you mean?" He gripped my upper arms.

"My blade. I always keep it strapped to my leg. Now it's not here. I think we left it at Costa's."

CHAPTER TWENTY-EIGHT

OLIVIA

"Are you absolutely sure you left the dagger at Costa's?" Roman asked me as I paced around the bedroom, with the sensation of snakes coiled in my stomach.

"One hundred percent," I said, then I stopped. "Okay, seventy-five percent. Okay, I think so. That's what makes the most sense. But everything's such a blur. I just don't know. Fuck!"

"*Amore mio*, please calm down." Roman swung his legs from the bed.

"How can I calm down? Losing my dagger is horrible. What if someone like Costa found it? I'm doomed!" I waved my arms wildly.

"Olivia!" Roman said, tone sharp.

"What?" I whirled to face him.

"Let's follow the steps. We'll start at Malik's, then take it from there, okay?"

He was right. I was freaking out, which wasn't helping. But when I met his gaze, the telltale signs of worry creased in the corners of his eyes.

"Oh, Roman! What if it's gone for good?"

Roman seized my upper arms and looked deeply into my eyes. "We don't know that yet. Let's just take one step at a time, okay?"

"Okay," I said, nodding, drawing strength from his calm demeanor. "Okay. We'll start at Malik's like you suggested."

Wordlessly, we dressed in clean clothes, then made our way downstairs.

The estate seemed quiet and empty save for the faint clatter of kitchen sounds.

I followed Roman through the dining room and into the large kitchen at the back of the house, where Beatrice was chopping vegetables.

She stopped when she saw us. "Good evening, Mr. and Mrs. Alexander. Did you sleep well?"

"*Sì, sì, grazie*," Roman said. Then, he proceeded to ask her where Count Montego was.

"I don't know. He left some time ago. I expect he'll return shortly for his evening meal," Beatrice said, resuming her chopping.

Roman nodded. "Mrs. Alexander and I are heading out on an errand. Please let him know."

"*Sì, sì,*" Beatrice said as she scooped the vegetables into her hands and tossed them into a waiting pot.

Roman and I left through the kitchen back door and headed to the stables.

We chose two swift, young horses and arrived at Malik's in record time.

Roman handed the sweaty horses to the groomsmen as I flew inside.

"Anybody home?" I yelled once I stepped through the front door.

"In the dining room," Malik called.

I rushed through the foyer and living room to find Malik and Rosie sitting around the dining table, teacups in hand.

I pulled up short, startled by the cozy family setting.

We were anything but a cozy family. We're a band of misfits with freakish abilities.

Malik sat his teacup in the saucer with a soft clatter.

"Are you in danger? What's going on?" he said calmly.

Rosie clung to Malik's side as if afraid I would take her away from him. Perhaps he told her Roman and I knew we were her parents in a past life.

"Olivia's upset, Rosie," Malik murmured to her. "I already told you she won't take you away from me. Right, Olivia?"

He flashed me a piercing gaze.

"Yes, of course," I said, calming my racing heart. "Malik is your daddy, Rosie. But you and I can be friends, right?"

She nodded and seemed to relax.

Malik dabbed at his lips with his napkin. "So, please tell me why you have rushed into my home looking like your skirt might be on fire? I assure you, there are no flames."

"Oh, but there soon might be," I said. "My dagger is missing."

Both of Malik's dark eyebrows rose. "I haven't seen it here. I've only seen your gun."

He lay his napkin by his plate.

"Maybe you missed it," I said, wringing my hands.

"I assure you, I don't 'miss' objects of significant importance, Olivia." He pushed his chair away from the table.

Roman strode into the dining room behind me. He and Malik exchanged a nod.

"Where else might it be?" Malik said.

I blew out a lungful of breath.

"Costa's," I said, and my body sagged.

"Oh, dear," Malik said. "That might be a problem. How would that have happened?"

"Olivia pulled her knife on me at the party. I had fooled her into thinking I was a stranger desiring her favor," Roman said, grimacing. He rubbed the back of his neck.

Malik threw back his head and laughed. "Good one, brother!"

"It's not good, Malik," I said, flames of impatient rage licking my insides. "It's definitely not good."

"I'm not making light of the loss, Olivia," Malik said, sobering. "I'm only making light of your capacity to resort to violence at a sex party."

He leaned over, kissed the top of Rosie's head, and said, "Can you go fetch the wooden puzzle I got for you? Once Roman and Olivia have departed, we will put it together."

Rosie nodded and scrambled off her chair.

Malik steepled his fingers in front of his chin. "You realize, without your dagger, you're stuck in this time, right, Olivia?"

"Just say it, Malik. Without my dagger, I'm *fucked*!" I stabbed the air with my hand. "What if it's destroyed?"

"That would be a problem, yes." He closed his eyes. When he opened them, he said, "But I don't think that it is."

I rushed around the table. "Can you see it? Do you know where it is? How can you be sure? Tell me!"

"I can't *see* it, Olivia. I just know it hasn't been destroyed. It can never be destroyed. No matter what you do to it, it can never be harmed or burned in any way. It's a magical, mystical weapon." He smoothed the cloth napkin next to the plate with his long fingers.

"We must go to Costa's." I directed my gaze at Roman.

He nodded.

Malik said, "You can't just rush over to Costa's in the state you're in. He and some of his men are still alive. You don't want to be discovered as a Timeborne."

"No, of course not," I said, my mind reeling. "I'm not an idiot."

I frowned, trying to come up with a plan.

"When you go there, make up a lie. Come up with a plausible story," Malik said.

"Any suggestions?" I asked.

A sharp rapping sound came from the entrance, interrupting our exchange.

Malik's maid appeared in the doorway to the kitchen and scurried past us to see who was at the door.

Count Montego appeared in the doorway, beaming.

"Count Montego," Malik said, giving him a cool-eyed gaze as he stood.

"Malik," the count said with a curt nod. "It's been a long time."

He crossed the room and shook Malik's hand.

"Too long," Malik said, keeping a secretive facade.

I watched the whole exchange, wondering what the nature of their friendship was. Something seemed unusual about their transaction.

"I was passing by," the count said to Roman, "and thought to inquire if you'll be staying here tonight. I could send for your things."

"That won't be necessary," Roman said with a wave of his hand. "Olivia has lost something, and Malik doesn't seem to have it. We thought to check with Count Costa."

"Oh? What did she lose?" Count Montego cocked his head.

My hand flew to my neck.

"It's a necklace. I got it from Queen Elizabeth," I lied, hoping my Tudor history was accurate.

"Oh, my!" the count said. "A necklace from the Queen! I shall accompany you. I'd like to see how Costa is doing after the tragedy. He and I have been friends for a long time."

"Excellent!" Malik said. "And now I must spend time with Rosie."

He departed.

"I came by carriage," the count said. "Ride with me."

We headed outside to be greeted by what promised to be a glorious sunset, though searching for my dagger in the light of the disappearing sun wasn't ideal.

I sat in the back of the carriage, chewing my nails.

Roman and the count kept up their idle chit-chat, yet Roman kept hold of my hand, offering reassuring squeezes.

At Costa's estate, we all climbed out of the carriage. The breathtaking sunset overhead was in direct contrast to the carnage and destruction before us.

Half of the villa was missing; the other half still stood. Dead bodies littered the ground. Men hauled the bodies into the backs of their wagons. At the same time, women fluttered about, closing the eyes of the dead and placing coins over their eyelids.

I shuddered. The memory of the burning building and its screaming participants flooded my mind with vivid intensity.

A group of men stood around the wreckage of Costa's home, talking animatedly.

Costa was one of them. He turned to us and glowered.

"Count Montego," he said, "did you see what happened to my beautiful villa?"

He swept his hand toward the burned lumber and debris.

"Yes, yes, such a tragedy," the count said, striding up to stand before him.

"Balthazar wants to destroy my life, but I will kill him," Costa snarled.

"So you think he's responsible? I left before seeing what happened," the count said.

Costa smirked. "We all know where you were, Montego —snugly sandwiched between two or more of my female guests. I heard the moans when I walked by."

The count didn't react at all other than to say, "I had a good time at the party. Too bad it ended the way it did."

Count Montego was having a threesome or a foursome? I was shocked.

"Indeed," Costa said, his gaze sliding toward Roman and me. "And who do we have here?"

He scanned my body with an unsettling, lascivious glance.

"These are my companions, Roman and Olivia Alexander," the count announced with a grandiose gesture.

"*Incantato*," Costa said, a devilish glint in his eye.

Delighted.

Costa lifted my hand to his lips; it was all I could do to not yank it away.

"Olivia lost a necklace here the other night. She was in attendance at the masquerade," the count said.

Costa kept a tight grip on my hand far longer than necessary.

"Was she?" he said. "It's a pity I didn't get to partake."

A feeling like crawling maggots rippled along my skin. I smiled, but it carried no warmth.

Roman simmered with barely controlled rage.

"How did you make it out alive?" Costa said, his dark gaze skewering me.

"We rushed to Montego's waiting carriage," Roman said,

stepping close to me and removing my hand from Costa's foul grip.

"The gods must love you," Costa said, sneering.

"Olivia thinks she lost a necklace at the party. Have you recovered any jewelry?" the count said.

Costa studied me with a calculating gaze. "You lost a necklace, you say?"

"Yes," I murmured, studying my husband's profile. "It was a gift from Queen Elizabeth."

"The Queen, you say?" Costa said in a condescending tone. "How is Her Royal Highness?"

I shrugged, scanning my brain for details about Queen Elizabeth I. "She fears that the French plan to invade England and put her Catholic cousin Mary, Queen of Scots, on the throne," I said. "She worries so."

I met Costa's gaze with a challenging glare. *Thank you, high-school history.*

He scowled at me, clearly annoyed at my "intimate" knowledge of the Queen. I was sure he hoped to catch me in my lie.

"What brings you to Italy?" Costa asked.

"My wife and I are explorers. We travel the world looking for notable artifacts," Roman said, tucking my hand in the crook of his elbow and smiling at me.

"Yes," I said, returning his smile. "We'll be returning home soon."

"And where is home?" Costa said, canting his head to the side.

"Great Britain," Roman answered.

I nodded. "I'm sure the Queen will want to see us again. Think how disturbed she'll be if I don't attend her court wearing the necklace she gifted me."

Costa narrowed his eyes as he looked between Roman

and me. He licked his lips like a predator. "By all means, then. Let's see if your necklace has been recovered."

Roman and I fell in step behind him, exchanging a nervous glance.

The count sauntered next to Costa, talking with him.

We walked across his courtyard, which was still intact, and entered the villa.

The stench of rotting bodies and charred wood overpowered me. I gripped Roman's arm. I had to cover my mouth with my hand to avoid vomiting.

How the men could move through this environment so calmly was a wonder.

We trekked through the estate with the char and debris on our right.

Costa led us upstairs to his office.

My heart thudded as I scanned for my dagger. *Where is it?*

"You have many interesting illustrations in here, Count Costa."

"Do I?" Costa said in an oily-sounding voice.

"Yes." I brushed my fingertips across one of the drawings labeled belladonna. "Do you have an interest in gardening?"

"Plant life has always fascinated me."

His penetrating gaze unnerved me.

"I've stored the recovered jewels here," he said, stooping to retrieve a small wooden chest. He procured a key from his pocket and fit it into the keyhole. He opened the lid revealing many fine jewels. "Do you see your necklace?"

I moved the pieces around until I found an emerald and diamond necklace. "Yes, I believe this is mine."

Costa's eyelids lowered as he retrieved a dagger from the sheath on his belt.

Oh, shit, oh, shit, oh, shit! That's my dagger!

I kept my face impassive, but I worried my thundering heart would give me away.

Costa studied me, gauging my reaction. He slid the deadly knife tip into the wooden chest and fished out the strand of emeralds and diamonds.

"This one?" He extended my dagger toward me with the necklace dangling from the blade.

"Yes, that's certainly mine." Using my fingertips, I carefully removed the strand of glistening emeralds.

"Pity," Costa said. "I had hoped to keep this piece."

"My God, what an exquisite knife," Roman said.

"Isn't it?" Costa turned the hilt back and forth. "I found it in my office. I was rather shocked. Someone was in here without consent.

"Further, I found several of my men with their throats slit. Who would do such a thing at a gala like the one I threw?" The tip of his tongue landed on his incisor and slid across his teeth. "Have you heard of the Timebornes? Timebounds?"

His face was void of expression.

"We might have heard of them in our travels," Roman said. "Olivia, are those names ringing any bells?"

"Not that I recall," I said, frowning.

"I'm afraid our friend here is obsessed with the Timebornes and Timebounds," Count Montego interrupted with a wave of his hand. "He's head of a mysterious group of people who hunt others."

He pressed his lips together.

Costa's nostrils flared. "They deserve to be purged from the planet."

A shudder ripped up my spine at his vehemence. "What did they do to you?"

He sneered. "They *exist.* That's all the motivation I need." He slid my dagger back into his sheath. "I found a Timebound here at my party. Can you believe that? What imbecile would willingly come to a masquerade thrown by a known Timehunter?"

"Obviously, one who didn't know your rules," Roman said.

Costa ignored him and looked at the count. "You must join us, Montego. We could use a man of your stature."

"Come, come," the count said, waving him off. "I'm an old man—nearly seventy-two."

"And yet, look how you took care of those females. The moans and groans that I heard are enough to know that you can give a mind-blowing orgasm at your age. I have no doubt they'd still be talking about you if they were still alive." Costa clapped the count on the back.

The count sighed heavily. "It's a shame they were lost in the fire. Nevertheless, thank you for your offer, Count Costa. We've discussed this many times before, and I must decline."

"Pity," Costa said, closing the lid to the wooden chest and locking it. A sly look flitted across his face.

"Would you like to go hunting with me?" he said, directing the question at Roman.

Roman faltered.

"No, thank you. I'm afraid we must be on our way." He extended his hand and said, "Your party was magnificent. I'm so deeply sorry it ended in tragedy. We'll never forget our time here."

Costa shook Roman's hand, coldly eyeing him like a snake sizing up its prey. Then he shifted his gaze to me, and I felt a chill run down my spine. It was clear that he didn't buy our story.

Riding back to Malik's in his coach, Count Montego said, "That's so wonderful you got your necklace back. It looks like a fine piece."

"I'm so relieved," I said, clutching the jewels.

"Costa is so strange about that order of his. All this nonsense about Timebornes and Timebounds. It's utter folly if you ask me." The count shook his head.

"Indeed," Roman said, gazing out the window at the night sky. He brought my hand into his lap.

"I'll drop you off at Malik's, if you wish, and have my manservant bring your things over in the morning. I'm sorry you have to leave so soon. I've enjoyed your company." The count smiled.

"Thank you," Roman said. "You have been most generous with your hospitality."

The count waved his hand. "Think nothing of it. It's been my pleasure."

We rode the rest of the way in silence.

At Malik's estate, he stood outside as if waiting for us, holding a torch.

Roman helped me from the carriage, and we approached Malik after saying our goodbyes to the count.

The shadows of night lined Malik's face, making him look more mysterious than ever. "What happened at Costa's?"

"He has the dagger on his person. We couldn't get it back," I said.

"We've given him a ruse," Roman added. "Told him we're explorers on a hunt for artifacts."

"And also told him we are to leave at once," I said.

"Yes, yes," Malik said, rubbing his jaw. "We shall all depart. Our work here is done, and none of us can stay behind —it's too dangerous. I'll find a way to get the dagger back."

Hope rocked through my heart.

"And we must head west and find the moon dagger," Malik said.

"That's the plan," I said, massaging my temples.

"Montego will bring all your goods from his house in the morning. We'll have a plan in place by then." Malik began walking toward his estate.

Roman and I followed.

Once again, I was on the run. Only, with my dagger in the hands of a mortal enemy, the circumstances were the direst they'd ever been.

CHAPTER TWENTY-NINE

OLIVIA

As I stood in front of the full-length mirror in my bedroom, anxiously dragging a brush through my hair, the sound of Malik's voice made me jump.

"Olivia? Are you decent?"

"Yes, decent enough," I said, glancing at my robe-clad form. I was getting ready to retire for the night but doubted I would get any sleep. There was too much going on in my head. My dagger was in the hands of a brutal killer. And Roman, Emily and I had to be on the run again.

My life in the twenty-first century had been so comfortable. The only significant stressors I'd experienced were income or relationship trouble. Running from demons and losing my means of time travel into the hands of said monster hadn't been a concern.

Malik appeared behind me in that mysterious way of his, his emerald eyes shining bright as he gazed at me in the mirror. He put his warm hands on my shoulders. "We'll be leaving at dawn."

I tensed beneath his touch.

"Don't worry, Olivia." He leaned down to kiss my shoulder, then backed away, giving me space.

Although my boundaries were firm, I still found my body responding to Malik from his potent presence alone.

"Just be happy we're all ahead of the game. Balthazar is on babysitting duty. Plus, he can't exactly time travel, now, can he?" He smirked, looking quite pleased with himself, like a cat that had just feasted on the fish set out for guests.

"I suppose," I said listlessly. After all, Balthazar was a demon, and monsters were treacherous and could defy logic.

I crossed the room to my armoire and retrieved the sun dagger which I'd rested at the bottom. I turned around with it in my hand and held it up for Malik to see. "Doesn't this knife seem dull and lifeless? I just can't imagine this blade is so powerful that it can possibly destroy all darknesses. It looks powerless."

Malik waved his hand in front of his face. "Don't worry, Olivia. Everything will work according to plan. Just get a good night's rest."

I gave him a wan smile and replaced the dagger in the armoire. When I turned around, I fell back on the solid, carved wood. "It's going to be hard to sleep tonight. I'm already so anxious. Traveling with a pregnant woman and a five-year-old will add to the arduous nature of the journey."

"Relax," Malik said, smiling. "Marcellious, Roman, and I take our duty as protectors seriously. You have nothing to worry about."

He pivoted on his heel and departed, leaving me in a frothy wake of fretfulness.

I wandered to the dark wood vanity, sat down, and resumed brushing my hair.

Roman entered the room. His smoldering eyes met mine in the mirror. Then, his gaze softened. "What's wrong?"

"Everything," I said. "I feel like an idiot for losing my dagger. What kind of time traveler does that? I mean, it's the most precious thing I own. It's *essential* to my ability to transport from place to place. You knocked it out of my hand, and I got so flustered, I completely forgot about it?"

Roman toed off his boots and began undressing. "We've dealt with worse, Olivia. Don't fret. We'll get it back."

I resumed brushing my hair, angrily yanking on a knot. "I guess. But I still feel like an idiot."

Roman removed a layer of clothing. "What was it that got you so distracted that you forgot your knife?"

I heard the tease in his voice.

"You," I said sulkily. "You got to me. Seeing you for the first time in forever I forgot about *everything*."

"My point exactly. You need a moment of respite. You need to forget the world." He stood, coming into view, completely naked.

I sucked in a breath, bowled over by his powerful body and his thick, stiff heat bobbing between his legs.

His eyes appeared dark and hooded as he stalked toward me, locking his gaze with mine in the mirror.

I licked my lips as he approached me, my core flooded with wet heat. All thoughts fled from my head. *Mercy.* I lay down the silver brush and pressed my palms to the surface of the vanity.

Roman's muscles shimmered in the gold-leaf-backed glass that served as a mirror. When he stood behind me, he massaged my shoulders with firm strokes. His sea-blue gaze reached into my soul with unceasing intensity.

I let my head fall against his solid six-pack. "That feels good."

"I want you, Olivia. I want you all the time. At every waking moment, I long to bury my cock inside you and make love to you," he said in a low, throaty voice. "When we were apart I thought about you incessantly. It hasn't stopped now that I'm with you. You're driving me crazy."

I rolled my head from side to side, feeling his hot, hard erection against the back of my neck. "I feel the same, Roman. It's like the more I have you, the more I desire you."

"Mmm, *amore*. Your silken hair all over my cock makes me want to come." He stepped away from me, withdrawing his hands from my shoulders. "But think of what a shame it would be to not linger in our love."

I pivoted on my seat, coming face to face with his shaft. It occurred to me that Roman and I had never engaged in oral play. His throbbing member dangling at lip level was too much to ignore.

Gripping the base, I lapped at the smooth glans.

"Fuck," he breathed, gripping my scalp with his strong hands. His fingertips massaged my head, melting me.

I gripped his base and fit my mouth over his shaft. Then, slowly, excruciatingly slow, I let my mouth slide down his erection.

"Oh, fuck, fuck, *fuck.*" Roman moaned, stroking my head with a firm, loving touch.

His cock pulsed in my mouth.

My core was completely wet, hungry for entry. But, I stayed put, sliding him in and out of my mouth, like I had all the time in the world.

He yanked away from my mouth and fisted himself, stopping the imminent orgasm. "Too soon for that, *amore mio*."

As soon as he got himself under control, he crouched before me, letting his lips drop to mine.

The sweet, honeyed taste of mead collided with my senses, as his tongue languidly twirled with mine.

"Mmm," he moaned.

"Mmm," I echoed, widening my legs without thought. Utterly entranced by his tongue, I fell into languorous intoxication. I could kiss Roman for hours.

His lips drew close, a breath away from my own as he teased me with expectancy. A fire raged within me, desperate for the touch of his, and I surged forward to meet him. But he pulled away, skimming the tip of his nose across mine while still keeping me in sweet suspense. The heat of the moment threatened to devour us both.

He continued to hold himself back, letting the warm air from his exhalations tickle my mouth. He shifted his mouth to my ear and whispered, "I love you so goddamned much, Olivia."

The words swirled through me, awakening an explosion of joy. "I love you, too," I whispered. "I never want to be away from you again."

"Never." He brought his soft lips to my face and kissed my cheeks, my eyelids, and my jaw. Then, his mouth was on mine again, devouring me. His fingertips pushed beneath the hem of my silk dressing gown and traced the inside of my calf, sending a jolt of current inside my leg.

I shivered, spreading my legs even wider.

His fingers circled the inside of my knee and stroked up my inner thigh.

Another shudder rocked through me. I was seized by wild tremors, as his fingers stroked the juicy folds between my legs.

My head fell back, and a long moan escaped my lips.

He lifted my gown and moved his face between my legs. His hair tickled my inner thighs as he positioned his face close to my core.

I was panting, on fire with desire. I lay back, falling against an unforgiving wooden bend in the vanity. My elbows rested against the solid wood and my head lolled against the looking glass.

Roman urged my legs even further apart with his palms. He took a long, deep inhalation. "You're my medicine, *amore*. My food, my daily sustenance."

The tip of his tongue met my clit, and I wanted to scream with pleasure.

Instead, I sucked in a breath and then panted, like a wild horse in heat, consumed by my desire.

"Roman," I whimpered. "Oh, Roman!"

He held the tip against my clitoris, just pressing it there without moving, breathing slow and deep.

I melted, completely gone a swirl of liquid heat.

He slid his tongue up and down my folds.

"Holy fuck," I whispered. This was all new for us, like discovering a new world.

Pleasure rippled through my skin and my head rolled back and forth against the mirror. Passion devoured me, licking at my soul, at my skin like hot flames.

We moved in harmony with one another, like rocking waves lapping against the shore. My hips undulated, pressing into the feel of his face against my core.

His mouth and his wicked, wicked tongue, met me thrust for thrust.

He slid one finger into me, and I gasped. Then, there were two fingers inside, then three. The fullness of his fingers coupled with the ecstasy of his mouth on my clit drove me insane.

We were one, giant throbbing organism, moving as one toward a river of bliss. The intense sensation thrumming through my core made me sit up and seize Roman's hair.

He growled, continuing to lick me and fuck me with his fingers.

Finally, I couldn't take it anymore and I cried out his name, as an explosion of fireworks rippled through my skin. "Oh, God, Roman!"

I was plugged into a current, that electrical bliss we all sought, riding high as I came all over Roman's face.

He let out deep, lusty moans of pleasure that vibrated through my core, sending me higher. Then, in a flash, he lifted me from the padded vanity bench and whirled me around until I stood facing the mirror.

He kicked the bench seat out of the way.

Our eyes met in the looking glass with smoldering intensity.

He slid the robe from my arms and tossed it aside. It fluttered like a feather to the ground.

Then, reaching around me, his eyes still pinned to mine, he untied the stays at my neckline and urged the garment down my shoulders.

It fell beneath my breasts, holding them aloft.

He held her gaze captive and took in a deep breath. "Olivia, you are incomparable to any other woman in this world," he declared with conviction. The intensity of his words settled like dark velvet on the air around us.

"Thank you," I whispered softly, surrendering to him completely.

"Press your hands against the looking glass," he said.

I obliged him and my breasts hung like ripe fruit, begging to be touched.

Roman held them in his palms, bouncing them up and down. Then, he rolled my nipples between his fingertips, all the while watching me in the mirror.

I gasped at the ache he elicited. It was a sweet torture.

He tugged the hem of my silk gown up over my ass. "Look at me, *amore mio*."

Our gazes locked.

"I want you to see my expression when I enter you." He palmed my round ass cheeks with his calloused hands.

I hissed and undulated, spreading my legs, never breaking eye contact.

"So beautiful," he breathed. He clutched his cock and slowly slid it up and down my folds.

I arched my ass, desperate to have him inside me.

A devilish grin spread across his face. "I think you want this. You want me inside of you."

"Please, Roman. I'm so wet for you."

He licked his lips as he fit the tip inside.

I writhed, wanting him deeper. I felt torn apart from the climax I'd just had, yet filled with longing for more. I wanted to be consumed by him, devoured by our passion.

He clutched my hips, stilling my frenetic movement. "Now, watch me. Watch me fuck you."

His nostrils flared as he slowly slid inside to the base of his cock.

We both let out a long, "Ahhh."

His eyelids grew heavy as he stood behind me. "So fucking beautiful. I'll never get enough of you."

"Nor I you," I whispered.

This strange sense of stillness surrounded us as he pulsed inside me, not moving, continuing to look deeply into my eyes.

My heart surged with joy. Our coupling was as erotic as it was vulnerable. There were no walls up, no pretense…

"Roman," I whispered.

"I feel it, too," he breathed. "You're my everything, Olivia. The pause between the heartbeats, the breath I draw into my body."

He withdrew his stiff shaft, then, still gripping me, he thrust inside.

"Oh, God," I breathed, my body rippling with pleasure.

We both struggled to maintain eye contact. The intensity sizzling between us was almost unbearable.

My heart felt torn open, bared, and vulnerable to this man. Never could I be this honest, this trusting, and this safe with anyone. Roman was my all and everything.

He began to thrust inside me, steady, rhythmically.

Our gazes danced as did our bodies, connecting and pulling apart, merging and separating.

"Touch yourself," Roman insisted. "Make yourself come again."

Leaning against the mirror with one hand, I brought my fingers to my core, feeling Roman's thick cock sliding in and out of me, in and out.

He smiled wickedly as his thrusts grew wilder.

"I love you so much," he growled.

"I love you, too." As I circled my clit with my fingertips, another climax began to build. "I won't last much longer."

"Come for me, sweet Olivia." Roman bucked and thrust.

I met each pounding push, working my fingers round and round. "Oh, God, Roman. Oh, God."

Roman roared out his release, hammering into me.

I exploded around his throbbing cock, coming apart with the powerful intensity. There was nothing but color and vibration, this ecstatic thrumming, taking us to new heights.

Like feathers drifting back to earth, I came back into the room, back into my body.

Roman pulled out of me and scooped me into his arms. He crossed the room and lay me on the mattress, then, slid in beside me.

Our gazes met and no words were needed for what we'd

just experienced. We'd been granted the profound gift of connecting with driving passion and complete openness.

There was nothing left to do but fall asleep in each other's arms.

I rode on stars and wild stallions through the night, stirring when Roman rolled away from me.

I opened my eyes and grimaced at the light poking through a slit in the heavy drapes.

"What time is it?" I said in a groggy voice.

Standing next to the bed, Roman pulled pants up his gorgeous legs and fastened them. Then, he leaned over and gave me a long, sensuous kiss.

"It's time to get up," he said, when he pulled away. "We've got to get on this journey."

"Can't we linger in bed a little longer?" I yawned and stretched my arms up over my head. I lay naked beneath the covers, my nightgown nowhere to be seen.

"I would like nothing more, but we have ground to cover. We must put a great distance between Balthazar, Costa, and ourselves." He pulled a long-sleeved shirt from the armoire and slid it over his torso.

I blew out my breath and rolled off the mattress. Then, I, too, proceeded to dress and prepare for the day.

As we all gathered downstairs, luggage packed, and a sparse breakfast in our bellies, Roman's eyes lit up.

"Ah!" he exclaimed. "I have something here for you, Marcellious." He extended a letter.

"Is it for me?" He wrinkled his eyebrows and squinted at him. "Who is it from?"

"Moon Lee. He gave it to me when I was in the twenty-first century. He told me to make sure and give it to you." Roman crouched and rooted through a knapsack. When he stood, he held an envelope in his hand. "For you."

He handed the envelope to Marcellious with a flourish.

Marcellious' wide-eyed expression conveyed something like shocked surprise. He stuffed the envelope away in a satchel.

"Aren't you going to read it?" Roman said.

"In my own time," he said, his eyes shadowed.

I was sure he wanted privacy to read the letter.

A knock sounded on the door. Malik's maid scurried through the archway leading to the kitchen, but he stopped her.

"I'll see who it is," he said, striding toward the entrance.

When he opened the door, there stood Count Montego, bags in hand.

"I've brought your goods, Roman, as promised." As he handed the bags to Malik, he said, "Where are you headed?"

"Great Britain," I said. "Wales, actually. We are on a quest to find a certain artifact."

Count Montego brightened. "How fortunate! That's where I'm heading, too! What do you say we combine forces and head out together? I have everything you need to transport safely."

I frowned, looking to Malik to decline his offer.

When Malik simply shrugged and stepped aside, I said, "That's a generous offer but we can't impose on you."

"Nonsense," the count said, waving his hand as he stepped across the threshold. "And who is this?"

He looked at Emily, beaming.

"I'm Emily. Emily Demarrias," she said, sadly. "I'm with child."

This morning, her pallid complexion and queasiness made it apparent that she was suffering from morning sickness.

"I'll send for a nursemaid who will see to her needs. We want Emily to be comfortable. It's quite a journey." The count firmly picked up two of our bags as if it was a final decree, causing me to glance sharply at Roman.

He silently shrugged in acquiescence, knowing full well that the decision had been made.

"I insist you accompany us to my villa in Wales," the count declared confidently. "It will be no hindrance, but rather a delight for me to have your company when I send for the nursemaid who will see to Emily's needs and make her journey comfortable." His voice took on a commanding tone as he stepped outside with our luggage, leaving us no choice but to follow.

CHAPTER THIRTY

OLIVIA

T wo months into the journey I'd become a liability to our progress. I didn't know where we were, didn't care. France, maybe? It had been slow going, what with Emily's growing belly and my exhaustion. I was constantly tired, continually sick to my stomach. I couldn't keep anything down and my attitude was dismal.

On one particular morning, I lay in the back of our wagon, unable to move. The heat of summer beat down on the leather covering the carriage, making it feel like a sauna in here.

I wondered if I was dying from some inexplicable sixteenth-century illness. Unable to do an online search, I scoured my memory for "sixteenth-century illnesses that could kill you." Things like diphtheria, pertussis, and typhoid fever came to mind. Then, my brain coughed up other, stranger illnesses like "English Sweat," a viral disease that affected Britain, and "the scherbock," a form of land scurvy found in Scandinavia and the Netherlands.

Have I been eating enough fruit? It's not like we've passed an abundant orange grove.

Roman sat next to me, wiping my brow with a cloth. "Count Montego says there's a town up ahead. I want to have a doctor examine you."

"Don't be stupid," I snapped, pressing my hands into my stomach. "I'm fine. I just need to get out and ride a horse. It's this lying about, the surge and roll of the wagon that's doing me in. I got carsick a lot as a child. I'm sure that's what it is."

Roman grew quiet, his jaw tense.

"I'm sorry I'm so bitchy," I said, burying my head beneath the covers. "I feel like death warmed over. This century had so many untreatable diseases. What if I've caught one of them? I can't even time travel back to twenty-first century Seattle for proper medical care."

Tears stung the backs of my eyes.

I could go from sunny and cheerful to growling and angry in less than a second. *What if Roman and I caught syphilis? Doesn't that affect the mind?*

Roman moved away from me, parted the leather curtain, and asked the driver to stop the cart. Once we stopped, he climbed out.

"Where are you going?" I said in a whiny voice.

"I'll be back," he said.

"You want to get away from me, don't you?"

He didn't reply—not that I heard, anyway.

I couldn't blame him. He'd been doing his best to care for me, but this illness made me unbearable. Even *I* was sick of myself.

We continued to lumber along with Roman riding horseback outside the wagon, while I slid in and out of slumber. Finally, an hour later, the wagon stopped.

The dull rumble of the travelers' conversations outside the wagon increased in volume, and I was about to look out the window when the horses lurched forward and broke into a gallop. The ground swayed beneath us as we flew through the countryside.

Finally, we stopped, and I was left with horrible queasiness.

The leather curtains parted, and Emily stood outside. "Get up, Olivia."

With her hands resting on top of her belly, she stared down at me.

Rosie stood by her side, smiling her little sunshine smile.

Now that we didn't have secrets between us, my relationship with Rosie had bloomed. I felt like her dear auntie who looked out for her when Malik wasn't around.

And Roman had fallen in step with the role as her uncle.

"What? Where are we?" I said, rubbing my eyes.

"At a healer's place somewhere in France," she said.

"What?" I repeated. "No! This was Roman's idea, wasn't it?"

"Yes, it was. But I seconded the motion. We need to get you checked out, sister."

"I don't want to go to a doctor. I'm *fine.*"

Emily turned down my covers. "Have you ever thought you might be *pregnant?* Believe me, I know what morning sickness feels like. I'm so glad mine is behind me."

Fear gripped me. What if I am pregnant? What if Balthazar finds me? What if he does something to cause me to lose this one, too?

Rosie withdrew her hand from Emily's and went off by herself. Emily clasped my fingers in a comforting grip. "I can see it in your face, Olivia: you're having those awful thoughts again. Balthazar is far away; he can't get to us. Roman, Marcellious, and Malik are always around, on guard for any danger. Please, get up now," she said, tugging at my wrist.

When I stood up, she handed me my dress then closed the

curtains so I could put it on. My stomach was doing somersaults as I stepped out of the wagon. "Do you know where the men are?"

"Getting supplies. Roman asked me to accompany you to the healer. Let's go." Emily turned toward Chiara, her nursemaid.

Chiara sat in the back of the carriage ahead of us. She opened the carriage door and Rosie crawled inside.

Emily called, "We'll be right back. We'll be in that house right there."

"Okay," Chiara said.

I blinked in the bright sunlight. Clouds hung on the horizon behind the humble cottage before us.

The two other carriages appeared empty, save for the horses harnessed to them and the drivers lounging in the sun.

"Where are they headed to gather supplies?" I said.

"Not far. Follow me."

A skinny dog slunk toward me, wagging its tail.

I held out my hand and it nervously licked me.

The dog lay down and rolled over, revealing several swollen nipples.

"Oh, look! She's a mama dog!" I said, crouching to pet the dog's soft head.

"I see that," Emily said. "Come. The healer is waiting."

An older woman, her hair bound in a colorful scarf, stood in the doorway of the cottage. Arms folded, she studied us without smiling.

I crossed the yard toward her, the dog trotting by my side.

Chickens scratched in the yard and a fluffy white cat sat solemn-eyed on a fence post, watching our every move.

When we were almost near the door, the cat leaped to the ground and padded toward the woman.

She scooped up the cat and continued to regard us, as solemn-eyed as the cat had done.

The dog scratched on the door and the healer opened it, letting her in.

"*C'est toi la malade?*" she said to me in a lilting voice.

You are the sick woman?

"*Oui c'est moi*," I said. *Yes, that's me*. I held out my hand.

She took it between the fingertips of her free hand and gave me a gentle handshake. Her clear light-blue eyes were sharp and penetrating as she regarded me. Then, she entered the house.

Emily and I glanced at each other.

"Should we follow her?" I whispered.

"I guess so," Emily said.

The inside of the house smelled fragrant with dried herbs, which dangled upside down in abundance from the ceiling.

The mama dog lay on furs near the unlit fireplace, eight puppies suckling at her nipples. She looked up at us, thumped her tail, then lowered her head with a contented groan.

Emily and I followed the woman into her medieval kitchen.

Like the front room, it was filled with herbs. Only, instead of hanging upside down, these bunches of herbs lay on every spare surface with numerous vials and glass bottles placed here and there.

A cauldron hung suspended over an ash-filled brick-lined fireplace.

The healer set the cat on the stone floor, plucked a stone bowl from the counter, and sniffed it. "I need you to pee in this bowl," she said in French.

I took the bowl and said in French, "Where shall I go?"

The healer waved her hand impatiently. "We are all women here."

I winced, turned my back to her and Emily, and squatted, positioning the bowl between my legs.

When I had released a scant amount, I stood and handed it to the healer.

The cat rubbed her legs, weaving around her.

The healer rested the bowl on the sturdy wooden table before her and waved her hand over the bowl toward her nose. She reached for some dried herbs spread across the wood and sprinkled them on the surface. Then, she intoned a chant. She lifted the bowl before her and cocked her head left and right. Then, her scrutinizing gaze met mine.

"What is your name?" I said in French.

The woman pressed her palm to her chest. "Thérèse Brès."

I smiled. "Olivia Alexander. And this is my sister Emily Demarrias."

The woman smiled before disappearing out the back door, bowl in hand.

Emily and I said nothing, exchanging worried glances.

When Thérèse returned, the bowl was dripping wet, but my pee was gone. She sat the bowl upside down on one of the counters and stood before me. "Yes, you are pregnant. Are you ill with the pregnancy?"

"Yes, very much."

She lifted vials from the tables and counters, inspecting them. She set three of them aside, tied a colored ribbon around each, and lifted each one at a time. "This one is for the nausea. Take six drops as needed." Thérèse waggled the one with the blue ribbon before my eyes. "This one is for fatigue. Three drops, three times a day." She handed me the one with the red ribbon, stating, "For the health of the baby and mother… To prevent miscarriage…"

I clutched this one to my heart. "Thank you, thank you."

A slight smile appeared on her weathered face. She gave a curt nod. "You're welcome. I serve all the women in this region. My medicine is very powerful."

I had no doubt. I asked Thérèse how we could repay her, and she waved her hand before her face.

"Bearing a living child will be payment enough."

She grinned, revealing two gaps where teeth once were. She reached out to hug me, enveloping me in her warm embrace.

I recalled the feeling of Amara, Roman's housekeeper, hugging me. It felt so safe and comforting.

But then Thérèse released me, shooing us both away.

Emily and I retreated from her house and strode toward the wagon.

"So, sister, mine. We're both pregnant," Emily said, grinning.

"I can't believe it. I know when it happened." My cheeks blazed with the intimate memory of our last night at Malik's house.

It had felt so magical. Now we were with child.

I removed the stopper from the yellow-ribboned vial and extended my tongue. Six drops fell into my mouth. I swallowed and tucked the vials of herbs into the corner of the wagon.

"I wish I had a Thérèse Brès when I was sick as a dog," Emily said, plucking a strand of long-stemmed grass and sticking it in her mouth. "All I had was a Malik. And then, Marcellious."

She flashed me a side-eye. "Don't get me wrong. I'm overjoyed to have Marcellious back. But, men are useless when it comes to morning sickness."

"I know. Poor Roman has tried to comfort me but there was nothing he could do." I leaned back against the side of the wagon. "It helps to know what we now know."

Malik whistled a jaunty tune as he, Roman, and Marcellious rode up the hill, their horses snorting with the effort. They rejoined us, each of them sporting lopsided grins, their saddlebags bulging with supplies.

When Roman saw me, he frowned and reined in his horse. Leaping from its back, he hurried toward me. "What did you find out, *amore mio*?"

Without a word, I seized his lapels and kissed him hard, hungering for his lips.

He responded in kind, our tongues tangling and our chests heaving against one another.

The stiffness of his erection ground against my lower abdomen and I wanted nothing more than to strip him and climb on.

Marcellious cleared his throat.

I drew back from the kiss and looked into Roman's eyes, grinning. Then, I placed his hand on my belly.

"Are we…?"

"Yes! We're pregnant!" I blurted.

His face grew sunrise bright, and he wrapped his arms around me, twirling me around and around.

"Oh, Olivia!" He exclaimed, his voice filled with a passionate joy. His arms swept me up in an embrace and crushed me to his chest. His lips found mine and lingered, exhilarating warmth radiating from them. "You...and me...and baby! We'll be a family!" Joyous tears spilled down his cheeks as he spoke and kissed me tenderly. "We're the three happiest people on the planet!"

He withdrew from me and looked over to Malik and Marcellious. "Did you hear that? Olivia's with child."

"How could we not hear it?" Marcellious grumbled. "Or, see it."

Malik's face beamed as he lifted Rosie from the wagon seat, her arms clasped tightly around his neck and a joyous laugh spilling from her lips.

This time, I would do everything in my power to bring the child to term.

Three months later, with my belly starting to show and Emily looking like she might soon pop, we arrived in Wales. We'd been significantly slowed by weather as the season transformed into winter. Although Count Montego had outfitted us in weather gear, purchased in Paris, the horses harnessed to the wagons and carriages struggled to pull everything through the snow or mud-soaked terrain. The horses had to forge through snow nearly up to their bellies at times.

Many times, we had to take refuge in a town or form an encampment next to a ledge until it was safe to continue. Once we had to make a treacherous passage across a raging river. I was forever indebted to our sturdy steeds.

We were all so tired of travel. We just wanted to be in one place, settled.

Our journey made me feel close to everyone, like we were one strange family traveling to distant lands.

For five months, we hadn't seen hide nor hair of Costa or Balthazar. It had been such a blessing to travel without the constant fear of Balthazar finding us or Costa ambushing us.

I'd begged to get out of the wagon and ride one of the horses. Now, slogging through the downpour, I longed for the covered buggy.

"I told you we'd be safe on this journey," Malik said, pulling his horse beside mine. Huge drops of rain dripped from the brim of his leather hat.

The skies had opened up, dumping rain on our heads.

Roman rode on my other side. Emily, Marcellious, and Rosie were in one of the wagons. "What's your definition of safe?" I said, pulling my fur-lined coat around me. I pushed aside a wet strand of hair.

"Not having a demon on our tail." He grinned.

The count slowed his horse so we could catch up. "Are we near your estate, Malik? I'll certainly feel better once the ladies are safe and dry."

"Indeed. My home is right over that rise there." He lifted his chin in the direction of the hill before us.

"Good, good," the count said.

When we got to the top of the rise, Malik frowned.

His estate had been razed, utterly destroyed. It looked like what was left of Costa's home.

He urged his horse into a gallop.

Both Roman and the count took off after him.

I kicked my horse's flanks and followed.

Malik reined in his horse near the rubble.

Rain continued to pelt our heads.

"What happened?" Roman asked, his forehead creased in concern.

Malik bore an expression of disgust. "I don't yet know. But whoever did this will pay dearly."

I shuddered, staring at the destruction all around me. What had once been a beautiful estate, I was sure, now lay in ruin.

Count Montego shook his head. "This is certainly an unfortunate occurrence."

A lightning bolt flashed in the sky, followed by the rumble of thunder.

"We need to get to safety. Come, you can stay at my place," the count said.

Roman opened his mouth to protest, but the count cut him off.

"I have a palace, Roman. There's plenty of room for all. Plus, we'll pass right by the caves you're seeking. We can take a moment to investigate." He spurred his horse and took off in the direction of the next hill.

We climbed higher and higher, with the wagons lagging behind.

The higher we climbed, the deeper the snow.

I started to shiver from the cold. Soaked to the bone, I just couldn't get warm.

"Hang on, Olivia. We're almost there," Count Montego said.

His horse strained to climb through the snow, its nostrils flaring with the effort.

My horse, too, struggled beneath me.

"Look!" The count pointed toward a stony structure. "There are the caves."

"Let's go check them out. Where is your palace?" Roman said, his sights set on the cave.

"It's that way. Just ahead. I'll head back and direct the wagons. We can go take a look, and then I know a shortcut to get to my estate. We should all arrive at my home at the same time," the count said.

Snow drifted from the sky, creating a pale, frozen landscape.

"He-yaw," he called, spurring his horse. He took off down the hill.

Roman, Malik, and I forged our way toward the cave.

When we stood at the entrance, we all dismounted, and led our horses to the mouth of the stony structure.

We peered in the opening, but it was too dark to see anything other than the vastness of the cave. It seemed to occupy the entire hill.

The chances of finding a dagger in there seemed slim to none.

CHAPTER THIRTY-ONE

ROMAN

Barely an hour had passed in our stay at the count's, and Olivia was begging me to head out into the snow and explore the caves together.

"No," I said, gripping her shoulders. "You can't go. We don't want anything to happen to the baby. Besides, you've got to care for Emily."

I kissed her nose, releasing her shoulders.

"Emily has a nursemaid, in case you haven't noticed over the past five months," she said, arms waving. She plucked a feather-stuffed pillow from the massive bed and threw it at me.

I batted it out of the way.

The room Count Montego had put us up in was by far the most opulent I'd ever stayed in. The bed, with its ornately carved headboard and bed frame, sat on a podium beneath a carved wooden canopy inset with jewels. A massive chandelier hung over the bed, complete with twenty or more "modern" oil lamps.

The maid assigned to us had to stand on a stool placed in the center of the bed to light and extinguish each one.

The rest of the room was paneled with the same blond-colored wood with dark walnut inlays. Intricately carved dressers and armoires held our clothes. The two windows, flanked by thick gold-colored curtains, overlooked a sweeping vista of immaculately tended gardens and surrounding hillside.

"We already lost a baby. I'm doing everything in my power to make sure we don't lose a second one. I refuse to let you go out in this weather and explore a treacherous cave," I stated in a no-nonsense voice.

"Everything in your power…*your* power? Which one of us is growing the baby inside her belly?" Olivia said, her voice rising.

I rolled my eyes toward the ceiling. Fighting with my lovely wife could be exasperating.

"We're no longer in your twenty-first century, my love," I said in a gentler voice. "Which means I can and will assume my role as your protector. Many men in your century would turn and tuck tail rather than face the challenges of sixteenth-century Europe. *I* am not that kind of man."

Her lips clamped shut in a firm line, and she crossed her arms over her chest. "Fine. I'll stay home with the women and children."

"Well, you're a woman, and you're with child, so that makes sense." I smirked.

I ducked out of the bedroom before she clocked me in the head with her fist.

Out in the yard, Malik, Marcellious, and I all stood next to our horses, surrounded by a pale world absent of color.

The horses blew white clouds from their nostrils.

Malik handed Marcellious and me a torch consisting of a piece of wood bound in rags that had been soaked in animal fat.

The torches burned brightly in the overcast light.

Malik kept one for himself.

We all mounted and set off toward the cave.

The snow had ceased falling, at least, and a weak sun punched its way through the clouds. A bitter wind lifted snow drifts and blew ice crystals in our faces.

I was glad for the woolen scarf I'd wrapped around my nose and mouth.

The horses slogged through the snow, laboring to find their footing in the hidden ground.

Finally, we reached the cavern.

We dismounted and ground-tied our steeds near the entrance. Then, torches in hand, we set off to investigate the caves.

The torches cast long, eerie shadows across the stone, which looked like it had been dimpled by a giant's thumb. A dank, damp smell came from the water that dripped from the ceiling and trickled down the rock walls.

We faced several archways.

"Let's each take a tunnel to explore," I said, feigning confidence. In truth, I'd never explored a cave system and didn't know rule one of how to conduct such an encounter. But, I figured we could each assess the terrain individually, return and put our collective thoughts together in a plan.

"Good idea," Marcellious said.

I set off toward the archway to the right. I took a step and nearly lost my footing on the slippery ground. After that, I tread more carefully, picking my way through the cavern.

Minerals dangled from the ceiling like brown icicles or protruded from the ground like icicles in reverse. The rock formations were a wonder to behold.

When I rounded the corner, I was faced with impossible egress: the stone tunnel appeared to go straight down. No way would I explore it without ropes and other equipment. I wondered if what I needed even existed in 16th-century Europe.

I pivoted and headed out of the tunnel.

Marcellious stood at the entrance to the cavern.

Malik was nowhere to be found.

"What did you find?" I said.

"Treacherous footing. There's a narrow walkway about yay wide," Marcellious said, spreading the thumb and forefinger of his free hand. "You?"

"A steep downclimb, impossible to make without equipment of some sort. I don't know what kind of ropes exist in this period. It's strange to know the technology from different centuries and not be able to access it in the century you're in," I said.

"I hear that. I don't yet have the privilege of the twenty-first century." Marcellious reached across his chest to grab the arm holding the torch. "That must have been something to behold."

"It was. They have these modes of transport that are out of this world. I want to get a motorcycle."

Marcellious gave me a side-eye. "What's a motorcycle?"

"It's a device with two wheels powered by an engine. It goes faster than a chariot or a galloping horse," I said, smiling as I recalled seeing one in Seattle.

"Really?"

"Yes, really. You know how when you're on a horse, racing across the plains? Imagine going twice that fast." I could practically feel the speed.

"Fuck, yeah, that would be fun," Marcellious said, his face brightening.

"Yes. Fuck, yeah," I said.

Malik emerged from the archway to my right. "Gentlemen, we have our work cut out for us, do we not?"

"What did you discover?" I said.

"A narrow passageway, not even a child could go through it. You?" Malik said, stopping next to us.

I made a gesture indicating straight down.

"Narrow passage with death on either side," Marcellious said. "Also, a lot of potholes. If we opened them up, we might find something below them."

Malik nodded. "I say we head back and see if Count Montego has any needed supplies. If not, we'll have to forge our way into town."

We slogged our way through the snow and returned to the count's palace. Smoke drifted from the chimneys, leaving blue-gray smudges trailing through the sky.

Upon dismounting, we plunged the ends of our torches into snowdrifts to extinguish them.

I stamped the snow from my boots before entering the mudroom at the back of the house. Then, I removed my coat, leather gloves, and scarf and hung them on hooks to dry.

Marcellious and Malik followed suit.

We tromped through the kitchen fragrant with the smells of a feast underway.

Kitchen maids stirred sauces in cauldrons over flames and rotated a pig and a deer on a spit.

My mouth watered at the thought of a good meal. Our fare on the road had, at times, been rather sparse.

The count met us when we entered the dining room. A cup of tea and a tray of sweetmeats and cheeses rested on the table in front of him.

"Our intrepid explorers have returned!" He clapped his hands together. "What did you discover?"

"We need much in the way of supplies," I said, pulling out a chair and sitting down.

Malik and Marcellious joined me.

"Would you like some tea to warm the old bones?" the count said. "I have plenty of appetizers."

He shoved the silver tray in my direction.

"Yes, please," I said, reaching for a morsel of meat.

Count Montego picked up a small bell resting near his plate and gave it a shake.

A plain-looking maid scurried into the room. "Yes, Count Montego?"

"Fetch my friends a pot of tea, would you please?"

She curtsied. "Of course, sir, straight away."

While I snacked, Marcellious and Malik explained our findings to the count.

The maid returned bearing a tea tray laden with cups and saucers, a silver teapot, and a small cake stand filled with tiny cakes. She placed the tray on the sideboard and poured each cup, setting the fragrant tea before us. Then, she set the cake stand in the middle of the table, curtsied again, and departed.

"So, how can I help you on your expedition?" The count rubbed his hands together.

"You can tell us where we might procure supplies. We need ropes, shovels, pick axes, and the like," Marcellious said.

"I see," the count said. "I know of a place in town, but it's a ways away from here."

Olivia appeared in the doorway. "You're back. What did you find?"

She crossed the room and worked a chair between Malik and me.

We briefed her on our progress and the discoveries we had made thus far.

Her eyes hardened as she looked at me. "Which means what, exactly, as far as gathering supplies?"

"Which means," the count said, "they'll be heading into town. It's a bit of a journey. And then, they'll likely begin their exploration of the caves." He beamed.

"And how long will that be?" Olivia said, rubbing her baby bump. Her eyebrows drew together.

"No way of knowing," I said, mentally preparing myself for her resistance.

Her head fell back, and a loud moan slipped from her lips. When she righted herself, she said, "No, Roman, no! I'm afraid you won't return to me."

Malik placed his hand on her shoulder. "Don't worry, Olivia. Roman will be with me, and he'll be fine. I already told you—I shall protect you, Roman, and now your unborn baby with my life."

Olivia huffed out a sigh.

"We'll only be gone a matter of weeks, not months," he said. "I will protect your husband. I know how much he means to you."

"So, telling you I forbid the journey probably won't make a bit of difference, will it?" Olivia said to Malik.

"No, Olivia. We came here with a purpose, and we must fulfill that purpose." He gazed somberly at her. "But I give you my word, Roman will be safe. We'll all be safe."

Olivia let out a long sigh.

I felt more grateful for Malik's friendship than ever. He actually seemed to be getting through Olivia's wall of defenses.

After resting and filling our bellies and saddlebags with food, we headed outside, where the groomsmen held our horses.

Olivia and Emily joined us.

SARA SAMUELS

Finally, reluctantly, Olivia shuffled over to stand before me. The air was charged with tension as we stood there, looking into each other's eyes. Our bodies were so close, I could feel her breath mingling with mine.

Without a word, I cupped her face in my hands and pressed my lips to hers in a tender, yet passionate kiss.

At first, our lips were soft and gentle, exploring each other's mouths. But then, the kiss deepened, and our tongues met, dancing together in a fiery tango.

Olivia ran her fingers through my hair, tugging at the strands, and I growled low in my throat.

The world around us fell away as we lost ourselves in the kiss.

Finally, we pulled away, gasping for air. I rested my forehead against hers, our eyes locked in an intense gaze.

"This kiss is my promise to you," I whispered, still breathless. "I *will* return."

She gave a slight nod.

"Okay. I believe you," she whispered back.

"Hello?" Marcellious called. "Is there a man named Roman about? Tell him we need to leave."

I flashed him an angry look. I could strangle my brother sometimes.

I didn't want to leave Olivia, but we had to find the dagger.

I murmured to her, "You know if I could take you, I would. But we don't want anything to happen to you or the baby."

"I know," she said, her expression set in resignation.

"I know you're strong and capable of helping us explore the cavern. We're both just trying to protect our baby," I said.

Gripping the lapels of my coat, she nodded. "I know that, too. That doesn't mean it doesn't suck."

She flashed me a wan smile.

I gave her one last kiss before mounting my horse. I glanced at Marcellious, who stood opposite Emily.

"You take care of my boy, you hear?" Marcellious said.

"How do you know it's not a girl?" Emily teased. "I have a girl's name all picked out."

"Well, I have a boy's name at the ready," Marcellious said, smiling. "I know it's a boy."

"We'll just have to see, won't we?" Emily twisted back and forth in a winsome manner.

"We will. I'll win," Marcellious said, laughing. Then, his expression became serious. He took Emily's hand in his and pulled her close, wrapping his arms around her in a tight embrace.

"I'll miss you," Emily said, her voice cracking with emotion.

He pulled back just enough to look into her eyes.

"I'll miss you too," he said softly.

He pressed his lips to hers. The kiss was short but passionate. When they drew apart, they looked into each other's eyes one last time before he stepped back.

"Take care of yourself," he said, his voice heavy with emotion.

"You too," she replied, her eyes filling with tears.

Marcellious cast a lingering glance over his shoulder before grasping the reins of his horse. "What do you want?" he growled at me. "What are you looking at?"

I laughed. "Oh, nothing except for you appearing tender with your wife."

Marcellious had changed so much from the hardened warrior he used to be. A new, softer side was shining through now.

"Yeah, so? I had to watch you getting all kissy-faced with

Olivia. Thought I'd return the favor." He mounted his horse with a scowl.

Olivia walked up to Malik. "I'm counting on you to protect Roman."

Malik met her fierce gaze. "I already gave you my word."

Olivia threw her arms around him and kissed his cheek.

Malik stiffened and then patted her back, but I could tell he was moved when he lifted his gaze toward mine.

I nodded in acknowledgment.

Olivia released him and then stood next to Emily, holding her hand.

The two women sniffled as we set off toward town.

The journey to town took many days. We were slowed by Malik's need to kill to keep up his strength. He always disappeared at night to spare us the sight of him murdering someone and inhaling their soul essence.

We dug snow caves to sleep in at night and then, after we got off the mountain, set up rain shelters near trees to sleep.

While I missed having Olivia by my side, I contented myself with knowing she was safe in the count's home. I was overjoyed at the prospect of being a father. I didn't want anything to happen to Olivia or the baby.

Finally, we reached town. We secured our supplies at the ramshackle establishment Count Montego had told us about, then decided to find lodging for the night. The skies were darkening and bloated with heavy clouds. It would be good to sleep in a warm bed instead of frozen or muddy ground for a change.

We found a place called *Hammer & Cross* with a tavern on the first floor and rooms upstairs. We tied the horses outside, but before heading inside, Malik said, "You two go on inside. I'll be inside shortly."

Marcellious and I exchanged a look, knowing what Malik intended. He would kill someone and consume their soul.

We nodded, and I opened the heavy wooden entrance to *Hammer & Cross*.

The noisy room was filled with patrons shouting over one another to be heard.

Marcellious and I pushed our way through the customers, heading for the bar in the back.

Dark beams spliced the white-plastered ceiling. The walls boasted identical black beams between plastered walls. Every table was overflowing with men downing ales or whiskey, smoking cigars, playing cards, or simply enduring the loud companionship.

A plump barmaid, her reddish hair piled high on her head, sashayed toward us. Her voluminous breasts were pushed high in her bodice. Coins clung to her sweaty skin from between her cleavage.

"Evening, gents. What will it be?" she said, revealing a gap-toothed smile. She wiped the bar top with a towel and propped her hands on her generous hips.

"Two ales," Marcellious said, fishing money from his pocket and placing several coins down.

The woman picked up the coins and retrieved the change from her bosom. She placed it before Marcellious, then whirled to fetch our ales.

As we waited, I turned to lean my elbows on the bar. My gaze landed several feet away on a young man standing at the edge of a circle of men.

The skinny young man gestured frantically with his hands and shouted. His skin appeared olive-toned, like mine, and his brown, almond-shaped eyes blazed with anger. A thatch of raven-black hair bobbed on his head as he yelled.

Marcellious bumped my arm.

I turned to see him extending a ceramic beer stein to me.

I took it and brought it to my parched lips.

"What's going on?" He lifted his chin toward the group of men.

"Don't know. Let's find out," I said, already crossing the room.

We hung back at the circle's edge.

"They took my beloved!" the man yelled.

"Who took her?" one of the onlookers asked.

"The Timehunters! They took my betrothed!"

Prickles of alarm raced up and down my spine.

Marcellious and I exchanged an uneasy glance.

"We're all in danger," the young man shouted, raking his hair with his hand. "Each and every one of us. The Timehunters are killing people mercilessly."

A few chuckles erupted from the circle.

"I'm telling the truth. We have to protect each other!" He swayed unsteadily on his feet. "The solar eclipse is coming soon, and we must be ready to face the Timehunters. Any baby born during that time will be in danger. The Timehunters will be looking for Timebounds and Timebornes. You must protect your wives and children!"

He clutched his hands beneath his chin, imploring the men to believe him.

"Timehunters, you say?" one man bellowed.

"Your wife probably left you," another jeered. "And you had to come up with an addlepated story. You're an asshead, Osman."

Still, another said, "What a fanciful tale." He jabbed the guy next to him with his elbow. "I'm done listening to his nonsense. Timebornes and Timebounds folly. Let's drink."

Others followed suit until Osman was left alone, rubbing his forehead with his palm.

I nudged Marcellious and tipped my head toward Osman. We shuffled forward.

"What seems to be the problem?" I said.

Osman waved his hand. "Just leave me alone and let me be in my misery. You're probably here to make fun of me, too, like those other men."

He spoke in a thick British dialect that was difficult to follow.

"No, no," Marcellious said. "We find your story fascinating. We've heard of these Timehunters."

Osman's jaw dropped. "You have?"

"Yes," I said. "I've learned of Timehunters, Timebounds, and Timebornes from a scholar. Come."

I patted his back. "Allow us to buy you a drink, and we can chat more about it."

Osman narrowed his eyes at me. "You're just trying to set me up."

"Not at all. If there's danger, we want to hear about it." I inclined my head toward the bar, conveying that Marcellious should fetch Osman an ale.

Marcellious nodded and handed his stein to me before departing.

I guided the young male toward a table that had been vacated.

"Why do you believe me? No one else in this room does," Osman said.

"Because I've seen some things," I said, leaning close to Osman. "I've witnessed the depravity of the Timehunters with my own eyes."

Osman's eyes widened. "Have you?"

He pressed his palms to the splintered wood.

Marcellious returned bearing a stein which he slid toward Osman before taking his seat.

"Thank you. You're both very kind. My name is Osman Suleyman Aydin," he said, puffing up his chest.

"Marcellious Demarrias," Marcellious said, hefting his drink before him. He took a long swig.

"My name is Roman Alexander," I said.

Osman glugged several swallows of his ale. "My future wife and I traveled here from the Ottoman Empire. We intended to be married." His gaze darted back and forth. Then, he lowered his voice. "My betrothed and I were looking for answers. We were in pursuit of something called the moon dagger."

My eyes slowly shifted to meet Marcellious'. His expression was unreadable, but an understanding seemed to pass between us in that moment.

"Go on. Why did you want this moon dagger?" I took a swallow of my ale.

"We were led to believe it might help us. My beloved is what is known as a Timebound." Osman let out a deep sigh. "And someone named Raul Costa found us. We got into a fight, and I haven't seen my Reyna since."

He pinched the bridge of his nose before picking up his stein and draining it. "I'm certain Costa has killed my betrothed." His eyes moistened, glistening in the smoky light. "I've looked everywhere for her. I can't find her."

He squeezed his eyes shut for a moment. "I have to kill Costa. He is now my enemy. I won't leave here until I find answers. Costa is a dangerous man. If he finds out that the solar eclipse is a few months away, he will hunt every woman who is bound to have a child and kill it. I must find a way to destroy him before the solar eclipse."

I tensed. Solar eclipse? Will my baby be born under a solar eclipse?

"When is that supposed to be?"

"Two months." Osman dragged his hand through his thick hair.

Two months. Olivia's not due to give birth for three months. My shoulders fell away from my ears.

"Well, don't worry, Osman," I said, patting his shoulder. "We'll help you find your beloved."

Osman said nothing. Instead, he stared at something or someone behind me, his eyes like chocolate drops floating in milk.

I turned to see what had frightened him.

A man pushed his way through the crowd before stepping into view.

It was Raul Costa, and he looked mad as hell.

CHAPTER THIRTY-TWO

ROMAN

A s Costa approached us, pushing through the crowd of noisy drinkers, Osman turned so pale he could have served as a lightbulb. His gaze darted back and forth as he looked for a means of escape.

Several other Timehunters flanked Costa's sides. They all looked mean and menacing as they sized up the room as if searching for their next victim.

"Get up and make your way to the back wall," I hissed to Osman. "Then, make your way into the crowd. We'll find you. We'll help you."

Osman stumbled to his feet, knocking the chair over. He moaned, righted the chair, and then disappeared.

Costa's gaze fixed in our direction as he approached. He beelined toward us as Marcellious and I picked up our ales and drank, feigning nonchalance.

Costa came to a stop at our table. "Why, what have we here? I *know* you."

He stabbed his pointer finger at me.

I lifted my gaze to him, arching my eyebrows as if surprised. "What a wonder to see you! I told you we were explorers. Our quest has taken us to this part of the globe. What brings you here?"

Costa ignored my question. "Where did your friend go?"

His vicious gaze scanned the room like a predator.

"Oh, he excused himself to relieve his bladder. He'll be back shortly." I smiled and took another swallow of ale.

The air here was dense with smoke and liquor fumes, clogged with the endless conversations around us. Costa's intense energy only added to the weighted atmosphere.

Costa glanced over his shoulder at his men. He muttered something to them, and they nodded, falling away. When he turned back to Marcellious and me, I repeated my question.

"What brings you here? This is a long way from Italy." I hefted my ale and took another swallow.

Marcellious appeared bored, but I knew he kept Costa in his peripheral vision, watching him, ready to make a move if warranted.

Costa narrowed his eyes as he regarded us. "I was told there's gold out here in some caves. I thought I'd see if I could increase my wealth. Restoration of my villa cost me a small fortune."

"I can only imagine," I said, trying to appear as if I were commiserating with him. I placed my hands around my mug and twisted it back and forth on the worn wooden table. "I've heard nothing about gold. Perhaps we can explore together."

And I can kill you once you're trapped in the cave with us. You've got to be here for the dagger, as am I.

I kept my gaze pinned on the table, pretending to be only marginally interested in this conversation.

Costa didn't reply.

Marcellious drained his ale, let out a satisfied sound, and leaned back in his chair.

"Who's your companion?" Costa eyed Marcellious warily.

Marcellious shifted his weight, drew himself up, and met Costa's gaze with a piercing glare. "The name's Marcellious Demarrias," he said in a low voice that reverberated throughout the pub.

He drummed his fingers on the table like he was playing a death march.

Costa curled his lips in disdain, his eyes lazily assessing Marcellious. "You look like you've just been dragged out of the jungle," he drawled.

"Why, thank you," Marcellious said, batting his thick eyelashes. "And you look like a—"

"Marcellious," I warned, interrupting him.

"Come now. I'm interested in what he has to say," Costa said, his eyes glittering with menace. "What do I look like?"

"Like an Italian prick. Even your accent reeks of pretense," Marcellious said.

The air snapped and crackled as Costa digested Marcellious' insult.

I clenched my teeth and let out a long breath. Marcellious had no idea who he was speaking to. *Or maybe he does.*

While traveling, I'd talked to him about the Timehunters, particularly Costa.

I cocked my head and gazed across the table at Marcellious.

A small, secretive smile flitted across his face.

He knows. He's playing with him.

I flexed and fisted my hands a few times. "I'm afraid I know very little about you, Raul. I told you all about my love of exploring and finding artifacts. Might you share something interesting about yourself?"

Costa let out a deep sigh and slumped on Osman's empty

chair. "There's not much to tell. I'm a wealthy Italian businessman."

He picked up Osman's half-full ale and glugged it down. Then, he waved his mug in the air until the barmaid scurried over to retrieve it. "Get us all another. I'll buy."

Marcellious and I drained our tankards and pushed them toward the young woman.

The barmaid gathered all the mugs and hustled away.

Costa got a faraway look in his eye. "A long time ago, I was married. My wife brought me so much happiness. We had a beautiful child together."

Why is he telling us the intimacies of his life? Is he drunk?

"Even though my wife brought me happiness, I loved someone else," Costa said. He scowled, still staring at his memories. "But she loved a *monster.*"

A chill prickled my insides. The only monster I knew was a demon named Balthazar.

A furrow of pain formed between Costa's eyebrows. "Our son—my wife's and my son—we lost him." He clenched his teeth. "He was *killed.* I loved him so much. I tried everything to erase the pain, but I couldn't. The pain was agonizing. Losing a child, especially your own child, is heartbreaking."

The barmaid reappeared, shoving her way through the crowd. She placed three fresh tankards before us and waited for payment.

Costa tossed a few coins on her tray, and she hurried away. He lifted his mug to his lips and drained half of it. Emboldened by the drink, he let out a sob.

"So much pain." He swayed back and forth in his seat. "Losing a child is hell. You can't understand it unless you've gone through it yourself."

Don't I know it, I thought but said nothing.

"But my lover…" Costa's eyes glazed over. "She returned to me."

He closed his eyes as if lost in memory.

"She was the love of my life, and she returned to me. I knew she would. And I knew I'd found a way to ease the pain of losing my son." Costa's eyelids flew open, and he regarded me with a shrewd glare. "Do you want to know what I did?"

I blinked in surprise. "Sure. Marcellious and I are always up for a good story, aren't we?"

"We live for stories." Marcellious snorted, but Costa seemed not to notice.

He was too caught up in his tale.

"My lover wanted to poison her child—the child she bore." His face transformed into a cruel visage like the event was still fresh and raw. "I loved her. I would have given her the world. But she chose *him* instead."

Blood pounded through the veins in his neck.

I tried to piece together the story but felt as if I was missing something. "What was your paramour's name?"

Costa's eyes formed slits as he studied me. "Her name? It was Alina."

He barked out a one-note laugh void of cheer.

Alina! I pressed my hands into the table to steady myself. He's talking about Alina. Which means the child she wanted to poison was Olivia!

The urge to tear Costa's limbs from his torso flooded me.

Marcellious must have noticed because he shook his head subtly.

I took a deep breath, trying to calm my racing pulse.

"So, I struck a bargain with her…with Alina." Costa licked his lips like a cat who just ate a rat. "I told her to give me a child, and I'd help her poison her daughter."

The impulse to launch toward Costa and wring his neck overpowered me.

Again, Marcellious shook his head.

"And did she oblige you? Did she give you a child?" I forced the words from my lips.

A secretive smile lifted the corners of his mouth. "Oh, yes, she did. Alina bore me a son."

Olivia has another sibling? How many are there? I clenched my hands when I said, "And where is this son today?"

Costa's eyebrows arched. "My son?"

"Yes, you just told me you and Alina had a son," I said.

"Oh, him. I'm afraid he didn't make it, either." His expression turned sly, devious. "I experimented on him with my poisons. I thought he was strong enough to endure, but I guess I was wrong."

He lifted his tankard and glugged the rest of his ale.

I sat reeling in my chair. Was Costa a sick fuck, or what? He purposely experimented on his own son with poisons? And for what reason? To punish Alina for having a child with another man?

The notion made me sick to my stomach.

"Speaking of poison," Costa said. "You know how Count Montego and I spoke of the Timeborne and my secret society?"

"Vaguely," I replied, still trying to reconcile the fact that not only was he Alina's lover, but he had also poisoned their child.

"Why don't you join us? An explorer such as yourself must find himself in all parts of the world. You could be an asset to the organization." Costa beamed at me.

"Not if it means poisoning people you love. Not interested." My ale turned sour in my stomach.

"Oh, that." Costa wiped the air with his hand as if erasing the memory. "It's essential that I keep up the craft of using plants for poisons."

Then, he made an abrupt about-face in topics. "Alina left me." His jaw jutted forward. "She just up and left me with our son."

He leaned forward slightly and grimaced. "She *promised* she'd stay and help me care for the child. What was I to do? I needed to experiment on someone, and Angelo was available. And, in the end, Alina got what she deserved—her monster of a lover killed her ruthlessly."

My God, this man had no morals whatsoever. He's psychotic.

"I don't want to be a part of your society." I pushed away from the table. I'd had enough of Costa and his twisted brain. "Well, it's been a pleasure running into you. I wish you the best of luck in your quest for gold."

I stood and extended my hand.

Costa stared at my hand in confusion. "Where are you going? I thought we were having a good talk."

"Be that as it may," I said, withdrawing my hand, "I have a wife at home. We both have wives."

I gestured toward Marcellious.

"Ah, yes, your beautiful wife, Olivia. It's a pity three-somes aren't in vogue today, or we could have a fine romp." Costa lifted his gaze to mine, appearing angelic. "Unless, of course, you'd like to set something up with me. I won't tell if you won't tell."

A wicked-sounding chuckle left his throat.

"Not in a million years," I said. Then, I inclined my head toward Marcellious. "Shall we?"

Marcellious got to his feet, and we both turned toward the exit.

A horrible chill cascaded up my spine as I looked toward the door.

Balthazar and Tristan had entered the tavern. They made their way toward us.

Damn. Could this day get any worse?

Marcellious blanched.

"Fuck," he muttered, stepping back between a couple of patrons.

Balthazar sauntered toward our table, smiling broadly. "My, my, my. What a pleasant surprise," he said, looking at Costa and me. Then, his gaze slid toward Marcellious, who stood with his head down.

"You!" he hissed. "You fucking bastard. You little bitch. You fucking *betrayed* me!"

CHAPTER THIRTY-THREE

ROMAN

As I stood near the wall in the smoke-filled, noisy pub, my body was jacked with crackling tension. Not only were we in the presence of the madman Timehunter, Raul Costa, but Balthazar, the ultimate evil, had joined us. This day had gone from bad to awful in less than an hour.

Marcellious shivered, like he stood in the middle of a blizzard, as he fixed his gaze on Balthazar. He huddled near a few bar patrons who studied us with half-hearted interest.

"Stop hiding like a child, Marcellious. Come out and face me, man to man," Balthazar said, his white teeth glinting.

Tristan stood behind his father, watching everything like an idiot trying to fix together giant puzzle pieces.

Marcellious swallowed and stepped away from the crowd.

A few men cocked their heads, eying us with curiosity, hoping for a good show.

I didn't want to oblige them, but a thick tension rolled around our weighted little circle, which consisted of me, Marcellious, Balthazar, Tristan, and Costa. A demonic war would soon erupt if I didn't devise a plan of escape.

"Leave my brother alone, Balthazar," I said. "We're just trying to live our lives and want no trouble."

"How do you know each other?" Costa asked, rising from his seat. "I thought they were explorers. I was trying to convince them to join me in my quest to eradicate the world from Timebornes and Timebounds."

Balthazar sneered. "You've been duped, Raul. You, of all people, should know—these two are *Timebornes*. How could you not tell?"

Costa's nostrils flared, and his eyes seemed to bug from their sockets. "You're both Timebornes? You fucking lied to my face!"

Right. Like we would willingly tell you, the time-traveler hunter, that we're Timebornes.

"We don't want any trouble," I said again. "We know you're bloodthirsty and want to kill all of us. But I beg you to make an exception and leave us be."

Like that would happen. What was I thinking?

"And why should I do that?" Costa stood very close to me, so near that I could smell the disgusting odor of his perspiration mixed with the tobacco and alcohol in the room.

The crowd silenced and shuffled in our direction, eager for a fight.

Balthazar thrust his hand into the air.

The atmosphere crackled and popped with charged electricity.

"Get out! All of you! Get out of here before I do something regrettable!" Balthazar bellowed, his thunderous voice echoing off the rafters and walls. An unseen wind buffeted his long coat, swirling it around him.

A din of noise surrounded us as the bar patrons fled. Chairs and tables were knocked askew as the men rushed for the door. Glassware and dishes shattered, and the metal tankards bounced with tinny thuds against the floor.

Within minutes, the place had emptied of both customers and staff alike.

Costa's six henchmen emerged from the shadows where they'd been skulking.

A strange silence engulfed us. It felt like a venomous snake slid out of the mud as we all tensed, waiting to see where it would strike.

I put out my hands. "Let's be smart about this," I said to Costa. "Balthazar is the one you should destroy. He's the source of evil here."

Who was I kidding? Costa was equally as depraved. He just wasn't as powerful as Balthazar.

Or was he?

"Oh, no. Don't let them fool you more than they already have, Raul," Balthazar said, pointing at me and Marcellious. "They're the ones you want. They're cunning tricksters of the worst kind. You and I have always been allies in the war against the Timeborne."

When Costa didn't move or acknowledge him, Balthazar disappeared and reappeared before Marcellious. He grabbed his neck and lifted him as if he weighed no more than a kitten.

Marcellious kicked his feet, grabbing at Balthazar's arms for purchase. His face turned bright red, and he struggled for breath.

"You motherfucker," Balthazar said, his eyes glowing red. "How dare you betray me? Where is my dagger? Where's my daughter?"

His daughter? Who is Balthazar's daughter? Please tell me it's not Olivia.

My feet seemed to be glued to the floor from indecision

and apprehension. Finally, I forced my mouth to work. "Who is your daughter?"

"Oh, you didn't tell him. I'm shocked you didn't share yet. Tell him," Balthazar sneered before dropping Marcellious. "Tell him who my daughter is."

When Marcellious' feet touched the ground, he staggered backward, barely managing to catch his balance before falling. His face turned apoplectic, and he tapped the band around his ring finger.

My jaw dropped open. Oh, God. How can this be? Emily is Balthazar's daughter!

Marcellious gave a slight nod, confirming my worst fears.

He barreled toward Balthazar like a bull.

I rushed forward, intercepting him, wrenching his hands behind his back. "Stop! He'll kill you!"

Marcellious' muscles bulged as he roared, his eyes flashing with fury and spittle flew from his lips. He struggled fiercely against my grip, the tendons in his neck standing out like thick cords. "I'll kill him," he seethed, his voice low and dangerous.

Costa's men surged forward, but Costa stayed them with a sweep of his arm.

"If you want to fight us, prepare to be poisoned. I carry it with me at all times. And the one I currently carry is the most potent one of all." He slid his hand inside his coat pocket and retrieved a vial, presenting it like a bomb. "I know you're here searching for the moon dagger. I'll think about not using this poison if you tell me where your and Marcellious' wives are. I want all of you. There is no negotiation."

"I will never betray my wife," I said, spitting the words out.

"I'll destroy you all one way or another," Costa said. He loosed his grip on the vial, so it dangled from his fingertips.

"Do you think I'm scared of Balthazar? He and his ridiculous son are weak. They're pathetic."

Balthazar's eyes blazed with red. "Who are you calling pathetic?"

Intense heat poured from his body in waves.

I was shocked to see Balthazar and Costa together, only this time Balthazar was not trying to kill him. The last time I saw them together, Balthazar burned Costa's villa and killed many people. How was Costa not enemies with him after that event? Why was Balthazar standing by and not killing him? Something wasn't right. If we didn't die by poison, we would soon be burned to death.

Costa slid the vial into his pocket.

Before I could react, he rushed me, backing me against the wall. With his forearm pressed against my windpipe, he yelled, "Where. Is. Your. *Wife*?"

I forced his arm back an inch or so with unrelenting force. "I'll never tell you, asshole. You're the one who's going to die. We're going to destroy your little hive of hornets."

I summoned my strength and shoved him backward. He staggered, falling against one of his men. The man steadied Costa, but Costa whirled away from him, glaring. He turned to me and said, "Who are you working with? Malik? Someone else? Who is it?"

I barked out a laugh. "Are you that stupid? You think I'm going to tell you? I'm not going to tell you *anything*. I would rather die with honor than submit to your demands."

"That's a big mistake, my friend." Costa sneered.

"Do you think we're friends? Not even close." I slid my dagger from its sheath by my side. Brandishing it before me, I said, "Alina couldn't destroy you, but Olivia will. Mark my words. You're a dead man, Raul Costa."

"That's enough!" Costa yelled. "Get them!"

Costa's men rushed toward me. I grabbed Balthazar, using him as a shield.

The heat radiating from his body was unbearable. I dug my fingers into his flesh, refusing to let go. He released a guttural scream of agony when I plunged the dagger deep into his back. He bellowed in defiance and grabbed me with his powerful hands, hurling me across the room with an animalistic rage.

My world spun out of control as fear engulfed me like a wave. I hit the ground in a roll and jackknifed to my feet.

Marcellious was poised to fight. But the odds were against us with Costa's poison and Balthazar's command of heat.

Still—I was a good soldier, and good soldiers never backed away from a fight.

My strategy was to pick off Costa's men individually and then go for Costa. I retrieved a small pocketknife from my other side and held both blades outstretched, aimed at one of Costa's men, a swarthy hulk of a man directly opposite me.

"You're a fool, Alexander," Costa said. "This will be fun to watch."

He crossed his arms and stood back.

The hulking goon bared his teeth.

Fear coursed through my bloodstream, seizing my muscles. Costa was right. I was foolish to think I stood a chance here. But then Olivia's face drifted through my mind. She carried our child. I couldn't let her down. Besides, I'd faced too many adversaries, men who claimed victory before they stepped into the coliseum arena. And where were they now? All dead, bones picked clean beneath the ground.

All it takes is one distraction, one mistake…a cough, a noise…something that catches the mind of my enemy.

I summoned my gladiator strength and cunning. None of these men ever faced what I'd encountered in the coliseum.

The goon charged me. I evaded him, stepping to the right.

He growled and swirled around. His movements were slow and sloppy.

This one will be easy to pick off.

We circled around one another like wolves until I glanced to the side.

He glanced, too, to see what I looked at.

Idiot. I rushed forward to slam my dagger into his chest with a satisfying crunch.

The goon clutched his ribcage before toppling to the ground.

Grunts and groans surrounded me.

Costa had been accurate in declaring Marcellious a savage.

Marcellious fought with cunning brutality, schooled in him by the Native Americans and honed by being tossed into the coliseum arena as a gladiator.

Three men, including the one I had felled, lay sprawled against the floor, dead or dying.

Another man, wiry and skeletal with a scarred face, took the hulk's place.

The circling dance began again.

Scarface seemed light on his feet, capable of moving with lightning speed. He held a dagger, too.

We charged at one another, slashing, then retreated.

My knife slashed across his face, grazing his jaw, and drawing a thin line of blood. His blade reciprocated with a vicious stab, slicing through my upper arm like butter. Blood gushed from the two of us, uniting in a crimson puddle that surrounded our feet.

The scent of it spurred me on. I lifted my arm and licked

SARA SAMUELS

the wound, smearing the blood across my lips. Then, teeth bared, I faced my wiry opponent.

A memory surfaced of wielding a siccae, a short scimitar blade used in the coliseum arena against scores of opponents. In addition to our human foes, lions and tigers were often let loose in the coliseum to join us.

Scarface could never compete with what I endured.

But then another one of Costa's henchmen slid from the shadows, wielding a sword.

Where was a retes, a weighted net, when you needed one? I could have thrown it over the guy to my right and dispatched the skeletal man before me.

The two of them exchanged a look and then powered toward me.

I whirled out of the way, knives a blur.

I caught the guy to my right in the neck before he impaled me with his sword.

Blood spurted from his wound.

He let out a roar and tackled me.

I fell, slamming upon my back and letting out a groan.

The bleeding man pinned his sword to my throat.

I hooked my foot behind one of his legs and rolled him. His blade sliced my neck in the process.

How nasty was the wound? I would find out soon enough, either by my death or victory.

Costa and Balthazar shouted from the side.

"Do it, Lucas! Come on, Marco! Destroy him! Take him down! It's two against one!" Costa yelled.

"If you don't finish him off, I will!" Balthazar screamed.

I bore down on Lucas' wrist until he released the hilt of his sword. Blood continued to gush from his neck in slow spurts.

He blinked as if trying to clear his woozy mind. The loss of blood had to be getting to him.

I slit his throat, finishing what I had started.

Marco lunged for the dead man's sword.

I shot to my feet and roared with rage as I launched myself at Marco. He spun around and lashed out with his foot, connecting with my hand like a sledgehammer. My dagger flew wildly in the air, smashing against the wall before it clattered onto the floor, where the blade bit deeply into the wood. Marco wielded the huge blade with deadly skill, ready to deliver a fatal blow.

I, on the other hand, was now armed with a pocketknife. I had to rely on my quick reflexes and cunning if I was to have any chance of surviving this encounter.

We circled warily, sizing each other up, and searching for any opening to strike.

Sweat beaded on my forehead as I tried to focus on my task. Blood seeped down the front of my shirt from my neck wound.

Marco charged forward with his knife, a murderous glint in his eye. I dove to the side, evading his attack and swiped my blade across him. He bellowed and took a step back, a bloody gash carved down his arm. With rage in his eyes, he advanced again, persisting in his onslaught. I scrambled to stay out of reach of Marco's savage stabs and jabs, desperately searching for an opening. In that moment, I surged forward, thrusting my knife deep into Marco's shoulder.

His primal roar shook the walls as he swung his blade madly at me, trying to drive me away.

I managed to duck and roll away, narrowly avoiding the deadly blade. I leaped to my feet.

We limped around each other, each of us seething with determination but barely able to stand. Gradually I began to regain my strength, weaving and dodging his clumsy attacks with grace as I closed in on him. Taking advantage of the opening, I lunged forward for the kill and felt a satisfying thud as my blade connected with its target. The light faded from my opponent's eyes, and it was over.

A curious scent wafted into the air, and I cringed. The bitter smell struck the back of my throat, making me want to retch. A foul smoke filled the air, obscuring my sight. I thrust out my hands, feeling for something, anybody.

"Marcellious?" I shouted. "Where are you?"

Someone grabbed my hair and yanked my head backward.

"I'm going to have a lot of fun with your brother. He fucking betrayed me, and now he's going to pay," Balthazar hissed in my ear.

The edge of the blade seared my side like a branding iron, causing me to crumple in agony. Through the fog of pain, I could make out Marcellious' writhing figure in Costa's menacing grip, bloody tears streaming from his eyes as he squirmed for freedom. A molten-hot headache pounded against my temples with each beat of my heart, filling me with intense rage.

Shit. Costa released poison.

The air around me seemed to thicken and my vision darkened until I could no longer distinguish between reality and dream. Costa and Balthazar flung the limp body of Marcellious into the street as a thousand spears of agony pierced my head, and I stumbled blindly to steady myself against the pain. And suddenly, out of the oppressive darkness trudged a figure toward me slowly, like a nightmare on two feet.

Is it Malik? Please let it be Malik.

My head spun like I was being held by my feet and whirled around and around. I tried to yell, but the words wouldn't come out. I fell to the floor, immobilized. The only thing I was capable of moving was my eyelids. I blinked through my watery gaze.

The figure approached me. Strong hands seized me and attempted to drag me out of the tavern. But my rescuer staggered as if incapable of movement.

I squinted, trying to make out the face of my savior. *Yes. It's Malik.*

I watched helplessly as Malik crumpled to the floor beside me, his body heavy with the effects of the poison we had unwittingly inhaled. I felt a peculiar numbness stealing over me, paralyzing my limbs, and rendering me mute. The bitter taste of the toxin still lingering on my tongue, I lay motionless, unable to move or speak.

Our eyes darted back and forth as we struggled to understand what was happening to us.

The room began to spin as the effects of the poison intensified. Panic set in as I realized the grave danger we were in. We had to get out of the tavern before it was too late.

I tried to move my limbs with all my might, but without success. Malik's body seemed as unresponsive as mine. I could feel my heart pounding as I desperately searched for a way to escape.

Malik let out a thunderous bellow that filled the room with an unrelenting primal energy. Every muscle in his body strained as he fought to break free from the grip of poison, pushing himself up inch by bloody inch until his quivering limbs were able to hold him upright.

"We've got to get out of here," he said through labored breathing.

I felt a surge of revival, buoyed by Malik.

Together, we dragged ourselves toward the door, each inch of progress requiring immense effort. Finally, we hauled ourselves across the tavern's threshold into the chilly, windswept night.

The world around me seemed to ripple and warp, turning increasingly hazy as my vision blurred and my strength ebbed away like water in the desert. I was lying beside Malik on the cold hard ground, gasping for breath and forcing myself to keep going while Malik shuddered with exhaustion next to me. Where would we go? What would be our next move when I had nothing left to give and Malik appeared unable to help?

CHAPTER THIRTY-FOUR

MARCELLIOUS

I awoke in a dark, dank dungeon, my arms chained to the wall. The cold metal links dug into my flesh, and I winced with pain. I closed my eyes and tried to focus on anything else.

My mind was consumed by the haunting memories of my past. The guilt of having killed so many people mercilessly swirled around me like a vortex of despair. Though I knew that I had done those terrible deeds in the past, my mind still could not reconcile them. My conscience constantly filled my head with voices condemning me as an inhumane monster, unworthy of any love.

Emily must hate me.

My memories weighed heavily on my shoulders, the haunting voices of my past like a never-ending chorus in my head. "You're not good enough," they whispered. "You should just give up." I felt every ounce of their words as if they were stretching and tearing at my chest, an invisible force that pressed down on me until I had no choice but to succumb. My body throbbed with agony as I tried to silence their taunts through physical pain. I writhed in my iron restraints, taking satisfaction as the rusted metal dug into my flesh.

However, in a moment of clarity, I saw an image of Dancing Fire, the man I called my father. He taught me survival skills I use to this day. I once hunted under his tutelage and learned to ride. We shared a bond that went deeper than familial upbringing.

Dancing Fire glared at me.

"What do you want?" I mumbled.

"You didn't give me a chance to explain myself before leaving me," Dancing Fire hissed. He loomed over me, ten feet tall. He pulled out a knife and thrust it at my heart. "You were the only son I had, but you *left* me."

"No, no, no! It wasn't like that! I had to leave." Regardless of my words, the pain and scars of my past activities serving under Emperor Severus continued to haunt me.

A thousand men lifted their arms and lashed me with their whips.

"You deceived us!" they cried. "You betrayed us!"

I cowered beneath their assault, feeling like it was my destiny to be so savagely beaten.

The memories continue to overwhelm me, driving me to madness. I desperately wanted the pain to stop, but it seemed as though I could never escape my many demons.

Costa clanged the iron door bars that sealed me into this small, horrible cell.

I tried to focus on him through the haze of a million haunted memories.

"I see the belladonna is having its way with you. It's a remarkable substance, conforming to the insanity each person carries in his or her mind." He leered at me. "And I only gave you a small dose. Wait until I administer the full amount."

His laughter cut off. "I can't stand you. I hate your kind.

People who time travel are disgusting, and I want you all eradicated."

Balthazar materialized beside him in a burst of smoke and fire. His gnarled hand clamped down around the iron bars like a vice, as he snarled menacingly through clenched teeth. "Let me in with him. I'll make sure his suffering lasts for eternity with my own special brand of poison torture."

Costa looked askance at Balthazar, frowning. "I've got everything under control. But thanks for the offer."

"Come on, Raul. We can help each other. We need to get Demarrias to talk, to tell us who he's working for."

"And I said I've got everything under control," Costa hissed through gritted teeth. His face had turned an unnatural shade of red as he balled his hand into a fist. He moved menacingly toward Balthazar, who stepped back and mirrored his pose, ready for confrontation. Just then, the thumping of several pairs of feet echoed off the walls, signaling the arrival of backup.

"We're ready, sir," a man's voice said.

"Excellent!" Costa said.

The jangle of keys followed. The clink of a lock turned, and the iron door creaked open.

Costa, Balthazar, and two men wearing masks entered.

The masked men stood tall, gripping their torches like weapons of war. Their muscles raged with each step, bulging, and flexing beneath their heavy chainmail vests. Towering like angry titans, they seemed invincible in the flickering light, warriors ready for battle.

Like the ghosts who haunted me, the flames cast long shadows across the room.

"Ugh. This place stinks," Balthazar said, wrinkling his nose.

"That's part of the charm," Costa said, chuckling. "It

fucks with their mind to wallow in their own filth. That and the poison really does the job."

Balthazar's body trembled with excitement as he pleaded for permission to inflict torture. His voice cracked with suppressed rage, desperate for bloodshed. His eyes blazed with fanatical delight as a sinister smile spread across his face, eager to relish in the agony of his victim.

"Not happening," Costa growled.

Balthazar retrieved a knife from his sheath and waved it at Costa. "I thought we were friends. But you deceived me, just as he did."

He waved the blade in my direction.

Costa batted the knife from his face. "Stop, or you'll be imprisoned in my dungeon next."

"Ha!" Balthazar cried out. "Think you can imprison me? Think again."

I sat hunched over my torso, trying to escape the assault on my olfactory senses. I was weak, shaking, trembling, all strength having fled my limbs. It did smell ghastly in here, like thousands of men before me had added their own human waste and vomit to the stone floor.

"You and I are a means to an end, that's all." Costa gestured to his men. "Unchain him. We'll take him to a cell with less ventilation so the poison can work its magic better."

The masked men approached.

I struggled against the chains that bound me to the cold granite wall of the dungeon. I knew that my captors were planning to torture and poison me further. I braced myself for the pain that was to come.

The masked men knelt on either side of me and unlocked the chains around my legs and wrists.

I was too weak to resist.

Then, each hefted one of my arms, and they dragged me across the unforgiving stone.

Costa and Balthazar stepped back so we could all pass. They followed, quarreling in quiet, angry whispers.

The stone tore at my clothes and bit at my skin, like I was pulled across a metal grate.

I gasped for air as I felt the overwhelming pain coursing through my veins. I had been thrown across the room and stranded in a seemingly inescapable space, with no windows or openings to look through. The six-foot-by-six-foot room was too small, and I felt like I was suffocating. The masked men arrived, securing me onto heavy chains that were protruding from the wall. As they walked out of the door, a wave of relief washed over me... but it was quickly replaced by fear of the unknown.

Balthazar entered the room, brandishing his knife and closing the door behind us, sealing us both in.

"Where's my dagger?" He slashed me, tearing apart my shirt and the skin of my chest.

Crimson red seeped from the wound.

"You son of a bitch," he screamed. "Where is my dagger? My beloved Alina's dagger is gone, too, and you're the only one who could have taken it."

"I don't know what you're talking about," I croaked. I steeled myself for the worst but refused to let him break my spirit. I had to do this for Emily, even if she despised me. I was determined to stay strong, even in the face of his and Costa's cruel and torturous methods.

As a gladiator, I learned to compartmentalize a brutal attack in my mind and resist the pain. I called upon that skill now as Balthazar's blade continued to tear apart my flesh. I knew I would be lost forever if I allowed them to break me.

"Who have you been helping and working with?" Balthazar yelled. "Was it Malik?"

My woozy, poisoned mind had its way with my tongue, and the word "Yes" slid from my mouth. *Shit. Why are you telling him anything?*

"You sought me out as your helper. I succumbed to you, contaminated by your lies. But Malik came along and told me the truth. Malik saved me." I couldn't stop the torrent of words falling from my lips. *It has to be the belladonna.* "If you kill me today, it won't matter. Emily will never know the truth that you're her father. The best part is you're never going to see your grandchild."

Balthazar roared, his body seeming to expand before my eyes. "Where are you holding my daughter?"

"I'll never tell you. I would rather die first," I said, groaning.

Balthazar backhanded me across my face, tearing my lip open. "I'm going to kill you, then."

Blood filled my mouth. "Go ahead. I've done enough betrayal. You can't hurt me anymore."

The agony of pain began to push against my defenses. I didn't think I could hold it back any longer.

Balthazar grabbed my ragged shirt and tore it away from my torso.

"Look at all these brands on your back! I think you need a few more." He bellowed. "Bring me a white-hot branding iron!"

I passed out, unable to withstand the torture.

I jerked awake from the searing pain of scorching metal pressed to my back. The stench of burning flesh, *my* flesh, assaulted my nose. The acrid scent of poisonous smoke surrounded me. It stung my eyes and made it difficult to see.

I didn't know how many days had passed or if it was still the same day.

Balthazar towered over me, waving the branding iron.

"Go ahead and kill me," I rasped. I was beyond weak and hallucinating.

The brand landed on my back, sending fiery pain rocketing across my skin. I howled. The flashbacks of my time as a gladiator erupted. My mind raced as I remembered all the chaos and trouble I had endured during those years in ancient Rome.

I was back in the thick of it. The smell of smoke filled my nostrils, and screams echoed in my ears. As I fought in the heat of battle, I couldn't help but feel conflicted about why I was there in the first place. Was I fighting for what was right? Or had I been sent to this war as a pawn for someone else's gain?

I remembered the fear gripping my heart as I watched comrades fall around me on the battlefield. But even through the chaos, I couldn't shake the feeling that something wasn't right about this conflict.

I shook my head, trying to clear the memories from my mind. But they wouldn't go away. They continued to flood my thoughts, overwhelming me with feelings of guilt and confusion. How could I continue fighting when every fiber of my being screamed at me to stop?

I struggled and tried to remind myself that it was all in the past, that I was safe and sound with Emily in our bedroom.

Then the branding iron struck my back again. I catapulted into the past. The memories were too vivid, too real. I felt like I was back in ancient Rome, fighting for my life.

Get it together. You can withstand this torture.

As the flashback faded, I took a deep breath and tried to regain my composure.

Balthazar's voice thundered through the room. "Where is my daughter? Where's Olivia?"

Raul said, "Let's poison him. I can make the belladonna more powerful."

I squeezed my eyes shut and tried to disappear into a safe place in my mind. But then the burn of poisoned herbs attacked my nostrils.

Balthazar's voice seemed to come from everywhere, from inside, from outside, reverberating through me and all around me.

"Where's Emily?"

The hallucinogenic properties of belladonna ravaged me. My mind was foggy, and my vision blurred. I struggled to breathe, each gasp of air coming in short, ragged bursts.

I felt my mind slipping away, the world becoming a distant haze. My mouth began to move of its own accord and I realized I was speaking, words tumbling out in a stream of incoherent babble.

Thoughts from deep within me bubbled to the surface and spilled from my lips, no matter how hard I tried to stop them. The poison had taken control of me, and while I wanted to fight it, I felt powerless against it.

"I didn't mean to kill all those people. I swear I didn't."

Balthazar's voice boomed in my ears. "Yes! Tell me!"

"I'm a monster. I'm a dark monster who enjoys killing. I tried to destroy my brother. I tried to kill his wife." I shook and sobbed, confessing all my horrible sins. "I lost the first love of my life, my child. I don't want to lose my Emily and our child."

"That's it," Balthazar encouraged. "Tell me everything, my son."

He spoke to me like a father, like a priest. I knew I could trust him with my secrets. "I want to be a father so badly. Not a father with dark ways. But I crave the darkness with every fiber of my soul. Yet, a part of me wants to be good. Emily makes me better."

Poisoned as I was, I couldn't tell fact from fiction. I couldn't tell if the things I saw before my eyes were real or figments of my warped imagination.

"Now you're going to tell me where Emily is. And where's my dagger?" Balthazar's words whispered through my ears.

I whispered in response. "She's with Count Montego."

"Who the hell is Count Montego?" Balthazar hissed.

"He's a count. A nobleman. He traveled with us and let us stay with him," I mumbled.

"Where's he live?" Balthazar whispered.

Costa's voice bounced against the walls. "What did he say?"

Balthazar's voice grew louder. "He says she's with Count Montego."

"Oh," Costa said. "He's just an old man. We can easily overpower him."

"I just want to be happy in my life." I began weeping. "Is that too much to ask?"

"How about you bleed him out?" Costa said. "He'll start talking then."

Balthazar grasped my arm and started to slice. "He'll be drained out soon enough."

"I'd rather die than tell you anything more," I muttered.

"Don't you want to see your child or become a father? We can all be allies again!" Balthazar said.

"No, all you do is lie. You don't have your dagger. We will win. We're ahead of the game. You're upset because you're losing." I didn't know where my conviction came from.

Indeed, I would die soon.

Costa grabbed me and pulled me close to his face. "I've seen a lot of time travelers. You're different, Marcellious. Join us. We're stronger together. Tell us where the caves are and then we'll work with you."

Costa swam before my eyes, his face disappearing and reappearing.

"You can kill me," I said. "You can destroy me. Emily, Olivia, and Malik will ruin you. We have a stronger team."

Costa shoved me away, and my head smacked against the wall. My vision blurred as pain wracked my brain.

"I'm going to check on Reyna, the other prisoner," Costa said. The door creaked open and shut behind him, leaving me alone with Balthazar.

I was too high to be worried.

"I'm losing my patience," Balthazar said in a low, soothing tone. "Tell me where Emily is. I want to know her. And who is Count Montego?"

My hallucinating brain coughed up the address.

Balthazar practically crowed. "I knew, in the end, you would come through for me. You're a good son, Marcellious."

He strode toward the door.

"Where are you going?" I cried out, afraid to be alone.

"What does it matter? I'm done with you." Balthazar slid through the opening and slammed the door shut, sealing me in.

I beat my head against the granite. I'd allowed the belladonna to consume me. And now, my beloved Emily and my child would soon be dead.

CHAPTER THIRTY-FIVE
OLIVIA

I wrenched open Count Montego's heavy front door, and stepped outside into the howling storm. The wind whipped my face with icy rain, blowing through my hair as I squinted against the whiteout, desperately scanning for any trace of Roman. The trees around me looked like frightened animals, their branches bowing in surrender to the relentless blizzard.

"Olivia!"

Emily's sharp-edged reproach cut through my despair.

"Come inside at once!" She seized my hand and tugged me through the open doorway, slamming the door behind me. "You'll catch a chill and come down with something."

"I'm just so scared. It's been nearly a month. They said they'd be back in two to three weeks."

I rubbed my aching jaw. I hadn't slept much this past week, clenching my teeth, and fretting over why Roman, Malik, and Marcellious hadn't returned. In the depths of nighttime, my mind always conjured up worst-case scenarios. My sleep was filled with nightmares of the three men, lying in a pool of their own blood or impaled by swords. I tried to reason with my own thoughts, praying that they had made it safely up the hill, but all I could see in my mind were images of them defeated and alone. As dawn pushed through the curtains, the bright light brought me back to the real world and away from my tumultuous dreams.

Emily grabbed my hand. "I know, sister mine. I'm scared, too. But we mustn't put ourselves in harm's way because we are distressed. Come with me."

Count Montego's Wales estate was more like a castle than a simple manor. The big house and the outbuildings were surrounded by an enormous wrought-iron fence that looked like it could have stopped a tank from completing its mission of destruction.

The house was a sprawling mass of gray stone and thick timbers, with four towers, each capped with turrets and flying pennants. From the outside you would think it belonged in a fantasy, but inside, the space was just as magical. Each room was cavernous and vast, and I often found myself lost as I wandered from room to room.

It was much like wandering through a castle straight out of a fantasy story.

The space Emily led me to was known simply as Noir. The high tray ceiling was all white and elaborately carved. Fleur-de-lis wallpaper in shades of gold covered the walls, while thick, carved archways in ebony surrounded each doorway and framed the fireplace, which housed a roaring fire. The chairs and high-backed sofa had been fashioned from the same ebony wood, gilded in gold leaf, and covered with gold floral velvet. The floor-to-ceiling arched windows were framed by heavy velvet curtains in a different floral print.

The massive room looked like it belonged in a fairy tale.

We trekked across the lush blush-and-deep-blue floral wool rug.

"Sit," Emily said, pointing to the sofa.

I sat.

She settled next to me, facing me, and grasping my hands.

"I feel I must start my own search, Emily," I said, clutching her hands like they were my lifeline to sanity. "I've got to do something."

"Absolutely not! Do you see that blizzard outside the window?"

The ice storm battered the pane with relentless tapping sounds. The wind howled around the eaves adding to the cacophony of noise.

"Of course I see it. I was just standing outside in that blasted storm, remember?"

She knocked the side of my head with her knuckles. "I just wondered since it seems you have lost your good sense."

She flashed me a reproving glare.

Then, she grimaced, clutching her abdomen.

"What is it?' I asked in alarm. "What's happening?"

She held up a finger and panted. Then, she said, "Contractions."

"Do you think the baby is coming?"

"No!" She waved away her concerns. "I'm fine. I keep having contractions but they're small and far apart—like days apart."

"Oh," I said, relaxing. "They're what are called Braxton-Hicks. That's your body prepping for the birth."

"It's more like a foreboding," Emily said, laughing weakly. "They hurt. But back to your concerns…Talk to Count Montego, then. I saw him wandering up the stairs a few minutes ago. Maybe he can help."

I stared at the tray ceiling. Count Montego had tremendous resources at his disposal. Maybe she was right.

Rosie wandered into the room, wearing a long-sleeve, one-piece gown that ended at her ankles. "Will somebody play with me? I'm bored."

"Of course, Rosie," Emily said, rising to her feet. "Let's find one of your wooden puzzles and assemble it. Olivia has to find Count Montego."

"He's upstairs. I heard him in his room," Rosie said, twisting back and forth.

"Then, that's where I'll head." I headed for the doorway, tapping Rosie's little nose as I passed her.

I ascended the staircase, a wonder of architecture, the same as the rest of the estate.

Constructed entirely of stone, the railing consisted of small archways interspersed with columns. Human heads and hands had been carved into small panels festooning the sides of the columns. As I progressed, a red, blue, and gold wool runner rug softened my footsteps.

Upstairs, I trekked down the hall toward Count Montego's bedroom. The door lay wide open, and no one was inside, so I proceeded toward his study. I grasped the gilded doorknob and opened it.

Count Montego let out a loud grunt as he thrust between the legs of one of his maids.

"Oh, god," I gasped, pressing my hand to my mouth.

The maid let out a squeal.

"Don't move, dear," Count Montego said to her, still balls deep inside.

His long-sleeved shirt hung on his torso, but he wore no breeches, affording me an up close and personal view of his rounded ass. The muscles of his legs and ass belied his age, looking like they belonged to a much younger man.

"What can I help you with, Olivia?" he said.

I whirled around to face the door. "I'm so sorry. It can wait."

My cheeks blazed with heat.

"Don't be sorry. It's my fault. I should have locked the door." He grunted again, no doubt wanting to keep the momentum going in his tryst with the maid.

She let out a moan.

"No, no. I should have knocked. My apologies. I can wait." I wanted to sprint from the room, but my feet glued themselves to the carpet.

"No apologies needed," he said, groaning in earnest. "We'll be through in a moment, and I'll come to find you."

"Sure thing, Okay, then. I'll be downstairs." And with that stumbling communication, I fled down the hallway with the carved panel of nudes at the end. When I thought about it, carved panels of nudes frequented the rooms of this estate.

That should have been a clue.

"Where's Rosie?" I said once I'd reached Noir.

Emily sat on the sofa, staring out the window at the unforgiving snowstorm. "She just left to help the cook in the kitchen. She's such a curious child, always eager to learn." She frowned. "What's the matter? You look as pale as a ghost."

I flopped down next to her. "Oh, God, Emily. I just found Count Montego in his study, screwing one of his maids!"

Emily gasped. "You're kidding!"

"I wish I was. I'll never unsee what I saw. I mean, I knew he had sex sometimes—he was at Costa's sex party—but knowing it and seeing it are two separate things." I fisted my eyes as if that could erase the memory.

"He's a good-looking man," Emily said.

I met her gaze.

"But he's so old," we both said simultaneously.

"They both seemed to be enjoying themselves immensely."

Emily made a face.

Heavy footsteps approached, and I turned to see the count, immaculately dressed once more.

"I'm so sorry, Olivia. I should have locked the door," he said, settling in the armchair opposite us.

"No, no, no." I swished my hands before me. "I shouldn't have barged in. It's all my fault. We can just forget it ever happened."

I wanted to move this conversation along to a new topic.

"Entirely my fault, Olivia. It shan't happen again." He clasped his hands and leaned over his thighs. With his beaming smile, however, he didn't exactly look contrite.

"Fine," I said. "Apology accepted."

Please, let's just move on.

"What I'm most concerned about and want to talk with you about is the three men out there somewhere. Namely, our two husbands and Malik…"

"Yes, I've thought of them, also. I, too, am concerned." Count Montego stroked his jaw with his long, elegant fingers.

I blinked away the images of those hands all over the maid's lithe body. "Are you? Any ideas on what we can do? It's pure torture just sitting around here and not doing anything."

"Understood, dear Olivia. You are an adventurous sort. But I'm sure you understand the merits of staying indoors and keeping the baby and you safe." He glanced at the ceiling.

He possessed a timeless elegance to his features as if they were sculpted. Everything about him spoke of noble bearing, but I knew nothing of his lineage. Who was his family? Where did they come from? I didn't even know his country of origin. Even his accent couldn't be pinned down to a single culture.

"I'm sure it comes down to the weather," the count said, interrupting my musing. "It's difficult to travel with a heavy load. I'm sure they're safe."

He gave us a reassuring smile. "However, if they've not returned by the end of this week, I'll organize a search party. I'll even join in the search."

My shoulders fell away from my ears. "Oh, would you? I would be most grateful."

"Of course, my dear. I don't want you to waste another moment fretting. All will be well." He rested his hands on the arms of the chair and propped one ankle on the other knee. "How else can I ease your minds?"

I thought for a minute. "Why don't you tell us a story? Clearly, you still can make a woman smile." I blushed the moment the words left my mouth. "What makes you who you are, Count Montego?" I stammered, hoping to redirect the conversation.

Count Montego's eyes twinkled as if enjoying my blunder. "I'm glad you appreciate my prowess with the opposite sex."

He chuckled, and my cheeks heated to broiling.

"First off, you must stop calling me Count Montego. Friends call me Mathias."

Does he consider us friends?

I glanced at Emily, and she gave a slight shrug.

"Okay, Mathias. What can you tell us about yourself?"

Mathias settled back in his chair as if preparing for a long journey. He gazed out the window.

At last, he said, "I will tell you my background—the story of my life and how I got to this point. Once upon a time, I was a delighted man. I had everything I ever wanted—power, friends, a team of soldiers, everything. My background is that of a teacher. I taught for a long time and was mastering my craft."

"What did you teach?" I asked, fascinated.

He looked down his nose at me. "Please don't interrupt me. Let me tell you my story in full."

I sat back on the sofa, feeling like a scolded child.

"You can ask questions later," he said gently.

I nodded but did not speak.

"I taught people how to fight and defend themselves... basic survival skills."

My eyebrows arched. *Me, too.*

"I taught knights and royalty. I was a consultant of kings and queens in war tactics." His eyes glazed as if he were right there in his past. "I opened my own training school, working with certain types of people who needed my help."

He met my gaze, his eyes haunted and hollow as if gazing out of a vast, empty cave.

"Something was missing from my life." Shadows fell across his face. "It was love. That was the missing equation. I never had time for a relationship. I was too busy, too focused, consumed with my mission."

He dragged a weary hand across his face. "And then I met the woman who would be my wife, Cora. I loved her with all my heart."

His eyes fluttered closed as he savored the memory. When his eyes opened, the pain had etched his face like someone had drawn on him with a feather quill. "Cora came from a poor family. It didn't matter to me. I gave her everything. She took that pain away from me when I had dark times, stressed with problems."

He rose, crossing the room to stand before the fireplace. He stared at the glowing embers as if seeking solace. Then, he crouched, picked up an oak log from the metal log holder, and placed it gently on top of the embers. Hands on his hips, he stared at the wood until small flames licked the dried bark.

Emily and I shared a look of sympathy for Mathias' tale. I had no doubt it ended in tragedy.

He returned to his chair and resumed his story. "I told Cora I could give her the world."

He cocked his head and studied Emily, a slight smile curving his lips.

"I see my beautiful wife in you sometimes, dear Emily. She was a sweet young woman, as you are."

"Thank you, Mathias," Emily said, gazing at her hands folded in her lap. "But surely she was a more remarkable beauty than me."

"Oh, Emily, if you could only see yourself as others do, you'd know what an exceptional beauty you are." He exhaled deeply and stretched out his legs. "But back to the story. For a time, everything was beautiful. Life was perfect. We got married and were blessed with a child. I gave my school's responsibility to someone else so I could focus on fatherhood. But, in truth, I was scared. The moment our child was born, I was frightened to my bones."

He scoffed. "Me, a man in the prime of his life who trained men to become formidable warriors. 'It's just a child,' I chided myself. 'I've trained warriors. I can handle a small squirming baby.'"

His face creased in sorrow, and his eyes grew moist. He stared out the window at the unceasing snowfall. When he spoke again, his voice emerged as a whisper. "But my wife was killed one month after we bore the child."

"Oh, Mathias," I said.

Emily made a quiet gasp.

Mathias schooled his features into that of a blank canvas,

void of personality. "I couldn't go on. I didn't want to raise the child, nor did I want any part of my offspring. I gave my child away to someone else. I thought I wasn't good enough for her. I had failed my wife in protecting her."

His voice sounded harsh and bitter.

The room was engulfed by silence. The wind continued to howl outside the like a screaming tempest, speaking to the misery Mathias had endured.

I glanced at Emily, wondering what her reaction was.

She squeezed my hand, her eyes filled with tears.

"Say something," she mouthed to me.

"Do you know where your child is? Is there any way you can contact her?" I said softly.

"No. I wanted to protect my daughter and give her the best life, so I gave her to good parents. I was too focused on revenge at that point. I wanted to kill the man who had taken my wife's life. I couldn't watch over my child, so she had to go." His eyes refocused on the room as if seeing it anew. He blinked a few times and met my gaze. "I knew where she was for a time. I made it a point to keep tabs on her, to watch over her."

His expression soured. "But then she fell in love with my sworn enemy. He was the man who killed my wife."

"Wait—so your daughter fell in love with the man who killed your wife?"

Mathias nodded.

"Did she know?"

Mathias shook his head. "She knew nothing. She was charmed by this fellow—utterly charmed. She knew nothing of my hatred for him or the suffering he caused." His jaw stiffened. "She loved the man who murdered her mother!"

He slammed his fist on the arm of his chair. Emily and I flinched.

"Her parents couldn't control her. My daughter was head-strong, wild, and willful. I continued to lurk on the sidelines, watching her. I'd ride my horse by her house. Or, I'd make up an excuse to deal with her father. Neither parent knew who I was. I had gifted them my daughter through a close friend. And when I was in her presence, I ensured she had everything she needed. She wanted for nothing."

That same haunted, hollow look reappeared in Mathias' eyes. "Her involvement with this man grew until she was utterly obsessed. In the end, he killed her, too."

Emily and I gasped in unison.

"That's horrible," I said.

He idly rubbed the side of his neck. "It's not a happy story, that's for sure. But I console myself with the knowledge that my beautiful daughter gave me grandchildren and great-grandchildren. I'm truly blessed."

"Where are they?" I asked.

Mathias smiled—the first smile that crossed his face since he'd shared his story.

"They're close by. I'm most fortunate to have them in my life." Abruptly, he rose and crossed to his ornate ebony wet bar. He lifted a decanter of amber liquid and said, "Would you care for some brandy? I've got a wonderful distillation made for me in the Royaume de France."

"No, thank you," I said, stunned by his about-face. One second he spoke of unbearable tragedy; the next, he offered us drinks?

"You, Emily?"

"No, thank you, Mathias. I am pregnant." Her cheeks and neck grew pink.

"Ah, yes." Mathias poured brandy into a crystal snifter and took a sip. "Warms the soul, does it not?"

Drink in hand, he wandered back to his seat.

"You've suffered so much in your life," I said. "How do you maintain such a positive attitude? I've never glimpsed you as anything but warm until today."

Mathias swished his hand in the air. "Over the years, I've learned to increase my wealth by giving to others. And you and Emily have given me joy. Since meeting you, I have considered you both my granddaughters. I so enjoy and want to help you however I can."

I closed the space between us and crouched to take Mathias' hand. "That's a beautiful sentiment. I had no idea you felt that way. I'm fond of you, as well."

Mathias cleared his throat, drew my hand to his lips, and kissed my knuckles. "I make it a point to be a better person."

I smiled and resumed my seat on the sofa. "I hope we've helped fill the hole in your heart." I hesitated before saying, "Did you ever avenge your wife's death?"

A frown flitted across his face and disappeared. "One day, I will. I think I can do it before I die. I'm old, my dear."

"You're not *that* old." The image of Mathias caught in flagrante with his maid earlier zipped through my brain.

Mathias chuckled. "Oh, but I am. Seventy-two is old for me. And I might have lived a crazy life, but I'm glad to have had a wife who gave me a beautiful, albeit willful, child and grandchildren. I try to present myself well and be a valuable resource to my community. My wife would have wanted that."

He exhaled a wistful sigh.

Emily bolted off the sofa, moaning in agony. Her long dress bore several wet splotches.

"Olivia," she wheezed.

"What is it, Emily?" I leaped from my seat to stand next to her. "What's wrong?"

"My water's broke," she wailed. "My baby is coming."

CHAPTER THIRTY-SIX

OLIVIA

Emily's legs buckled, and she crumpled to the rug. Mathias sprang to his feet.

"Let's get her upstairs." He lifted Emily from the floor. "The servants are gone for the day—I dismissed them early—but there's still a maid around here somewhere."

I blushed, once again recalling Mathias thrusting his hips between the legs of that young woman. "You go and find her."

I didn't want to look the maid in the eyes—not after seeing her naked body.

"I was very close to someone a long time ago. She was a midwife. I'll dust off my brain and see if I can remember anything she taught me." My heart clenched, remembering my dear friend Amara.

I guided Emily a few steps before she screamed and fell to her knees. "It hurts, Olivia! God, how it hurts."

"I know, I know, Emily. But we've got to make it upstairs to the bed."

There was little time between contractions, so our

progress up the stairs was slow. Each time her stomach convulsed, we had to stop until it ceased.

Finally, we made it to the bed chamber.

The young maid—the same one I'd caught with the count —was already in the room, fussing about and preparing the feather-and-down-filled mattress. She stripped the bed of linens and replaced them with several thick pieces of wool.

"Madam," she said in a lilting French accent. "Allow me to introduce myself. I am Anne Geneviève."

"Olivia," I said, curtly.

"Please accept my apologies for earlier with Comte Montego, Olivia. He has been my lover for a time. He knows how to please a woman. But we thought we would not be interrupted."

I almost clapped my hands over my ears and uttered, "La, la, la." This was a TMI moment, for sure.

"Count Montego has gone for help."

"*Oh cher. Dans cette tempête?*" I said, slipping into French.

Oh, dear. In this storm?

I glanced out the window at the darkening sky. Snow and ice continued to pelt the glass.

"He will be safe," she said with conviction.

"We need to get Emily undressed and into bed. Can you help me?" I said, redirecting the conversation.

"*Bien sûr*," she said.

Of course.

Together we managed to get Emily on top of the wool sans clothes. Another contraction seized her, tightening her stomach into a hard knot and making her cry out in pain.

"Breathe, Emily. Like this."

She slowly inhaled and exhaled.

Emily took in a shuddering breath and slowly let it out.

"Better," she wheezed.

Anne Geneviève turned to me and said, "I brought the silk thread to sew up the torn skin after the baby arrived."

My eyebrows arched in surprise. "How do you know these things?"

"My mother—she is a midwife."

I nodded, hoping together, we could serve Emily's needs.

But then Anne Geneviève produced a brownish stone wrapped in a crude silver setting. She tied it to Emily's thigh.

"What's that?" I said.

"It's an eaglestone. Meant to expedite the birth."

I almost rolled my eyes as another contraction rocked through Emily. *It's a little too late for that.*

Anne Geneviève bit the end of the extra thread attached to the eaglestone. She gripped Emily's hand and demonstrated slow, steady breathing once more.

Emily tried to emulate her, but then she let out a howl.

"It hurts, Olivia!" she screamed.

"I know, Emily. I know."

"I'm so scared. Marcellious promised me he'd be here for the birth." Fat tears streaked her face as she writhed on the bed.

"Spread your legs," Anne Geneviève said.

When Emily complied, the maid crouched and peered at Emily's crotch. "The baby—it is almost here."

I rushed to the maid's vantage point, shocked to see a vernix-covered head crowning. Exultant joy flooded my heart.

"Emily! She's right. You've got to push now."

Emily let out an earth-shattering scream followed by a loud groan.

I thought the windows might shatter.

The baby's head inched out.

More groans and cries followed until the new Baby Demarrias slid into my arms.

Tears of happiness tracked down my cheeks. "It's a boy, Emily! You've got a son."

I rested the squirming infant on Emily's belly.

Anne Geneviève and I snipped the cord, sewed the tear between Emily's legs, and cleaned up.

Anne Geneviève departed, carrying soiled supplies.

I sat beside Emily and her baby.

Already, he was nuzzling her nipple.

Emily and I both had tears streaming down our faces.

"Almost a year ago, we were running from that demon and seeking Malik in another part of the world at another time," Emily said, her voice quivering. "And now I'm living in a castle with a baby boy at my breast."

I stroked her shoulder. "Isn't it a miracle?"

I wiped my eyes.

"I can't believe Marcellious was right about the gender of our baby." She laughed through her tears.

"Oh, he'll probably gloat about it," I said, chuckling. I reached out to touch the baby's back. "Your son is so beautiful. What are you going to name him?"

"Marcellious wants to honor his father, Moon Lee, and name him Leo."

A soaring sensation shot through my heart. "Oh, what a wonderful name! And Moon Lee would be honored."

Emily began to cry again. She blinked away her tears and said, "I'm so happy, Olivia. I only wish Marcellious was here to see his son."

"I know, sweetheart. I know."

We basked in the afterglow of birth before I rose, saying, "I'm going to go get some fresh linens."

Emily smiled as she stroked her infant's head.

I was near the stairs when a blood-curdling scream erupted from Emily's room. I sprinted back down the hall and stopped in the doorway. My heart cleaved apart in terror.

Balthazar and Tristan stood next to Emily.

Emily clutched Leo to her chest, her eyes wide with fright.

"Get out of here!" I roared. "Leave us be!"

Tristan's head snapped to attention as he heard my voice, a smirk plastered across his face. "Ah, my sweet little girl-friend. How nice it is to see you again."

"Get out!" I screamed, rage radiating from my body like a wildfire. "This isn't an opportunity for you to bring us down and make our lives a living hell!"

I thrust my finger forward with such force that it seemed like it might go right through the wall. My entire body quivered with rage.

Emily's breath emerged in short bursts like she was hyperventilating.

Balthazar leered at me. "Don't worry, Olivia. We're only here for a short time. I'll be taking my daughter and grandson to my place."

He reached for Emily.

"No!" Emily shouted, shielding her tiny baby.

Shockwaves rippled across my skin. "What did you say? Emily is not your daughter."

Another leer split the demon's face. "Oh, but she is. Ask Marcellious."

Emily's expression crumpled into one of anguish. Sobbing, she blubbered, "Oh, God! Say it isn't so. I'm the spawn of this foul creature, and my husband knew this whole time?"

I lunged toward Balthazar, seizing his arm. "Emily is *not* your daughter, you bastard! Stop torturing her!"

Balthazar laughed, shaking free of my grip. "Emily is most certainly my daughter. Alina gave birth to her. That's the missing part of the journal." He sneered. "She was with Philip at the time. Should I read it? So you know I'm telling the truth?"

A sheen of sweat covered my skin. Fear paralyzed me as his words sunk in. *My mother had Balthazar's child?*

"You're lying," I said, forcing myself out of my paralysis. "That's what you do. You lie and manipulate."

Balthazar slid his hand into his coat pocket and procured a couple sheets of paper the same size as Alina's diary. "Here you go. Here's your proof."

He thrust the paper my way.

I took it with trembling fingers. My voice shook as I read aloud. "I have been keeping a dark secret. I'm pregnant with Balthazar's child. I've fooled Philip into thinking it's his, but it is indeed the seed of my true love."

I flung the papers away, and they fluttered to the floor. "My mother's a fucking bitch! How could she? I'd nearly forgiven her, but now *this!*"

"No," Emily wailed. "I can't be your daughter. That makes me a monster, too!"

"Your eyes, child," Balthazar said almost tenderly. "Your eyes are the same color as mine. And now I will take you home and care for you."

He pried Leo from Emily's grip and cradled him in his arms.

Leo began to wail.

Balthazar rocked him and cooed and spoke to the infant in soft tones. "Who's a precious baby? You are. You're going to be my finest protege."

Tristan's mouth gaped open in shock, and his eyes blazed

with wounded indignation. "But I thought I was your best protege!"

Balthazar sneered coldly and spat out, "You were my biggest mistake." He crooned softly to the baby.

Emily tried to retrieve her infant, but Balthazar blocked her advances.

"Fear not, my love. I shall take the utmost care of you and your son Leo. Yes, I have done many horrible things—I even tried to kill you a few times—but it doesn't matter because you remind me of the one woman that I could never forget. I will raise your son as if he is my own flesh and blood, having him assume the place of next Timebound prince."

As if summoned by fate itself, a glinting necklace sparkled around Leo's neck.

"Behold our proof," Balthazar cackled darkly. "He may be Timebound, but I shall use his powers to make him strong."

Emily continued to sob.

My mind raced and whirled. I didn't have my dagger anymore, since Costa had it. And bullets wouldn't work on Balthazar. I was helpless against his wickedness.

"Tristan! Help your sister out of bed!" Balthazar commanded. He rose and stepped away from Emily.

Tristan blinked out of his stupor and lurched toward the bed. He seized her arm and tried to wrestle her from the mattress as she fought and screamed.

"Shit! I can't do this!" He flung up his hands.

Balthazar scowled. "You're pathetic, you know that?" He bounced the baby up and down, cooing, "Who's my sweet boy, huh? Who's my sweet boy? I can't believe I have a grandson."

I lunged for Balthazar.

Leo continued to scream and wail, his face red and his body arched.

Balthazar rounded on me and hit me with the back of his hand, his expression a cruel mask. "You should be glad you're still alive, bitch. The only reason you're still breathing is that my daughter cares for you."

I reeled back from the viciousness in his tone and the sting of his slap.

A dominating voice thundered into the room. "Balthazar! Give the child back to Emily!"

Mathias stormed through the doorway, eyes blazing.

Oh, no! Mathias can't get in the middle of this.

I rushed toward Mathias, grabbing his forearm. "Don't, Mathias! This man is dangerous!"

Mathias shrugged me off with a flick of his arm, his gaze pure fire.

I followed his line of sight to see Balthazar, pale, frozen, and unblinking. My head swiveled back and forth between Balthazar and Mathias.

What the holy hell is going on here?

Emily's and my gazes met in uncomprehending bewilderment.

I directed my attention back to Mathias. I could just *feel* the darkness emanating from him.

Who are you, Mathias Montego? Is that really your name?

"I have waited such a long time for this moment," Mathias said, his voice low and menacing.

Balthazar managed to get his mouth moving. "You... you're alive!"

"Very much so," Mathias said. "Unlike your son will be if you don't return the child to its mother."

He faded from sight and reappeared behind Balthazar with a blade to his neck.

My limbs trembled, shaking until I feared toppling to the ground.

Mathias is the darkness!

I reached out a hand to steady myself against the wall.

"You wouldn't kill my son," Balthazar said, his gaze flicking to Tristan and back to Mathias.

"Go ahead and test me," Mathias said, pressing the sharp knife into Balthazar's neck.

Several crimson drops trickled down the demon's neck.

"I would, and I will because you put my granddaughter in pain," Mathias hissed into Balthazar's ear. "Give the child back."

Balthazar erupted in maniacal laughter, his cackles echoing off the walls. His eyes flashed with barely contained rage as he spat out his words. "You have no power here. Think I'm scared of you? You can deceive these two if you like, but not me!" he sneered.

Mathias carved a slit in Balthazar's neck. "Give the child back, *now.*"

Balthazar extended Leo to Emily, who snatched him up and pressed him to her chest.

Mathias faded from view and reappeared clutching Tristan from behind.

Emily rolled away, pulling the bedding over her head, shielding her and Leo.

Tristan yelled, his arms flailing. "Father, do something!"

Balthazar lunged toward Tristan.

Mathias slid his knife through Tristan's neck with so much force the head fell from Tristan's body. He caught it by the hair before it fell to the rug.

The rest of Tristan collapsed to the floor with a loud thud.

I screamed.

"Here," Mathias said to Balthazar. "Catch."

He hurled the head with such force that Balthazar had no time for thought or reaction. A wave of anger and revulsion tore through Balthazar as he caught the head midair, his face twisted in rage, his eyes blazing with fury.

Balthazar stood before me, his furious grip clenching the head of his son, whose face was forever frozen in a never-ending scream.

My mind went numb as I crumpled to the ground, helpless and hopeless. I buried my face in my hands, trying to block out the horror that surrounded me, but the screams continued to echo in my mind like a haunting melody of death.

As Balthazar approached me with a twisted grin on his face, I could feel my soul shattering into a million pieces. Tears streamed down my cheeks as I realized that this moment would be forever burned into my memory, an endless reminder of the cruel fate that had befallen us all.

I placed my hands over my eyes, trying to erase the macabre image that was burned into my memory. With each sob, the weight of reality pushed down on me until I felt like I might suffocate under its crushing force.

My head spun as I tried to comprehend the convoluted family tree in front of me. Mathias, my mom's biological father, was Emily's and my grandfather. Balthazar was Emily's dad, while Tristan had been born from Balthazar's blood and an unknown mother.

Confusion flooded my mind as I realized that I had no idea who I really was or where I belonged.

CHAPTER THIRTY-SEVEN

MALIK

I lifted my head from the corpse beneath me and inhaled deeply. The body's essence coiled into my nose, bringing life and sustenance.

I sighed, sliding the blade from the dead man's chest, and rising from my crouch.

Standing on the cobbled street in the waning light, I paused. I'd killed four people tonight. That should be more than enough to sustain me, but the craving to feed on human souls roared through me like a lion tearing the flesh from its victim's bones. I had to find another soul to consume…and another…and another after that. I was insatiable with hunger.

I stalked up the empty street, sniffing, searching for my next victim.

I'd practice my so-called "morals" for years—only killing the weak, the morally corrupt, and the depraved. Were all those I'd murdered tonight from that category? I didn't know and didn't care.

The poison I'd ingested inside the tavern had compromised my nervous system, making me indiscriminate in my feeding frenzy. Even after four souls, my brain was still muzzy and unclear.

Goddamned belladonna.

The street, grim and foreboding, offered no solace to those who ventured down its length. I cast my gaze toward one of the houses at the end of the block, where a pale, yellow light shone from the windows like a beacon. That would be my destination this night.

My feet quickened as I circled around the cottage, searching for an entry point. A predatory smile curved across my lips as I caught a peculiar scent in the air. My next victim was close.

Definitely live bodies in there. Two, if I'm not mistaken.

I slung my fist through the thick windowpane shattering it. Then, I leaped through the opening with the grace of a large cat. I pounced at a male who stood inside the room.

"No, no, no! Don't! I know what you are. I'm on your side!" the man blubbered, stumbling backward. "Go kill someone at the tavern. There are many bad men there."

I blinked to clear the haze from my vision.

"Who are you?" I said, seizing him by his upper arm.

"My name is Osman. I'm a friend of Roman Alexander's." The man clawed at my hand, trying to pry off my hold.

My love for Roman and commitment to protecting him overpowered the craving to kill. I shoved Osman away from me, and he fell to the floor.

"Do you have Roman? Where is he?" I looked around at the tidy front room with a blazing fire in the hearth and a few shabby pieces of furniture scattered about.

"Yes, yes," Osman said, scurrying to a curtain draped over the opening to the next room. "He's in there, recovering. I gave him the antidote to the poison."

I stumbled across the room, my heart pounding so hard I could feel it in my throat. In the doorway, I paused and looked over at Roman who lay still on the bed, his body almost angelic in its repose. A surge of love filled me from head to toe and my breathing became shallow, my feet glued to the ground with emotion.

He's alive, thank God. But he barely looks conscious.

Slowly, so as not to disturb his slumber, I crept across the room and knelt at his side. I swept my palm across his head, letting my fingers tangle in his thick hair.

His chest slowly rose and fell with each breath. His skin looked the color of snow at night in the shadows.

My head felt like a giant boulder, weighted and dense. I struggled to hold it upright.

"God's bones, the poison has made me nearly immobile," I whispered. "I feel like hell. It's no wonder you look half-dead."

My body trembled from hunger. Saliva pooled in my mouth as the need to feed roared to life.

I lurched away from Roman and staggered into the front room, where Osman lingered.

"I've got to consume more souls. My teacher taught me not to kill innocent people, but you might be next if I don't find a soul fast." I placed my hand against the wall. "Where can I go?"

"The tavern," Osman said, backing away from me. "I told you—there are terrible people there."

He pointed toward the door.

"Malik!" Roman screamed, his voice desperate and hoarse.

I dashed back to him, my heart racing. "You're awake!"

"I'm coming with you." He tried to stand, shaking with determination.

"No!" I yelled, pressing my palm firmly against his chest. "You're still weak. You can't go—you must stay here and heal."

Roman shoved aside my hand with surprising strength. "I'm not staying. I heard what you said, and I'm coming to keep you safe." He lurched to his feet, grasping my arm, and pushing us toward the door.

The cold mist of rain blanketed my coat, beading on it like tiny diamonds on black velvet.

My craving for souls was insatiable, but I pushed ahead into the night air, knowing that Osman was following closely behind me.

I wanted to leave him behind in the darkness, but with every step I took, he was there just a few paces away from me.

My cravings thrummed through my bloodstream, begging for restoration from the spirits of the dead. I began to run as the scent of humans teased and tormented my nose.

In front of the tavern, I seized my knife from its sheath and plunged it into the back of a man looting a corpse's pockets. I inhaled his soul before his body hit the cobblestone. But that was only an appetizer. I continued my killing spree, murdering the gawkers, the looters, and the bystanders, heedless of good or bad, moral or immoral. I had to restore my strength, and this seemed the only way to do it.

A man let out a guttural scream. "Good lord, there's a monster among us!"

People pointed at me, stared in horror, or ran for their lives.

Moving like a madman, I caught each one and killed him or her, panting between inhaling their souls.

After everyone had been slaughtered, my body pulsated with strength.

The massacre stretched out before me, and my heart sank.

I fell to my knees, striking the hard stone. "What have I done? I'm truly a fiend."

Corpses lay draped over one another, their eyes sightless. Blood oozed from the gashes I had inflicted on each one.

The village air was pungent with the iron tang of blood as I held my head in my hands. "How can I live with myself? How can I continue to be Rosie's father, or Olivia and Roman's friend and protector?"

Slow footsteps echoed, approaching me.

Roman and Osman, hands outstretched, moved cautiously forward.

"Are you all right, Malik?" Roman said in the way one might soothe a cornered wolf.

"I'm despicable," I wailed. "You must be disgusted with me. All I ever wanted was to live a normal life as a father. How can I pretend to care for Rosie after what I've done?"

The light rain mixed with the blood, and crimson rivulets trickled away from the bodies in intricate patterns.

Roman kept his palms out as he approached.

Osman hung back.

The storm raged overhead, accompanied by an eerie and blinding light. As I stood in the pouring rain, I felt nothing. Satan himself could take me away in that moment and I wouldn't care.

Roman crouched next to me, his own face streaming with rivulets of water from the heavy downpour. His voice was soft yet desperate as he said, "You didn't choose this destiny for yourself. It was forced upon you."

But even as he said it, I felt no emotion—only a deep emptiness inside.

I picked up my knife, which I must have dropped next to me.

The blade gleamed, washed clean of blood.

I stared at it, not comprehending what I held in my hands.

Roman swayed, falling to his hands and knees.

Osman rushed forward, waving a vial in the air. "This is the antidote. Roman needs more of it."

I frowned. "Who are you that you know so much about poisons and antidotes? Are you a Timehunter?"

"No! I'm a scholar and a healer." He knelt beside Roman. "Tip your head back and open your mouth."

When Roman complied, Osman poured some tincture into his mouth.

"You'll start to feel better soon." Then, he turned toward me. "My betrothed came here for the moon dagger. She was taken by Raul because she's a Timebound. We were staying at the cottage where you found me."

He waved his hand in the direction of his tiny home. "I came to the tavern because I was getting nowhere. That's where I met Roman and Marcellious. They protected me."

I nodded.

"The solar eclipse is coming soon, and the Timehunters are going to be hunting for Timebornes and Timebounds," Osman said. "None of you are safe."

I shuddered.

"You're not afraid of a solar eclipse, are you?" Roman said, sitting back on his haunches.

"I'm concerned about the solar eclipse," I said. "That's the only day the darkness isn't the darkness. We have no power for twenty-four hours."

"You're kidding," Roman said.

"I wish I were. I'll be hiding on that day. We're not even human—we're forced to lock ourselves up and not come out. That day for us is complete misery." A strange weariness came over me even though I was bloated with the spirits of the dead. "Where's your brother, Roman? Where's Marcellious?"

Roman frowned. "I don't know."

Osman started to speed-talk. "I came upon Roman and Marcellious in the tavern. And then Costa came in. And then some man named Balthazar. I'm pretty sure he took your brother, Roman. And then I watched you help Roman get out and saw you were both affected by the poison. We can help each other. I've already been helping Roman for several days."

The pelting rain started to get to me, so I pushed to stand and reached out a hand to Roman.

He stood as well, and then the three of us stood under the eaves of the tavern, sheltered from the rain.

"How do you know so much, Osman?" I asked.

Osman leaned forward and shook the rain from his black hair. When he straightened, he said, "I already told you I'm a scholar and a healer. I come from Anatolia, where the Timehunters are known as the Black Assassins. Their society in Constantinople is more powerful than the one here. Their tortures are far worse—way worse than Costa and his men. My betrothed and I came here to find answers about the Timehunters and the moon dagger. And now we're stuck."

He shoved his hands in his pockets. "I don't know where my Reyna is. They probably already killed her. I'll probably never get her back."

A growl formed in the back of my throat. Goddamned Montego. He promised me everything would be okay if he traveled with us. He swore nothing would happen to my companions. But now Marcellious is gone, and Balthazar and Costa are here, wreaking their savagery.

"We have to get back," I said, shaking free of my despair.

"We must get on the road if we're to find Marcellious. He can handle anything. He's been subjected to worse."

I turned to Osman and said, "You're coming with us. If fate has intervened in our acquaintanceship, we must heed it."

I began to head toward his dwelling, my long legs eating up the road in my haste to depart.

Roman kept up with me, despite his weakness.

"Wait!" Osman called, racing after me. "I'm honored to be invited into your company. Might I know your name?"

I flashed him a scorching gaze. "I'm known as Malik."

Once we stood before Osman's home, I said, "Gather your belongings. You'll never be coming back. If you think the Timehunters have your betrothed, you can be assured they are watching you."

Osman's eyes widened into pools of fear. He blinked himself back to the moment and raced into his house.

"Nothing like putting the fear of God into a man," Roman said, adding a chuckle.

I slid my gaze toward him. "We both know that *God* is not the one he needs to fear."

We both shared a dark laugh.

Once Osman rejoined us, we hastened to the stable where we'd procured horses to carry our cave-exploring supplies.

A stableboy leaped to his feet from a bed of hay when we entered the barn. "Good sirs, how may I help you?"

"Prepare these horses for us." I fished in my pocket and tossed him a coin. "And if you hire someone to bring our supplies to where we are staying, there will be more gold for you."

The lad's eyes glittered in lust as he stared at the gold in his palm. "Right away, sir."

Once the horses were saddled, we set out, galloping through the darkening landscape.

When we reached the foothills, a light snow fell. As we climbed the hill, the snowfall gave way to drifts.

The horses struggled through the snow midway up their legs, so the going was slow. But, at last, the count's enormous estate came into view, a looming structure beneath the moonlight.

We dismounted in the stables, giving the horses welcome flakes of hay. And then we made our way to the front door.

When I opened it, I was met with the absence of sound— no maids or cooks bustled about in the kitchen. There was no sign of Olivia, Montego, or Emily.

I followed some quiet hums into the Noir room.

Rosie sat quietly, playing on the carpet.

"Sweetheart," I said, crouching before her. "Where is everyone?"

She shrugged. "I was told to stay down here and play."

"Okay, well, you must do what you're told." I tapped her nose, kissed her head, and rose.

"Something's wrong," I hissed to Roman and Osman. "One of you stay with Rosie."

"I'll stay! I'm good with children," Osman said.

I charged out of the room and up the stairs, Roman at my heels. We stopped in the open doorway of Emily's bedroom.

Balthazar cradled Tristan's lifeless head, with blood cascading down its neck in a steady stream.

Mathias stood before them like a sentinel, his towering figure filled with unbridled power and rage.

So he's revealed himself.

Olivia gazed at Roman and me from her position on the floor. Then, she promptly fainted.

CHAPTER THIRTY-EIGHT

OLIVIA

I stirred in my husband's arms, my body tense as chaos reigned around us.

"You're here," I said with a dry sob, trying to shut out the pandemonium all around us.

"I'm here." He gazed down at me with blazing eyes that burned with a thousand fires.

Balthazar unleashed a howl of rage that shook the very foundations of the earth, his voice jarring with such intensity that it felt like shards of blazing lightning were lancing through our bodies. "You killed my son!" he shrieked, his eyes burning hotter than any fire as an anguished tear ran down his face. "Another one of my children gone," he roared as anguish and wrath radiated off him in waves.

My throat caught as I guffawed. After all the suffering he'd caused my loved ones, his thunderous tantrum felt like karmic justice. But still I was astounded by his deafening diatribe of rage.

But still, Tristan, the man I'd once loved and had sex with, had been beheaded.

A shudder of disgust rippled up my backbone.

Little Leo continued to scream and wail as Emily shushed him beneath the covers, shielding him from the horrors around us.

I let Roman help me to sit as Mathias' voice boomed through the room, chanting the ancient scripture that sent chills through my bones.

My hair prickled across my scalp.

As he intoned the scripture, Mathias held a blade, pointing it at Balthazar.

Balthazar's face grew slack, and he dropped Tristan's head. It landed with a dull thud at his feet.

Mathias lunged at Balthazar, plunging the dagger into the demon's heart as gracefully as if he were practicing fencing in a university gymnasium.

Balthazar let out a silent scream. He, Mathias, and all remnants of Tristan disappeared in a cloud of black smoke.

"Oh, my God, oh my God, oh my God," I wailed, writhing in Roman's arms.

"Shh, shh, shh," Roman soothed. "I've got you, my love."

I wrestled out of his arms and lunged to my feet. I stood there, speechless.

No signs of the horror I'd just witnessed remained in the room. I rushed to the bed and wrapped my arms around Emily's body covered in bedding. "Emily, you can come out. The demon and his spawn are gone."

She sobbed as she flung back the covers, clutching the baby. "I'm the spawn of a demon. *Me.*"

Shit. Poor choice of words.

"You're nothing like Balthazar, Emily," I soothed, knowing nothing except what I'd already seen.

What if she has latent demonic tendencies?

I shook that thought from my mind. Emily was a good and loyal friend, and a loving sister.

"Will someone inform us what just happened?" Roman said from behind me.

Malik stepped to the end of the bed. "Emily, my darling. I'm sorry I didn't tell you. We wanted to protect you from the truth."

"But the truth always comes out in the end, doesn't it?" Emily said through a bout of ugly crying.

"I'm so, so sorry," Malik said gently. "And you don't have to worry about Mathias. I assume he told you what he is?"

My head swam with all the unprocessed new factoids swirling through my brain.

"Yes, he's the darkness, and he's Emily and my grandfather." I slumped on the bed next to Emily and her now-quiet baby.

Leo snuggled into his mama's breast, greedily sucking.

"Yes, Mathias is your grandfather. And he cares for you very much," Malik said, his eyes like liquid jade.

"So you knew all this time?" I said.

"I did."

Anger flared like a bonfire inside. I was so tired of discovering truths I should have known.

"I've been helping him all this time," Malik said, regarding me impassively. "He saved me when Balthazar imprisoned me. He trained both Balthazar and me. He is the man who's the most important here. I'm one of his students trying to destroy Balthazar."

"So, we're all just pawns in your game," I said with a snarl.

Ignoring my snide remark, Malik just stood there, his face

a mask. I peered through the doorway to the hall. "Where's Marcellious?"

Roman and Malik exchanged a glance.

"Where's Marcellious?" I repeated, hands on my hips.

"Marcellious has been taken by Raul," Malik said evenly. "Don't worry. We'll find him."

"Oh, no!" Emily cried, her sobs increasing.

The baby began to cry again, and the room erupted into turbulent, unceasing noise.

The sounds amped my anxiety until I thought I'd blow up.

"How can you say that so calmly?" I said to Malik. "If Costa has Marcellious, he could be dead by now."

This only made Emily cry louder.

I let out an exasperated moan. "Enough! Let's leave Emily and the baby and give them some peace. No more discussions in this room."

I pointed at the doorway.

"Emily!" I begged, my voice desperate and cracked. I leaned in close, my hands trembling with the knowledge of what I was asking her to do. "You have to believe Malik. I shouldn't have opened up my fears like that."

Her eyes were full of sorrow as she looked at me. "I come from the dark, Olivia," she whispered. "Maybe I'm destined for it as well."

There was nothing I could do but plead with her silently, hoping she'd make the right choice. "Don't blame Malik," I whispered. "He's only doing what he's doing because Mathias told him to."

"Okay."

"And don't let the knowledge of who your father is affect you. All will be well." I squeezed her hand.

"I hope so," she said, wiping her eyes.

Malik, Roman, and I tromped into the hallway, closing the door behind us.

Downstairs, Mathias' voice thundered, coming from the kitchen.

I no longer regarded him as a kind, benevolent person. Yet again, I had encountered another possessive, controlling darkness, perhaps the most powerful of all. Truthfully, he terrified me, grandfather or not.

"You must take care of Emily! Treat her with utmost respect!" Mathias roared.

"I have been, sir. I helped her birth her baby. I am doing my best!" came the equally heated response from the maid.

"Bring her some tea, some comfort...anything!" Mathias shouted.

"At once, sir," Anne Geneviève said, in a voice equally as loud.

Oh, boy, I thought with a roll of my eyes. *A lover's quarrel...*

Mathias stormed through the house and met us when we stepped onto the first floor.

"*Mon Dieu,*" he said, raking his hand through his hair. He took my hands. "Dear Olivia, I wish you hadn't found out about me in such a ghastly manner. I assure you—you have nothing to be scared of. I am so very grateful to have you in my life."

He leaned forward and kissed my temple.

"Come," he said, turning to walk away. "Let's sit somewhere comfortable, so I can tell you more of my story."

Numb, unsure what to say, I followed him, with Roman and Malik trailing behind. My mind struggled to fit together all these new pieces. I only wanted to fall asleep, wake up, and have all of this over.

Once we'd settled in the Noir room, warm from the crackling fire, Mathias said, "I'm sorry I've been dishonest with you." His gaze flitted between Roman and me. "I am the first darkness to ever be created. The monster I created is Balthazar. I need to assume responsibility for my creation."

I fell against the sofa back, stunned. My grandfather was the first darkness ever created?

"I'm the mastermind behind everything. Now that I have Balthazar, he's inhaling the belladonna in my dungeon. All I want is to have my family back—Cora and Alina. Yes, I am the darkness—happiness will always elude me—but neither of you should be afraid."

I shook my head. "I don't want to be here. You could have told me, Malik!"

Malik met my gaze with green-eyed calm; it was like looking into an emerald, cold and impassive. "I'm sorry I couldn't tell you anything. Mathias is Alastair, my mentor. He and I will destroy Balthazar. We've been plotting it for quite some time now."

"It's true." Mathias leaned forward. "But believe me, I would never harm you or Emily. I am nothing but grateful to have you in my life. Everything I do is for you, so you will never have to deal with this again. I promise I will make things right."

I should have been overjoyed hearing his words, but a numb apathy took over. I entirely shut down. It didn't feel safe to allow any vulnerability or openness.

"Where is Balthazar?" I asked.

Mathias' gaze darted back and forth before meeting mine. "He's…downstairs. I have a dungeon below."

Of course, you do. It's probably got torture devices.

"I want to see him," I said.

Mathias looked at Roman.

"It's not his decision. It's mine," I said, standing.

"As you wish," Mathias said, inclining his head.

I turned toward Roman and said softly, "I'd like to do this alone…without you."

Roman frowned. "But…"

"I'll be safe. I'll be with the darkest of the dark," I said, smiling for the first time in what felt like forever.

Roman rose and gave me a quick kiss. "I'll go and check on Rosie and the friend that we brought with us."

"Thank you." I hugged him.

As I followed Mathias through the many rooms of the estate, fear began to push its way through my body.

Mathias was undoubtedly ten times more powerful than Balthazar.

So what made me head downstairs to see my worst enemy with this unknown darkness, without Roman by my side? I couldn't answer that.

We stopped before a carved wall decorated with slender, nubile maidens prancing around horses and flying on the backs of dragons. The porcelain was pure white, like alabaster.

Mathias fit his fingers into specific places in the carvings and muttered strange words I could barely hear.

The wall creaked open.

I jerked, startled. Of course, the darkest of the dark would have a creepy dungeon protected by a secret wall.

Mathias turned to me, placed his hands on my shoulders, and said, "Now, don't be frightened. Balthazar is subdued in his cell. He can't harm you, okay?"

It was strange to look into the eyes of this man, my badass *grandfather*. Should I say, *Thank you, Grandpa? No problem, Gramps? Copasetic, Granddad?*

None of those seemed fitting for a man who scared the living daylight out of me. Instead, I opted for a simple, "Okay."

We tromped down smooth stone stairs lit by wall sconces.

In the foyer, stone faces leered at me, their eyes seeming to follow me as I scurried behind Mathias.

We came upon a doorway fashioned of metal.

Mathias procured a key from his waistcoat and fit it into the lock. He twisted the key, and the lock mechanism snicked and gave way.

As soon as the door opened, a bolt of fear shot through me.

"Mathias, wait!" I blurted, then shame draped over me at the slip of my tongue.

"Yes, my dear?"

"I'm scared."

Of you, of Balthazar, of everything this place now represents…

He regarded me with such tenderness I nearly cracked. Then I remembered his controlling demeanor beneath his refined appearance. Could I really trust him if he was the ultimate darkness?

"I will not let anything, or anyone harm you. Not now and not ever."

His words gave me no comfort.

He pushed the door all the way open and stepped across the threshold.

We entered a small chamber cleaved from the substratum beneath the earth.

I faced an enclosure of nearly a foot-thick glass, behind which Balthazar lay like a ragdoll on the smooth crystalline floor.

White mist drifted from a tiny hole near the bottom of the cell, coiling in lazy wisps around Balthazar.

Is that the belladonna? Or some other kind of demonic poison?

Mathias pulled a slender red cord from the ceiling, and a big brass bell clanged inside the prison cell.

Balthazar's eyes opened, and he gave me a heavy-lidded gaze, much like a lizard. With effort, he pushed to sitting in slow, awkward movements.

"Finally, after all these years, I caught you," Mathias said, propping his hands on his slender hips. His voice appeared to carry through the thick glass, as evidenced by Balthazar covering his ears with his hands.

"Stop screaming," he said, barely audible.

"I'm not screaming." Mathias smiled. "I'm merely savoring the victory."

Balthazar's loud, phlegmy cough made me gag, shooting bile into the back of my throat.

"What's the point?" Balthazar croaked in the voice of an old man. "I still won—I beat the teacher."

I strained to hear him. How Mathias could project his voice through the dense silicate was a mystery to me. But then, nearly everything about the darkness was mystifying.

"How so?" Mathias said, crossing his arms loosely across his chest. "What makes you think you've won?"

Balthazar clawed his way to standing and staggered toward the glass wall.

I shrank back as he came closer.

Mathias held his ground.

Balthazar steadied himself with his palms and said, "I killed Cora, took over your school, and made all the darknesses as evil as me. I seduced your beloved daughter Alina. I got her. I took her for myself. If only you knew Alina and her true colors."

He threw back his head and cackled until the laughter ended in a coughing fit. The violent outburst made him crumble to the floor.

Clutching his abdomen, curled in a fetal position, he continued speaking. "Now I know who this mysterious Count Montego is. Yet, I can see I've won. I killed the most precious thing you ever knew—destroyed your wife and daughter. I killed..." His eyes fluttered shut. "I killed them both."

Mathias laughed so hard, tears streaming down his cheeks; I thought he must be crazy.

Balthazar pushed his way up to an awkward position, propped on his hands, his head hanging like a sick dog. He tried to stare at Mathias, but his eyelids fluttered as if they were too heavy.

"Oh, Balthazar! You're still the biggest idiot to think you beat me. You're utterly pathetic. Don't you see? The master won the student. You think killing Alina would make you victorious?" Mathias wiped his eyes. "Let me tell you a secret I have been keeping for a long time. What if I told you that Alina has been alive all this time?"

I jerked at his words.

Balthazar continued to blink like an idiot.

Footsteps clattered down the stairs.

I whirled around, my heart jammed in my throat.

Two figures glided through the open doorway.

There is no way in hell. Are you fucking kidding me?

I rubbed my eyes with my fists, trying to clear my vision. "Mom? You're alive?"

My mother glanced at Moon Lee, who stood next to her.

Then, she flashed me a warm smile. "Yes, honey, I've been alive this whole time."

The Journey Continues….
Blade of Shadows Book 3.5: Wicked Lovers of Time
Balthazar and Alina's Story

TIMEHUNTERS (BOOK 4)
(COMING SPRING 2025)

THANK YOU FOR READING!

Enjoy *Timebound*? Please take a second to leave a review!

OTHER BOOKS IN THE BLADE OF SHADOWS SERIES
TIMEBORNE (BOOK 1)

DARKNESS OF TIME (BOOK 2)

TIMEBOUND (BOOK 3)

WICKED LOVERS OF TIME (BOOK 3.5)
Balthazar and Alina's Story

TIMEHUNTERS (BOOK 4)
(COMING SOON 2025)

LOST LEGACY OF TIME
(FINAL SAGA BOOK 5)
COMING SOON

JOIN THE BLADE OF SHADOWS!
https://www.authorsarasamuels.com/

Join the Club!
Blade of Shadows Book Club (Facebook Group)

TikTok
Instagram
Facebook

THANK YOU

Goodreads
BookBub

APPRECIATION

Writing *Timebound* was a profound joy for me, a journey filled with twists and turns, secrets unveiled, and a story that resonated deeply within my heart. My gratitude to my incredible team knows no bounds; without you, this story would have remained untold. From the core of my being, thank you for embarking on this journey with me and granting me the honor of sharing this tale with the world.

To the ever-supportive Chaela, your constant guidance, steadfast friendship, unwavering love, and continuous support have been instrumental in my journey. I cherish every moment and gesture, and my heart brims with gratitude for your presence in my life.

Rainy, your editorial prowess is nothing short of a gift. The canvas of my manuscript has been transformed into a masterpiece through your keen eyes and meticulous comments. I am indebted to you for sculpting my thoughts into their best form.

And Charity, words fall short to express the magnitude of my appreciation. Your invaluable feedback has been a cornerstone in enhancing the essence of my work. Your role in this venture is immeasurable, and my gratitude for you knows no bounds.

A heartfelt thank you to Krafigs Design, whose artistic touch graced my book cover, turning it into a thing of beauty.

Sarah and Liam, the brilliant narrators of my story, have breathed life into the characters through your duet narration. I am profoundly blessed and grateful to have both of you on this journey.

Finally, to my phenomenal beta readers, ARC, and the street team: your unwavering support and passion for this series have been my driving force. The energy you put into every post, reel, comment, and video has set the virtual world abuzz. My heart swells with gratitude for each of you—my most ardent and dedicated fans. Your support is truly immeasurable.

ABOUT THE AUTHOR

SARA SAMUELS is the author of the Blade of Shadow series. When Sara isn't daydreaming about her stories and time travel, she spends her day reading romance, cooking and baking, spending time with family, and enjoying life. Sara loves to connect with readers on Instagram, TikTok or by email, so feel free to email her, or message her on social media because she will reply back! Follow her on Instagram or Tiktok @storytellersarasamuels to get related updates and posts. Email her at sara@authorsarasamuels.com

Visit her website at https://www.authorsarasamuels.com/ and sign up for the mailing list to stay informed about new releases, contests and more!